AMBITION and SONDER

Rain and Ash

Yvonne A. Bulger

Copyright

ISBN 978-1-0688325-0-5

Simunye Publishing 2024 All Rights Reserved

To my GG, Simunye until the end.

The Earth is a very small stage in a vast cosmic arena. Think of the endless cruelties visited by the inhabitants of one corner of this pixel on the scarcely distinguishable inhabitants of some other corner, how frequent their misunderstandings, how eager they are to kill one another, how fervent their hatreds. Think of the rivers of blood spilled by all those generals and emperors so that, in glory and triumph, they could become the momentary masters of a fraction of a dot.

-Carl Edward Sagan

Author: Carl Edward Sagan – The Pale Blue Dot: A Vision of the Human Future in Space – Published by: Random House Books 1994.

Contents

Acknowledgements

To my husband Gord; who had unending patience, who inspired me to finish this novel, and when things seemed a little topsy turvy, encouraged me to stick to the journey I started. I thank you from the bottom of my heart for your extraordinary motivation and your unbroken love.

To my friend, and editor Susan; Thank you for your incredible support, encouragement and the hours you dedicated to turning my words into a book, how can I ever thank you enough?

And lastly, to my doggie, Laika; who patiently kept me company, and sometimes slept away the hours on my desk, a lifetime's worth of treats for you my lady.

Part Map of Kearthat

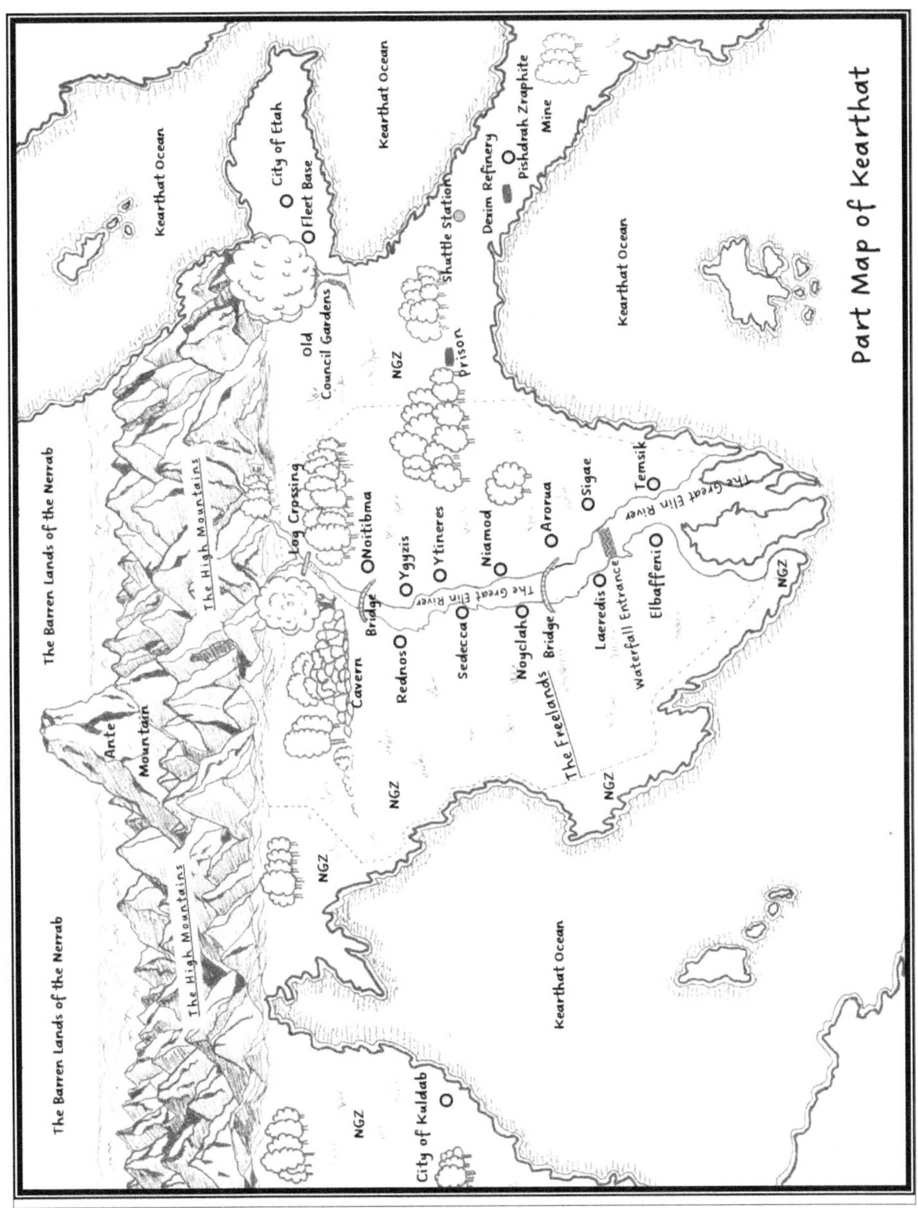

King Family Lineage

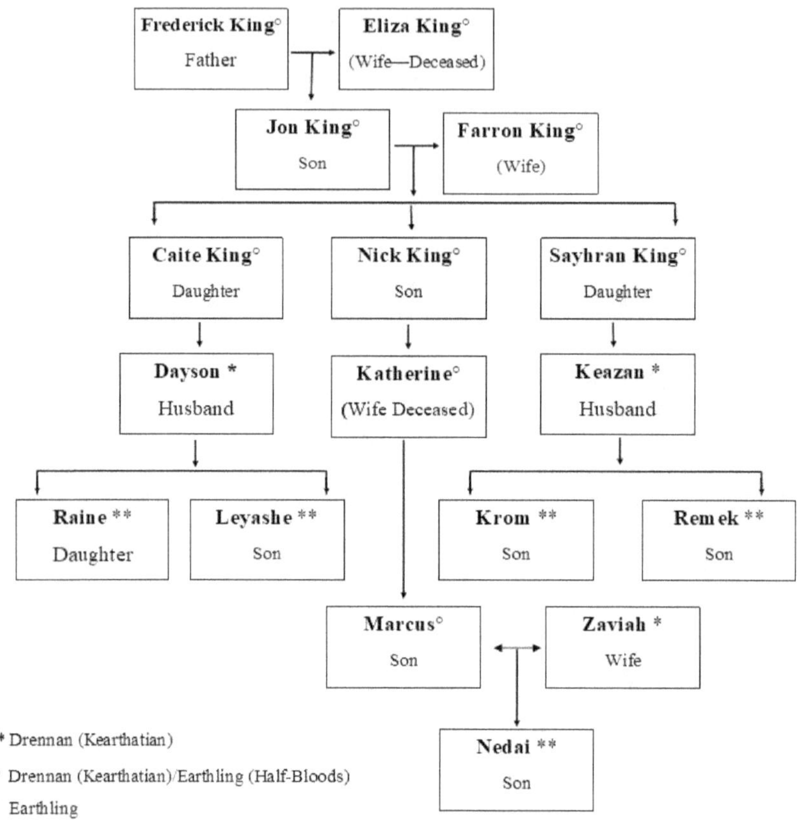

* Drennan (Kearthatian)

** Drennan (Kearthatian)/Earthling (Half-Bloods)

° Earthling

Prologue

The year 2071. Many countries are at war and savage dictatorships have culminated in the suffering of billions. Earth is burdened by disease and frequent destructive weather events. Climate refugees beg for entry into other countries as their shores shrink, but admission is fiercely blocked everywhere. The lack of uncontaminated water and food scarcity is heartbreaking. Sadly, those with excess selfishly ignore the plight of the many.

Back in the Year 2031. A young scientist named Frederick King made a discovery that could alleviate the suffering of millions around the globe, but self-seeking people in power thwarted him.

Almost 40 Years later. Frederick's quest to save humanity is complete as five giant spaceships prepare for launch. Each homeship carries five thousand humans. Among them are Frederick's son Jon, and his wife, Farron. Unbeknownst to them, it will take seventy years to find their way to the planet Kearthat and the enigmatic Drennan.

The five spaceships are catapulted into a strange void and transported to an unknown point in intergalactic space. It will be Farron King's dreams, filled with mysterious visions that guide them to a planet called Kearthat.

Eighty days after landing on planet Kearthat, the planet is invaded. For many years, these alien attackers enslave and oppress the remaining earthlings and Drennan of Kearthat alike while they plunder its riches.

Then, Leyashe, an earthling descendant, makes a discovery that will free their people from the clutches of the aliens. He and his sister Raine unearth the hidden secrets and riddles that Kearthat has kept for two thousand years, and a surprising, fantastical quest ensues.

x

PART I

Chapter 1 - It's Going to Rain

It is the year 2043. Somewhere in the Far North of North America.

"Come now, Farron, we have to get going," Rick Brand tells his five-year-old daughter.

As if oblivious to her father's need for haste, the little girl fiddles with a folded paper aeroplane she calls her rocket.

Rick has had a lot to cope with since he has been caring for his daughter on his own. Seemingly simple tasks quickly become time-consuming, like tying up her long blonde hair and twisting the hair tie between his big, uncooperative fingers until he had a perfect ponytail fashioned. It had taken months to perfect just this one small task.

Farron fidgets, making swishing sounds, waving her paper rocket around in swooping motions as Rick pulls on her socks. He notices that today's choice is a 'dog-hero' character, the other a princess from a movie they often watch together. To minimize dressing time, Rick has learned that it is easier if Farron chooses what she wants to wear; apparently, mismatched socks are a thing kids do deliberately.

So much to learn when a mom is suddenly no longer there.

"Where are we going? I don't want to go," Farron adds without waiting for an answer to her first question.

"We are going to have lunch with Freddy, and he won't be happy if we're late," Rick explains.

It only takes a split second for Farron to decide that this is a good outing, after all.

"I'm going to see Jon, goody goody gumdrops," she squeals, immediately replacing the pout on her face with a smile. All resistance is now history. She slips on the pair of shoes her father passes to her.

Hopping off the chair, Farron tosses her rocket through the doorway into the next room. The paper creation rises to a surprising height, then nosedives towards Rick's study. Bullseye! It is a perfect landing into the pencil holder on his desk.

Frederick King's son Jon and Rick's little Farron were more like brother and sister now. They had contact almost every day since the horrific light aircraft crash that claimed both of their young mothers.

Rick sighs; it has been a trying day. Earlier, a booster on ship number four had not performed as expected for the second time in a week. That morning, Frederick seemed upset and impatient, a trait very uncharacteristic of him. But Rick was sure it would soon be water under the bridge. Freddy would figure it out.

He and Frederick have been going through a rough time. Not only were they keeping up with gruelling work schedules, but they were raising children, and it was not easy. As it was, Rick had already taken on the enormous task of getting Stal Settlement humming like a finely tuned V12 Jaguar engine, giving Frederick King the freedom to immerse himself into Project 25K.

"Daddy, we must take the umbrella. It's going to rain," Farron tells her father, and his thoughts return to the present.

"It's not going to rain, love," Rick assures her as he glances out the window on a clear, calm, sunny day.

"Come on, Farron. We have to hurry up, princess," Rick pleads, his voice remaining calm.

"But daddy, it isssss going to rain. I know it is," the little girl persists, her tiny voice anxious to convince her father of the impending raindrops.

"Don't be a silly-billy, Farron Brand. Put down that umbrella. We are already late."

"I am not a billy-silly' Farron protests comically, pouting as she drops the umbrella back into the flower pot, which doubles as a container for several umbrellas beside the front door.

With Farron's little hand, Rick closes the door behind them. He does not lock it; in Stal Settlement there was no crime.

An hour later, dark clouds replaced the white fluffy clouds of earlier, and the sky greyed over. An almighty clap of thunder announced the rain. Rick and Farron Brand were soaked through by the time they returned home.

Chapter 2 - The Contract

It is the year 2036. Going back in time.

Frederick's first call is to The Department of Environment and Climate Change. He calls The Department of Science and Economic Development when there is apparent disinterest.

Three weeks later, he called more than thirty government departments, including the Prime Minister's Office. The silence is deafening, leaving him with mixed feelings swaying between despondency, how dare they, and to hell with them.

It is inexplicable. Why would no one be interested in hearing him out? His discovery could lessen the suffering of billions. The only explanation is that they think it is a hoax.

A week later, Frederick is shocked when he receives a call from the Department of National Defence. He has a meeting with a Lieutenant-Colonel by the name of Tremblay. The voice on the other end tells him it is concerning his call to the Prime Minister's Office. Frederick gets the impression that it is not an invitation.

Three days later, Frederick finds himself waiting outside of Tremblay's office. On his arrival at the impressive building, he was escorted by a young soldier in a perfectly pressed uniform and gleaming black shoes.

As he sits waiting for Tremblay, Frederick reciprocates nods from people who pass by. The hurried men and women glance briefly before disappearing down the hall with a deep green, well-worn carpet that tapers to who knows where. It is a sunny day, and it gives away the fact that the window sill opposite him has not been dusted in a while. It is in steep contrast to the dust-free shine everywhere else.

The door opens, and Frederick winces. A prominent figure dressed in an impeccable uniform stretches out his hand but does not give Frederick the time to stand.

"Tremblay", he announces.

"Please, this way, Mr. King," he gestures with the other hand.

Frederick rubs the hand that Tremblay just shook. The man's grip was firm, and its confidence lingered in his fingers.

Lieutenant-Colonel Tremblay is a well-set man, his deep voice matching his large form as he towers over the slender five-foot, ten-inch frame that makes up Frederick King.

Tremblay gestures to a chair opposite his large oak desk, and Frederick takes a seat. He keeps his bag containing his precious presentation on his lap, then extends a barely audible "thank you," adding "sir" as an afterthought, immediately regretting it.

Tremblay takes his time to settle into his big black leather chair before he points to a grey-green folder in front of him.

Frederick studies the impressively laden desk, its piles of neatly squared correspondence and precisely stacked folders, a sign of an orderly mind.

"I've been informed that you are making a right nuisance of yourself," Tremblay says, the leather chair making little noises as he keeps readjusting himself, his eyes never leaving Frederick's face.

Frederick can feel the heat rising from his neck into his cheeks. He clears his throat and then is surprised at how strong his voice is.

"I would not call it making a nuisance of myself", he declares, meeting Tremblay's gaze, angry at the man's suggestion that he is a pain in the ass.

"May I?" Frederick asks but does not wait for Tremblay's answer.

Frederick produces his laptop from a worn brown leather satchel. The Lieutenant-Colonel moves quickly to rescue three piles of green folders. Frederick puts the laptop down and pounds down on a key to give the machine life.

The laptop seems to take forever as they wait for it to load in the ensuing silence. Then, a 'bing' sound and the presentation Frederick prepared many weeks ago pop onto the screen. He turns the laptop to face Tremblay, taps once on the keyboard, and sits down.

Tremblay is silent as he watches the video. His expression changes between deep frowns and raised eyebrows, his eyeballs darting back and forth as he follows the presentation. The military man seems deeply immersed, and Frederick's nerves undulate as he studies the man's face intently.

When the presentation ends, silence returns to the room.

Tremblay leans back in his squeaky chair. The Colonel rubs his chin as little grunts, hisses, and muffled whispered words escape his lips. Frederick is certain that there is more than one expletive between the hisses.

Frederick is perplexed. Is Tremblay assessing what he just saw? Is he organising his words? Will he thank him for coming in and then dismiss him like a soldier without rank? Frederick wonders if it is the latter, as perhaps Tremblay did not understand the technology he was trying to present? Although he had taken great care to set out his findings in layman's terms.

Tremblay sits upright in one decisive motion, he lifts up a piece of paper hiding a red button on his desk, presses it, and barks, "Captain Stevens, find out where the General is and get the Prime Minster on the line for me."

It all happens so fast; one minute, Frederick is accused of being an annoyance, and the next, he is sitting opposite five men, one being the Prime Minister. He finally has his audience in a 'top secret' meeting held in an imposing conference room.

This time, his presentation is projected onto a big screen. Two hours later, Frederick begins to realise his government's blatant self-interest. It was apparent they had a get-together prior to meeting with him.

They want to keep his discovery a secret from the rest of the world, thinking more about using his breakthrough in weaponry. They are men of war, not science.

They are so ignorant Frederick wants to scream, and he begs that they reconsider. Elaborating, he explains that not only can his discovery save the world from most of its current problems, but it can advance space exploration to the point where finding an alternative Earth can be a mere few years in the future. The latter idea is dismissed swiftly without discussion, and it shocks him.

In his hotel room that night, Frederick feels defeated. He is happy he finally got someone in his government to hear him out. But it has snowballed into what can only be described as a monumental disaster as far as he is concerned.

Day two, and discussions continue. Frederick is exasperated. He cannot get through to the men wearing their medals and chevron-adorned uniforms. Why can they not understand that his discovery is meant to benefit humanity? And it is his breakthrough, not theirs.

"We cannot hide this from the world," Frederick defends. "There are billions that will benefit from this, please," he begs at his wit's end.

"You cannot do this," he pleads on day three, as discussions continue but mostly stall as Frederick continues to talk to a brick wall.

By the end of day four, Frederick's resistance is met with veiled threats, leaving him with little choice but to protect his family, so he enters into a secret agreement with his government.

Friendly, then congenial, the last meeting with Tremblay had finally turned malicious.

His discovery would be used for a purpose against everything he believes in. He is making a deal with the devil and regrets ever setting eyes on Tremblay. And there is nothing he can do about it.

His only consolation is that he has not capitulated on some critical issues. His discovery would remain his secret; he would choose the location to fulfil the contract, and Frederick wanted to own the land. He would decide on those who would work closely with him. Lastly, he would receive substantial remuneration under the agreement. They found his request to own land crazy, but he was beyond caring what they thought by then.

In early 2037, the work on Stal Settlement gets underway. At the same time, work begins on five enormous rectangular underground silos.

Dwellings to house the men and women working alongside Frederick and the military mushroom. The speed at which everything takes shape is mind-boggling. A small town springs up within months, with many of the amenities one would find in any small community.

In no time, structures are being painted an appropriate green, camouflaging the above-ground buildings from commercial and other aircraft. Frederick develops a defence system that secures the secret settlement, ensuring near invisibility to outsiders. The system has a warning capability that alerts the military stationed at the facility if anyone dares enter the perimeter.

The government allows Frederick to pick twenty scientists and engineers to work with him. As per the agreement, they go on the government's payroll. The engineers he chooses are signed to a damning contract, and their immediate families are uprooted and brought to the settlement. It is, to put it mildly, a never-ending nightmare. Many of the scientists he chooses are people he has met before or worked with collaboratively on various projects over the years. He has been forced to stoop low. Many will never forgive him, of that he is sure.

Chapter 3 - Freedom

It is the year 2039.

His country's administration was ousted three years after Frederick signed the contract. The incoming government is unaware of the contract. He finds himself thankful he had insisted the wilderness on which Stal Settlement is deeded to him. He now owns a stretch of land extending two hundred kilometres in each direction, almost fifty-thousand acres of remote, mostly boreal forest.

Released from his obligation, the departure from his contract leaves the very first shipment of arms sitting on pallets in the silos. The weapons will never be sent outside of the compound.

All but four of the military troops stationed at the settlement leave when they hear that they no longer answer to Tremblay. In contrast, all but one of the government-employed scientists and engineers remain.

That evening as Frederick sits alone in his office in Silo number one, he has a lot to think about. He has an incredible sum of money at this point, but it is only enough to fund work on the spaceships he plans to build for the first two or three years. Then what?

Unexpected karma has left Frederick at peace. Yet he finds himself with a new responsibility, a new dilemma.

Chapter 4 - Project 25K

It is the year 2039 continued...

Frederick calls a meeting with the remaining people of Stal Settlement. He explains what he plans to do going forward. They quickly jump at the chance to work and see out Project Twenty-Five Thousand. But he also explains that he is considering sharing his discovery with several governments. He is surprised when a majority are adamant he is making a mistake. The consensus is that it will fuel more conflict and greed among autocratic leaders, resulting in more war, and consequently, more suffering.

Frederick agrees to keep his secret for now, but it does not alleviate his feeling of guilt. The following day, work begins in earnest on Project 25K.

The plan is to build five spaceships, one in each silo. The goal is to accommodate and sustain five thousand of mankind's most like-minded, talented people, skilled in all fields.

Frederick calculates the project should take approximately four decades to complete. Away from prying eyes, their focus is now solely on the project and the continuance of the human race. The cache of weapons designed and manufactured thus far for the government has become a good start in forming Stal Settlement's first armed force.

Time passes quickly in Stal. In the rest of the world, misguided philosophies still flourish. Regressive thinking going more than twenty years slowly stifled innovation, law and order, and humanity's progress in all forms.

In the year 2042, another deadly virus kills millions. Many die because of the continued lack of trust in medical science. Conflict and war in various countries become responsible for agonising despair; refugees flee in their thousands just to find they are unwelcome in most nations. The alarming shifts in weather patterns add to the misery.

Earth is rebelling. Humankind is paying the price.

Empathy is dying, and a kind of crazy is taking its place as wealth has a say in governments across the globe.

Then Project 25K runs out of cash, and the fate of the people living and working in Stal hangs in the balance. Frederick is on the verge of telling the faithful few who have believed and worked so hard on the project that it is over.

Help arrives from the most unexpected source just when P25K seems irrevocably lost. The government officials who had initially negotiated the awful contract with Frederick arrive in Stal with their families. The ex-prime minister appeals to Frederick's compassion to allow them to stay. They would work for passage on one of the spaceships. When the ex-pm said he knew Frederick would use the money for spaceships when he was ousted, Frederick had to smile. The quiet man who had said so little in 2036 was clever and a listener.

In exchange, the ex-pm and his compatriots would introduce Frederick to a potential financier. So weighed down with the responsibility of the people of Stal, he agrees to meet the mystery money man.

He instantly finds a progressive thinker in Rick Brand. The man shows almost immediate curiosity in Frederick's vision for Project 25K. Rick is easy to talk to, educated, knowledgeable, and has a bloated bank account. It takes mere hours for the two men to cement an agreement that breathes new life into the project. Rick consents to funding the project to completion and agrees to relocate to Stal with his wife and baby daughter. Rick will oversee the steel shipments and various components for the project under Frederick's guidance. He will also recruit the people who will build and work on the spaceships, educate the children, serve in the busy community and ultimately be passengers on one of the giant homeships.

Friendship and mutual respect grow rapidly between the two men. Frederick immerses himself into the enormous task of building spaceships, and Rick becomes the giver of millions of dollars and the recruiter of brilliant minds. It is a perfect 'marriage.' As he brings more and more like-minded people to live and work in Stal Settlement, the pace increases substantially.

While P25K forges ahead, climate change, now commonly labelled a hoax, does not stop harsh weather events. The lies spawned in the past two decades that created a sub-generation of humanity, an oddity of mankind who perceive science as mostly a myth, remain subservient. Disrupters on the internet, directed and somehow steered by the wealthy, continue to exploit the poor and disadvantaged. The filthy rich becoming even more prosperous and powerful on the backs of those who now have even less.

A hard lesson, a lesson too late.

Rick snaps up men and women from all walks of life from many countries worldwide. Not only scientists but also builders, carpenters, welders, many in the arts, and those in medical fields. He is determined to find twenty-five thousand people with the knowledge to start over in an undiscovered world.

Stal Settlement expands rapidly and blossoms into a wonderfully self-sufficient town. Twenty-four hours a day, seven days a week, it is designed for undeterred productivity. 'Frederick's rule,' secrecy first, then honesty, followed by democracy. It is an axiom everyone in the settlement lives by proudly. People are happy. There is no intimidation, no hate, or duplicity, only individuals dedicated to working on a common solution.

Jon, Frederick's young son and Rick Brand's little Farron, who had only ever known Stal Settlement, absorbed knowledge in vast quantities in a community filled to the brim with clever people. They observe the giant spacecraft evolving daily in the giant silos, a place that had become their playground after school.

Chapter 5 - Planet Kearthat

It is the year 2051.

Somewhere, in a galaxy many light years from Earth, the Drennan people of the planet Kearthat go about their peaceful lives. They are as unaware of the beings on Earth as humankind is unaware of them.

At a celebration held for the latest batch of graduates from the Kearthat Starfleet Academy, Bryzon and Dayson look dapper in their uniforms. The twins have concluded their years of training. Skilled in combat, and qualified spacecraft pilots of the Starfleet, but they are not quite done yet.

Kearthat is a serene planet, and their trading partners, two nearby planets, are similarly docile. While their elite forces have yet to see combat, it does not mean that they are not battle-ready.

Today holds another special significance for Bryzon and Dayson. On this day, having recently reached their twenty-sixth year since their birth, they will be granted a special gift. A gift that passes to all the sons and daughters of those born to privilege on Kearthat.

The secret ritual conducted by the It-Ha, the mystics of Kearthat, will gift them a long-life and the ability to regenerate from any injury. Being *Xennes* will forever set them apart, assuring them of generations of longer life than their mortal Drennan brethren.

Chapter 6 - Jaenus

It is 2071, back on Earth.

Pages from the Journal of Farron (Brand) King.

A grown Farron King feels the need to start a journal before she says goodbye to Stal Settlement and the only planet she has ever lived on.

She writes; Day One. I feel the need to document our journey into space and share for the first time a secret I have kept all my life. So here goes.

For as long as I can remember, I have had vivid dreams. In my dreams, a 'shadow figure' makes his appearance and goes by the name of Jaenus. He has been an intrinsic part of my dreams since I was a child. Leaving me cryptic messages, Jaenus has predicted many events affecting my decisions and unknowingly that of my father and Frederick.

Jaenus has always managed to be rather ambiguous, leaving me to decipher his messages on my own. As I grew older, I became quite adept at knowing what he was trying to tell me. Don't get me wrong, I am no fortune-teller. How and why Jaenus appears to me and looks after me and those around me is a mystery. I only know that I can never imagine what it would be like if he just ceased to exist; to me, he has become a sort of cosy blankie.

I have only ever shared the existence of Jaenus with one person in my life: my husband, Jon. This has created a strong bond between us, so I guess Jaenus is our dream friend.

That said, let me tell you about my father, Rick, and Frederick, who I call my 'number two dad'. Our fathers did their best to raise Jon and I after our mothers died in the awful plane crash, but we were the children of many helping hands. The people of Stal instilled in us what they perceived as meaningful to our futures. It was a good but brief childhood. We prospered but entered adulthood at a young age, and I suppose Jon and I were always destined to marry.

We know every nook and cranny of the spaceships. The enormous towering metal giants contained inside the massive silos that became our second home while our fathers worked on getting P25K into motion.

My father, Rick, passed on in 2069 after a short illness.

On his untidy desk, I found several letters. In my father's familiar cursive handwriting, one of the letters was addressed 'To my Princess.' Another to the people of Stal Settlement. Frederick read the letter to the people as they stood silently in the town hall at the end of Main Street on a rainy afternoon.

It read;

To all the brave people of Project25K, I cannot impress on you enough the importance of completing the work Freddy started. It is our only chance to allow humanity to continue. The part I played in my friend's vision was one of the greatest achievements of my life, the other being my dearest Farron, and I know I have all of you to thank for that.

Look forward, my friends, always look forward. May you soon find a new home, and may it be as beautiful as Earth once was.

Take care of each other, remember how fortunate you all are, journey safely, and thank your lucky stars. Cheerio, my friends.

Rick Brand.

Even after death, my father's humour prevailed, leaving everyone smiling through tears at his final message.

There was a note to Frederick, and he shared its beautiful words with Jon and I after some time had passed.

It read:

Frederick, old chap, take good care of my daughter Farron. You have always been her second dad.

I could not have wished for a better life partner for my Farron than your boy Jon. He is a fine young man. You raised him well, my friend.

I cannot thank you enough for involving me in P25K. It was a pleasure to spend my smackers on something so brilliant, something so worthy. I recently calculated that there will be just enough money to complete the job. Hurry up, Freddy, before it dwindles to nought.

I will be watching from afar, cheers old man. Abeona be with you, and do not be saddened by my untimely expiry; it was one helluva ride.

Rick.

My father worked hard to realise his and Frederick's vision, yet he always found time for me, and his brief note to me did not come as a surprise.

It read;

My dearest Farron,

Princess, you know that I have always loved you more than words can express. Keep dreaming, love. Promise me you will never stop. Do not mourn your old dad, Farron Brand King! Please promise me that, my girl. Celebrate the wonderful years we had. See you on the other side, kiddo.

Always, your loving Dad.

I found it strange that my father would choose the words: keep dreaming. It was as if he knew my dreams were responsible for my many unconventional actions growing up. Actions that sometimes saved the day. Umbrella Time, he called it, when I was prescient about some future event that he could not imagine at that moment.

A folded paper aeroplane was included in the envelope when I opened my note. On one wing, my dad had written 'Courage,' and on the other, he had written 'I love you' and the date 2043. I admit that I wept like that same five-year-old child who played with that paper rocket. The thought of him keeping such a silly thing safe for so many years sincerely echoed my importance to him.

Chapter 7 - The Attack

It is the year 2071 continued...

Stal Settlement. Pages from the Journal of Farron King.

October 18th. It was past midnight when Jon and I heard what we immediately recognised as several helicopters flying overhead, their reverberation slowly disappearing into the distance towards Stal Settlement.

Jon told me to go to the Arc Room and wait for him there as he raced to dispatch our fighters to the now-empty settlement.

It did not take long for others to emerge from their quarters. People were tripping over each other in the passageway, dressed in their nightgowns and pyjamas, with confused faces.

By the time the emergency warning sounded in the spaceship loud explosions could be heard in the distance. The com clicked shortly afterwards, Frederick's calm voice requesting that everyone confine themselves to their quarters and keep the walkways clear.

The grind of our spaceship's large bay doors opening caused a shudder beneath our feet, letting us know that our pilots would meet the intruders with force. I knew our soldiers and flyers would make sure that those who came to do us harm would never get near the spaceships.

Sitting in the dark, looking out of the big porthole in our conference room, I desperately tried to understand what was happening. Who was attacking the settlement?

I could see the flames hungrily licking into the night sky toward Stal, and urgent chatter between the pilots and Commander Jean Bouchard confirmed that we were deliberately being attacked. There were chilling sounds in the background over the coms monitoring our forces. Shouting and gunfire, the echo of someone in pain, then silence, it was not hard to translate what was happening.

At some point, the battle turned in our favour. A squad commander of one of the ground units reported confusion on the part of our assailants. They were slowly beginning to understand that the settlement was deserted.

We had been living on the homeships for several weeks now. The silos were empty, and the compound that was so busy now uninhabited. Our timing, I suppose, had been impeccable. Our enemy was puzzled that their quest led to a deserted town and empty silos.

An hour and twenty minutes after the first explosions, it was silent. The sinister quiet brought people out of their quarters in droves. Their whispering, however, continued. It was as if they believed that the slightest noise could be heard by those seeking to harm us.

In the distance, I could make out sporadic gunfire, and I knew it was our soldiers taking care of unfinished business.

Dawn, October 18[th.] It is a bright, sunny morning. If not for the smoke snaking into the sky from the direction of the settlement, one could almost believe it had all been a dream.

Safe for now... but no longer feeling secure; we are all anxious. After so many years, it is hard to think that our secret is no longer ours to keep. The settlement has been discovered, and we are at risk.

Jon told me that no one would be sent to douse the flames destroying Stal. Our work on Earth had been completed.

Our one-way ticket is booked; it looks like we will be leaving sooner than we initially anticipated.

A large aircraft circling our location at a short distance was shot down by our military during the attack on Stal. We hope this aircraft will give us a clue as to our attackers' identities.

Dusk, October 18[th.] The ground forces sent to find the downed aircraft returned a short while ago. Aboard, they found the bodies of seven men and six women. There were no survivors.

We must conclude they likely hoped to hijack or forcefully demand passage on one of our spaceships. Who knows, perhaps they just wanted to destroy us and everything we have achieved. The world was no longer a trusted place.

Chapter 8 - Courage

It is the year 2071, Earth.

Pages from the Journal of Farron King.

October 20th. My dreams last night were filled with darkness, leaving me with foreboding. I am hesitant to share them with Jon as I don't understand them yet. My instinct is to say nothing, so I am keeping it to myself for now.

Earlier today, Frederick announced that our departure has been moved forward yet again. As I write these words, preparations are underway for the lead spaceship to launch at three o'clock tomorrow afternoon. The other four will follow at fifteen-minute intervals. We are currently at T-minus nineteen hours and counting.

October 20th. Continued...

The countdown was interrupted by an announcement from Frederick earlier. Anyone with doubts about leaving Earth was given the option to leave their respective homeships. No one disembarked, and locks have now been engaged.

Today had initially been planned as a day of celebration, where names for our homeships were to be announced, but plans changed after the attack.

Only a few of us had the opportunity to take a last walk to breathe Earth's air before the hatches and bays on the ships were secured. Jon and I were among those fortunate to say goodbye to the only world we have ever known.

Standing beside the white grave marker under the tree where my father chose to be buried made me profoundly sad. However, I believe his spirit is somewhere among the stars he loves.

I cannot imagine the stress Jon, Frederick, and so many people responsible for our lives are going through right now. We are on high alert; our fighter pilots are suited up and ready to engage anyone who enters our air space. Orders have been given to shoot down anyone who tries to prevent our departure, including our own government's forces.

The spaceships were named an hour ago.

"A successful society must have unity, equity, virtue and resolve, which can only be achieved through courage. We, the people of Stal Settlement, have achieved this. The lead spacecraft will be known as Courage. In launch order, the other homeships are named Unity, Equity, Virtue, and Resolution. Inspired by these words, we leave Earth to search our galaxy for a new home," Frederick announced. Then he cleared his throat, and I knew he would say something about my father.

"We will forever be grateful to Rick Brand, without whose investment in our futures and Science, the completion of Project25K would only ever have been a pipe dream. He was a man of vision, a man of his word, and my dear friend. And lastly, may we never forget the innocent who we leave behind to an uncertain future," Frederick's voice changed, and we all heard the sob he let out before the com clicked off. My throat burned as I shed tears for my father, for Frederick and for being forced to leave my home.

I could hear loud cheering from the hallway outside our living quarters as the T-minus count resumed. We were finally leaving.

Chapter 9 - Hope

It is the year 2071 continued...

After the launch, Frederick stares out into the dark.

 He is sitting at one of the many consoles displaying dozens of buttons that monitor every inch of Homeship Courage. Around him, those on shift monitor the consoles before them, deftly pressing and flipping switches when necessary. The light in the control centre is dimmed to a comfortable hue. The rush is over.

Used to always having one or the other crisis to deal with, Frederick feels a little lost. Long ago, he told Rick that his mission was to save humanity come hell or high water. Well, here he was, no hell, no high water, just a low hum coming from Courage, and the colourful buttons and beeps that propel it.

Looking down at Earth from his vantage point, it had to be the ultimate deception. The planet looks so serene, and there is not an inkling of the hardship and suffering it is experiencing.

It all started with Star Trek movies as a kid, then the years of study and endless lab work followed by many years of dedication in Stal with a singular goal. Quite the journey thus far, but he had done it. No, he and Rick and the humans held in the bellies of each of the spaceships had assured that the project had come to its conclusion.

Something beeps close to where Frederick is sitting. Second Lieutenant Ambrosia comes over, smiling at him. She gives the blinking light a glance and then retreats to her seat; it does not beep again.

Frederick wonders if any of the heads of state have received their parcels yet? He wishes he could see their faces as they realise how important the information is. The presentations explaining how his discovery of regenerative energy works and the actual visual proof are sure to make their heads spin.

By now, most of the world knows that five huge craft have left the planet. There is no doubt in Frederick's mind that it will breed new conspiracy theories. Rumours about Project P25K had appeared on social media in the past. Luckily, the tales had found their way into the labyrinth of lies, deceit, and willful rubbish spouted by so many. The rumours that immersed themselves into one of the many conspiracy theories belched out by the ignorant of the world had managed to shield the project throughout its process.

Frederick had sent parcels to governments he still considered to have a semblance of democracy and integrity, the means to tackle and fund the solutions humanity desperately needed. He had handed it to them on a platter. One thing he is confident of is that he will never know how it turns out.

He stretches as he leaves the big leather seat meant for the commander of the current shift. It is time to rest for a few hours while they circle Earth, waiting for the exact time to leave its orbit. Satisfied with the knowledge that he has left behind a copy of his life's work, it is up to a few good humans to change a planet in chaos. He had given them the blueprint to save humanity. All he could wish for was that none follow the path his government had so many years ago.

Chapter 10 - Lost

It is the year 2071 continued...

Pages for the Journal of Farron King.

November 9th. I am settled into my seat at the porthole window in the Arc Room. From here, I can barely see the remains of Stal Settlement, but I know we leave behind a burned-out ghost town.

As I listen to the final minutes of the countdown, I am certain all aboard the five home spaceships believe they are doing the right thing. Soon, we will accept the vast universe as our backyard and our spaceships as our planets.

Update, November 9th. It all happened so quickly; I could see grass and trees and the destroyed buildings of Stal Settlement, and then I could only make out green, brown and blue patches between white clouds. Then, all too quickly, it was black all around us.

It has been a few hours since we left Earth, and everything is quiet. From where I sit, our home planet looks peaceful. It is hard to believe that so many struggle to survive on this tiny dot floating in blackness.

I can see another of our ships in the distance. We will soon be bona-fide space travellers, and only time will tell where or when we will set foot on terra firma again.

November 10th. It appears we were somehow guided to leave the surface just in time. Reports from Earth speak of a massive earthquake in the Pacific Ocean, the disruption of the ocean floor triggering a mega-tsunami. Unrelated to the earthquake, an unprecedented dust storm in North Africa is making its way across the continent towards the Atlantic Ocean.

My dream last night again predicted what is happening today. In my vision, I saw dust blocking out the natural light and people trying to run from it as daylight turned to night. Then, I was sitting on the wing of a large gull, swooping over the ocean. Below me were white beaches. Quite suddenly, all this changed; all I could see was water, and the beaches were gone.

I catch a glimpse of the devastation as we orbit. North Africa to the equator is doused by a brown cloud of dust moving East to West, the front of the monster beginning to block out the Atlantic Ocean's blue.

November 12th. Earlier, our countdown to break away from Earth's orbit was aborted. Even before Frederick announced it, I somehow knew that our departure would be delayed. Call it a feeling or a remnant from my many dreams. An error was found at T-minus forty-five minutes. Our launch window, so meticulously determined, now inexplicably indicates our trajectory optimal transfer time is off.

November 13th. The error has been corrected.

A while ago, we heard on the radio that the tsunami on Earth had reached many shores. Millions are without a roof over their heads, and hundreds have succumbed. The ocean has, as in my dreams, demanded more land and more lives. The earthquake was the largest ever recorded.

November 16th. What started as jubilation moments after we broke from orbit changed instantly. We have awakened to emptiness. There are faint glimmers of what we think may be distant stars, but we cannot be sure as they are ever-changing. The only certainty is that we are being propelled forward at an exceedingly high speed. This is all happening without our homeship's power. 

Our spaceship, Courage, shows no signs of damage, but we cannot communicate with the other homeships. I fear we may be all alone. An absolute and profound feeling of being lost has overtaken everyone. The eerie silence is deafening. Blackness surrounds us; in it, a milky light-purple haze swirls as if wrapping us in wisps of smoke. In the distance, we can see spots of indistinct light shapes; We have no point of reference.

Jon and Frederick think they may have an idea of what occurred. We do not appear to be in any immediate danger. Everything is functioning well on the spaceship, and we are extremely grateful.

The last thing I remember is when the countdown reached zero, and Commander Bouchard announced, "Launch window, breakaway. Voilà mes amis."

I had been looking at the partial outline of Northern Africa and the lingering cover from the dust storm at the time of the breakaway. Suddenly, there was a blinding light; it seemed to envelop everything. I think it came from Earth, but I am not entirely sure. Briefly, I thought the ship was ablaze. I know I felt dizzy for a few seconds, and then nothing.

When I awoke, I was lying on the floor next to my seat at the porthole. Managing to sit upright, I felt disoriented. The strangest thing is that my first feeling was an unbelievable thirst. My legs felt heavy, and I found it difficult to stand. Jon burst through the door a few minutes later, frantically calling my name.

Later, Jon shared Frederick's opinion that our predicament was not unlike being in a tunnel or void. He did not need to spell it out for me. I knew what they were thinking. A phenomenon yet unproven, but here we were, what else could it be? It had to be a wormhole!

We speculated that perhaps an enormous explosion on Earth had reached us via a ripple effect, the wave moving us off our trajectory. While our computers indicate we had experienced some radiation during our break from Earth's orbit, everything was working as it should be. I know I should be terrified, but instead, I feel strangely calm and unafraid. I checked the time and date; we had all been in an unconscious state for three days.

Could this be the beginning of the end? Will we die before we have had the chance to explore our galaxy? And what about Earth? Are there any survivors? Did the explosion come from Earth, or was it something colliding with Earth, but that is so unlikely? Was this what Jaenus was trying to warn me about many dreams ago? And where are the other four homeships?

Chapter 11 - The Nothingness

It is the year 2078.

Pages from the Journal of Farron King.

After seven years of unyielding nothingness, a weird way of life has evolved on Courage. People get up in the morning and work on the different levels of the ship, be it at the hydroponic farm, the medical centre or the school. It is a strange normal, and awfully odd when you think we are going somewhere at an unfathomable speed, yet it feels like we are standing still.

There have been weddings, several babies born, and Frederick's nephew got engaged to a charming young girl named Petra who works on the fourth level as a baker. Life goes on.

My dreams are filled with messages from Jaenus telling me to advise Jon that we must take to hibernation for fifty years. My dream friend is asking for patience from us. Could he be leading us somewhere? How in this new world are we to convince everyone to take to the pods?

Continued...

Frederick put the idea of hibernation to the people on the homeship. To my surprise, there was an overwhelming affirmative outcome when the votes were counted. We are all desperately hoping that when we awaken, we will find this current nightmare a thing of the past. We, so want to continue our journey of discovery.

Jon and I are among the many who have volunteered to maintain the ship during this period, and each of us will be required to do at least one, six-month shift. We will be woken together when our turn comes. We do not yet know the effects of such a long period of cryogenic suspension. For the first time, we all fear what could happen, yet another unknown.

We dare not think about what our future holds if we awaken to the same predicament. We can only hope that our big sleep will outwait this strange singularity.

Chapter 12 - The It-Ha

Planet Kearthat, somewhere in an unknown galaxy.

Meirah, Bryzon's woman smiles at him. He and his twin, Dayson, are about to board the transporter craft that will take them to the secret place where they will go through the ritual of receiving long-life, the rite that will make them Xennes.

At the grand gathering, a celebration in honour of the graduating class from the Kearthat Starfleet Academy Meirah will await Bryzon's return. She knows exactly what he will experience on this night, as she went through the same ceremony two Kearthat years ago. Her heart is full of love for him, and soon, they will be of equal standing in the eyes of the elite of Kearthat. Then her father will accept him and give his blessing for them to undertake the ceremony that will join them as one and be together for the rest of their lives.

Last to board the transport shuttle are the three mystics of Kearthat. High It-Ha Solaarr, It-Ha Layrrah and It-Ha Sihuun. The three women are similarly dressed in dark purple dresses that flow to the ground. The fine fabric wafts as they walk, their matching cloaks reaching the floor; Capes hide their faces partially. Their long black hair is held back by numerous strands of gold shimmering as they move. Although different in appearance, they are all beautiful women. Unchanged since the day of their becoming It-Ha, they remain youthful. They, however, are ancient; no one knows exactly how old, and no one has ever dared ask.

Their destination is somewhere high up on Ante Mountain's cliffs, known only to the It-Ha. The pilot of the shuttle, and the graduates will find that they cannot remember its whereabouts when they awaken tomorrow. The It-Ha are women of great magical ability, and such trivial spells were easily cast.

The clearing where the shuttle has landed is barely big enough for the transport craft. They are surrounded by big trees and brush. High It-Ha Solaarr waves her hand towards a narrow path that has appeared out of nowhere. The graduates follow the mystic women in silence. Their path is being lit by the light of hundreds of Firemoths.

The moths had materialised as if called, and Bryzon could feel the magic in the air surrounding them.

When they reach the cave entrance, Bryzon looks at Dayson; without speaking, they know they will be very different when they exit.

A short walk brings them to a clearing, and Bryzon can hear the water rippling before he sees it. The water is so clear he can see every little pebble at the bottom of the shallow flowing stream.

The It-Ha ask the graduates to form a line and then go down on their knees at the water's edge. The mystics begin to chant, and Bryzon and his friends watch in amazement as the It-Ha begin to float upwards and drift to the centre of the stream. Their pupils aglow, flickering between yellow-green; their chant achieving oneness with the rhythm and sound of the ripples of the water. Then, several narrow spouts of water rise out of The Cigam-like arms. They grow longer and longer, reaching towards each of the graduates where they stop. Dayson taps his brother on the back and smiles. They have never witnessed magic before this night; it is indescribable, beyond words.

It-Ha Layrrah breaks away from the chant and floats back to the edge of the stream; small wooden cups float out of the dark to each of the graduates. Stunned, they look toward the It-Ha, her pupils still glimmering green.

"Drink of the roots of the Enoce tree and receive renewal," she tells them, gesturing to take hold of the cups floating in front of them.

Ambivalent at first, Bryzon discovers the dark brown liquid smells of the forest, and it is almost tasteless.

"Now drink of the waters of the Cigam and become Xennes It-Ha Layrrah tells them, her voice lyrical, but at the same time almost hollow sounding.

Bryzon puts his mouth to the water spout before him and swallows a good-sized gulp as little droplets spatter his face and Starfleet uniform. He waits; at first, he thinks the ritual is complete. Then it happens, and he is taken by complete surprise. His body begins to heat up, and just when he thinks it is unbearable, it goes the opposite way. He is cooling down, and fast, he can see his breath in front of him. Bryzon feels his mind go into a state of panic, and then it dissipates. He lets out an audible sigh. It takes mere seconds before he feels quite normal again.

The two It-Ha floating above the stream stop their chant and float back to the shore. Their eyes have returned to the natural deep green that gives away the fact they are It-Ha.

Bryzon waits for something else to happen, but there is only silence until the It-Ha smile and extend their well-wishes to each of them.

It is done, they are Xennes. He and his brother will live for a thousand Kearthat years, and if they ever experience injury, they will feel the pain, but their bodies will heal. They are impervious to harm. They are the elite of Kearthat. Long-life and regeneration have assured them a wonderful future.

Returning to the festivities, they celebrate their new status. Bryzon and Mehira disappear into the Supreme Council Gardens, and hugs turn into kisses under the largest Trigga tree known to be growing on Kearthat. Finally, they are free to join their lives.

But sadly, little do they know that one's future is never assured.

Chapter 13 - Expelled

It is Earth Year 2128, October 2nd.

Pages from the Journals of Farron King.

Today, we awoke from our pods to find that we had finally been expelled from the vacuum that had held us captive. It has been almost fifty Earth years since we took to hibernation. It is strange to know that I should rightfully be in my eighties. I look and feel unchanged. However, Frederick did not adhere to his promises to Jon and I. He stayed awake for long periods at a time; he is now a frail old man. Jon is heartbroken.

We have not seen or heard from any of our other homeships. We can only hope they will materialise soon. The prospect of returning to exploring and finding a new home might become a reality once more.

Our powerful telescope on Courage has been busy. We can only hope we can soon pinpoint where we are in the universe. Until then, we wait in anticipation for the other four spaceships to emerge from the mysterious vortex that has us trapped for so long.

October 4th. This morning, the doctors on Courage completed a battery of tests on Frederick. His sister Mary, Jon's aunt, has not left her brother's side for a moment. We fear that the years of shuttling between a state of suspension and a state of wakefulness have taken its toll on him.

October 6th. Resolute joined us from out of the void. A recon ship is readying to transport Jon to the spaceship to assess their situation. Frederick is not well.

October 8th. Equity, Virtue and Unity have reappeared; no words describe how thrilled we are. After boarding the other spaceships to ascertain their circumstances, Jon was able to establish that they mysteriously dealt with their situations much as we had. I am convinced that Jaenus must have somehow had something to do with their decisions.

Miraculously, there have been few deaths among the five ships. Somewhat disturbing is that two of my friends on board Unity chose to stay awake longer than planned. They are now many years my senior.

Earth Year 2129, February 27[th.] We have concluded that we must have been propelled far beyond our solar system, we have yet to identify our position.

The wormhole could perhaps have sent us thousands of light-years from Earth. No decision has been reached yet as to how we should proceed from this point on. We could be destined to search this unknown part of the universe for many years. We have to be certain of our decisions before we begin exploring. Our ability to be self-sufficient continues undeterred, but our desire to find a viable planet remains paramount.

April 4[th.]Jaenus has finally given us a cryptic message to follow. I have interpreted it to be a star cluster. I am now sure we are no longer in the Milky Way.

With the homeships able to engage at a phenomenal speed, which we call DIPPS, it will take us approximately eleven Earth years to reach the star cluster we have been guided to. Perhaps when we awaken, a viable planet we can call home will await our arrival. I am trusting in my dreams, and in Jaenus.

Again, volunteers have agreed to remain awake for the first three months in preparation for our journey, after which all of us will take to our pods and be awakened in shifts to run the ship.

After Jaenus left me with directions to follow, he has been absent from my dreams of late. I feel lost without my shadow friend.

April 8[th.] Today, it saddens me to write that we said goodbye to Frederick. His health suddenly deteriorated. Our hearts are shattered by his loss, and Jon's grief is hard to witness. Thoughts of my father keep me awake at night. I so wish he were here.

July 25[th.] I am mapping the point where the wormhole released its hold on us. This has come about because of a dream I had; Jaenus is back. I have interpreted it to indicate that perhaps, one day, our descendants may want to retrace the path that brought us to where we are now.

Earth year 2130, Jan 2[nd.]

With my mapping done, Jon and I will take to our pods later today. My dear Journal, be patient, my paper friend. I will write again in eleven Earth years.

Chapter 14 - Home Sweet Home

It is Earth Year 2141.

Kearthat Year unknown.

It is late afternoon, which is usually a busy time in the City of Seccus on planet Kearthat. Today is different; everyone has stopped what they are doing. The Drennan are captivated by the spectacle above their city.

Bryzon has just left the base and is making his way home, his mind preoccupied. As he nears the underground exit to his sector, he hears the sirens go off at the base. By the time he makes it back, there is frenzied activity.

His friend and second in command at the Starfleet base, Ohre, is acting in his stead. Orders for fighter craft to surround the giant spaceship hanging like an imposing bug above Seccus have already been given.

He is quickly brought up to date. The spaceship, Bryzon is told, entered Kearthat's airspace without the slightest detection. It had simply appeared as if by magic. He learns that several attempts to communicate with the craft have yielded no response.

Immediately he takes to the sky in a weaponized transporter to get a closer look. Bryzon's ship approaches the enormous grey intruder, a bay door opens on the foreign vessel, revealing bright light emanating from its interior. Silhouetted against this vivid background, a figure stands next to him, and a small craft waits.

Looking through the lens of his enlarger, Bryzon can discern a humanlike creature, much like the Drennan, with both arms in the air. Recognising the stranger's gesture as a sign of surrender, he immediately orders the fleet surrounding the intruding craft to pull back just a little.

He evaluates the situation; the foreign vessel has retracted its bay doors and he concludes that the man seems to be indicating that he comes in peace.

Bryzon watches through his enlarger as the white-haired man straddles the tiny craft next to him and begins his descent away from the big ship. Only then does he instruct the pilot of his craft to follow, landing a short distance away.

When Jon King dismounts from the SpaceBike his father Frederick so long ago designed and built, he immediately raises his arms in the air.

Jon kneels keeping his hands behind his back to signify total surrender. Only then does he lift his head and look directly into Bryzon's eyes. He smiles, a suggestion from Farron. The earthling's smile is disarming, just as Farron predicted it would be. The submissive behaviour works, and Bryzon approaches Jon. He nods a greeting at the stranger. His greeting is quickly reciprocated by Jon, who responds with a sort of exaggerated kneeling bow to emphasize his purpose of being one of peace.

Jon King is helped to his feet; from there, he is taken to the base. Several Kearthat Starfleet fighter craft circle above the earthling homeship, which has since landed a short distance outside of the city. A large contingent of Kearthat's armed force quietly guards the alien ship. Leaving Bryzon, Dayson and Oreh are tasked with establishing who the strangers are, and what their intentions may be.

Chapter 15 - The Elder Council

Seated in the grandiose Council Chambers with its enormous, gilded fixtures and lavish furnishings, the twins have no idea what the council will decide. To Bryzon and Dayson, the light-haired pale stranger, although odd at first, had started to look remarkably normal to them. He was a man, much like them.

The Earth leader begins by turning the electronic tablet he brought with him to face the Elders. It runs projects a presentation he and Farron painstakingly put together. The idea was that no matter the language, it would convey that they came in peace and were looking for sanctuary.

The Elders are at first amused, then finally bored.

This is when High It-ha, Solaarr, steps in. She bows to the Elders and makes her way towards the encumbered stranger. Jon at first does not notice her advance on him; when he does become aware of the tall woman in her lengthy, deep purple robe, he stops, he is mesmerised by the beautiful woman floating a few inches off the ground. He takes a single step back and watches as she raises her arms in front of her in his direction, her palms turned up. The light in the grand room dims, and she begins to chant, her pupils glimmering deep yellow.

Bryzon can see on Jon King's face that he realizes that it is the It-Ha who had somehow dimmed the lights.

Two balls of pale pink mist emanate from It-Ha Solaarr's palms. The perfectly rounded swirls slowly drift towards the motionless earthling. The tight balls of mist rotate while they hang in the air just above his head. Jon tilts his head back just in time to see the pink balls explode, silently showering him in a spray of tiny sparkles. His reaction is to close his eyes. He immediately wipes his face when he opens them, but there is no glitter anywhere. It has all simply vanished.

Solaarr ascends the stairs to rejoin the council. The light returns to the room, leaving Jon dumbfounded.

The High It-Ha addresses Jon King in Drennan, and Bryzon can see the shock on the man's face when he realises he can understand her. The languages are magically translated.

Putting his hands together in a sign of appreciation, Jon bows to the Elders of the council sitting above him and then towards Solaarr in a gesture of thanks. Speaking his language, he knows it is the Drennan tongue the elders hear.

Those on the council are shocked, sitting upright and attentive. Before long they are enthralled by the space traveller's story. The hours pass quickly as Jon relates the epic journey of Project25K to them in short form. He assures the Elder Council of the trustworthiness of his people, and the elders are captivated.

Jon confesses that the only home many of his people have known are the spaceships, and none had put their feet on solid ground in almost seventy Earth years. He explains that they were hurtled through space at incredible speed by some unknown force.

Then he makes the first mistake. Jon offers to share earthling technology in exchange for the right to stay on Kearthat. Things immediately turn a little sour.

The sharing of technology and Jon's theory that the homeships had inadvertently been catapulted into some wormhole has the elders buzzing with frenzied discussion. Jon is left staring at the backs of most of the council members as they huddle in discussion.

Bryzon is aware that the senior leaders are suspicious of almost anything, let alone technology or some unknown magic from another world. To his horror, he quickly learns the elders are more prone to destroying what Jon has to offer than embracing it. They are also suspicious of Jon's feckless disclosure of 'this wormhole.'

When asked about the distance of Earth from Kearthat by an elder, Jon respectfully admits he has no idea and that Kearthat could be many thousands of light-years from Earth.

Then, for some unknown reason, Jon tells the elders that Kearthat is larger than Earth but does not have the same tilt. Bryzon becomes concerned when he adds more frivolous information to his story.

Jon had managed to confuse his previously enthusiastic audience. Kearthat was the superior planet among those it traded with, and the elders knew nothing of tilts or planet sizes. Kearthat was, in their eyes, perfect in every way. No one was going to tell them otherwise.

Finally, the earthling is dismissed and handed over to Bryzon for further questioning. Bryzon houses Jon close to where he has easy access to him. He is keen to learn more about the man with the white hair from another world. He now must gain as much information as possible to report back to the elders.

Chapter 16 - Recollection

Jon tells Bryzon almost everything about their journey that led to finding Kearthat. How they had been the recipients of horrible experiences, their losses occurring at different intervals during their mission. The sad occurrence of leaving fifteen thousand men and women of all ethnicities for dead, three of their spaceships lost forever somewhere in the universe.

Unknown to Bryzon, the only secret Jon would hold back would be Farron's dream friend, Jaenus. The dream shadow who pointed the earthlings to Kearthat.

As he learns of Earth, Bryzon is speechless.

Earth had once been beautiful. Humankind has created many advanced societies with subtle differences. Living on one planet, their world was separated into pieces of land divided by a great ocean. They were a species that innovated constantly. There were great cities and vast lands where beautiful and strange creatures roamed. There was privilege and immense wealth, but it had all begun to change.

One man's lies, Jon explains to Bryzon, created a new breed of human. Humans who were violent and destructive, who demanded a departure from democracy, and held no empathy towards the unfortunates of Earth.

Jon describes how his planet was neglected by leaders who put the accumulation of wealth above the needs of the people. Deceit and corruption gained a firm foothold, creating poverty and misery. A culture of hatred and violence, and how all science was slowly suffocated. The effects were so extreme that a once modern and progressive world was slowly stripped of years of advancement. Bringing about a regression that began to stifle the planet.

But it is the bright light radiating from Earth when they left that Jon can't explain, which is the strangest of all Jon's stories, leaving Bryzon both fascinated and dismayed.

Only five-thousand three-hundred and forty-seven earthlings were aboard the two homeships that made it to Kearthat, Bryzon learns. Jon insists that, without the help of the time tunnel, they would never have found Kearthat.

Recounting the loss of the three homeships to Bryzon in detail was heartbreaking for Jon. Bryzon could see the sadness in the man's eyes as he recalled the memories. Jon explains that two of their ships were lost after being struck by an unknown force that must have moved invisibly at an incredibly high speed. In his opinion, the velocity at which the ships were hit was the reason there was no trace of debris. Many thousands of beings on the two craft had been killed instantly, or so he believes.

It was the third spaceship, lost under incredibly sinister circumstances, that Bryzon finds most perplexing.

The loss occurred when the earthlings thought they had found a habitable planet. One ship was sent to the planet's surface while the other two ships waited at a safe distance.

A research team reported that the habitat appeared to be much like Earth. Lush vegetation, rivers and streams, breathable air, it all seemed idyllic. Yet there were no life forms, no birds, animals or insects. Then suddenly, excitement turned to panic. In less than a day, everyone on the first ship to land on the planet had succumbed to an unexplained event.

Jon tells Bryzon that they sent several armed transporters to investigate after not hearing from the spaceship Unity in two days. When they reported back, Jon explains, it felt as if his soul had been ripped from him. The spaceship was devoid of life. It was empty.

The remaining two ships waited ten days, hoping for some kind of contact, for his people to re-emerge. None returned. In time, after a unanimous vote, they left the homeship Unity on the strange planet's surface and with it, the strange secret that stole over five thousand lives.

Jon shakes his head, and tears form, which are quickly wiped away by the earthling.

The first time they saw Kearthat from up close, Jon tells Bryzon, it reminded them of Earth again. They were, however, extremely cautious. They waited and watched from afar until some weeks later when they saw a spaceship approaching Kearthat. Forty-eight hours later, a different spaceship left the planet. Eventually, a united decision was made by the people on the remaining homeships, who voted to take a closer look at what this world had to offer.

They chose to land where there seemed to be no activity on the planet. Unknown to them, they had landed in the Nerrab, the Badlands of Kearthat.

When the reconnaissance team reported back, it was good news. They had landed in the desert, but it seemed like paradise to everyone on the homeships; the air was good, and they were hopeful. They decided one spaceship would approach a large city while the other would wait in a position of relative safety.

"We knew we could engage DIPPS to escape at any sign of danger", Jon says and smiles. Then the earthling finds that he has to explain DIPPAR Speed to the Drennan man who sits quietly while he learns of the genius of Frederick King.

Chapter 17 - Unfair Deal

The earthling' ability to make their spaceships blend into their surroundings, and their mysterious capacity to travel at amazing speed has Bryzon excited. But he knows this is not sitting well with the elders. They were old and comfortable in their ways, thinking of Kearthat as the only planet of greatness in their galaxy. Strange, advanced technologies made Kearthat look lesser, and to the elders that was unacceptable. It was best that these ridiculous technologies were destroyed to restore Kearthat to its original glory, the leader of their galaxy.

After Bryzon, Dayson, and his friend and second-in-command Ohre report back to the elders, the council decides that if the strangers are to stay, the ships would have to go, and with it, all the strange technology 'and magic' from this other world.

Many hours of discussion are held. The oldest of the elders, well into his nine-hundred and tenth year, has the final say in the matter. He remains adamantly opposed to earthling technology.

The decision vexes Bryzon and Dayson. Nothing had changed much as far as the Elder Council was concerned in over two thousand years. It was clear that only innovation invented by those on Kearthat was appropriate.

Bryzon is shocked and angry. He expresses his disappointment to his father. Destroying the earthling technologies would be an opportunity lost, a chance for Kearthat to learn, he begs. While Dayson and Ohre stand by his side in support, Bryzon listens to his father defend the decision of the elders. There is nothing Bryzon can do to negate their unified decision.

The elders entrust the task of destroying the earthling ships to the mystic women, the three It-Ha, who serve at the pleasure of the most senior and oldest Elder.

Chapter 18 - The City of Seccus

It is Earth Year 2141, March 3rd.

Pages from the Journals of Farron King.

We have finally left the homeships for terra firma.

The Drennan are fascinated by us, and we find them equally out of the ordinary. There seems to be a lot of staring by both sides and as rude as it may seem, I suppose no one can blame the other for behaving in this manner.

The only animal I encountered close-up since our arrival was a little pinkish ball of fur that I glimpsed when we first entered the City of Seccus. I decided it was perhaps a cross between a Pomeranian, with maybe a smidge of hedgehog. Through its long fur, I could see that its eyes were bright yellow, most unusual. Amusingly, it seemed to be going a hundred miles an hour on its six short little legs. I am not sure if it was the equivalent of a small dog, but the little creature was too adorable.

Shortly after we settled in, they gave us each a computerised tablet of sorts. Jon would soon learn that it translates to Enscriptor, in their language. At first glance, the technology seems far more advanced than our computers. When Jon and I were shown how to turn on the Enscriptors, we found very few similarities to our gadgetry.

March 4th. Dear Journal, I am continuing with the Earth date and time. Why, I am not sure as yet? I must confess that the written text and spoken language here are overwhelming. It will take us years to converse; perhaps that is why I am continuing my old ways.

I managed to turn on the Enscriptor and navigate to pictures of animals, and by pure chance, I found pictures of the night sky. I fear I am none the wiser of our location. It is frustrating to be unable to ask the questions that pop into my head whenever I look at something new, but the language barrier makes one positively mute.

For now, we are grateful that Jon has understood Drennan when they speak and vice versa. I find it hard to digest the incredible magic of a woman they call the High It-Ha Solaarr. We want so much to fit in. But magic? Who thought?

March 6[th.] Jon introduced me to Solaarr today. I felt immediately close to this mysterious woman who seemed sincerely concerned for our well-being. Within minutes, she used her magic to enable me to speak to and understand her. It has changed everything. I was soon overwhelmed at her generosity in relating answers to anything we asked about Kearthat and its people, animals, and geography. She speaks of their galaxy as Ade~mordna.

I, of course, had a gazillion questions, the first being about their moons and suns. Much like Earth, but in some ways vastly different, Kearthat is a marvel. They have three moons, which I was sure played a part in their ocean's tides; however, they are rather distant from the planet I have learned, and the disruption was not as drastic as I thought. Their two suns are intriguing, but as with their moons, their dominant star, and also their second star are far more distant than that of Earth. They talk about 'the cooling and the darkening' here. From what we can understand, it is when eclipses occur. I can't wait to experience it. This might eventually explain the pale pink daytime sky, cream clouds and the tropical weather.

My heart is filled with great optimism for the future. At the same time, I feel sad that my father and Frederick are not here to witness the fruits of all their hard work. I know that many of us were silently beginning to wonder if perhaps we were the only evolved beings in the universe, but here we are.

High It-Ha Solaarr finds my hair fascinating, and several times without asking, she has run her fingers through my hair, leaving me blushing with embarrassment. Her actions don't seem to phase her, though. All the men and women here have straight black hair; my lighter hair is obviously quite the anomaly.

Our lodgings are more than adequate. The food is delicious. They are meat-eaters; I dare not think from what animal. Their vegetables delight us. The fruit is a gift to our senses as we experience new flavours and smells.

The Drennan, although advanced, seems oddly old-worldly in a way. Of course, our accomplishments as far as the homeships are concerned are far superior to theirs. Jon told me they could learn a lot from us. I imagine how Frederick and my father would have embraced such a place. We could not ask for a better world to end up in.

The closet in our housing unit is filled with new tunics. All practical, all serene colours. Footwear is simple, but the men in the Starfleet wear uniforms and boots that somewhat resemble those in old Star Trek movies. Jon looks quite handsome in his tunic, and I must admit I have never worn anything as comfortable.

Kearthat has never seen war. We were dumbfounded when we discovered that two planets near Kearthat are populated, and we were overjoyed to discover both are considered friendly. Jon has been fortunate to be introduced to several beings from the planets Kaldu and Ibromne. Apparently, they were startling, definitely what we would call alien, Jon told me. He insists they remind him of a cross between Greedo of Star Wars and a Tapir but with more grey matter. I must admit his description had me in stitches, and I will not begin to describe the picture that came to my mind.

The Drennan only live on a small portion of their planet; the other, almost two-thirds, is mostly desert and mountainous. The reason for this, we understand, was an enormous quake several thousand years ago.

The air here is pristine, as is the water. It is apparent that Kearthat has never been exposed to the pollution of fossil fuels, that is, if there are any. However, they mine a mineral called Zraphite, a magical naturally occurring inorganic that supplies power to everything they use.

March 10th. We were warned up-front but never thought it would be this soon; we experienced our first Kearthquake this morning. It lasted for less than a minute before it was followed by two smaller shakes, as they refer to them.

A gigantic volcano that towers thousands of feet and forms part of a mountain range that is the backdrop to Seccus, is said to be dormant. But something is quite obviously stirring somewhere. The Drennan, however, seemed quite unperturbed by the movement below their feet. They have assured us that we need not be concerned; we take them at their word.

Since being on Kearthat, my dreams have been disturbing, full of terrifying alien beings and war. Perhaps everything has been too overwhelming since our arrival. My mind, I think, has been dwelling on too many of my fears. I am ignoring my nightmares. I cannot for one minute entertain the idea that we would ever again experience war in our lives. The Drennan are gentle people who appear to be explorers first and soldiers second.

But accepting this planet as our 'forever' home will take time.

Earth Year 2141 continued...

March 11th. The destruction of the ships will apparently be left to the three It-Ha who have sworn to us that we will be safe on Kearthat. It is a grave price to pay, but we are desperate to have a normal life, and this seems pretty normal to us.

April 16th. It is lovely to get up in the morning, see the soft pink sky, and feel the suns. It is tropical and warm. I am ageing normally now, but it is a fair trade if we are allowed to live out our lives in peace. And who knows, my dreams of having a family could soon be realized.

The Drennan and Xennes alike have otherwise shown us only kindness.

April 30th. We have begun to feel quite guilty, and we asked how we could contribute to our new society. We are ready to show our appreciation. Jon and I met with Bryzon earlier, and I told him that we would do whatever was asked of us.

Without hesitation, Jon asked if he would be allowed to work on the Starfleet base permanently.

At first, I was a little reluctant, afraid that Bryzon would think of me as presumptuous, as I explained that astronomy had brought me to Kearthat and that I would like to continue my work in that field. I also expressed that I would very much like to study the florae on the planet as I had a great interest in the medicinal uses of plants.

He seemed quite happy with my request. Jon later told me that Bryzon was in awe of the colour of my eyes, and I could have asked for anything I wanted.

The remainder of our people will be offered various choices to contribute to the Drennan way of life. We were assured by several of Bryzon's people that they would consider everyone's skills and what they could offer to Kearthat. Bryzon expressed that he wished to please each person.

Jon is the happiest I have seen him since we left Earth. However, for the life of me, I cannot understand the attraction of boarding a spaceship so soon after getting off one.

The Drennan Xennes twins, Bryzon and Dayson, are quite different from their parents, who Jon has told me are elders. We got the distinct feeling the twins were not happy with the elders' decision to destroy our homeships.

Chapter 19 - All is Lost

Kearthat, Earth Year 2141.

Pages from the Journal of Farron King.

May 21st. I am not sure what I am about to write will ever be read by anyone.

Ignoring the warnings Jaenus has been giving me since we have been on Kearthat has brought us our worst nightmare. The city has been attacked by aliens who are unknown to the Drennan. I fear my blunder has cost the lives of many thousands, including that of our own people.

We woke up to chaos in the middle of the night with the sounds of explosions. For just a moment, I thought I was back in Stal Settlement.

I am in what I think is a bunker under the city with hundreds of older Drennan, young children, and pregnant women. There are a handful of people who arrived with me on Homeship Courage. Jon is with Bryzon. Where? I do not know. All around me, I see terrified faces. We are not sure what is happening outside and that in itself is frightening.

Our people are scattered all over the city. I hope there are more bunkers like this one where they can be safe, at least for now. I do not know how long we will be in here before we get news of what is happening.

Ignoring the warnings that Jaenus was giving me in my dreams is unforgivable. I was complacent, too content not to believe it. The horrible creatures I saw in my dreams seemed improbable to me, and now I am powerless to change what was happening to us. It is too late.

May 22nd. Still no news from Jon of what is happening outside. We keep hearing explosions and other noises that we cannot identify. I don't have the words to express how wretched I feel today. I nod off every so often, but Jaenus does not appear. I need to speak to him. He must tell me what we must do. What did we do to deserve this?

May 23rd. No news yet. I miss Jon. There are long periods of silence. We can hear the droning of spaceships as they pass overhead. I can only hope that they are Drennan craft. Is Jon still alive?

May 24th. The door to the underground bunker opened today. Jon and Dayson, accompanied by some Xennes soldiers, are taking us to the Starfleet base. We will use the underground tunnels before they close them off for good. We are hoping to escape on one of the Kearthatian spaceships. The Drennan are retreating; the aliens have won. The plan is to get to the planet Kaldu.

May 25th. This is my last entry. Jon and I are two of several thousand caught trying to escape the city. We have been taken by a vile, alien species. There are dead everywhere. I fear Jon and I may not live to see the end of this day. I am so scared. I can't imagine what these disgusting creatures have in store for us. I hope tha.....

PART II

Chapter 20 - The Invasion

There was barely time for Jon and his people to settle into life on Kearthat. They had been living on their new planet for a mere eighty days when the attack came from the Eslaf. An unknown enemy and species to the Drennan of Kearthat.

The Kearthat forces tried bravely to hold back the onslaught, but the Starfleet and ground forces were overwhelmed. The aliens came at them with everything they had, which was a mighty force. It did not take long before it was evident that they had come to purge the people from the planet.

The earthlings had again suffered a great loss of life. For those who survived, it had been fortunate Jon King had chosen Seccus, as it was the only city on Kearthat that the alien Eslaf from Ludinia chose to spare. Jon and his wife Farron had miraculously escaped death together, one of the very few couples saved in an indiscriminate slaughter.

By some miracle, Bryzon and Dayson were two of the few thousand Drennan who were taken prisoner. Kearthat had lost all but four thousand five hundred lives. It had been a massacre.

Unknown to Bryzon and the few Drennan survivors, it had been the magic of It-Ha Layrrah invoking the power of The Veil that safeguarded Jon and Farron. The enchantment of invisibility had protected the earthling couple.

Few Xennes survived the Eslaf invasion. Courageous men and women fighters met their deaths as a result of Eslaf weapons. Their Xennes ability to regenerate was taken from them in an instant when they were fired upon by the alien weapons.

The three It-Ha, with their ability to see into the future, had failed Kearthat's people when it came to alien attack. Bryzon was unable to fathom how Solaarr, Layrrah and the third It-Ha, Sihuun, never saw a vision of the invasion.

Xennes fighters finally had to accept they had been defeated. The struggling Kearthat Starfleet ceased fighting, and their ground troops were conquered.

In Seccus, the fear was palpable as they were being rounded up. Many begged on their knees to be spared but were cut down, while others were chosen randomly to be herded onto waiting alien ships. To this day, Bryzon believes he and Dayson were spared because the Eslaf soldier deciding on their fate could not fathom how they could be an exact copy of one another.

Many Drennan tried to flee to the rural areas of Kearthat, but there was nowhere to hide. Hunted down like animals, they, too, met their fate. Thousands of bodies lay scattered; to the absolute horror of those who remained, the destruction was horrific.

In the days leading up to the surrender, a band of brave Drennan Xennes fighters led by Meirah and a handful of soldiers, which included some earthling volunteers, kept attacking the Eslaf from outside of the city. But soon, the fighting stopped, and Bryzon knew. His heart broke into a million pieces, but there was no time to mourn.

From the alien spaceship where he and Dayson sat forlorn, they could see small towns and farm settlements ablaze below them. The twins knew then that thousands had lost their lives. It left no doubt that it had been an eradication!

Bryzon and Dayson could not tell where the alien ship was taking them. They held each other close, crying openly for the loss of their people, friends, and family. Bryzon shed tears for the loss of his fellow Xennes and the City of Kuldab beyond the sea that lay in ruins. His heart was on fire as he cried for his beautiful Meirah. But these would be the last tears Bryzon would shed for a long time. His heartache would soon harden into intense, searing hate for the aliens who took everything from him.

When the alien craft landed, they found themselves on the plains of Kearthat, west of the capital of Seccus. Bryzon was perplexed. The Freelands were colourful; Ripening crops ready to harvest stretched as far as the eye could see, laden with fruit and vegetables.

The survivors were paralyzed with fear. They surrendered helplessly to their captors, doing everything they were motioned to do without question, as if in a trance. They were mentally overwhelmed by what had happened to them, their families, and their homes, lost forever.

Menacing, the fearsome grey aliens guarded their every move, and Bryzon knew they were more dangerous and uglier than any creature had, or would ever know.

The Eslaf wore body protection made of highly polished material. Their full-body armour clung to their bodies as if imbedded into their flesh which created an illusion that they were even bigger and more intimidating. When Bryzon saw them for the first time he had been repulsed. Big, tall, large drooping ears, they were startling to witness. Their heads, were a gruesome oddity with long, irregular-shaped protrusions dangling from their faces, these flaccid pieces swinging haphazardly as they moved. It was hard to imagine that the dangly bits served any purpose other than to add some comedy to their alarming exteriors perhaps. On seeing the Eslaf up close, Bryzon changed his mind; his first impression had been incorrect. The Eslaf were more bug-like than reptilian.

Fear motivated a small group of survivors to make a run towards a forested area. Within minutes of their attempted escape, the sound of alien weapons reverberated. Later, it was discovered that all the dead were alien survivors from the planets Kaldu and Ibromne, who had the misfortune of being in Seccus trading when the city was attacked.

Closely guarded by alien soldiers, the survivors began to transform the look of the open landscape. Using nearby vegetation, they constructed simple shelters to keep the harsh rays of the suns at bay. But mostly, they just sat or stood around waiting. Waiting for what? They did not know.

Then the aliens did something unexpected. An enormous vessel arrived, setting down near the newly formed rudimentary camp, and all the soldiers guarding them boarded the craft.

As the spaceship ascended, the survivors looked up in confusion. Suddenly, it crossed their minds they were going to be executed. Bryzon and Dayson bid each other farewell as they waited for their death. One  minute passed, then five. Finally, the large, noisy alien craft seemed to give birth. The drones that came down from the alien craft hovered a few feet above them, their sound quite deafening by the sheer number of them.

When the first shots rang out, everyone hit the ground. Bryzon and Dayson dove into a shallow ditch for cover. Some held their heads. Men tried to shield women and children close to them with their bodies. When the attack mercifully stopped, there were bloodied bodies everywhere. The murder of more innocent people had been a cruel and unmistakably a message to the survivors. The demonstration, it seemed, was to ensure that the survivors understood the power of their captors.

The large ship and the Eslaf soldiers left, but the droids remained. It was clear escape was not an option. They buried four hundred and eighty-seven in the coming days; many were earthlings.

Elder Moss, the only surviving Supreme Council Elder, approached Bryzon and Dayson, suggesting they hold a Xennes Evalc, a gathering of the chosen. The count revealed that only three-hundred and fourteen Xennes had survived; the rest of the survivors were mortal. At this point, the Xennes were fully aware that the alien weapons made them as vulnerable as anyone else.

The dithering elder seemed mystified, repeatedly asking anyone who would listen how it could be possible that the Xennes could die at the hands of the alien weapon. His question remained unanswered as Bryzon dealt with the many other immediate issues. Finally, It-Ha Layrrah angrily informed Elder Moss to consider the living before questioning the reason for the absence of the dead. To make sure he would stop his incessant talking, she put a spell on the elderly man, taking his voice away for several hours. After that day, Moss bore a visible grudge towards It-Ha Layrrah.

The dishevelled survivors left it up to It-Ha Layrrah and the Xennes to make all their decisions for them. Of course, with the permission of the ever-present Elder Moss. The earthlings withdrew from the rest of the survivors as they mourned their loss in their way.

The first contact between It-Ha Layrrah and Jon King did not go well. Jon was sceptical of her. His friendship with It-Ha Solaarr as his intermediatory in Seccus had become a close one, and he found it difficult to trust the last magic woman of Kearthat.

Solaarr and Sihuun had, they assumed, lost their lives at the hands of the Eslaf. Thus, Jon and Farron could no longer communicate with the Drennan, their ability having vanished with that of Solaarr's demise.

Every action the survivors took was being watched by the droids that hummed above their heads. The Drennan soon referred to the dangerous and irritatingly noisy drones as Idlers, because of how they hovered. Running or sudden movements were avoided, and children were kept in the centre of the group to prevent any misunderstandings that would confuse the machines into killing another child.

Unbeknownst to Bryson, Layrrah had many visions during this challenging time. Her dreams showed settlements surrounded by high walls, a great beast her people would fear. She saw another alien race walking about on Kearthat.

Finally, the It-Ha's dreams were visited by the Red Firemoth, bringing with it disturbing visions of destruction in the future. When she awoke, it was the first time in two thousand years that the It-Ha wept like an infant. She chose not to share this with Elder Moss, or Bryzon.

The Xennes men salvaged tools to assist them in improving their miserable existence, always under the watchful eye of the Idlers. They encountered gruesome scenes; the bodies of the dead were everywhere. Some were ravaged by predators, while others were hard to look at after being in the heat of the suns for some time. The carnage they came across was horrible. The Xennes agreed not to disclose what they encountered and silently went about burying their people.

After twenty days, the survivors held a ceremony to honour the dead. They maintained the Drennan practice of laying down rocks in a pile that quickly grew tall. To Bryzon's surprise, the earthlings participated in the ceremony as if they had been born to Kearthat.

To this day, Bryzon has never let his mind roam to what happened to his mother, father, or Meirah. He simply forced his mind to remember them as they were when they were alive.

In a state of constant unease, time passed slowly as the survivors in the Freelands watched Eslaf ships fly high overhead, ignoring them.

Being disregarded by their captors puzzled and scared everyone. Fear became as normal as breathing, forcing them to live each day as if it would be their last. The dishevelled group fell asleep each night, accepting they could awake to their execution. At the same time, it was almost as if the Eslaf had forgotten about them.

Were it not for the Great Elin River close by and the fields of vegetables and trees bearing ripe fruit, they would surely have succumbed. The days passed, then weeks passed as the Idlers watched as two highly evolved species struggled to surrender to the open grasslands.

Chapter 21 - The Colonies

On day thirty-six, two large spaceships landed near the makeshift settlement, and hundreds of Eslaf soldiers disembarked. The unkempt survivors on the Freelands were surrounded, weapons at the ready; the intimidating aliens in dark green shell suits were prepared for any resistance.

When the tight formation broke near Bryzon and Dayson, an alien in a deep-red suit stood towering over the Drennan nearest him. He was undoubtedly the leader. The creature came within twenty feet from where Bryzon was before he stopped. The alien shouted something in a deep, resounding voice. No one knew what to make of it.

It took Bryzon a few seconds to realise the Eslaf leader was speaking a now familiar-sounding tongue; it was earthling. A woman nearby said something in a soft voice, prompting the grotesque creature to take a step towards her. She quickly stepped back, mimicking his advance. The Eslaf spoke to the earthling woman, then waved her off with his big gloved hand. There was dead silence as frantic calls for Jon King could be heard in the crowd. Before long, the woman reappeared with Jon by her side.

As minutes ticked by, Bryzon could make out from Jon King's mannerisms that the conversation with the Eslaf was a negotiation. The alien in deep-red armour, he learned later, was called Cirabrab, who informed Jon that the survivors were to be spared with conditions.

It-Ha Layrrah remained hidden behind the throng of people while the alien was speaking to Jon King. Her magic was hard at work. She understood every word the Eslaf leader said to Jon. When the aliens left, the survivors had still not been told why they were on the Freelands, but Cirabrab would return.

The first-ever gathering, an Evalc of the Xennes and their last Elder, now included a being from another planet. Under the shade of a large leafy Koa tree, Layrrah let her powers go to work. The magic of the It-Ha surrounded the Xennes, attending the gathering of the gifted. When the pink mist dissipated, the Xennes men and Elder Moss found they could communicate with the earthling Jon King, and conversely so.

"We have been chosen to live, but we must obey their rules. The hideous creature was clear. If we disobey, they will kill us," Jon King told the gathered Xennes. "They will be back with instructions." No one asked how the nefarious aliens knew of the English language; they were too busy dealing with other, more immediate matters, like staying alive.

In the days that followed, Jon proved to be a natural leader, suggesting to Bryzon that the Xennes keep secret their abilities at all costs and that the existence of It-Ha Layrrah protected at all costs.

When the Eslaf in red returned, Bryzon and his fellow survivors learned they would be tillers of the soil. The Eslaf had invaded Kearthat for its vast reserve of Zraphite. They were alive simply because the Eslaf needed them to harvest and continue to grow more crops to feed the prisoners working at the Zraphite mines. This was when they discovered that the alien Korak of Dirha had been invaded and brought to Kearthat to work in the mines. Yet another species the Drennan had been unaware of from their galaxy.

It-Ha Layrrah knew then that her visions were going to come true. She feared things were only going to get worse.

Not long afterwards, the Eslaf delivered the first Korak prisoners to help build the colonies and three bridges across the Elin River. The poor creatures arrived chained together. The sight of the tall, ungainly aliens walking off the Eslaf transport ship added to their feelings of dread.

The Korak were awkward in appearance; they looked as if their extremities were joined together by extra-large bone joints, but at the same time, they were muscular. Upon closer inspection, their most peculiar affliction was their small ears that constantly twitched and turned. Their big heart-shaped heads were largely taken up by enormous dark oval eyes. Their heads tilted constantly from side to side as if they begged to understand what was happening around them. The Korak were grey-green, perhaps leaning more toward a shade of olive.

In all the madness, Bryzon heard that the City of Seccus would now be known as Etah. The Freelanders were given details regarding the No-Go Zones and were informed many more Idlers had been deployed. There would be no mercy for those breaking the rules set out by the Eslaf.

Left to establish the sites of the twelve colonies the aliens insisted upon, the survivors began to strategize how they would please their new masters.

It-Ha Layrrah chose where the colonies would be erected, claiming that the Red Firemoth had come to her with a vision of the exact locations. Then, much to the disgust of Elder Moss, the It-Ha insisted that Farron and Jon King name the colonies. Bryzon was more concerned with each colony's distance from the other as per the direct instructions from the alien Cirabrab.

Bryzon knew why the aliens were splitting them up; it was a common-sense strategy. With smaller groups, more than an easy walking distance, it minimized collaboration against the aliens. The Eslaf were way ahead of them yet again.

The survivors chose Thirty-six leaders among the Xennes, including the earthling Jon King. They divided the population into twelve communities and allocated one leader and two lesser leaders to each colony. Their first obligation was to harvest the current yielding crops and ensure the right crops would keep producing. The colony leaders honed their focus on feeding the prisoners working in the mines, making sure everyone obeyed all rules while doing so.

Five Eastern and seven Western settlements were built on opposite sides along the Great Elin River. This would give them easier access to water, ensuring healthy yielding crops for the large hungry Korak.

The first colony to be completed was Rednos Colony, close to where the Freelanders were deposited after the invasion.

The Xennes were careful not to show they could heal if injured and were even more careful not to get shot by the alien weapons. The It-Ha hid in plain sight, using her ability to cast the veil of invisibility when the Eslaf were near. And so the list of secrets grew as they tried putting some semblance of routine and reason back into their lives.

The Eslaf established a grim reality for the survivors. For every death in the colonies, one birth would be allowed. The population of the prisoners of the Freelands was never going to be allowed to grow unless otherwise ordered by their masters. Disobedience, they learned, would culminate in death for any unauthorized babies born. Destined to live with the dread of not pleasing their new leaders, Kearthat's free prisoners put their backs into the tasks set out for them. They were trapped.

When all the colonies were established, Cirabrab sent a message to Jon King. The earthling leader was to be permitted three offspring if he so chose. Cirabrab stated that the reward was in recognition of Jon's cooperation.

Bryzon found it difficult to comprehend the bizarre act of respect the creature had shown towards the earthling. Cirabrab was never heard of or seen again, and the Freelanders assumed he had returned to Ludinia from where the Eslaf hailed. Many different red-suits took his place over the years, but none as 'generous' as Cirabrab.

Jon King became the leader of Rednos Colony, and all of the earthlings chose to live under his leadership. When Jon asked Bryzon and Dayson if they would be his Lesser Leaders, they accepted without hesitation.

The Inter-Colony Shuttle Service was introduced by the Eslaf to improve the establishment of the settlements at a much later date. Someone at Eslaf headquarters had re-thought the difficulties such remote settlements caused, or so Bryzon assumed.

The colonists feared failure. Failure meant punishment, so they worked hard to please the Eslaf. This approach was soon rewarded when the aliens largely ignored them as long as the colonies produced and ran smoothly.

The few Korak at the colonies laboured relentlessly while remaining grateful for the kindness shown to them by the Freelanders. And so it came about that the colonies were later allowed to negotiate for a small amount of legal Zraphite for their own use. The mineral made pumping water to the settlements easier and provided power and hot water. But it did not take long for the Freelanders to discover that self-improvement had limits. The Eslaf were not about to give them an endless supply of Zraphite.

When some young Freelanders built vehicles from pieces scavenged from the long-ago burned-out farm settlements, the Eslaf were furious and destroyed their mechanised inventions. This act was a message; the Freelands would never be allowed to progress in any way. They were stuck in an era they had overcome long ago. Deprived of exercising their extensive knowledge of space travel and other advanced pursuits, those who were once engineers, spaceship pilots, and masters of many different skills settled into the understanding they would only ever be farmers.

A bizarre, disgruntled order began to emerge. Crops were planted and then harvested. Animals to feed the colonists were reared, and the Nexo herds grazed on the lush grasses outside of the settlements for the colonists who were meat-eaters. Hunting within the confines of the Freelands and the lowlands of The High Mountains was eventually permitted. So days became months, and then years began to pass.

Those not possessing the gift of being Xennes passed onto the next world as they aged, and new babies came into this bizarre way of living. A system was devised to pick who would be allowed to have a child next. Their new society became, although unusual, somewhat tolerable. As years passed, the Freelanders gradually gained more trust from their alien masters. The Eslaf pulled back significantly, but the rage and distrust for the aliens never diminished. The Xennes lived a long time, and they would never forget.

It-Ha Layrrah spent countless hours with Jon King at Rednos Colony, where she chose to make her home, always in disguise as a mere Freelander. Bryzon remembers them sitting under a large tree in the centre of the colony. They would talk for hours. This was before It-ha Layrrah seemed to vanish for short periods of time.

55

Chapter 22 - Mixed Bloods

Long after the invasion of Kearthat.

Bryzon's twin, Dayson, had been mesmerized by the earthling girl Caite, the eldest daughter of Jon King. The attraction prompted the earthling leader to warn Dayson in no uncertain terms to stay away from his young daughter, then only eighteen years old.

Undeterred, Dayson waited patiently for Caite to grow up. Her eyes, the colour of the light blue pollen found only in a Mura flower, had Bryzon's brother helplessly swooning every time he saw her. He was irreversibly in love. In her twenty-first year, a wonderful day of festivity saw Jon King give his daughter's hand to Dayson.

The smile on his brother's face said it all. His wait had been rewarded. Bryzon had never seen or witnessed a man so taken by a woman. Dayson loved his Caite with the dedication of a hermit. Sadly, Dayson knew he would eventually outlive her by decades. At this point in their lives, earthlings would have judged the twins to be no older than twenty-eight; yes the Xennes aged incredibly slowly.

By blessing his daughter's union with Dayson, the earthling Jon King set an example for others. Not long after, Sayhran, Jon's second daughter, took Keazan, another Xennes as her husband. From these unions, a new generation began to emerge, a generation of mixed-bloods.

Chapter 23 - Nick and Marcus King

Farron King, who became almost invisible after the invasion, passed to the next world having always been a bit of a mystery to Bryzon. She was a woman of endless compassion, tending the sick; she was the first healer of the colonies. Farron took care of Jon and bore him three children. After her firstborn, Caite, came Nick, followed by Sayhran.

Bryzon found Farron quiet and withdrawn as if she carried a heavy burden after Kearthat was invaded; her voice had regressed to almost a whisper, her eyes downcast most of the time as if she was hiding something. When she passed, his best friend, Jon King, was shattered. He and Farron had shared their lives since they were infants. At Farron's burial, It-Ha Layrrah had whispered to Bryzon that the earthling woman had died of a melancholy born out of regret, but the It-Ha never elaborated before vanishing as she did from time to time.

Jon lived for many years after the invasion. He had by then led his surviving earthlings and their offspring through the most trying times of their lives.

He laughed one day as he told Bryzon he was the oldest earthling to have ever lived.

By unanimous vote, Jon's son Nick King took over leadership of Rednos Colony after Jon passed. Caite and her sister Sayhran were deeply saddened by the loss of their father but took solace in the fact that he achieved what he set out to do. He had found a habitable planet so that his kind would live on, even though it was not perfect.

A few years later, Nick King suddenly became ill. He called for Bryzon, who was then living in Noitibma Colony. A messenger informed him that Nick had an urgent communication and to bring his sisters to his bedside. By the time he, Caite and Sayhran arrived in Rednos, the ailing leader was unable to speak.

Bryzon hoped there would be something the It-Ha could do to improve Nick's health, but this was not to be. The following morning, Bryzon was saddened to find that Nick had died during the night. The urgent matter he sought to share with Bryzon remained untold.

When the people of Rednos Colony gathered to choose another leader, they chose Nick King's son Marcus with unanimous support. But Marcus was still a boy. So it came about that the earthlings of Rednos chose Bryzon's Xennes friend, Ohre, as interim leader while they waited for Marcus King to become a man.

At the laying to rest of Nick King, Bryzon had intended to ask the It-Ha if the gift of long life might be considered for all. But when the time came, he couldn't remember why he wanted to talk to her. After Nick King's honouring, Bryzon discovered Layrrah had again vanished into thin air. As his mind began to clear, he knew she had anticipated his request; she had tricked him by putting a brief spell of forgetfulness on him.

Several years later, after completing his *time-of-learning*, Marcus King went before his people. The earthlings of Rednos had not changed their minds, and Marcus became the youngest leader of all the colonies. Marcus would, in time, have a son of his own.

Chapter 24 - The Uprising

Thirty Earth years after the invasion of Kearthat.

It has been many years, yet each day, Bryzon regrets how poorly he and Dayson had planned the attack on the Eslaf. The mistakes he and his twin brother made should never be repeated. The uprising had been a deadly mistake.

He and his twin banded together with Sahdmar and Bryzon's good friend Pateeo. They planned to form a rebel force to attack the Eslaf-held spaceship base in the now alien-held city. The intent was to attack from under the city, using the walkways sealed off by Bryzon during the invasion of Kearthat years ago. The aliens, he was sure, had not yet discovered these secret passages.

Sadly, Bryzon and his rag-tag Xennes rebels were discovered on their way to the secret entrance that would take them into the passageways. A drone had spotted them. The Eslaf poured into the area and within minutes, they were overwhelmed. They were badly outnumbered, and their meagre self-made weapons were inadequate against the Eslaf soldiers. All that was left was to make a run for it.

Never could Bryzon have imagined that he or his twin could lose their lives. When his brother Dayson was hit in the chest by shots fired from one of the ugly grey beings, Bryzon was shaken to the core. It took all his strength to pick his brother up and run. Without thinking of the danger, he headed for a nearby forested area, shots sounding around him.

Once in a place of relative safety, he knelt over Dayson. He was confused and alarmed as he watched the gaping hole in his brother's chest pump out a stream of blood. It was not healing; Dayson was dying.

On that day, he made a promise to his brother to take care of Caite and their children, Raine and Leyashe. A promise he would not fulfil for many years.

In the thick cover of the forest, he and a fragment of his men hid from the aliens who searched for them mercilessly until the light faded. By then, he had spent many hours looking at his brother's lifeless face. Bryzon buried his brother in the dark near the large Trigga, where he had kissed his precious Meirah. Now overgrown, the once grand Supreme Council Garden had become one with the forest.

He left a simple stone marker to remember where his brother's body lay. Before dawn, he turned for the last time to look at the mound of dirt, knowing he was leaving half of himself behind.

After bidding farewell to Dayson, the rebels moved stealthily up into The High Mountains, regrouping in the cave where they had prepared for their attack on the Eslaf a few days earlier. But as the men began to arrive at this rendezvous point, Bryzon was notified that more Xennes lives had been lost.

Among the dead was Sayhran's husband. The news of Keazan's demise came as a blade to Bryzon's heart.

The Xennes tried to lay their dead to rest when possible. Bryzon was informed Keazan was buried near a stream in a tranquil setting. The men had made sure that the brave fighter faced the Freelands. That night, Bryzon's heart ached for each loss; the rage he felt was comparable only to the shame he felt. His error in forming a rebel force against the aliens had come at an overwhelming cost. He found it difficult to process the loss of his brother, brother-in-law, and some of the bravest men he had ever known.

Time passed, and the Eslaf troops got closer each day to apprehending them. For what seemed to be time interminable, they constantly stayed on the move, always only one step ahead of the aliens. The more time passed, the more mindless the cycle of survival became. Eventually, Bryzon had to admit that their situation was hopeless. The reality was that, ultimately, they would be apprehended or fight to the death.

Oblivious of the circumstances of the rebels, the colonists in the Freelands below The High Mountains had their own problems. They had begun to encounter a creature more dangerous than anything they had ever known. The Freelanders were being hunted after dark. The Night Creatures had arrived. Unbeknownst to Bryzon, It-Ha Layrrah's visions of so many years ago were still coming true, one after the other.

A gathering of the colony leaders led to a decision to erect high walls around the settlements. Before long, the Freelanders were locked in at night while the Night Creatures roamed Kearthat sunsset to sunsrise. During the day, these mystery creatures disappeared. Where to? No one knew.

The Eslaf watched as the high walls around the settlements were built, higher than the beast could jump. They never stopped the colonists and did not interfere in any way. The Night Creatures discouraged any possibility of communication between the rebels and the Freelanders. Again, the aliens were one step ahead.

Oblivious to what was happening in the valley, Bryzon and his men spent countless months hiding. Day after day, they watched through the forested canopy as alien spotter craft circled, looking for them.

Bryzon wondered if Dayson would still be alive if they had allowed the earthlings to join the uprising. The earthling men had beseeched the Xennes to permit them to enlist. They wanted revenge for their losses in years prior as much as the Drennan. But the display of bravery and the willingness of the people from earthling descendants was rejected. Elder Moss had again wielded his power; his single vote nullified all those who voted in favour of the earthlings joining the fight. Elder Moss also forbade the Xennes women from participating in the rebellion. Angry at first, Bryzon would later be grateful Moss had voted against the women taking part.

As the days passed, Bryzon and his men were systematically driven to the fringe of The High Mountains. He knew if they crossed over, they would never return. The Jagged Mountains of The Nerrab stretched for hundreds of miles beyond The High Mountains. All that existed between the ocean and the mountain range was an empty rocky desert and an ocean that would not be of any salvation to them. These lands had been declared a No-Go Zone by the Eslaf after the invasion, but there had been no need. The entire Nerrab was a natural deterrent to anyone trying to escape. It was an inhospitable place with no food, water or shelter from the elements. They were trapped. They had to go over the mountains or surrender to the aliens. The fact remained that the Eslaf knew the desert would solve their problem.

Bryzon sent Ohre, accompanied by a small contingent of men, to make the dangerous trek down the mountain. Their mission was to get back to the nearest colony in the dark. Ohre would carry a message from Bryzon to the Xennes colony leaders and Elder Moss. Part of the letter expressed his profound regret for failing his people. As he waited, all he could hope for was that Ohre and his men would not be killed before delivering the communication.

Bryzon patiently scoured the Freelands from the mountains each night until finally, the signal came; Ohre had made it.

The answer Bryzon waited for came as three wood pyres burned high and bright in the night sky. He and his men knew that the flames came from Noitibma Colony from its position. The three fires indicated to Bryzon that Elder Moss and the Xennes leaders had decided the men should surrender rather than attempt crossing into The Nerrab. The decision meant he and his men would trade terrible suffering in the wasteland for perhaps worse at the hands of the Eslaf.

To this day, the Eslaf have never been aware of the involvement of Ohre and the few that made it back to the colonies. No one has ever spoken of it again. It was a small victory as they saw it, even though the aliens were unaware of it.

The day they surrendered, Bryzon told no one he somehow felt a sense of relief. Finally, he could mourn his brother, however short the time was before the punishment of death by the alien weapon known as the Nobrac befell him.

Chapter 25 - The Korak

After they were captured, Bryzon and his men were taken directly to Noitibma Colony, where they were lined up in the center of the settlement. Two red-suits arrived on a spotter craft not far from where the men were waiting in silence for their execution. With them came a big transporter craft and a contingent of armed Eslaf green-suits.

The aliens in charge were not satisfied they had apprehended all of Bryzon's men. They threatened to kill all the colonists. Bryzon was given a five-minute ultimatum to give up the men still hiding in the mountains or watch as the Freelanders were killed.

After much pleading and reassuring that all his men were accounted for, Bryzon could never have imagined what would happen next. Four randomly chosen colonists were pulled out from the crowd of watching innocents. They never saw it coming; the two red-suits walked up to the four confused colonists and shot them in the head as everyone watched in horror.

Bryzon remembers screaming at the red-suits, and rushing forward, but several soldiers were on top of him in seconds. He went down on his knees in front of the Eslaf and begged them to stop the killing.

He can still picture their enormous dusty boots as his face was held down in the dirt, recalling the taste of the sand in his mouth as the creatures stomped on his hands. They kicked him until he felt and heard several bones crack under their vicious attack on him.

When eventually his head was violently yanked up by his hair, Bryzon became aware of the anguished looks on all of those watching. He caught a glimpse of Sayhran, who was not far from him. He tried to scan the area for his brother's wife, Caite, as he was being dragged by his hair as if he were a child's toy, but she was not there. The terrified faces looking on, the sound of women and children crying, and the harsh heat of the suns added to the bad dream, a nightmare he seemed unable to awaken from.

Bryzon swore to the Eslaf red-suit that no other fighters were left in the mountains, but the aliens remained suspicious. They insisted they had repeatedly counted all the adult males in the colonies, concluding Bryzon was lying. The truth was the Eslaf did not know how many had taken part in the uprising. They had become complacent, but this was about to change. They were bound to reimplement the counting of the colonists on a regular basis.

Bryzon begged the Eslaf in the red armour to execute him, imploring the aliens to spare the colonists. It became evident his pleading with the ugly grey creatures was fruitless. Convinced they were going to kill him, and then execute everyone in Noitibma Colony, Bryzon loudly asked the forgiveness of the Freelanders looking on.

To this day, Bryzon can still feel the blow that struck him on the top of his head. He fell face down, searing pain coursing through his jarred neck, warm blood gushing from the wound running down his face, neck and arms. He did not dare move in fear of antagonizing the Eslaf even more. He hoped the alien would not notice his wound heal in all the confusion. His saving grace had been the sheer amount of blood loss acting as a concealer.

Confused and bloodied, Bryzon saw Noitibma's Leader and his friend Keeland step out of the crowd. Clearing his throat loudly, Keeland raised his hands in a sign of peace. The Noitibma leader walked right up to the Eslaf in red before kneeling. Softly placing his hand on Bryzon's shoulder, he never looked away from the brutal alien. At Bryzon's side, Keeland offered his life to the aliens for those of the Freelanders, with a promise they would never again rise up against the Eslaf, assuring the ugly being that Bryzon was telling the truth.

After what felt like hours of debate among the Eslaf, it was decided that Bryzon and his men would be punished by going to work in the Zraphite mine. Miraculously, the aliens chose to penalise rather than destroy them. Keeland was warned he would be the first to die if anyone in the colonies ever stepped out of line again.

As Bryzon and his men were hauled onto an Eslaf transporter, he recalls the horrified look on Sayhran's face. The last glimpse of her was with a very young Leyashe in her arms, Raine by her side, and Krom, and Remek, Sayhran and Keazan's son's faces stained with tears clinging to their mother's tunic. His brother's wife Caite was nowhere in sight.

A peculiar peace existed between the colonists and aliens until the uprising. It was a fragile trust built over years of negotiating with the Eslaf, first by Jon King, then by Leader Keeland of Noitibma. Now, it was in jeopardy.

Bryzon could read the anxiety in Sayhran's face; the tears he knew were for her husband Keazon. Unknown to Bryzon, Sayhran also feared what would befall the Freelanders now that the trust had been broken.

Caite had passed while Bryzon was hiding in the mountains. Sayhran had been unable to convey this information to him. For almost five years, Bryzon would assume Caite had not been able to look at him, blaming him for Dayson's death. And yes, the first thing the Eslaf did was take away all access to Zraphite, making life extremely hard for the colonies.

When the transporter took off from Noitibma Colony for the prison on that fateful day, Bryzon watched through a small window as the many faces from his home settlement stared up at the craft. Expressions of disillusionment. The picture he saw confirmed he had jeopardized everything by creating the insurgency.

Flying over the colony, he caught a glimpse of the four lifeless bodies, innocent men and women who had been chosen to bear his punishment. They had died for what he had known right at the beginning of the uprising, had been a ridiculously small chance at freedom. The motionless bodies lying in the dirt in the middle of the colony in the hot suns would haunt his dreams for many years.

Bryzon remembers the surreal feeling he had when they landed at the prison for the first time. The whole scene, the debris being whipped up by the craft, the uncertainty of their fate, it had always remained with him. The reality was they were prisoners with no freedoms, slaves to the Eslaf, destined to be there until they were killed by the aliens. It was surreal.

He noticed the height of the fences at the prison first. No walls, just a thick lattice of Zraphite-powered cables strung between metal posts. The interwoven mesh gave everyone a view of freedom they could not enjoy. There were four look-out towers from where the Eslaf soldiers could see every move the prisoners made. There was no possibility of escape.

Beyond the enclosures, beautiful green forested areas were out of reach of the captives. Bryzon knew it would be a long time, if ever, that he would touch a tree or walk through the cool shade of the forest again. Later, there were days that he found it hard to look at what extended beyond the electrified fence. He and his men tried to absorb the reality of their predicament. The acrid smell of dust mixed in with the body odour of thousands of prisoners was impacting. A feeling of total helplessness prevailed.

Later that night, he would hear the growl of a Night Creature, and silent tears would sting his eyes for the first time since the invasion. Unbeknownst to Bryzon, It-Ha Layrrah's visions continued to prove true.

Chapter 26 - Namow

The shock of so many Korak overwhelmed Bryzon and his Xennes compatriots. It took some time before they digested the thought of living and labouring beside three thousand Korak. Days passed, then weeks, and the Korak prisoners proved docile. Bryzon soon discovered a friend in one of the tall, olive prisoners.

Namow had taken a liking to the Drennan man who was so small beside her.

On the flip side, befriending Namow and learning her language was deliberate initially; Bryzon wanted to form an alliance with the Korak. The fire of hate that burned in him towards the Eslaf, combined with the long, tedious hours, never deterred Bryzon from building countless uprisings against the Eslaf in his mind. He mourned his brother each waking day as regret ate away at him.

The kind Korak, Namow and Bryzon agreed that the Eslaf were cunning. The alien carnage on Kearthat and Namow's planet, Dirha, had been perfectly synchronized. They had invaded Dirha for strong, able-bodied workers for the mines on Kearthat, taking prisoners to grow the food needed to sustain the several thousand Korak prisoners. The rest of the slaughter had been an eradication for the mere purpose of their well-orchestrated plan. It had always been a constant struggle for Bryzon to reconcile the lunacy and extreme cruelty of it all.

The planet from which Namow hailed was unknown to Bryzon. In the dirt, she had one day drawn a rough sketch of the galaxy, showing Bryzon her home. It was almost directly opposite his planet, in their galaxy, but many light years away.

This meant only one thing to Bryzon: the Eslaf had a means of incredible speed at their disposal, or they had access to a wormhole, similar to the void that Jon King had described to him many years prior.

Bryzon later learned that Namow, her brother and several hundred others had managed to evade the Eslaf for some time. She had been brought to Kearthat after the first groups of workers had arrived. During this conversation, Namow neglected to tell Bryzon that she had been taken prisoner after the Korak spaceship that she had escaped on had been captured by the Eslaf, where they were trying to hide from their invaders in an asteroid belt.

However, she does tell Bryzon that the ignorant Eslaf had not considered some of the female Korak being with child. Namow herself had been one of those unfortunate females when she was brought to Kearthat. Sadly, a few days after she had birthed a tinier version of herself, she watched in horror as her offspring was forcefully taken from her, never to be seen again. Unaware that the Korak babies had ended up in Noitibma Colony to be raised by the Freelanders, Namow was ecstatic to hear her child may have survived. Her friendship with Bryzon was sealed from that moment on.

The Korak infants grew up significantly slower in the colonies than their human counterparts. When they reached what the Noitibma's Tutor Layhne assumed was a mature age, they were made to attend class, sitting side by side with the human children at night. To the wonder of everyone in the colonies, they thrived. Taking on the ways and knowledge passed on by the people of Kearthat.

Bryzon, quite by chance, found out in conversation with Namow that there had originally been more alien species brought to the mines, the Korak being the only ones to survive. The other two species, Namow, led him to understand that all had perished not long after they were brought to prison. The consensus was that poor air quality in the mines had caused their demise, but she admitted she did not know this to be a fact.

At Bryzon's request, Namow tried to discover more about those who had perished. When she reported what she had discovered, Bryzon had no doubt they were the inhabitants of Kaldu and Ibromne. Kearthat's trading partners had met the same horrible end.

As Bryzon and Namow's friendship grew, he learned how devastated the Korak were each time the Eslaf burned the bodies of their dead. She and her kind believed the burning of the bodies robbed their life force of the opportunity to move to a higher plane of existence. Her large eyes filled with alien tears as she confessed her fear of meeting a similar fate.

As time passed, Bryzon and the alien woman understood each other more and more. He began telling her about his Kearthat before the invasion, and he discovered that Namow's brother had been taken away from the mining prison, and she had not seen him since. She assured Bryzon he was still alive, as she could feel his presence. Bryzon wondered then if Namow's child was, in fact, dead, as she did not feel his presence. Another oddity to Bryzon was that his Korak friend referred to her brother as her father's son, something he could not comprehend.

Many Korak were brought to the colonies at different intervals to work in the fields since the colonies were established. Once delivered, the aliens seemed to forget the Korak men were there. A management flaw on the part of the Eslaf, Bryzon assumed, or did the Eslaf not imagine that alliances could form between the Korak and the Freelanders, their species being vastly different? Perhaps this was a mistake on the part of the Eslaf, he thought.

Bryzon had fleetingly considered telling Namow of the Korak adult males at the colonies but found himself withholding the thought as he had no evidence that her brother was one of them, so he kept it to himself.

Namow and Bryzon shared much, but the secret he and his men had sworn to keep remained untold. He could not bring himself to tell her he was Xennes, that he would live hundreds of years, and that his body was capable of regenerating from injury. Well, almost every injury.

It had crossed Bryzon's mind several times that Namow could have been someone of high standing on Dirha. He mustered the courage to ask her outright if she had been a leader on her planet. It was then that he heard a sound that passed as a Korak laugh for the very first time. Her answer, "Namow, jus Namow," she had insisted.

In return for her kindness towards him, Bryzon continued teaching her his language. He, in turn, persevered with endless patience, learning the difficult clicks and sounds that made up the Korak tongue. It took a long time, but Bryzon and his olive friend could now converse quite satisfactorily.

Chapter 27 - The Prison

The siren goes off, and Bryzon is jolted from his sleep. He bolts upright and surveys the prison camp. Over in the visitor enclosure, he can see that the morning siren has woken his nephews. He watches as Krom and Remek shake the dust from their overnight blankets, then stuff them into a bag.

Bryzon had recognized the leather bag when he saw it slung over his nephew Remek's shoulder the previous evening. It had once belonged to his twin brother Dayson. Later, he was happy to discover the familiar satchel contained sweet bread sent to him by his sister-in-joining Sayhran.

Bryzon waits until he has his nephew's attention. He raises his arm in the air and then taps his chest twice with a clenched fist. The greeting of the Drennan people of Kearthat is returned. Krom and Remek are mixed-bloods, part Drennan, part earthling, but they have embraced the ways of the Drennan.

On that special day in Noitibma Colony so many years ago, when Jon King's youngest daughter Sayhran joined as one with Keazan, Bryzon could never have imagined he would be in prison, and Keazan would be dead. The fact that his nephews Krom and Remek were here on a visit was in itself a miracle to him. He did not deserve such forgiveness and he knew it.

The suns barely show their glow over Ante Mountain, but it is already hot. Within no time, perspiration challenges Bryzon's brow as he gathers his belongings. Dust being kicked up by the thousands of feet in the prison camp makes it hard for him to fill his lungs with a breath of fresh air. He runs his fingers through his shoulder-length hair several times before haltering the black tangled mass with a leather thong. He does not take his eyes off his nephews and notices Remek covering his mouth to stifle a yawn. Their movements are slow, and both young men are suffering from a lack of sleep.

Bryzon wishes he could stay and talk more to them, but the collar around his neck prevents him from going to the electrified fence for a final farewell.

Disobedience is not tolerated in any form by the Eslaf guards. Instead, Bryzon grabs his cot and folds it in half, then hurries to the East corner of the vast prison. He weaves and dodges as he darts through the throng of prisoners as quickly as he can.

Bryzon enters Cell Block 3, where his locker and allotted indoor space are located. He punches his code into the keypad, opening the tiny metal box containing his meagre possessions. He gives his treasure a glance and with a sigh, picks up the hand-drawn likeness of Meirah. It is a good portrait of her. It shows her long black hair and kind dark eyes, just as he remembers. The picture does not show her slender waist, which was so small he could almost wrap his arms around her twice. She had been a good soldier and life partner, their future was stripped from them when she perished during the invasion.

Bryzon shoves his blanket into the locker and reaches for his boots. He places the picture of Meirah back onto the narrow ledge at the back of the locker, which doubles as a rudimentary mirror. He hurriedly sorts out the annoying strands of hair left uncaptured earlier. His reflection is blurred, but he can discern his light brown body tone and the beard that makes him appear older. The eyes that stare back at him are deep brown; his face reflects that of his twin brother Dayson. On each waking day, this image reminds him of the circumstances surrounding the loss of his twin, a memory reinforcing his searing hate for the Eslaf, and burning regret at having involved his family and friends in the thought of an uprising.

Bryzon strips off his nightshirt, revealing a lean, muscular body, before pulling on his other clean but dirty-looking tunic. He had requested a new set two months ago, but his requisition had been ignored. With less than eight weeks before he and his men will be released from prison, he will be wearing his nightshirt when he goes home.

The thought of finally being allowed to go home to Noitibma Colony does not yet ring true for Bryzon. How could he trust the Eslaf after everything he has been through?

He waits until the click confirms his locker is secure before pulling his cot open. Bryzon places it in the exact space allocated to him in front of his locker. He seldom sleeps in this allocated space indoors, and the intense heat makes most prisoners choose to sleep out in the open, taking advantage of the cooler night air. There are sixteen identical cell blocks in the prison compound, and C3 was where the Drennen were allocated. Bryzon estimated the Korak prisoner count to be well over three thousand.

As he exits the building, he hears a noise coming from behind him. He swings around to see who it is. It is an Eslaf guard. The tall, ugly, grey creature yells something in a deep voice, but Bryzon does not stop. Pretending not to hear, he increases his stride until he is out in the morning sunlight, disappearing into the muddle of rushing bodies.

He joins the line for the morning meal; at the same time, he will be provided with a pail containing a meal to take to the mine. Bryzon looks up at the sky; there are no clouds.

"We need rain," a voice says behind him. It is his friend Sahdmar who had planned the uprising with him.

"May the day welcome you, Sahdmar. I agree, my friend; it is going to be another hot day," Bryzon answers, looking up at the man slightly taller than him. Bryzon has profound respect for his fellow prisoner. As Base Commander of the Kearthat Starfleet, he had seen firsthand how Sahdmar fought bravely during the invasion of their planet. His friend suffered greatly at the hands of the enemy, losing not only his wife but also their young son. Yet when Bryzon asked Sahdmar to help him form the rebel force, the Xennes man never hesitated.

Bryzon's turn in the lineup comes, and he is handed a plate of fried vegetables and two hunks of bread. He also accepts the container of daily rations. He knows it is a stew of vegetables and Nexo meat and another two thick slices of bread. The meal is always the same for the Xennes prisoners.

Ready to leave the lineup, he nods towards Sahdmar and purposely finds a spot where he can be alone. He eats quicker than usual and heads to the water supply station to fill his canteen.

When the piercing sound of a second siren fills the air, Bryzon runs to line up for the shuttle heading to the Zraphite mine, the shuttle that takes him and his men to misery and hardship day after day.

Fortunately, the slight rise in the terrain where the shuttle waits each morning gives him a view of the visitor enclosure. If he is lucky, and the Eslaf are slow with their duties, he might get an opportunity to wave to Krom and Remek one more time.

Bryzon keeps an eye on his lineup, hoping it will not move too fast as he watches the visitors' pen. Finally, both boys look up in his direction and wave. He reaches as high as his arm will stretch and waves back, then they are hidden by the trees, and a second later they disappear altogether. The path will take them out of the prison gates, a short walk through another treed area, and then the final stretch through grassland will take them back to the Inter-Colony Shuttle Station, where the next shuttle craft will take them home.

High-pitched cries interrupt Bryzon's thoughts. The commotion is coming from behind him. A Korak prisoner is stirring up dust, his limbs flailing as horrible screeches escape the large alien's tiny mouth. An Eslaf soldier towers over the shrieking figure. The Korak's huge eyes are closed as the guard repeatedly strikes the unfortunate prisoner on the head with the back of his weapon. The Korak tries to shield himself with his long arms, but to no avail, and the pounding persists. Bryzon knows that the cries of pain are not only because of the beating. The docile alien's collar is pulsing bright red as it inflicts additional discomfort.

Bryzon turns his back on the horrible scene, his anger too great to watch. A few minutes later, the screams calm to a whimper. Mercifully, the punishment has ended.

Seething, Bryzon balls his fists; it takes all his strength not to erupt. To distract himself, he focuses his thoughts back on Krom and Remek, wondering if they will travel by land Traxid to Noitibma Colony if the shuttle is full. Either way, he knows they will share space with the crops transported daily between the prison, the colonies, and the city. At night, all shuttles returned to base in the city.

Bryzon glances to the back of the line just in time to see the unfortunate Korak, who was punished, being helped to his feet. His punisher waving his weapon at the Korak prisoner, indicating he must rejoin the line.

"Not long, not long to go," Bryzon whispers, trying to keep his temper in check. Then he hears a Korak prisoner behind him click his tongue; it is Dulf. The kind alien tilts his head sideways, his big dark eyes looking into Bryzon's face questioningly. Bryzon apologizes in the best Korak he can muster, then wonders why he is apologising and shakes his head. The look he gets from the olive-skinned being speaks volumes; the gentle giant thinks he is crazy for talking to himself.

As the line gets closer to the craft, Bryzon begins to mull over the events of the previous evening. Most of the night was spent talking with Krom and Remek about Noitibma Colony and what the family has been doing in the last three months since he had seen his nephews. They discussed Bryzon's imminent release, talking about it in the early hours of the morning. It was only when, to Krom's amusement, Remek could be heard snoring while sitting upright that they lay their heads down for a very brief rest. However, Bryzon felt quite refreshed when he awoke. The ability his body had to regenerate was working its magic. Being Xennes had its advantages.

A visit from his family always provided Bryzon with many hours of pondering as he laboured in the mine. The visits left precious thoughts that would allow him to get through the many tough hours under the watchful eyes of the Eslaf soldiers.

To avoid the Night Creatures, all visitors who came to the prison had to arrive before the suns set behind The High Mountains. Those who journeyed from the colonies to visit inmates willingly allowed the Eslaf to lock them into an enclosure next to the prison yard to ensure their safety. It also guaranteed them an all-night stopover with the prisoners they were visiting.

Bryzon sighs loudly as he leaves behind the morning that started with familiar faces, but no one notices except the Korak male behind him. He smiles at the peaceful creature and nods.

When he finally reaches the walkway of the ship, Bryzon looks back one more time in the direction of the visitor enclosure, but it is empty. He enters the craft and files into his seat, making sure to put his food container between his feet first. Then he lowers his arms and rests his hands on his knees.

He has a good view of the bay door where dozens more prisoners pour onto the transporter. Soon, he finds himself squinting as the bright glare of the suns bounces off the metal walkway. Everyone aboard, the shiny access ramp begins to hum as it retracts into the belly of the craft. The hatch closes with a thud, and loud locks automatically engage to secure it.

The sound of thrusters fills the air, and Bryzon feels the craft rock slightly under his feet. The guards take their seats on either side of the hatch. A series of low-pitched alien commands are exchanged with the pilot of the craft, signalling that they are ready for takeoff.

At the same time, the row of seating Bryzon occupies suddenly swings around without warning, jerking everyone's heads with its force. Bryzon grips his knees a little harder to absorb the rough transition. Every alternate row now follows suit. He is now facing a different row of prisoners. A metal bar descends without advance caution and stops at chest height, locking the prisoners in. Barely able to move, they are helpless for their short journey to the mine.

The female Korak prisoner sitting in Bryzon's line of sight obscures most of the view gifted to him by the narrow, elongated window behind her. The alien woman tries to muster a smile that exposes her dark, pointed teeth. Bryzon nods to acknowledge her Korak attempt at a humanlike greeting.

When they take off, a haze of debris billows out from under the craft, blocking out the view of the forest his nephews had disappeared into earlier. Bryzon had realized long ago that being twenty-second to thirty-third in the morning lineup guaranteed him a seat where he would get glimpses of the Freelands through the small window. Each day, a precious view of the ocean or The High Mountains was akin to a jolt of sanity, helping to dissipate his almost constant anger since he was imprisoned. Looking past the Korak's large head, Bryzon makes the most of the scenery, however limited.

The craft levels out, the noises on the ship limited to the occasional deep-throated mumblings of the Eslaf soldiers. Prisoners are forbidden to speak on the shuttles, which mercifully provides Bryzon with the semi-quiet he hankers after.

He can see trees in the distance come into view. Further from the prison, the Freelands suddenly appear, and Bryzon's heart soars at the thought of going home. He imagines walking through the lowlands where the tall Lattgrass grows. He closes his eyes and tries to envision the wonderful solitude of the forest. To hunt again or just walk among nature again will be pure joy.

Not far into the journey, the ocean appears. Bryzon tries to imagine the feel of a cool breeze, even cooler water, and the soft black sand between his toes. Long ago, he and his brother had spent many hours with their friends and family, enjoying the fresh air and water. He remembers swimming in the safety of the shallow pools between the rocks where they were protected from the dangerous creatures that swam the depths of the dark water. The dark water that was beguiled by Kearthat's moons.

A short while later, Bryzon feels the tilt of the craft; they are about to descend. The ever-present weariness on the dejected faces surrounding him is a reminder of the despair the Eslaf brought to their planet. Bryzon's good friend Pateeo, who sits diagonally opposite him, turns up the corners of his mouth. Bryzon identifies the slight smile as an offer of commiseration, a recognition of their mutual suffering.

In the distance, he catches a glimpse of The High Mountains. Ante Mountain stands watch majestically as it towers above the rest of the vast mountain range. Once an angry volcano, it had lost a third of its size two thousand years ago after an eruption. Regardless, the giant remained the highest in the range, a splendid backdrop to the Freelands of Kearthat.

The shuttle arrives at the mine and Bryzon's daydreaming ends abruptly. Without forewarning, the bars holding the prisoners in place all retract at the same time. The transporter's hatch slides up, the hot morning air rushes in and the jostling to disembark begins. The prisoners reach for their food pails, making their way to the exit. This time, the walkway does not extend; they must jump onto the dusty patch below the hovering craft.

When their feet touch the ground, they turn their backs to the loud ship and scamper towards the mine entrance. Using their arms and lunch pails, they try to protect themselves from the dust and debris churned up by the hovering craft.

"Thank the galaxies; there are not many of these cursed days left," Bryzon says under his breath. The noise drowns out his comment as his mouth takes in fine dust. The transporter does not linger, and when the last set of feet hits the ground, it ascends. Through a curtain of eyelashes, Bryzon watches as it leaves, on its way to bring more captives to the mine.

The Eslaf soldiers assigned to their crew shout above the noise, pointing their weapons to force the prisoners to move faster. The tallest of the three grey beings prods Bryzon in the small of his back while shouting 'in alien' at him. Bryzon swings around and gives the guard a look that would cut a man in half. The Eslaf gives Bryzon a dead, bug-eyed, unemotional stare in return. Then Bryzon feels himself being propelled forward by a strong arm. It is Pateeo practically lifting him off his feet.

"Not worth it, my friend, not worth it," Pateeo says, keeping his voice low as he tries to save his friend from sure punishment.

"Sorry," Bryzon whispers, his anger towards the alien causing him to sound a little hoarse. They speed up, putting distance between them and the soldier. Bryzon glances back at the ugly being, its dangling bug-like protrusions swinging from its ridiculous face, an absurd sight to take seriously anyway.

The incident reminds him that any confrontation could cause the Eslaf to change their minds about releasing him and the men who have already served seventeen years for their defiance against the Eslaf. The last thing Bryzon wants to be responsible for is to destroy the chance of being reunited with his brother's children, Raine and Leyashe, his sister-in-joining Sayhran, and his nephews, Krom and Remek.

Chapter 28 - The Secret

Raine shakes her head at her brother Leyashe, and his stride outpacing hers is evidence that he is a young man on a mission.

"I am going to show you something that will make your head spin, Rai," he had told her excitedly the night before. After hours of pleading, he finally persuaded her to accompany him to a 'mysterious place' that he had declined to describe.

Signing the register at the gate before leaving their colony just after dawn, she had again pressed Leyashe for a hint of their destination. All he was willing to disclose was that they were heading to a spot near their special tree, the answer yielding a tiny clue as to which direction they would be taking.

Leyashe's eagerness makes Raine curious. 'What on Kearthat could be important enough to demand so much secrecy?' she thinks to herself.

Sometimes, it was difficult to get her brother to leave his bed in the morning; it was refreshing to have him wake her. His usual Drennan greeting of, 'May the day welcome you', replaced by, "You are going to be completely blown away, Rai."

"Blown away?" It is not part of our tongue, brother," she had admonished.

"If Tutor Layhne were to hear you now, he would question if your time-of-learning was truly nearing its end." As expected, Leyashe's response to her joking about his linguistics produced only a mischievous little smile and a roll of the eyes.

Her brother's eagerness for the day ahead has Raine thinking of Bryzon, who will soon be released from prison. With Leyashe's eighteenth year just passed, Raine hoped he would take it upon himself to guide her brother into adulthood in the Drennan ways.

Leyashe's voice calls out to Raine in the distance, and it tugs her from her thoughts.

"Hurry, sister," he urges, and then adds, "Please," trying his best to soften his impatience.

"Do not be so intolerant, brother. It will get you into trouble someday," Raine cautions as she lengthens her stride to catch up to him.

Having a combination of Drennan and earthling traits, the siblings were attractive. Both have straight, long black hair and the darker complexion of their Drennan father, Dayson. Their light blue eyes inherited from their earthling mother Caite, distinguishing them as unique and affording them many second glances.

Earlier, at the colony, two young girls at the gate were whispering and giggling when they saw Leyashe. Raine smiled inwardly when her brother pretended not to notice them, but it confirmed he was no longer just her little brother.

"I thank the galaxies that you will be home soon, Bryzon; I need you," Raine whispers as she walks. "Leyashe needs you," she adds a few seconds later, continuing a conversation with an absent Bryzon. Raine shakes her head and smiles, 'What would Bryzon think if he knew she had taken to speaking to the wind of late.'

Everyone relied on the agreement reached between the aliens and the colony leaders, hoping the Eslaf would not suddenly back out of the fragile deal. Bryzon and his men were desperate to return home to their families. Raine could not wait to see him freed from the awful prison.

When Raine looks ahead, she finds she must hurry again to catch up to Leyashe, who is just entering the tree line to the forest. Taller than Raine, his stride longer than hers, she struggled to keep up with her brother's hurried walk.

Once in the forest, the temperature drops considerably, and Raine can feel the ground give way under her feet. A thick, spongy moss grows on the floor of this damp, eerie world, all life here held captive by an almost impenetrable ceiling of leaves. In no time, Raine feels the chill on her bare arms and legs. She keeps her pace going as she carefully places her steps, her right hand on her short sword, in the event of unexpected predators.

As if drawn by an unknown irresistible force, Raine stops and looks up. The huge trees all appear in a desperate race, each striving to be taller than the other in their quest to reach the suns. She marvels at the sight as she tilts her head as far back as possible. When she looks down again, her indulgence has rendered a price; she can barely discern her brother's silhouette in the dim light. A few seconds later, Leyashe disappears entirely from her view.

She is about to start running when she hears a distinct crack.

Raine stops in her tracks and listens. In the silence that follows, she can feel her heart rate increase. She remains quite still certain it was not her brother who made the sound. Taking deep, slow breaths, she steadies her nerves.

She surveys her immediate surroundings before meticulously extending her line of vision further away; she does not see anything.

Then another sound, a twig snapping, this time much closer. She backs up to a tree behind her, her movements deliberate, her eyes darting about in the semi-darkness. She assesses her situation while raising her short sword, holding it high above her head. She is ready to strike. Then, the culprit is revealed. The silhouette of a large Agnak feeding on the moss becomes visible, and Raine relaxes.

The harmless Agnak's jaws, chewing moss frantically appear ferocious in the dim light, but it is one of Kearthat's more docile creatures. When the animal senses Raine, it sprints away, the dark forest swallowing it up as if it were never there.

Raine must make up for the lost time. Dodging branches, she becomes more annoyed at Leyashe with each step. She decides to scold him the moment she catches up to him. He should have realised by now that she was no longer behind him.

She steps into the sunslight, and in the distance, she can see Leyashe. As she gets closer, she finds him sitting on a log, tossing pebbles aimlessly into a small pond covered by beautiful deep purple Atolfs; the big floating flowers and their leaves cover almost the entire surface of the water. When he hears her approach, he looks up and smiles. With her brother's current level of excitement, she decides a reprimand may only find deaf ears. Her anger scatters in the suns' early morning light as she chooses not to tell him of the Agnak.

When they reach the rushing water of the Great Elin River, it means their journey is nearing its end. Where they are about to cross, a gigantic Trigga tree has fallen across the wide expanse of the river. The collapsed tree provides a natural bridge for those brave enough to cross it. At first a challenge for the four cousins, Leyashe, Raine, Krom and Remek, they had learned to cross the raging river's expanse many times despite warnings laced with  consequences coming from their aunt Sayhran.

Leyashe climbs up onto the now-dead exposed roots of the giant tree at the edge of the river. He extends his hand to his sister, and then begins crossing, but he turns to look back at his sister's progress at the halfway mark.

"Are you coming, Rai? I mean today," he shouts, cupping his mouth to raise the sound of his voice above the roar of the water.

"Just wait until I get over there, brother," Raine shouts back, but she knows her softer voice has been drowned out by the sound of rushing water over the waterfall a short distance from the tree bridge. He has not heard her playful threat.

Not to be outshone by Leyashe, Raine increases her pace, placing her feet on the mossy bits of the log and keeping her balance honed. She welcomes the cool mist of hundreds of tiny spatters that the gushing water throws up at her as it makes its way to Kearthats waiting ocean.

Apart from the shallows of the ocean between the rocks, the ocean on Kearthat was not a place to befriend. Dangerous beasts swam about in the deep dark water, creatures that prevented the people of Kearthat from ever using the ocean on their planet.

"Well done, sister, you made it. I thought perhaps a giant Ekans had leapt from the Elin River and swallowed you up," Leyashe quips, mocking his sister playfully. Raine lunges at her brother the moment her feet hit the ground, and he is forced to make a quick getaway, avoiding what he knows will be a lighthearted slap.

"Giant slithering creatures are afraid of me, brother," Raine shouts back, and the chase ends in laughter as they enter an area with high brush. Enormous blooms surround them, and they are careful not to disturb the towering stems to appease any large, bad-tempered bugs. Walking in silence, the scenery changes from brush to trees, and then their Trigga tree comes into view.

The siblings had begun to spend time here not long after their father, Dayson, had been killed in the uprising. Around the same time, Raine and Leyashe also lost their mother, Caite, to a sudden illness. Their aunt Sayhran, in her endless wisdom, had brought them here in the hope it would be a place of healing, a place of solace as she mourned her husband Keazan.

Together with her cousins Krom and Remek, Raine and Leyashe grew to love the giant Trigga tree and the unusual outcrop of large smooth rocks nearby. And somehow, as if by magic, they found peace in the one place on Kearthat where they experienced freedom.

A short distance from their tree was a memorial dedicated to the fallen of Kearthat. Here Sayhran taught them to honour those who died at the hands of the Eslaf. Now, there were few visitors to the memorial, represented by a huge pile of small, individually placed rocks. It had  become a place where only the birdsong and the breeze rustling the leaves in the trees eerily paid homage to those purged by the aliens.

The Trigga tree they call 'theirs' stands almost four hundred and fifty feet tall, boasting an abundance of large purple and green foliage. None had thus far braved a view from its top, or so Raine thinks, completely unaware Leyashe had recently conquered the giant. Leyashe, having decided that his accomplishment would remain his secret, in fear of what he sometimes jokingly referred to as 'the wrath of Raine'.

When they arrive at their destination, Raine notices the Trigga tree has seeded. It is a sight that takes her breath away. She immediately believes this is the surprise her brother has meant for her to witness.

A Trigga tree only ever bears seed once in its lifetime, and their tree's epoch had finally arrived. Big pods hang from the branches, their duty to repopulate well underway. Raine picks up a pod the wind has managed to coax down. She turns it over, and hundreds of Trigga seeds, each with a feathery tail, escape, fluttering to the ground. She smiles as she visualizes the seeds taking flight in the wind, finding a suitable spot where they will grow into the next generation of giant trees.

"Do you see the pods, Rai?" Leyashe asks, his back turned to his sister as he puts down the heavy pack he has been carrying.

"I do, brother. They were worth the long walk to see, thank you."

On this scorching day, the long branches of the big tree are unmoving. The shadow it casts below its long, leafy limbs provides an enormous welcoming patch of shade, the temperature immediately dropping under its huge parasol.

"What is so funny, brother?" Raine asks, confused at the amused look on her brother's face.

"The Trigga tree seeding is a wonderful surprise, Rai, but that is not why I brought you here," he informs her. "Once we have cooled and rested a while, not for long," he clarifies, "then I will take you to see the true surprise. It is going to blow …" he begins to say, but quickly decides to change his words to, "you wait and see."

Raine is about to sit down and enjoy the reprieve of the cool air when a Torrap flies out from somewhere above her. She instinctively covers her head, but its long tail feathers touch the top of her hands as it makes its hurried getaway. The squawking, brightly coloured bird disappears behind her, leaving her heart beating just a little bit faster for the second time on this day.

Raine thinks back on when they finally were old enough to come to play here alone, Sayhran's warnings still ringing in her ears.

"You must go the long way and use the proper bridge, and not so high in the tree, please," her aunt would say. They, of course, had chosen to always cross the river by clambering over the log, climbing their Trigga tree as high as their nerve would allow.

Raine leans back against the gigantic trunk, shifting her thoughts to the present. It is so quiet that she can hear the waterfall cascading onto the rocks. The sound of the swirling whirlpool and its treacherous waters is quite audible even at this distance. She closes her eyes and soaks up the peace.

She wonders if the waterfall near Sigae Colony could be heard from a great distance. Raine had been there once as a small girl, but it was so long ago, and she could not quite recall it. She knows the falls are far, far larger than this one. How is it possible she does not remember? She scrunches up her face as if she is willing her mind to cooperate, then shrugs her shoulders.

She does recall that as children, their games here at their Trigga tree included pretending to kill the Eslaf, their game extending to dumping the slain aliens into the churning froth of the waterfall. The ugly aliens had died horribly from feigned wounds inflicted by wooden swords and spears in these hours of play. Sadly, wooden weapons and dreams were always left behind in their tree house when they returned to the reality of the colony. In those days, the thought of the next time they would be allowed to return to their special place kept the cousin's minds off their misery.

"Enough rest, Rai, time to go," Leyashe announces, cutting into Rain's thoughts and pulling his sister away from her childhood recollections.

They pass a patch of Mura flowers in full bloom, and Raine stops momentarily to breathe the fragrance filling the air. A huge Flutterbug settles on one of the bright red flowers a short distance in front of them. The bug almost covers the flower with its huge black and yellow wings, seemingly oblivious to their approach. Its eyes shining in the sunlight it quivers as it draws nectar from its willing donor. Leyashe bumps the blossom's stem with his pack as he passes by. Too close for comfort, the beautiful Flutterbug takes flight, showering them with blue pollen. Raine shakes her head at her brother's clumsiness.

"Careful, Ash, it will leave stains if you do not dust carefully. Blow it off if you can; do not rub it in," she adds to a string of instructions.

Her brother tries to dust himself off but only manages to make things worse.

"Well, this is going to take much scrubbing," Raine comments as she hurries to catch up to her brother, who has abandoned his futile mission to rid himself of the blue mess.

When they reach the rocky outcrop, Raine cannot help but look down and study the damage done to her tunic. When she looks back up, Leyashe is nowhere to be seen.

"Where on Kearthat have you gone, Leyashe?" she says under her breath with slight annoyance. She is about to call out again when he answers her.

"I am here, sister," she hears, but she still cannot see him. She spins around to look behind her. When she turns back, Leyashe is standing directly in front of her, no more than two inches away.

"Do not do that, Leyashe, son of Dayson, not one more time today, do you understand me?" she scolds, looking up at him. "We have to stay together when we are away from the colony. The use of his father's name alerts Leyashe. It translates to, 'Your sister is extremely irritated with your behaviour.' He raises his hands, then lowers them, a gesture of silent apology.

"So, brother, why are we here? Raine asks quite sternly. I have been waiting patiently; what is the big secret?" Raine deliberately deepens her voice to emphasize the words 'big secret'.

"I have discovered a doorway, Rai," he tells her with a huge smile on his face. He reaches out, grabs her hand, and drags her along with him into a space at the back of the thick growth, right up against the towering wall of rock.

"This is it," Leyashe says, waving both hands towards the rock face as if presenting a play.

"A rock, Ash, why have you brought me to see a rock?" she asks, confused.

"No, Raine, I brought you to see a door that opens into the rock. Watch this," he declares as he reaches with his arm into a narrow crevice. Straining and stretching, he presses his face flat against the solid surface, extending his arm as far as it will go. Raine watches keenly, hoping nothing that bites lives in the narrow space.

Suddenly, a low grinding noise fills the air, and part of the rock in front of them slides away from the rest.

Raine's first response is one of utter disbelief. She leans forward to peek inside. It is dark. She looks back at her brother, and her mouth opens, but she finds herself momentarily searching for words.

"How did you know this was here? How, how did you find this, this door?" Raine exclaims, her eyes wide in surprise while pointing at the open space. Instead of answering his sister, Leyashe walks through the opening.

"Come, Rai," he urges, motioning to her to follow.

Raine keeps looking back as she moves forward as if not completely committed. Leyashe does not give his sister a chance to decide whether it is a good idea or not. He grabs her by the arm and pulls her inside. Immediately, the rock door begins to close, and the bright sunslight disappears as she watches in silence.

Then she hears an Idler. She grabs Leyashe by the arm with one hand and puts her finger to her lips, indicating that he should be quiet. She panics, wondering if the drone might have caught their movements in the final moments of the rock entrance closing. She presses her ear to the exit, holding her breath, she listens. She can hear the whirring sound of the drone outside. Just when she thinks they are being scanned, the sound begins to get fainter and fainter. She lets out a sigh of relief.

Raine re-adjusts the belt around her waist and feels for her short sword. In the semi-darkness, she bends down to find her bow and a pouch of arrows she had dropped earlier. A faint glow is coming from the walls around her, and the walls are vibrating. She takes a step back while her brain tries to grasp what the movement can be. It does not take long for her eyes to adjust, and she recognizes the Firemoths. The moths cover every inch of the walls and roof, their phosphorescence generating enough light to illuminate their surroundings. The siblings have grown up watching these large, gentle bugs as they feed on the Freelands at night.

"Bryzon was right," Raine whispers.

"Right about what?" Leyashe asks as the area fills with light from his torch.

"When I was a little girl, he told me that Firemoths were one of Kearthats mysteries. He said they hid underground during daylight, and he was right."

"Raine, the rock door, it is not rock," her brother tells her, changing the subject. The cavern around them is silent as she waits for her brother to communicate what is on his mind.

"I studied it carefully yesterday," his face serious. "It has the same texture and colour as the surrounding rock. It is strong, but it is not made of rock," he repeats. "It was made a long time ago in old Kearthat, I think? We could never accomplish this now," he adds.

"Do you suppose the Eslaf..." Raine begins to say when Leyashe cuts in.

"No, Rai, no, this is not the Eslaf. Why would the aliens do this? What would be their reason?" he debates.

Raine thinks about it and agrees the aliens would not need to hide things in caverns; they were in charge. Anyway, she doubted the large creatures would want to be in any cave.

Raine follows Leyashe, as he leads the way. There is an adjoining space that is much larger. Immediately, she notices a wall to the left that is distinctly blue.

Some of the trees and brush growing on the rock outcrop above have been very busy. Hundreds of long dead root vines hang lifeless; many have successfully conquered the void anchoring themselves to the ground, forming eery haphazard, crooked pillars.

The hair on the back of Raine's neck and arms stand on end, a strange sensation. A feeling that this place is special, the emotion washes over her like warm water. She is surprised that a place so dark and mysterious would make her feel so at peace. She slowly pivots on one foot to take it all in.

"How is it possible? We have climbed these rocks above us so many times, not knowing the existence of the cave below?" she asks her brother, but Leyashe does not answer.

Raine lights a second torch. The extra light exposes the extent of the masses of tangled roots, but she can make out the far wall through them. She wrestles through the vines and taps the wall with her short sword.

"It is solid rock," she confirms loudly, and there is a slight echo in the space around her.

While Raine looks around, trying to comprehend it all, she can hear Leyashe hacking away at the roots covering the peculiar blue wall.

Raine's scream fills the cavern. Leyashe races towards his sister's voice. He finds Raine kneeling beside the biggest Tenlegs he has ever seen. His sister's short sword neatly embedded into the middle of the creature's head, the bug's many eyes oozing little streams of thick green blood. The wound Raine inflicted on it was deadly; the creature's ten long hairy appendages quiver for a bit before they go limp. The siblings look at each other, their eyes wide. Where there is a female of the species, there is sure to be a male.

Raine cringes as she pulls her weapon out of the bug. They step over the seeping creature and make their way back to the blue wall. She is pretty shaken by the encounter but tries not to show it as she wipes her weapon on one of the thick vines closest to her.

Leyashe picks up a small rock from the cavern floor and taps the blue wall. It sounds hollow at first, but when he taps lower down, the sound becomes dull in places, suggesting a gap behind the metal wall.

"It must have a door. I am sure this is it!"

Raine puts her hand on the cold surface, running it along the ridged edge that Leyashe has exposed using his knife. She agrees it is a metal box of sorts, and it could be an entrance.

Leyashe uses his hunting knife to cut at the vines. Raine was still oblivious that this very same knife brought him to discover this mysterious place.

"Ok, stop, stop, stop!" Raine exclaims, her voice echoing slightly in the cavern.

Leyashe looks up, wide-eyed. "Why, what is wrong?" He scans the area to see if something else may be lurking in the dark.

"You have to answer some questions, brother. How did you find this place, and how are we going to get out now the exit has closed?" assuming her role as his big sister.

He is about to answer when Raine continues with another question. "And why did you not tell me about this place? I could have been prepared for this, whatever this is?" She stammers before she adds, "Your turn to speak," sounding a little out of breath.

Leyashe stops what he is doing and leans back against the blue wall, stretching his legs out in front of him.

"I was on the rocks above cutting some dried meat when I dropped my knife. Before I could grab it, it slid down between the rocks."

"I thought I had lost it forever, Rai," he says, frowning, as he relives the moment. "It is the knife Bryzon gave me," he exclaims as he holds up the knife. "The one he was gifted by Greatfather Jon, you know, it comes from Earth," repeating something she is well aware of.

"I climbed down after I calculated where it could have landed. I was worried that my arm would not reach it at first. I could feel the tip of the knife, but I had to really stretch. When I pulled it out, the rock door opened. I swear this on my honour." Leyashe goes silent and waits, watching Raine's reaction. She does not comment, so he continues.

"I knew I had set off a mechanism of some kind, so I investigated and found this to be true," Leyashe smiles triumphantly.

"I know where the lever is to open the door again from inside. I am not dim-witted, dear sister," her brother adds, shaking his head, his voice mocking her as he adds a playful teasing tone and smiles.

"Oh, and lastly, Rai, would you have believed me without seeing this place for yourself? Would you? You thought I had brought you all this way to see Trigga tree seeds?" he repeats with raised eyebrows. Happy with his explanations to his sister, he turns back to the task at hand, roots flying in all directions as he hacks away at them.

Raine concedes; her next question delights her brother. She knows he would much rather be talking about what is behind the wall when he finally gets it open.

"I wonder what we will find inside? It would be wonderful if it were filled with amazing things from old Kearthat that we have never seen before."

Countless stories of Kearthat from before the invasion never mentioned any secret caverns. Of that, Raine is certain. It raises the question of whose secret place the cavern might be, and would 'they' return? Shaking her head, she takes her sword and joins her brother in the struggle to clear the stubborn growth from the blue wall. Judging from the busy, long-dead vines, no one had been here in a long time.

For some unknown reason, her mind wanders to thoughts of their mother. "Caite was a beautiful earthling," Raine recalls. Sadly, she had only seven short years with her mother before she passed to the next world.

Bryzon had told Raine how her mother insisted she knew her husband Dayson would not return from the rebel war against the Eslaf. She also predicted the attack on the aliens would not end well. But the twins went ahead with their plans anyway.

Little did Bryzon know it would be the last time he would see Caite alive, and his twin brother Dayson, her father, would indeed die. Sayhran raised her and Leyashe together with her two sons, Krom and Remek.

In her eighteenth year, Raine was finally permitted to accompany Krom to the prison to visit Bryzon. Every time she visited the prison after that, he would tell her more about her parents, and Raine swooned when she heard how her father waited years to take her mother as his bride. It was the most romantic story she had ever heard.

It was not long before Raine understood that Bryzon and her earthling grandfather had been like brothers. Their struggle to survive the alien invasion and the years that followed built an unbreakable bond between the men from different worlds.

Bryzon spoke many times about the three mystic women, Rain's ears perking up each time to hear of the magic the It-Ha possessed. He relented every time they requested for him to re-tell the story of how he became Xennes.

She found out that Elder Moss still wielded much power among the Xennes and Drennan mortals alike. The Xennes, she understood, were sworn to obey the conventions of long ago and that Moss was holding them to their oath. She discovered that the old grey-haired man with the long silver-grey beard had the final word on all matters.

For Raine, it was hard to imagine the magic that the It-Ha possessed. When Bryzon recounted to her how the last surviving mystic had abandoned the survivors, taking with her the only magic left on Kearthat, Raine was appalled. She decided that if High It-Ha Layrrah was indeed real and still alive, she had to be the most selfish person on Kearthat. The crunch came when Raine found out It-Ha Layrrah and her grandfather had been close friends. It boggled her mind. It just did not make sense to her.

On many occasions, Bryzon echoed how her grandfather was an honourable man and a brave earthling,' and among the Drennan, Jon King was a hero and considered one of them.

"Do you think the Yraif could be responsible for this?" Leyashe smiles, interrupting Raine's train of thought.

The Yraif, everyone knew from Elder Moss's endless stories, had all supposedly perished in the huge Kearthquake more than two thousand years ago.

"Ah, now let me think, brother. Could it be," Raine mocks, preserving the tone her brother has set?

"Well, let me see." Raine scrunches up her lips, distorting her mouth and raising her eyes to the cavern roof as if summoning an answer from the roots above.

"We know they liked the dark and only ventured out after the stars dotted the sky. They were very fair in complexion, with long white hair and slightly pointed ears." Raine mimics pointy ears with her fingers. Leyashe laughs at his sister's facial expressions as she talks, prompting him to add what he knows of the mysterious First Ones of Kearthat.

"The Yraif had eyes made up of many colours that shimmered in the dark and ..."

"Do you know why their eyes were like that, Raine?" this time Leyashe interrupted. "It is said that they would steal the twinkle out of the night sky," he tells his sister, feigning Elder Moss's stern, deep storytelling voice.

"Elder Moss told you that? I must have missed that tale." Raine giggles.

"Yes, Rai, more than once, he seemed quite certain it was true," Leyashe says with a chuckle. "What else do we know?" he encourages as if willing the conversation to keep going.

Raine plays along. Her brother is enjoying the silliness of it all.

"Well, I know only what old Moss told us when we were children, but was it all true?" she questions mockingly and laughs.

"The Yraif were excellent swordsmen and women, and they beyond doubt knew how to use a bow. They were here long before the Drennan came to Kearthat. Among them was a mystic woman who possessed extraordinary magic. Moss said that she was incredibly beautiful; she was the High Yraif," Raine recalls from the reservoir of tall tales told by the old man.

"Wait, wait," Leyashe interrupts, "I remember something else now." It is said the High Yraif's anger at Ante Mountain when it erupted is why the mountain went to sleep, as it feared her retribution."

"The fury of Ante Mountain's eruption created the Jagged Mountains and the Barren Lands of the Nerrab, making more than two-thirds of Kearthat uninhabitable," Raine says, bringing reality back into their conversation.

"So, in conclusion, Ash, my dear brother, I would say that the Yraif, if they were real, could make a big blue box and put it in a cave with a pretend rock door. But enough jesting, brother, what do you truly believe?" she asks, putting an end to the light-hearted banter.

Before Leyashe can answer her question, he stares at her, his eyes huge.

Behind her, a Tenleg twice the size of the one she had killed earlier hangs from a vine less than two feet from Raine's head. Leyashe leaps towards her and buries his knife deep into the head of the creature. A loud squeal fills the cavern. At the same time, Raine moves, trips and falls face down, but she is back up on her feet in a split second. She moves fast, plunging her short sword into the creature's head beside Leyashe's hunting knife. The Tenleg lets out a final eery screech before it drops to the ground. It is massive, its stinger the length of Raine's hand. The creature's long extremities spasm for a time before it finally gives in to death.

When Raine turned to look where she was sitting, the distance covered by her brother seemed impossible, but he had done it. It is as if he attained the speed of light. His quick action saved her from a bite she is sure would have been fatal. She shivers, a crawling sensation taking hold of her as she rubs her bare arms, trying to erase the creepy feeling.

Leyashe grins triumphantly. The Tenlegs lying conquered, his grandfather's knife sticking out of the creature's head, gives him a sense of pride, a feeling of satisfaction after saving his sister.

They carry the Tenlegs by holding their weapons that are still stuck in the bug's head, making sure that its lifeless hairy legs don't touch any part of their bodies; the creature joining its partner at the back of the cavern, "out of our sight, out of our minds," Leyashe tells his sister.

After the nasty episode, they settle down and continue hacking at the growth on the blue wall. Before long, Leyashe is chuckling with excitement.

"I think I have found it, Rai. Take a look here; there is a definite gap. I think I have found the entrance!"

"You might be right, Ash, but it feels quite stuck."

Raine tries to pry at what looks like an opening with her fingers, but it does not budge. Next, they try using the edge of Leyashe's knife and Raine's short sword together, but the opening remains stubborn and will not yield.

"We will have to return with the right tools," Raine suggests, frustrated at the lack of equipment needed for the task. She gets the feeling that they will be forced to leave their curiosity unsated.

As they make their way back to the exit, her brother reaches into a small crevice to the right, and the door suddenly groans. The expectation of blinding sunslight quickly dissolves. The suns hang low in the sky; the day is soon to bid farewell.

"We should have first listened for Idlers. Come, the hour is late. We must hurry, brother," Raine sounds a little flustered. "We will return tomorrow."

"I will make sure to check for drones next time, Rai, and I will not disappear on you again. I swear," Leyashe tells her as if anticipating the berating she had planned for later on.

Raine is disappointed she has not kept better track of the time. She tries to reassure herself that her panic is the cavern's fault. It had distorted time, but she knows it is not a valid excuse. The urgency to get back before the Night Creatures begin to stir scares her. If the colony gates closed before they reached the settlement, they would not be allowed in. It was the rule.

The siblings feel twinges of haste but decide it is worth spending the time to brush away their footprints around the rocky outcrop before they leave.

On entering the big gate at the Noitibma Colony, Raine feels relief. They made it back just as the suns were about to settle behind The High Mountains.

The siblings head to their three-room cabin at the Eastern wall of the colony. Whilst Raine prepares a simple meal of fried vegetables and bread, she smiles at her brother. He has been talking non-stop. He poses questions but does not wait for answers; he simply answers them himself. Without her input, Raine notices many 'maybes' in the one-sided conversation, and she knows he will find it hard to wait for the safety of dawn. She does not say it, but she, too, feels eager to return to the cavern.

When they sit to eat their meal, the frenzied chatter from Leyashe renews. Finally, he suggests he find the tools they need for the next day. She reminds him to check in with Sayhran, and Raine is glad about the ringing silence that ensues.

She pushes their small table surface where they have just had their meal up towards the wall and hooks it into a latch, revealing Leyashe's bed beneath it.

Raine goes to the modest washroom, closes the door, undresses, and steps into the small tub filling with warm water. The water feels good on her skin. After she scrubs her slim body and rinses her freshly washed hair, she scrunches up her legs and lays back, staring at the roof.

Rid of the dust of the day, her mind goes back to when the pleasure of warm water and other small comforts had once been taken away from the colonies. She was very young, but she recalls how Sayhran struggled. After the uprising, when refined Zraphite bars were removed from the colonies as punishment, the Freelanders were left to struggle without heated water. Countless hours were spent collecting wood to cook their food, and further monotonous hours making candles, catching Shiftaf and extracting their oil to light their small homes took time too. It was a period when she and her cousins Krom and Remek struggled to read their lessons in the poor light. Lessons taken at night, in fear of the aliens discovering the children were receiving instruction in many subjects, and in the ways of old Kearthat.

Her bedroom is welcoming. Raine is tired after the anxious pace she and Leyashe had set to get home before the gate closed. She is eager to rest. She knows her long hair will not dry properly; it will wait for the morning when the suns complete the task.

With her hair still damp, the slight breeze through the small open window makes her feel chilled. Raine pulls the soft Trungo fur over her, leaving only her face peering out from beneath it. But it is not long before she abandons the furry cover for something thinner.

She yawns, but her nightly ritual of devoting thoughts to her parents keeps her from giving in to sleep. She starts by trying to recall her father's gentle, deep voice, a voice so different from that of his twin, Bryzon.

Raine digs deep into the memories she formed as a little girl. She randomly picks a day when she remembers her father forging a short sword. She can clearly remember the heat coming off the hot coals and the hiss of the steam when the hot metal met the cool water, but not his voice. She panics and hastily reaches for the only picture of her parents which she and Leyashe possess.

Hand drawn by a man in the colony with a talent for sketching from memory, Sayhran had assured Raine that the image was an excellent likeness of her parents. The drawing has started to wear from the many times she and Leyashe have held it. The charcoal portrait of Dayson and Caite has smudged slightly, but it does not hide the fact they were a handsome couple. After studying their faces for a short while, Raine carefully puts the picture away.

The smell and the colour of her mother's hair are what Raine remembers best. As if spun from the gold strands of a Tenleg's web, her mother's hair shone like jewels in the sunslight. Raine conjures up the one memory that stands out. It is of her mother hanging freshly washed clothes on the line, tugging and pulling to straighten each item to ensure they would dry unwrinkled.

"One day, the Eslaf will pay for what they did; this, I swear," Raine whispers as she reaches to extinguish the light on the small bedside table. She pulls the cover over herself. The Trungo fur slides off the end of her bed onto the floor with a 'plop'.

Strangely, Raine's weariness is put on hold as she ponders how dangerous it must have been for her father to hunt this giant animal for its fur. She had seen drawings of Trungos when she attended her lessons as a child. Ten feet tall or more, they were sturdy, with furry skin and thick, solid legs carrying their weight. They were dangerous beasts when cornered, Bryzon had once told her. Trungos, it was said, made such deep rumbling sounds their presence could be heard for miles as their sounds reverberated on the breezes blowing through the Freelands.

Sadly, these once-respected animals were hunted down and killed to extinction by the Eslaf. No one knows why, but it is thought this animal might have resembled a creature from their home planet, their creature perhaps far more dangerous than the unfortunate Trungo of Kearthat. A feeling of pure hatred for the disgusting aliens enters Raine's whole being when she thinks of the audacity of their actions. She had never had the chance to see a Trungo alive, even as a child.

She hears Leyashe return and shouts, "Until dawn, brother."

"Sayhran sends her greetings. Until dawn, Rai," he replies and then adds. "I love you."

She smiles.

"Love you more, Ash," she responds as she listens to him preparing his bed for the night.

Raine feels fortunate their adventure has come during her break from her regular duties. As an Overseer in Noitibma Colony, she usually worked many days in succession before having time off. Luckily, she has a break from her duties for two more days, making it possible to take another trip to the cavern.

However, there was one duty she had agreed to before she went on her time-off. She would have to be back at the colony to attend a gathering at the end of the following day. This was sure to upset Leyashe. She had deliberately put off telling him, as she did not want to cut short her brother's excitement.

"Too late now," she whispers to herself, and it does not take long for her to drift off into a deep sleep, all thoughts of Trungos, secret caverns and oversized ten-legged bugs fading away for now.

Chapter 29 - The Storm

Dawn breaks and Raine awakes with a start, not knowing what has roused her from her deep sleep. She lays in her bed, not moving, listening to the silence. She squints to look through a narrow gap where the shutter does not entirely cover the tiny window beside her bed. It still looks dark outside. She sighs and snuggles into the covers, uncertain if dawn has met the new day.

It does not stay quiet for long before the sound of clanging comes from the next room.

"Ash," she says under her breath, pulling the blanket over her head. But her eyes refuse to stay shut as her brain recollects the previous day's events. She jumps out of bed and gets dressed. She finds her brother waiting patiently for her when she opens the door. His long hair was tied into the latest fashionable knot, his pack ready at the door, a smiling Leyashe eager to leave.

"May the day welcome you, Rai. I made you something to eat." The enthusiastic look on his face is priceless, his eyes telling of his anticipation.

"May the day welcome you, brother."

Raine has to smile when she accepts the plate, and she giggles inwardly. A large portion of cold fried vegetables left from their evening meal and a slice of bread thick enough to stop a charging Trungo fills the wooden bowl.

"I packed food for our journey," he tells her proudly.

She loves this brother of hers, and she knows she would give her life for him. The colony had granted her considerable support during the first few years after losing their parents. Sayhran had been more than generous and had cared for them selflessly during their young years until the colony leaders had different ideas. When Raine reached her eighteenth year, she was called in by the three Noitibma Colony leaders and declared, as they had put it, 'no longer a fledgling.'

After much protest from Sayhran, the siblings were moved into a cabin of their own. Now, many years later, she was grateful for the decision made by Noitibma's Leaders, Keeland, Nowber, and even Elder Moss. Their harsh decision had created a special connection between her and Leyashe.

As her brother grew up, it became clear to Raine he would eventually need the guidance of a strong male figure. Krom, being the older male cousin, did his best. However, she was elated when Leader Keeland recently announced that he had, with the help of her cousin Marcus King the leader of Rednos Colony, negotiated with the aliens to release Bryzon and the men involved in the uprising.

"What did you have to trade for the tools, Ash?" Raine asks her brother before taking another bite of her cold food.

"I traded three Tibbar and a Xiso. I will have to go on a hunt soon, but it was a good trade," he insists. Raine knows that hunting the slow-hopping, four-eared Tibbar would be easy, but Leyashe would have to be cunning to track and cull the fast-running Xiso.

Raine manages to eat half of her meal, then excuses herself. Her next mission was to tie her slightly damp hair into place before they set off for the day.

Looking into a large broken piece of mirror, her mind is filled with what the day could bring. If there were treasured items behind the blue wall her colony could use, she would be overjoyed.

As her thoughts drift, Raine cannot help but imagine how different it must have been before the invasion, before her people were forced to become farmers living under the watchful eyes of the Eslaf. She has heard so many stories from the Xennes of how magnificent the cities were.

Tugging tightly, Raine secures her tresses with strings of cleverly braided Ylock leaves and tucks the stray bits behind her ears. As an Overseer, Raine was used to putting her hair up, and looking tidy. An Overseer's duties were to make sure that the colonists followed the rules set by the aliens and by the colony leaders. They were the regulators who ensured everyone's safety from the cruelty of the Eslaf. It was a bizarre way to live, but it worked best. It was common knowledge that one could be executed by the alien soldiers for the slightest infraction. It was up to the Overseers to protect their people from these harsh punishments.

But Raine was not only an Overseer. 'Your job is twofold,' Leader Keeland told her on the day she graduated from the challenging training. She was to be the first Observer. She was chosen for this special covert undertaking because of her exceptional skills in noticing things others normally did not. At a private meeting with the three leaders of Noitibma Colony, her mission was explained to her, and Raine welcomed it with open arms.

When Raine next visited Bryzon in prison, she confided in him.

"Study them well, Raine. The day will come when your 'watching' will be of great value to us," he told her.

Raine was dedicated and worked hard to prove she could fulfil her job as an Overseer and Observer. She was determined to use every encounter with aliens wisely. She would find their vulnerabilities. She was tough. She had bow-handling skills, her hand-to-hand combat training was faultless, and her observance skills were unchallenged. Surely, watching would be the easiest thing in the world?

She did not disappoint; Raine was the best Observer the leaders could have wished for.

Overseers boarded the shuttlecraft several times a day to check on the cargo. They were fortunate to drive the rugged Traxid vehicles used to transport goods and colonists between the two closest colonies to Noitibma, and they spent a great deal of time in close proximity to the enemy.

Raine's quest to learn everything about the Eslaf gave her purpose. She made detailed drawings of the different Eslaf transporters, shuttles, and spotter craft that landed at Noitibma. She made notes, many times making notes about the existing notes.

She observed how the aliens walked and how they talked. She kept schedules of their incoming and outgoing homeships as they passed overhead. This way, she knew when new aliens were shipped to Kearthat, and others departed for their home planet, the spaceships transporting Kearthat's Zraphite were different, she noticed in time. Soon, she was able to discern a pattern to everything. One thing that stood out was that during the time of 'the cooling, and the darkening' the sky was clear of alien craft.

At first, she found it difficult to identify the markings on the Eslaf soldiers she encountered on the shuttles; they all looked so alike. But quickly, she was able to tell them some of them apart. Others she felt were odd. Odd how? She was yet to establish.

Some months later, she was convinced that some Eslaf had to be Android. She waited until she had the least doubt in her mind that she was right and told the Noitibma leaders. They raised an eyebrow and told her to keep up the good work.

Later, she discovered that it was not always the same Eslaf who came to the colonies. After some months, she could report to Keeland, Nowber, and Elder Moss that there was some kind of rotation system. Information Raine reported, however, was never spoken of again, and she finally conceded that the leaders knew there was not much they could do with the knowledge other than ask Raine to keep it secret. This did not deter her, and she continued to keep up her scrutiny of the vile creatures. Her reports to the council were met with enthusiasm, gratitude, and a pat on the back. She never felt the urge to abandon her mission, and out of respect for the colony leaders, she never questioned their inaction.

Driving the Traxid between the colonies allowed Raine to roam the Freelands, to experience what it must have been like before the invasion. She loved interacting with the Freelanders on these trips. She made friends in Rednos and Ygyzis Colony. Short visits with her cousin Marcus in Rednos added to a feeling of belonging, family, and just a tiny bit of freedom.

"Raine, how long are you still going to be?" Leyashe shouts from their small kitchen.

"On my way, brother, patience please," she answers as she turns off the light.

"I have to be back in Noi by three hours past the mid-hour, Ash," she announces. Not giving Leyashe time to protest, she adds, "It is the monthly gathering of all the near colony Overseers, and I am expected to attend, even on my time-off, brother," she states in a serious voice, making it official. "There could be schedule changes that I may need to know about. It is not good for me to make excuses," she continues, trying to get him to understand the importance of the meeting.

"Oh Rai, nooo, can you just not go?" Leyashe begs, drawing out the words to show his dismay, knowing his sister will not budge. Raine had integrity; her duties came first.

"It will not take us long if we run, Ash; there is more than enough time. Come, let us be on our way," she reassures him. Leyashe rolls his eyes at her, huffing and slinging his pack over his shoulder. "I thought you had the whole day off, Rai," he pleads while moving towards the door.

Today would be short, but it would be enough time to open the door and see what is on the other side of the blue wall; of that Raine is positive.

Leyashe was still free from a full schedule of chores while attending the last of his required classes at night. This would be over soon. Before long, the leaders would find a job for him in one of the colonies that needed an extra pair of hands. If he were lucky, he would remain in Noitibma. Raine knew he wanted more than anything to follow in her footsteps and apply to be an Overseer. However, only a few of these jobs ever became vacant, and he would have to wait until there was a need again.

She closes the door to their cabin and then checks to see if anyone has left a note for her in their message box.

"The gate is already open, sister," Leyashe says impatiently.

"Yes, brother," she says, shaking her head at him. "We stick together today, Ash, or I turn back. Do you understand me? You must be more patient Leyashe, son of Dayson," she adds as an afterthought.

"Sorry," he answers, immediately regretting his manner towards his sister.

They leave the colony without as much as a second glance from anyone. It is a normal, busy morning. The Freelanders are going about their daily chores as dawn breaks into day over The High Mountains.

A challenge awaits Raine and Leyashe; they have a wall to defeat. Five minutes after exiting the colony gate, they set off at a steady run. Raine looks up at the pale pink sky. It is a beautiful morning; pillowy cream-coloured clouds float gently overhead, birds are chirping in nearby trees, and there is only a slight breeze. She smiles, 'it is going to be a good day,' she whispers to herself.

Raine thinks of the Firemoths in the cavern. Do they watch the Night Creatures from above at night? What do they see? How do they get in and out of the cavern? All these questions make her wish she could fly. What a wonderful gift that would be as she tries to envision it, and then smiles at her silly thought of having wings instead of arms. No, that would not work, she smiles.

Leyashe keeps his promise to be at his sister's side. When they arrive at the outcrop of rocks, it looks untouched. Just a few minutes and they will be inside the cavern again. They keep quiet, not moving. All they hear is the waterfall in the distance and the sound of bugs soaking up the morning suns. They cannot hear any drones or alien craft. When they are sure they are completely alone, they enter the cavern. The Firemoths are still there as if they have never moved.

Leyashe kneels in front of the blue wall, handing his sister one of the flat metal bars from his pack. "They weighed me down, so they had better work, Raine."

"Insert your bar into the gap at the top near the corner, and I will put one into the gap halfway down. When I say go, you push ahead with all your strength and your entire weight," Leyashe repeats.

Raine allows her brother to take charge, confident they will succeed. She knows he must have been awake half the night planning the strategy to beat the stubborn door into submission.

Unbeknownst to the siblings, the weather outside is suddenly changing drastically. A storm is brewing. The gentle clouds of earlier have become dark, and there is an ominous purple sky beginning to blanket the Freelands. The birds have long ago fled to places of safety; the wind is picking up speed rapidly. The wide branches of the gigantic Trigga tree not far from the cavern sway as the gusts become stronger and stronger. Any seeds on or under the big tree are scooped up violently and sent on their way, destination unknown.

Time passes quickly. Oblivious to the outside world, Raine and Leyashe battle with the blue door. It opens a small amount each time they strain, but it stubbornly holds firm, refusing to yield completely. They take a break to drink from their canteens, excited and frustrated at the same time. Neither mentions that the tools are beginning to show signs of stress or that they are not paying enough attention to any bugs that could still be lurking. Raine begins to wonder if they will succeed before it is time to return to the colony or if one or both tools will break under the pressure they are putting them under.

The lightning comes first. Silver lines race across the sky, the jagged white veins light up Kearthat and thunder growls. The vibration is suddenly felt inside the cavern. The siblings react in sync; their expressions turn to wide-eyed horror as they both assume, Kearthquake?

"Out, we have to get out now!" Raine screams. They drop everything and run for the exit of the cavern. As the simulated rock door grinds open, they are dismayed that the earlier light has been replaced with semi-darkness. Fierce wind rushes into the cavern, and drops of rain splatter at high speed into their faces and bodies. They are in disbelief; they are trapped. Leyashe pulls the lever and the exit begins to close.

Raine slips on the wet ground and falls. When she tries to get up, her wet hands make it difficult; Leyashe reaches out and helps her up. Another huge flash followed by a blinding light and a thunderous crash. They lose their footing as the ground beneath them heaves. A massive lightning streak in the sky shakes Kearthat, followed by a profound silence and a lull in the wind. Then they hear it, a great big thump nearby as the wind resumes its ferocity.

"I think a tree fell across the entrance. I hope it did not cover our exit," Raine panics.

"Do you want me to open it again and take a look?" Leyashe asks.

"No use, brother. We are trapped here for now anyway. There is no sense in us getting soaked again," Raine adds breathlessly.

"It is a storm, Ash, a big, big storm. We should stay a while. It is dangerous out there. It is dark enough for the Night Creatures to be released. It must be safer in here for now," she decides. Hoping it is the right choice, she looks over at her brother, who nods in agreement.

"We can wait out the storm for a while, but the moment it clears and lightens up a little, we have to run for home before the night comes. Let us gather what we need, brother," Rains says breathlessly. Leyashe obediently starts gathering items he wants to take home.

Suddenly, there is a loud crash, and then there is only darkness.

Raine opens her eyes slowly. For a few seconds, she is disoriented. She can make out her brother lying on his back. He looks peaceful, as if he is sleeping. She scrambles over to him. As she reaches him, he bolts upright and gasps, causing her to jolt.

"What happened, Rai? What happened? Did the lightning strike in the cavern?" Leyashe asks.

Raine tries to stand, but her knees feel weak. She holds onto the wall for support and immediately realizes the Firemoths are gone. Drops of water coming from above drip on her arm. She looks up at the roof of the cavern, and realisation dawns.

"I think the rain must have stopped long ago, Ash. The Firemoths are gone, which means it is dark outside."

When she looks back at Leyashe, she gulps. His pupils are glimmering. Luminous-green pupils are staring back at her. At the same time, her brain tells her she can see all around her, even though the torches are out.

"Rai," Leyashe screams, "Your eyes, they are… they are glowing," he shouts, moving back a step as if afraid of his sister, "Rai, your eyes…" he repeats.

"I know," she says, "Yours are too. I think the lightning, or the cavern, or something, has changed our eyes," she repeats, trying to find a plausible answer.

"Why?" Leyashe asks, as if his sister has any inclination.

This I do not know, Ash. I just do not know," she declares. "I just do not know," she says again, sounding defeated. "What I do know is that it is dark out there. We were supposed to be back hours ago, and I have missed my gathering," she tells her brother. "By now, everyone knows we have not returned to the colony. It has to be in the middle of the night or later. Who knows how long we were unconscious?" she says, sounding awfully worried.

Leyashe comes over to his sister and puts his arm around her; resting his head on hers, he hugs her. He stays silent, not quite sure if he is consoling his sister or himself.

It is the usual practice that all Freelanders sign the register when leaving their colony. The siblings had done so, stating they were going hunting. If they did not return before nightfall, it would be assumed something terrible had happened to them. There would be a search party in the morning, and Raine was certain of that. They would have to hurry back as soon as the suns rose over the mountains.

Their decision not to include Sayhran in their plans now seems to be the biggest mistake they could have made. Her aunt was a kind, caring, gentle woman, and Sayhran was sure to be out of her mind with concern. A twinge of panic sets in, a feeling of dread that she failed in her responsibility to take care of her brother unnerves Raine. They hold hands and walk back to the bigger cavern. They avoid looking at each other.

"We need to light the torches," Raine suggests, "In case there are more Tenlegs. They are afraid of the flame," Raine says. Although they both can see quite clearly in the dark, they light the torches to be safe. The warm light fills the cavern and immediately lifts their spirits. For some uncanny reason, their eyes appear normal in the light. Raine notices distinct relief on her brother's face.

They cannot hear anything from outside, but inside the cavern, the sound of water trickling arouses their curiosity. A small stream has formed near the edge of the stone wall, disappearing under the blue wall. They exchange a glance that needs no words. If the water goes in under the wall and disappears, something must be under the blue wall. Where does it lead to?

Raine and Leyashe pick up their tools simultaneously, almost bumping heads on the way down and again when they lift their heads. This time, their effort must count. They heave, twist and push. There is a loud crack and the door swings open.

"I give you the door," Leyashe giggles, feigning an ushering gesture. Raine rewards him by grinning from ear to ear. She is happy about the achievement, although their predicament is otherwise dire. Neither notice their physical strength has increased ever so slightly. Their excitement at finding a way into the blue box has overwhelmed their senses.

They move at the same time, squeezing through the newly discovered entrance. Once inside, their eyes immediately become accustomed to the low light.

They have left the torches behind in the cavern. When they look at each other, Leyashe sighs and returns to bring both torches and his pack. He does not say a word, but the frustration of this new dilemma is evident.

The siblings find themselves looking at metal containers of all sizes stacked one on top of the other. The containers fill three sides of the room from floor to ceiling. Leyashe calculates the size of the space. He does not share the information with his sister, but it is quite a large room.

"It is so clean and tidy, Rai. It looks as if it was sealed up yesterday," Leyashe comments as he moves from one stack of containers to the next, touching them lightly with his fingertips. Then he sees an object sitting on a small metal table in the room. They approach it cautiously as if it were something dangerous. Leyashe notices the name on the flat, rectangular, thin and grey 'thing.'

"It is an Asus," he giggles, pronouncing it 'ass-us,' and his sister taps him lightly on the head.

"I wonder what that stands for? What do you think, Ash?

"It is an Enscriptor of some kind. I am almost sure I have seen this in one of the earthling books we have in Noitibma." He runs his hands over the top before discovering it is made up of two halves. He pulls the two pieces apart to reveal a scriptboard.

"There are no tethers, but ..." Leyashe begins to say while pulling open the only drawer of the table. As hoped for, he sees a cable, and immediately knows that it is the source of power for the machine. After turning the item every which way, he finds where to plug it in. All he needed now was energy.

"I have a piece of Zraphite. I will find a way to power it. This means we will have to take it home with us, sister," Leyashe announces, picking up the machine and the chord. "It is not that heavy," Leyashe quips as he slips the laptop into his bag without waiting for approval or objection from his sister.

"We should get ready to leave the moment dawn comes. Let us go and check if the moths have returned. They will be our guide that daybreak is near," Raine prompts. She is still worried there is a tree over the entrance, mentally preparing for the difficulty.

"Raine, can we open one of the big boxes before we leave," Leyashe asks, tilting his head to prompt a yes. But Raine is adamant they have no time.

"We will have a lot of explaining to do, brother. I need time to think. Let us be on our way," Raine tells him. On the way out, Raine spots a tiny box on the only shelf in the room. She picks it up, hesitates, and then decides she is taking it with her. Leyashe smiles. It is exactly what he would have done.

They close the blue metal door only partly. Reluctant to leave, they know they must face whatever consequences await them. Suddenly, a soft whirring sound comes from behind them. They spin around just in time to see the blue door closing itself.

"There must be a mechanism that opens and closes it, Rai. How dim-witted am I?" Leyashe admits, shaking his head. They begin looking around for a lever or a button, something that could possibly open the blue door again.

Raine decides to feel around the opening of the bigger cavern. She runs her hands over the rock. It takes no time at all to find what she is looking for. Closer inspection reveals a metal square with a narrow, raised button. She pushes the button down, but nothing happens; she pushes it to the right, and the door snaps open.

"Well done, Rai, you found it!" Leyashe exclaims with delight. He immediately wants to test the door and lever again, but Raine stops him.

"We must go now, brother. We can examine this tomorrow or when we next return," she insists. Leyashe does not argue the point, deciding it is best not to test his sister's patience. The stream they had earlier watched travelling under the blue box has drained away. They both notice, but neither comment as they leave their unexplored treasure behind.

The Firemoths are back, and Leyashe reaches to open the exit. Daylight is just beginning to pour over The High Mountains. They are relieved to discover that nothing is blocking the exit. Brother and sister notice two things: their eyes are back to normal in the daylight, and everything around them looks like a war zone.

Setting a steady pace, they stop briefly at the river to fill their canteens. They cross back over the log bridge. The water rushing below their feet is considerably higher as the excess storm runoff makes its way down from the mountains to the waiting Kearthat Ocean.

They are shocked as they survey the damage that meets them mile after mile, confirming the fierceness of the storm.

While they sprint, they get their story straight as to why they never came home. They were not in the habit of lying, but this was different. They will use the sudden storm as an excuse and explain that they took to hiding in their treehouse in the big Trigga tree. The closer they get to home, the more worried Raine becomes. The Freelands have suffered, the crops have sustained great damage, and she begins to fear the Freelanders may have suffered casualties.

To her relief, there is a flurry of activity when they enter the colony. Several familiar faces look elated to see them. It does not take long for Raine to realise that most thought she and Leyashe had succumbed to the violent storm or the Night Creatures.

Chapter 30 - The Mine

A crowd forms as the prisoners wait to board the mine's tunnel transport. Bryzon inhales deeply; it will be the last clean air before the long day begins in the underground mine.

The previous day, he had spent endless hours erecting roof supports for a new section of tunnel running deeper than any before. The last task had been to move the cages that would protect the prisoners in the event of a Kearthquake. Several years ago, many alien soldiers and Korak alike had lost their lives in a particularly violent shake. Those deadly tunnels remained sealed to this day.

When the Tracker arrives, they push and shove to get seated. A shuttle meant for eighty seats a hundred with a squeeze. The Eslaf guards shout continually in the crazy shuffle of prisoner bodies, their guttural alien verbiage blending into the chaos. Over the years, Bryzon has come to understand that the soldiers' shouting had only a few meanings: get to work, hurry up, or move along.

Once the mine Tracker is full beyond capacity, they hold on tightly in anticipation of its speed. The bucket, as the Xennes prisoners prefer to call it, jerks as it starts up and their short journey into the belly of Kearthat begins. Ironically, it is the very Zraphite they dig for each day that runs the whole system.

Bryzon glances back at the alien guards languishing in a Tracker all to themselves, following directly behind them. The alien guards have more than enough legroom. He can feel his anger grow, but then he remembers his promise to Peteeo. His friend was right. The slightest provocation could make the aliens change their minds about releasing them from prison.

The Eslaf soldiers' green body armour appears black in the dull twilight depths of the tunnels.

The colour-coded armour of the aliens pointed to a society with defined social hierarchies. Bryzon concluded that this most likely ensured the best chance of species survival; it was a hive mentality.

Most of the Eslaf are green-suits; they make up the largest cog in the Eslaf's fighting machine. The grey-suits at the Dexim Zraphite Refinery and those working in the city were the workers, the easier positions. Leaving the fewer red-suits to direct all the operations on Kearthat. Somewhere, Bryzon knew, there had to be a supreme leader or leaders that gave the red-suits their instructions.

The ugliness of the Eslaf knows no bounds. However, the sophistication of the Eslaf spaceships and weapons point to a highly evolved species. The barbaric and brutal character of their race confirmed that the Eslaf should never be underestimated.

With a jerk of their heads, the Tracker abruptly stops, and Bryzon is yanked from his thoughts. The prisoners move quickly. Every man and Korak grabs a shovel from the back of the Tracker, all aware that if you are left standing without a shovel after the bucket leaves, it results in ... you guessed it, more punishment.

Bryzon tucks his ration tin under one arm, and with the other hand, he manages to grab extra shovels for the prisoners carrying water pails. The pails filled at the mine's entrance are now only half full. The rough, hectic scramble has again spilled much of the precious liquid meant to sustain them for the last half of the day.

For Bryzon and his men, another long, hot, hard day begins. Within minutes, shovels are scraping the black rocks hiding within it the sought-after Zraphite. Loaded into carts under the watchful eyes of the Eslaf guards, the full carts leave on an outgoing line while empty ones find their way back on an incoming rail. A concert of monotony is orchestrated each day by this routine.

Once on the surface, the black dirt will automatically tip onto the conveyor system. The destination of the fruits of their labour is the Dexim Refinery, which is not far from the prison.

Soon after the colonies had been established, Bryzon heard that both male and female Eslaf were seen working at the refinery. To him, the presence of females meant the aliens would be staying for an undetermined time. Their intention, he knew, would probably be to remain until the mine stopped producing.

An hour of reminiscing passes before Bryzon is drawn out of his thoughts of the past and the future that awaits him. He stops shovelling and lets out a huge sigh as he wipes his forehead with his forearm.

"Damn this mine, damn the tunnels, damn the heat and the Eslaf," he says loudly. "Damn it all to the void beyond Ade~mordna." The intolerable conditions in the mine has Bryzon struggling with his feelings, damning the aliens to a place beyond his galaxy, demonstrating his feelings well.

Close by, he can hear a peculiar, unrelenting sound. It is the sound of a Korak prisoner coughing and Bryzon knows it will only be a day, or maybe two, before the prisoner is unable to work. When the Korak dies, an ugly smell from a large fire will reach their nostrils at the prison. The Korak will burn to ashes, having died far away from the peaceful planet he once called home. His soul adrift in the wind, with nowhere to go, Namow would remind Bryzon afterwards, as she always did.

Bryzon pulls his neckcloth off. He feverishly rubs at the sweaty dirt on his arm as if it is to blame for his discomfort. Peteeo watches his friend from the corner of his eye, his heart heavy.

"Rightly so, my friend, I too wish them to die on the dark side of a far planet without suns," Pateeo sympathizes. Everyone in earshot manages some form of disparaging comment about the Eslaf, and Bryzon is somewhat comforted by the commentary that is in sympathy with his feelings.

Namow, Bryzon's Korak friend, stops digging when the Eslaf soldiers are distracted. She reaches to pat Bryzon on the shoulder with her large, bony hand, a gesture of empathy for his suffering.

Her big dark eyes narrow slightly as she looks to where the guards are directing a digger to move forward. Namow's distinct Korak scowl meant for the Eslaf soldiers amuses Bryzon. She had managed to lighten the moment somewhat. The working conditions in the mine at this depth are horrendous, and the air being pumped into the tunnel is not enough to sustain them adequately. The heat was unendurable.

Namow tries to form a human-like smile meant for Bryzon. The grin she manages to emulate is almost comical, but the result of her effort leaves him content to call this kind alien his friend.

Beads of perspiration run down Namow's large olive forehead, forming little dust-filled paths down her heart-shaped face. She removes her neckcloth, revealing the collar all prisoners are forced to wear. The green light shines bright in the semi-dark of the tunnel. She wipes away some of the dirt and perspiration. When the guard returns to his post, he looks directly at her. Namow quickly ties the neckcloth back into place, her long alien fingers working as fast as possible. Then she picks up her shovel and the drudgery continues.

A while later, a loud commotion draws everyone's attention. A series of shouts from the Eslaf guards triggers a work stoppage, and everybody looks up to find out what is happening. The problem, it turns out, is two rail carts have somehow become stuck to each other, the full cart dragging the empty one along with it. The guards stop the power to the tracks, and shouting and waving of weapons culminate in orders to fix the obstruction. Several prisoners act on instinct and jump into action to remedy the situation.

"A terrible day, ruined by bad attitude on their part, do you not think, Bryzon, my friend? Peteeo says with a straight face.

Bryzon finds himself chuckling inwardly at Pateeo's staid, blackened face. The light moment brought about by his friend's natural ability to produce humour is appreciated. Still, there is little reprieve from the miserable part the heat continues to play in the day's sad tragedy.

As the dusty air continues to mix with the hot steam rising from the ever-hissing vents below their feet, the men and Korak alike transform. Bryzon surveys the area and sees only eyes around him as the bodies of the men begin to blend into their surroundings. The occasional white-toothed smile by a Xennes prisoner is a strange sight indeed. The olive-skinned Korak in contrast, with their dark eyes and teeth, become one with the black rock and dirt surrounding them.

Bryzon desperately longs for the short shower they are allowed at the end of their shift.

Finally, conquering the burden of the heat that clings to him, Bryzon manages to force his mind to drift back to daydreaming. He imagines what it will be like to be free again, concluding he would rather die than see the inside of this mine again.

The red light in the tunnel flashes, signalling a work stoppage yet again. The interruption is a Tracker arriving carrying four Eslaf soldiers; one of them is a red-suit. After some alien jargon is exchanged with the guards on duty, mayhem ensues as they grab a Korak prisoner and drag the wide-eyed alien towards the waiting bucket.

Immediate silence follows as Namow raises her hand in the air. The echoing clicks of the Korak language fill the tunnel. The only voice comes from the unfortunate alien who is being hauled away. His eyes locked onto Namow; the creature clicks too fast for Bryzon to fully understand what he says. Namow remains still while the Korak is deposited into the Tracker, which speeds away. Bryzon notices Namow's big eyes begin to shine. Two large alien tears spill over onto her cheeks forming new streaks as they challenge the dust on her face. He waits patiently until the guards are distracted before asking Namow what happened.

"He wan die," Namow tells him, shaking her large head. "He take anuhda mans tings, day not his, he put in hiz locka, he mak shuh Esluf see him," she relays to him.

Bryzon can read Namow's sorrow by the exaggerated tilt of her head. He was learning something new about the Korak. Self-killing is not the way of the Korak, but death by the hand of another is accepted. The Korak male had simply given up. He had deliberately broken the rules. Rules he knew would ensure his execution. He had chosen death over working in the mines.

Bryzon hurries back to his ever-mulling thoughts of old Kearthat, willing his mind to blank out what happened. He cannot wait for his release.

After all these years, Leader Keeland of Noitibma Colony and Marcus King, leader of Rednos Colony, have negotiated their freedom. On one of his visits to Bryzon, Krom explained how Marcus and Keeland had bargained for their release. The leaders had used the reasoning that the adult numbers at the colonies were dwindling, and this was true. Still, it took the Eslaf almost a year to be convinced of the sincerity of the two leaders' request.

Bryzon, refusing to be in the here and now, continues his reminiscing as he begins to tear apart the ways of the world he grew up in.

Although Bryzon felt a great and undying love for his advantaged mother and father, he resented that for which they had stood. As members of the Elder Council, choosing who would live a long life and who would die naturally after a shorter life had been indescribably wrong.

Each time his nephews and niece visited, Bryzon observed as they grew to adulthood. Soon, they would grow old while he remained young. He knew he had to find a way to share the gift of long-life with the colonists, a way to rectify the past injustices. But there was the matter of locating the only surviving mystic. High It-Ha Layrrah, the only person on Kearthat who knew how to perform the ritual of the Cigam, the only one who knew where to find the Enoce root. Where was she hiding?

Bryzon's thoughts wander to the day the first visitors were permitted to the prison after five long years. It had been a total surprise to him when the first caller he received was his nephew Sayhran's eldest son, Krom. The hours were filled with his many questions, and Bryzon could not stop staring at the boy's resemblance to Keazan.

Bryzon was shocked to hear that his brother's wife Caite had passed to the next world. Then astonished to hear that the Freelanders thought of the imprisoned Xennes as heroes. It was something he found hard to believe, or understand. He and his men had accepted they had failed their people.

In a letter sent to Bryzon, Sayhran wrote she did not bear any resentment towards him, wishing only that she had been able to bury her husband closer to the colony. However, Keazan's final resting place in the serenity of The High Mountains had brought some small comfort. "He looks down over the Freelands and down on his boys growing up," she wrote, and Bryzon's heart had broken into a thousand pieces at her words.

That night, he held the letter close to his chest as he wept like a small child, knowing he did not deserve the kindness or forgiving nature of his earthling sister-in-joining, or the people of the twelve colonies.

As the years passed, first Raine, then Remek, joined Krom on days he was allowed to receive visitors. Finally, Leyashe came to visit. A smile creeps onto Bryzon's face when he thinks of Remek. The ever-smiling, joking, talkative second son of his friend Keazan. The young man always left him feeling light-hearted after each of his visits.

Raine had turned into a beautiful, passionate young woman, while Leyashe looked like a younger version of his father. His mannerisms were unmistakably that of Dayson. He recalls how Leyashe described having tamed a deep-black, long-maned Inop to ride on the Freelands. The whinnying beast, was a remarkable animal that took bravery and patience to subdue, and Bryzon was impressed.

Krom and Remek had dark hair and their father's darker complexion. But their mixed-blood, gifted Keazan's boys with light brown eyes. Sayhran and her light blue eyes were somehow ignored by her union with the Xennes man. Krom was the most physically strong and perhaps a little too serious. But his staid demeanour reassured Bryzon, who was head of the family, that Keazan would be proud of his eldest son.

"Watch out, watch out," Pateeo shouts, grabbing Bryzon by the arm not a second too soon. Bryzon is brought out of his memory-induced trance in an instant. He swings around barely in time as a large rock hurtles towards him from the direction of the tunnel digger.

He jumps to his left, crashing into a quake cage, turning his head sideways and flattening himself as much as possible. The runaway passes him, but not before he feels it brush the fabric of his tunic and the hair on the side of his head.

"That was close, Pateeo hisses through his teeth. "Thank you," Bryzon answers, knowing that his friend Peteeo has just saved him. He had narrowly avoided healing from an injury in front of the guards.

Bryzon is slightly shaken but returns to his endless pondering after the incident.

Thinking back in time; After the purge, life changed in an instant after they were rounded up by their enemy.

All mechanization had been destroyed by the aliens during the invasion, and he and his brother worked long hours. Not used to menial labour, they suffered under these conditions at first. Eslaf soldiers were everywhere, watching them day and night. But when the first 'cooling' came, the Eslaf retreated to the city, leaving the drones to watch over the Freelanders. Something frightened the aliens about the events.

After that day, defying the rules of the Eslaf, Bryzon and a group of men from Noitibma Colony entered the nearest No Go Zones looking for anything they could use in the colonies. The eclipses were an advantage they had not expected, and they were determined to make use of it. As they risked their lives rummaging through the debris in the burned-out towns, they dodged the Idlers above them while recovering as much technology as possible.

Luck was on their side; they found intact Enscriptors and small amounts of refined Zraphite to power them. They were soon educating the children in the colonies. Hiding places were cleverly built into the walls and floors of the cabins to secure their treasure. The fact that the Eslaf were unaware of the instruction of the younger generations has since given Bryzon immense pleasure.

It saddened Bryzon that the only time a Freelander ever boarded a flying craft was when they used the Inter-Colony Shuttle Service. When the shuttles were full, the colonists turned to the next available transport, which was the Traxid vehicles.

Bryzon remembers well when the Traxids were brought to the colonies. It had been unexpected that the Eslaf would allow them to use such vehicles to lighten their burden. Not long after, the Freelanders started calling the vehicles worms because they swayed when all their trailers were hooked up.

The worms had embedded devices to alert the Eslaf when the vehicles left the Freelands. The first time a Traxid accidentally left a designated area by a mere few feet, it was swiftly destroyed. The explosion took all the lives on it and near it. It had been a hard lesson. The aliens never spoke to the leaders about the incident; they simply revelled in their power and delivered a replacement Traxid to Temsik Colony.

The Eslaf had thought of everything. There was no way a Freelander could escape, either by crossing the mountains or the ocean. And, the question always remained, escape to where?

Chapter 31 - The Shakes

Bryzon wakes when the siren goes off. At the same time, an alien homeship is passing overhead. The ground below him vibrates as the noisy metal giant moves slowly over the prison. It is barely dawn.

When an Idler hovers over Bryzon, he halts in place. The machine takes its time. He can feel the familiar vibration on his neck collar; the drone is verifying his whereabouts and identity. It is a reminder that he is disposable. He lets out a sigh, his shoulders relaxing when the droid finally moves away.

Waiting in line for food and shift rations, Bryzon feels rested. His Xennes abilities continue to do their duty, and his body has healed from the damage done in the depths of Pishdrah the day before. Today will yield new injuries, but they too will mend themselves.

The chaotic routine of the morning is much like the previous almost five thousand days. An hour later, it is as if Bryzon never left the dark tunnels of the mine.

Back at the same dig zone as the previous day, it does not take him long to distance himself from his miserable surroundings as his mind sinks back to the past. His reminiscing, however, gets him into trouble with Pateeo.

"You will not get a reward, my friend. Slow down," Pateeo pleads, and Bryzon stops his frantic excavating.

"You dig that fast, your shovel will catch fire," Pateeo insists, his face un-amused.

Bryzon wipes the sweat away between the neckband and his skin, removing some of the grime already caking his body.

"Not long, Pateeo, not long then we will be free of this dark place," Bryzon replies. He regrets his statement the moment Namow looks at them for a few seconds before she turns her head away.

Yes, he was going home, but Namow would remain. He feels ashamed that he chose to talk about leaving prison in front of his alien friend. He puts his head down and immediately picks a reference point in the past to recall. Bryzon would rather be drawn far away in thought than look at Namow right now. Her eyes said it all. For the Korak, there was no escape from the mines.

Going back in time, a time when the Eslaf began erecting high walls that made the now alien city of Etah impenetrable from land or ocean. They were using the original Starfleet base for their own operations. Small bits of information came via the few who delivered goods to the alien city's gates. What they saw when the large city gates opened briefly was startling; the aliens had transformed it. In only a short while they had erased the City of Seccus as the Drennan knew it. Etah was dark and ominous. However, most of the goings-on in the city of Etah had remained shrouded in mystery since the invasion. All that anyone could be sure of was that spaceships arrived empty and left loaded with refined Zraphite.

The Eslaf chose not to include the once Supreme Council Gardens or its enormous Trigga tree as part of the city. The same gardens he and his men had tried to reach during the uprising. The very same tree where he had kissed his Meirah all those many years ago.

Here in the now overgrown gardens, a secret trapdoor to the tunnels below Kearthat lay waiting as a prize. Bryzon intended to ask the very same men who had risked their lives in the uprising to place their trust in him again. Once released, he hoped to entice his men with his new war plan, which would again include the secret walkways under the old Starfleet base. However, this time, he intended to have the backing of High It-Ha Layrrah and her powers, and his plans would exclude Elder Moss.

The break siren rings out, and Bryzon is jerked from his thoughts of war and 'nulling' Elder Moss.

The prisoners rush for their rations, sitting down on the hard dirt. Two Eslaf soldiers put their weapons aside and begin the obscene ritual that passes as eating. Four guards remain where they are, their eyes unmoving as they stare ahead.

Bryzon watches the strange practice the Eslaf use to nourish their bodies. Their food has the consistency of thick syrup; it is repugnant. Out of the corner of his eye, he can see their long alien tongues roll out of their mouths, devouring the awful sludge that passes as food. It is a disgusting spectacle.

Pateeo looks up from his food, noticing Bryzon's revulsion.

"The droids are fortunate, my friend. I can smell that stuff from here," he whispers. Bryzon nods his head but does not comment.

As soon as the siren sounds, everyone gets back to work immediately.

Bryzon blocks out the heat and the noise. The smell of the alien food lingers in the stale air. Soon forgotten, Bryzon's almost dream state makes him think of the Night Creatures. They were a problem he had yet to solve in his planned attack on the aliens.

Pateeo shakes his head at his anguished daydreaming friend. Namow tilts her big head, her oversized eyes questioning, as she watches her 'fren Brizo' return to his trance-like world.

During daylight hours, the colonists could travel freely between the colonies. The alien guards patrolling the Freelands let them pass by, provided they have a good reason. If it was not a work-related journey, a note from the colony leaders was required to explain the Freelanders' time-off. The colonists had freedoms again, and Bryzon was about to use this complacency to his advantage.

Tendrils of black powder rise from the ground; it is a warning. Bryzon is immediately drawn out of his thoughts as he recognizes the louder hissing sounds coming from the vents in the ground nearest him. A split second later, he throws down his shovel as he and Pateeo shout for everyone to take cover. He grabs Namow's long arm, and with the other arm, Bryzon tries to cover his head as they run for the protective structures behind them.

Rocks crash as the ground wobbles from side to side as if they are standing on solidified day-old Ylock porridge. The metal forms protect them from the larger pieces of debris, but small rock fragments and dust rain down on them. The ever-present vents on the tunnel floor spray huge plumes of steam up towards the tunnel's ceiling, and an awful stench fills the air. The combination of vapour, dust, and steam in the air creates tiny, messy mud spots squirting in all directions, and the pressure from underground causes it to reach as far as the cages.

Suddenly, the rumbling stops, and it is eerily silent. The red lights along the top of the cages can be seen through the haze of dust as they flash on and off. It is a signal for everyone to remain where they are. They wait for the smaller shakes that normally follow. First five, then ten minutes pass, but none come.

Large pieces of rock litter the area where they worked a few minutes before. The vents are back to hissing softly, their anger of earlier reduced to steam columns no higher than before the quake began. The dust is thick in the stale air, and Bryzon pulls off his sweaty scarf and covers his nose. As soon as the fine dirt in the air settles, they will be cleaning up the mess left by the shake.

The powdery dust takes its time to make its way to the ground, and Bryzon leans back on the cage, taking advantage of the repose. Looking up, he can see several fair-sized rocks littering the roof of the structure, many big enough to have taken lives.

The lights turn green. The guards that fled with their prisoners into the cages are the first to leave. Soon the soldiers are shouting orders, signaling the prisoners to get back to work. Low murmurs from the work crew express relief that no one was killed. They will have to move the big pieces of rock before their shift is permitted to end. The fine dust persists, as does the incessant orders being given by the Eslaf guards.

That night, the temperature is unusually hot after the suns have set. With Ante Mountain being extinguished so many years ago, the scientists of Kearthat had deduced that the lava trapped under them would one day form a new mountain. They had predicted it would take hundreds of years. It had not yet happened, and Bryzon was amused to find that he had imagined a new fiery mountain forming exactly where the Zraphite mines are situated. He knows that this would surely guarantee the departure of the aliens.

He lies back on his cot. The guards walk up and down along the fence. The grey beings have little or no expression on their unpleasant faces. Their beak-like mouths make him wonder how they even form the words of the earthling language, but his thought is interrupted by sleep.

Chapter 32 - Going Home

The main gate at the prison slides open. The Eslaf soldier gestures for Bryzon to exit, but he is hesitant. Earlier, when his neckband was removed, he thought he would be executed. The unexpected announcement of his freedom, much sooner than the rest of his men, came as a shock. He had repeatedly asked, What about my friends? Why were they not being released? But his questions were ignored.

Bryzon looks back at the guard, then at the gate. He can feel the point of the alien Nobrac in his back, pushing him, "Go, you go now," the red-suit repeats.

The first thing that hits him is the distinct aroma of Mura blossoms, then the thought of the next shuttle or Traxid taking him home makes him feel a little at a loss. The prison gate slams shut behind him, and his heart skips a beat. He waits for the shots to ring out, but he only hears birds chirping in the trees nearby and his heavy breathing.

He is free.

It feels strange to be putting one foot in front of the other, propelling himself away from the prison. Soon, Bryzon walks faster and faster, trying not to run. Several hundred paces from the prison gate, he hears a drone gaining on him. He wills himself not to look up. His heart is pounding, sweat running down his forehead, dripping into his eyes. They are stinging, but he does not slow down to rub the pain away.

"Why me, why only me?" he asks aloud, aware he will not get an answer to his question. His tunic is soon clinging to his body, perspiration drenching him as the drone persists it's mission.

Keeping pace directly above his head, the Idler is still with Bryzon as he arrives at the shuttle station. The two miles he covered felt like ten. He is exhausted when he finally finds a shady area and sits down.

No shuttles or worms are waiting; he will have to be patient. The airborne droid hovers for a few seconds longer then shoots away. It takes time for Bryzon's breathing to settle into an even, slow rhythm and his heartbeat to reach a comfortable pace. The slight breeze is hot even though he is in the shade. He closes his eyes, his mind skipping from one thing to the next as he tries to fathom why only he has been released.

The long wait eventually makes him feel as if they could arrest him again at any minute. Each time an Eslaf passes close by, Bryzon feels his freedom will be short-lived. When a shuttle finally appears, he relaxes a little.

It is not long before the craft lifts off, and silent tears run down his cheeks. They catch Bryzon by surprise, and he quickly wipes them away.

He recognises two women from the line where meals are handed out to the human prisoners. They are seated not far from him. They nod and smile. After a brief greeting, Bryzon looks out of the window, his mind too full to seek interaction with others.

The transporter makes it to Temsik Colony, where Bryzon exits the shuttle. He immediately begins walking away from the colony's gate in the direction of a treed area. There he gathers edible root vegetables and fruit, they will be used as compensation to show his appreciation for a night at the visitor's lodgings.

The feeling of freedom is exhilarating, and the pure joy of uninhabited space overwhelms his senses. A few yards into the trees, Bryzon sees a small pond. He smiles broadly. He looks about to make sure he is alone, strips and walks waist-high into the refreshing water. When he feels energised, he changes into the slightly more presentable tunic he owns. He digs a hole and buries the unsightly rags he left the prison in. He is lucky to spot a wild Ellpa tree before he heads for Temsik Colony and picks a few of the ripe fruit to add to his cache.

Bryzon asks a young boy where he can find the Visitors Lodge. The wiry child with huge brown eyes directs him to a building in the East corner of Temsik. Bryzon remembers where it is, but the interaction with the child adds to a feeling of freedom.

A friendly, old woman with long grey hair, a wrinkled face and a smile greets him at the door.

"Welcome, traveller. We have a bed for you for the night and good food. Come in, friend, come in," she invites. The old woman is true to her word. The building is filled with the scent of wonderful flavours, and Bryzon's stomach rumbles.

"You can put your belongings in the second room to the left, and when you are ready, come to help yourself," the woman offers. He does not find it odd that she looks at him from head to toe just a little longer than an old woman should. The sound of laughter and chatter around him makes him feel a little disoriented, almost as if everything is happening far into the distance. It does not feel quite real to him; he in fact feels quite muddled.

He thanks the kindly old woman and hands her the fruit. Bryzon bows, his right hand placed fisted on his chest. The old woman smiles and nods. She knows the Xennes gestures of old Kearthat very well.

The room has a bed, neatly covered with a blue blanket. There is an inviting pillow, something Bryzon has not had the luxury of for many years. A clean grey-blue tunic, exactly his size, is neatly laid out on the bed. He shakes his head, but his thoughts cannot fathom what to make of it. Something tells him that the clean set of clothing is meant for him. It is strange, somehow not right, but he does not seem to be able to dwell on it.

Another room leads off the bedroom. Bryzon walks over and peeks in. It is a washroom. He stares at the shower. He can almost feel the warm water running over his body, warm water that will come with no time restriction. On a small table, there is a straight razor with a wooden handle and a bar of soap that smells mossy and fresh, like freshly sawed Radec wood.

Clean and refreshed with a smooth face, Bryzon emerges from his room. He is ravenous. His stomach propels him toward the smell of the food, but several bodies block his way. It takes him a few seconds before his mind identifies the faces. In his path to the dining area stands Ohre and several of the men who once called him Commander.

"Bryzon, my friend, it is you," the boisterous voice says as two huge arms come forward to enfold him. Bryzon reciprocates, overwhelmed with emotion as he recognizes his friends. They are the brave men who evaded the Eslaf during the uprising. Ohre's baritone voice insists that Bryzon come to his cabin. He accepts graciously, asking only that they give him time to have his meal.

 When he arrives at Ohre's cabin, Bryzon can hear his friend's deep voice inside as he knocks on the door. Once inside, it does not take long before the uprising lives once more. Bryzon and Dayson are hailed as heroes. Ohre and his men were fortunate to escape the wrath of the Eslaf, but as is the way of the Xennes, there is no resentment towards those who did not pay for their disobedience towards the aliens.

Much later, Bryzon is persuaded to eat again. Drinking his fill of the locally brewed Reeb he listens to the stories of the past. Reciprocating, he tells them of Namow, conveying that he views the Korak as harmless, as allies.

He jokes that he noticed during his time at the mine that the Eslaf had not grown any prettier, a comment earning a roar of laughter. Smiling broadly at their response Bryzon laughs with them. However, he cannot help but feel he is betraying his friends. His participation in light-hearted banter is almost deceitful. Bryzon is concealing his true intention. He wants to involve them in yet another war against the Eslaf.

It is late when they finally allow him to return to the Visitors Lodge, where a restless night lies ahead. Bryzon's dreams are filled with horrific scenes of the uprising, snippets of him, his niece, and nephews lost in The High Mountains, and scenes of his dying brother. They are searching for the High It-Ha Layrrah, but they find only large holes in the ground filled with writhing snake-like creatures the Drennan of Kearthat call the Ardyh.

The banging of pots and pans brings Bryzon out of his restless sleep. He bolts upright and runs his fingers through his long hair. It takes him several seconds to remember where he is. A sigh of relief washes over him when he comprehends he is still a free man. No whirring of drones, no prison camp noises, just the smell of food reaching his somewhat unhappy stomach.

"Ugh, Reeb," he complains as he swings his bare feet onto the cool stone floor.

But it doesn't take long for the sick feeling in his stomach to disappear. As regeneration takes place, his body quickly rids itself of the toxins he had consumed the night before. Bryzon eats his morning meal as he watches the very normal goings-on around him. He feels sad for Pateeo, Namow and the rest of the prisoners readying for a hard day in the mines, still dumbfounded as to why he was the only one released.

The kind old woman bids him a safe journey when he leaves. Ohre, now a leader in Temsik, and several of the men who were at Ohre's home the previous evening walk with Bryzon to the shuttle station to see him off on his journey home.

Huge disappointment comes over him when he discovers the shuttle will only be going as far as Sigae Colony. The frustration dissipates when Bryzon decides to take solace in the knowledge that it will be the last stop before reaching Noitibma Colony the following day.

Upon reaching Sigae so early in the day he decides to hunt for something to trade for the night's rest. After a short search near the colony, he becomes aware of the ever-darkening sky above him. It does not take long before the ominous clouds are accompanied by a strong wind. He decides to head for the colony gate as quickly as he can. He is soon forced to pick up his pace as daylight turns dark. Streaks of lightning light up the sky. The menacing clouds above roll and churn while the thunder growls louder and louder. He reaches the gate just in time. A minute later, he would have been locked out. The Night Creatures are sure to be let loose as the skies grow more threatening.

The lightning strikes, jagged lines illuminate everything for miles. Loud cracks follow the deep rumbles, and with each mighty roar of thunder, Bryzon can feel the ground vibrate. The ever-increasing wind hastens him to find the visitors' lodgings. For a brief second, his thoughts go to the shuttle for the next day, and he wonders if there will be any transport if the storm persists.

The young woman who greets him at the lodge eagerly accepts the bundle of wood Bryzon has to offer. This time, he finds his room somewhat basic. It has a bed, a lamp on a narrow shelf, and a washbasin on a table in the corner with a jug of cool water. There is no clean tunic on the bed here, and he will share the only shower with others.

Instead of first washing up and returning to eat, Bryzon deliberately steers clear of anyone who might recognize him. Ten minutes later, he retreats to his room with a large plate of food. The storm worsens; as time passes, he starts to fear for his family in Noitibma. The dark-purple sky lights up repeatedly, the deafening cracks and low rumbles persist as the thunder booms, the wind making ominous whistling sounds through the colony's structures.

Bryzon can hear branches crashing into the side of the building and the sound of trees crashing down in the distance, making him feel uneasy. He stares through the small window to the outside but sees nothing as the wind drives the raindrops against the pane. He lies on the bed, the rain loud on the roof, the blinding lightning bolts illuminating the small room. The roar of thunder continues for hours. Several more times, he gets up to look through the window, but the rain does not relent, and it is impossible to see anything.

Bryzon hears anxious voices in the room next to his. Hours later, the storm starts to grow silent. It rains softly for a while and then finally stops. When there is total silence, Bryzon drifts off into a deep sleep. For the first time in many years, his sleep offers no dreams.

In the morning, he eagerly accepts the food offered but rushes through his meal. When he awoke, Bryzon was not sure if the suns would be out, but now he could see it would be a cloudless day. He is elated. He is going home today.

When he leaves the Visitor's Lodge, the colony is a hive of activity. The destruction left by the storm is evident everywhere he looks. The people of Sigae are feverishly cleaning up the leaves and branches and picking up many other objects scattered far and wide. Their frenzied action leaves him wondering what damage Noitibma Colony may have sustained. He leaves with a feeling of excitement, but at the same time, he is sad to see the devastation around him.

Eventually, a shuttlecraft comes into view, but when it lands, it is a big goods transporter ship, much larger than the normal shuttles. Bryzon is overjoyed to learn that the craft will be going to the most westerly colony of Elbaffeni, passing Noitibma on its way. However, the storm has taken its toll, and it takes longer than usual to offload and reload the transporter. When the hatch finally closes, Bryzon counts eight colonists aboard and four Eslaf soldiers. He makes sure to sit at a window. The stop at Arorua Colony comes quickly, and he remains on the craft.

When they stop at Accedes Colony, Bryzon again decides to remain seated. He uses the time to study the Eslaf, who are directing cargo in and out of the ship. Bryzon decides to test a theory. When the nearest Eslaf looks his way, he grimaces at the creature. The alien does not realise Bryzon is doing something that would normally be unacceptable or strange behaviour. Bryzon tries something different. He suddenly moves to wipe his forehead, which elicits a different response. The alien looks directly at him and raises his weapon ever so slightly. It takes a few seconds for the creature to conclude that Bryzon is doing something innocent, and the alien lowers his weapon.

After a while, the Eslaf ignores him, returning its attention to the movements of people coming in and out of the shuttle. He is amused at the alien's reactions. He knows it is silly, but he feels good, even if it was a droid that he was unsettling.

Bryzon stares up at the high wall as he enters the heavy gate that protects Noitibma. The frustration of stopping at all the colonies on the way begins to fade. He is finally home. His family are going to be so surprised.

His shoulders automatically square up and a feeling of belonging fills his whole being. He finds himself trying to put names to every face he sees, but no one pays him any regard. They are all hard at work; Noitibma is still busy dealing with the storm's aftermath.

A young Korak female passes Bryzon and smiles. "Worst storm ever, nothing but clean up for the next few days," she says and keeps walking.

'After I bow to the Council, I will go to Sayhran's house to see my nephews and niece,' he thinks. Bryzon's heart beats faster with each step that brings him closer to the Council Lodge. He is as excited as a child who cannot wait for sweet cakes at a celebration. He has missed his good friends Keeland and Nowber; he cringes at the thought of Elder Moss.

Bryzon would have to get permission to stay permanently as a member of Noitibma Colony. He had hoped to obtain consent, although the thought had crossed his mind several times in the past two days that he may be forced to seek another colony to call home.

Chapter 33 - The Code

The leaders of Noitibma look troubled. The events of the past few hours were indeed concerning. First came the Kearthquake, then the storm, and now Raine and Leyashe have not returned from a hunt. If that were not bad enough, the aliens expected the colonies to clean up and return to normal by day's end.

Elder Moss whispers to Keeland before speaking from the slightly raised platform where the leaders are seated.

"Did they say anything?" the elder asks, looking directly at Sayhran. "Did Raine and Leyashe tell you anything that could help us find them?" he reiterates.

Sayhran's eyes well up. She shakes her head, trying desperately to control her tears.

"No, I do not know where they could be, Elder Moss," she answers in an unsteady voice.

Keeland next questions the Overseer who has been asked to investigate. The young man who works closely with Raine confirms that the register at the gate disclosed the siblings would be returning before dark. He adds that the Gatekeeper and some of Leyashe's friends had no idea as to Raine and Leyashe's intended direction for the hunt.

"Not knowing the path the young ones took…" Moss begins to say but then abandons his sentence as he often did. Instead, he mumbles, "Um, yes, not good, not good at all," while stroking his long silver beard. The old man, perplexed at what should be done to resolve the dilemma, was looking to Keeland for a solution.

"It begs the question, how far did they venture from the colony? And why would they leave at such an early hour?" Keeland poses, sounding frustrated at the lack of information.

Nowber and Keeland, who had once served with Bryzon as Starfleet officers would put together a search party, of that Sayhran was sure.

"It would make no sense to send Overseers on a directionless search," the elder mumbles, his gloominess seemingly endless at this point. Keeland acknowledges the old man's remark by nodding but does not comment, leaving Moss's negativity unchecked.

The Night Creatures are on everyone's mind. If Raine had not found somewhere safe for them to hide, the creatures might have tracked them down. Sayhran does not want to think of something as awful as that, but Moss is looking at her as if it were her fault her niece and nephew are missing.

The three men discuss what they can do, and it leaves Sayhran to recall a story she was told some years ago. An elderly Drennan woman of Rednos Colony had divulged to her that Elder Moss had left his family as a young man to be with a girl he had fallen in love with. The girl in question came from a family with no standing, a mere Freelander, a mortal. Moss's father, an elder on the supreme council, wasted no time expressing his displeasure and ordered his son home. But Moss went against his father's wishes, choosing to work and live among the Freelander people. He later took the woman to be his wife.

When Moss outlived his wife, he returned to Seccus after his father passed to take his place on the Supreme Elder Council, much to the disgust of those on the council. Opposite to what would have been expected of Moss, he began to embrace the unjust practice of allowing only some Kearthatians the gift of being Xennes, going as far as wanting to make it law that Xennes men could only marry Xennes women. Unable to oust Moss from the council, he was loathed by his counterparts.

Sayhran's thoughts of Moss's distant past is interrupted when he speaks her name, and she flinches.

"Sayhran, we will ponder the question of a search; do not become anxious, woman of Keazan," Moss assures her, his manner suddenly that of a supreme leader of sorts.

Sayhran respectfully excuses herself. Two steps into her departure, her knees almost buckle under her as she takes in the sight of Bryzon. He is standing at the entrance of the council building, outlined by a halo of light from the door behind him.

"Bryzon," she exclaims, "Is it you?"

Sayhran never once went to the prison to see Bryzon. She knew she would not be able to bear the sight of him as a captive. Instead, she had waited patiently for what her eyes were seeing at this moment.

"I am here for all time," he tells his sister-in-joining, dragging her into a close embrace. Bryzon immediately notices that Sayhran has aged somewhat, and his heart fills to the brim with sadness.

"The young boy outside tells me that Raine and Leyashe did not return to the settlement last night. Is this true, Sayhran?" Bryzon asks. Sayhran nods, her eyes shiny with tears she wipes them away, and sniffs softly.

Bryzon releases Sayhran and moves towards where the leaders are seated. She takes a seat nearest him, determined not to let her brother-in-law out of her sight.

Elder Moss, Keeland and Nowber make their way down the platform with broad smiles. All trepidation Bryzon might have had faded in an instant. The leader's expressions had without a doubt conveyed that he would be welcomed back into his old community.

"If only circumstances were better," Elder Moss comments, continuing his downcast bearing.

"It gladdens our hearts to see Bryzon. Welcome on behalf of the Freelanders of Noitibma Colony. We will feast and celebrate your homecoming when the children return," Keeland promises.

It is Nowber who asks the obvious question, "Where are Pateeo and the rest of the men of Noitibma?"

The reaction is one of shock when they hear Bryzon is alone. Keeland is immediately angry. It appears that the aliens have broken the pact with the Freelanders. Or have they? Bryzon had been released early. Are they waiting to see if Bryzon obeys their rules before releasing the others on the date originally promised per the agreement?

Bryzon requests that he accompany a search party to look for his niece and nephew as soon as it can be arranged. He bows, showing his respect for the Xennes leaders, and he and Sayhran head for Raine and Leyashe's cabin, a place Bryzon has never seen but may hold a clue as to where the siblings can be found.

Overcome with emotion, Bryzon surveys the small quiet, tidy cabin. He shakes his head and runs his fingers through his hair. A sigh escapes his lips, highlighting his frustration. The tiny home is not revealing any clue as to the whereabouts of his niece and nephew.

Bryzon asks Sayhran's consent for Krom to join the search party but is disappointed when he finds out that Remek and Krom had been called to Rednos Colony for a day, their exact return to Noitibma unknown to Sayhran.

There is a commotion at the door. Regor is howling, and an excited young person's voice can be heard calling Sayhran's name. Sayhran swings the top half of the cabin door open and almost trips as her foot catches on the now barking Eninac. The historian's son who is inflicted with a bad stutter acts as a runner for the Noitibma leaders.

"I s..s..saw them," he tells Sayhran, trying to gulp air into his lungs. "Rai aa... and Ash, they, they are b...b...back, they are o...on th...th... their way, they are sss...safe," Kergann spits out.

Bryzon can see Raine and Leyashe walking towards the cabin. His face stretches into a smile; the young people approaching look like Caite and Dayson at this distance.

"They are their parents," he says softly.

"Yes, they are, Bry, so they are," Sayhran agrees, thankful at the sight of the siblings, her eyes filling with tears, her small hands cupped over her mouth.

The moment Raine sees Bryzon, she is stunned.

"Can it be true?" she shouts, running towards him she drops her pack, her arms outstretched. They hug while Leyashe waits patiently to embrace Bryzon.

"Finally, we are together. No more fences between us. I thank the galaxy that you are free," Leyashe tells his uncle, smiling.

"Come, let us sit opposite one another," Bryzon requests of Raine and Leyashe as he moves towards Sayhran's big wooden kitchen table. "I want to look at you. I want to make my eyes believe," he repeats. For wordless seconds, he and the siblings sit staring at each other, holding hands before their delighted laughter breaks the silence.

"Ok," Sayhran says with a serious expression, taking advantage of a lull in the laughter. "Where have you been? Everyone in this colony has been demented with worry for you."

"We will tell you all, but I ask that you excuse us, Sayhran. We need to go and clean ourselves. We are not fit to be seen," Raine pleads.

"Very well, go. And hurry so that you can tell us your reason for not returning to the colony," Sayhran chides when, in actual fact, she is just so unbelievably grateful that they are back unharmed.

Unknown to Bryzon and Sayhran, the siblings are biding their time. Time to decide whether they will tell the truth or lie. Regor has followed them home, and Raine gives the Eninac a quick scratch under the chin. The pampering is short-lived, and the confused animal is soon left staring at a closed door.

Raine looks down at her tunic, then up at Leyashe. They are a dreadful sight. Their clothes are filthy, muddy, and covered with spots of blood from the Tenlegs they slew. The burning barrel will be busy; it is the second set of clothing they will forfeit due to their recent adventures.

Regor is still there when Raine opens the door for some air. He has not moved an inch.

"Good Eninac," Raine praises as they return to Sayhran's cabin.

When they are done with their evening meal, it is time for the siblings to tell Sayhran and Bryzon the reason they did not make it back to the colony. Raine is about to speak, but she is shocked to hear Leyashe's voice in her head. 'I wish we could just tell the truth,' she hears her brother thinking. She gasps. 'That is what I would prefer,' she thinks, stunned when her brother answers. His eyes are large, and as he looks at her, she distinctly hears, 'It is better we tell the truth, Rai.'

Raine gets up to close the door to give herself time to recover from what just transpired.

Leyashe asks if they can all move to Sayhran's bedroom. Sayhran raises her eyebrows but diligently submits as she leads the way. Bryzon, also confused by the request, follows without a word.

Sayhran sighs as she sits on the stool in front of a broken mirror where she usually brushed her hair. It is not the most comfortable seat. Bryzon chooses the only chair near the window, and Raine and Leyashe hop onto Sayhran's bed, just as they had done so many times when they were growing up.

Raine glances at Bryzon. She feels a twinge of sadness. He looks so much like her father. She also notices how much older Sayhran looks compared to Bryzon. They had been approximately the same age when he went to prison.

Leyashe puts his hand on his sister's shoulder, and she knows her brother has heard her thoughts and felt her sorrow.

"You know the place where the big pile of rocks is for the fallen? Where the big Trigga tree is just across from the river?" Leyashe begins.

Bryzon and Sayhran nod, looking a little confused at Leyashe.

"Just beyond where we used to play as children, there are those giant smooth rocks?" Leyashe continues to echo.

"Yes, Ash, of course, we all know the memorial well, get on with the story, boy," she says impatiently, readjusting her body on the small, uncomfortable stool as she sighs again quite audibly.

When Leyashe gets to the part of the knife falling between the rocks, he stops to look at Bryzon. "I knew I had to find it, Bryzon. It is the special one, the one you gave to me, the knife that came from Earth, that belonged to Grandfather Jon," confirming yet another well-known fact.

Bryzon smiles. "I am proud that you tried to find it, Ash, but if it is lost, so be it. It was not done purposely. We will go together to see if we can find it," he offers, revelling in the idea of spending time with his nephew.

"Well," Leyashe says, taking a deep breath, "That is just it. I found it."

Leyashe shuffles uncomfortably on Sayhran's bed. Uncrossing his legs, he swings them freely off the edge. He stretches his back, squaring his shoulders before he continues.

"When I reached in between the rocks, I could feel the knife. I pulled it out, but my hand touched something. A kind of mechanism," he continues, wrinkling his face in an odd expression.

"What is a mechanism?" Sayhran asks immediately, the odd question accompanied by an exaggerated confused expression on her face, which has Raine smiling inwardly at her aunt.

"Well, something opened an entrance into the rocks, a sort of door into a cavern," Leyashe tries to describe. There is silence. His supposed discovery of this mysterious entrance has Sayhran and Bryzon quite baffled.

"Of course, being the most curious person on Kearthat," Raine cuts in as she rolls her eyes at her brother, "He had to go inside and explore this place."

Leyashe playfully tells his sister to 'shush' and then continues to describe exactly what he saw, how one cavern led to another opening, and the mysterious blue wall.

"Are you telling us the truth, Leyashe, son of Dayson?" Sayhran demands, her face revealing her scepticism for her nephew's wild story.

"It is so, Sayhran. I thought the blue wall to be more of a huge metal box when I examined it further. I decided to tell Raine and pleaded with her to come back with me to confirm my doubt."

"I was meant to find this place, Bryzon. I truly believe it," Leyashe tells him.

Leyashe looks at Raine, and she carries on from where he left off with the story. Again, they exchanged thoughts without having to speak physically. Going through every second of the adventure, Raine explains exactly what had happened when they found out they were trapped by the storm. She tells them how she had decided it was safer to wait out the storm, fearing the release of the Night Creatures.

Neither mention what happened to their eyes, and that they could now communicate without talking, or that they had brought back objects from the cavern. The killing of two of the biggest Tenlegs ever seen is not revealed in fear of Sayhran's reaction; her fear of Tenlegs was well-known.

Much has changed in just three days. The deliberate lying troubles Raine, and having her brother included in the deceit makes her feel worse.

"Bry, what do you think?" Sayhran asks.

"I am not sure what to think," Bryzon admits, rubbing his chin.

"Did you open any of the containers? Did you see anything that would reveal who may have put them there?" Bryzon asks.

"No, we were more concerned about getting home before someone sent out a search party for us," Raine concedes.

We need to go back, Bryzon, as soon as we can," Leyashe implores, and Raine nods her head several times in agreement.

"You could be right; it could be something from old Kearthat. Who knows what treasures could be hidden the colony could use?" The prospect of finding out what the children have discovered has Sayhran forgetting how uncomfortable the small stool is at that moment.

Bryzon paces the tiny space between the window and the bed. He is about to speak when there is a noise. A wet nose pushes the door open, followed by a yellow-furred face. Regor and its enormous wagging tail fill the limited space at Sayhran's feet.

"Oh, Regor," Sayhran exclaims, there is no room for you, you silly Eninac." Regor lies down immediately as if fearing immediate eviction, its large eyes looking up at Raine over the top of its nose.

"Oh, ok, but you stay still, or you are out," she mutters, pushing the door closed with her toe. Bryzon grins at the Eninac's victory over Sayhran, his heart warmed by the normalcy that this simple act brings.

"We must plan. We must think of a good reason for all of us to go to the cavern. A good excuse, one that looks less... what is the word?" Sayhran snaps her fingers, looking for the lost expression in the air.

"Less suspicious," Leyashe offers and smiles. And just like that, another lie is set in motion, and it quickly becomes a family event to tell untruths.

"I think we should wait a few days so everyone can forgive the two of you for disappearing," Bryzon suggests as he points in the direction of Raine and Leyashe.

"Raine, you must beg Keeland's consent for a time-off, and soon, for all of you," he corrects. You will tell Keeland and Nowber that you wish for me to be with my family to celebrate my return. I do indeed wish to visit with your cousin Marcus in Rednos Colony. We will stop at the cavern on the way there," Bryzon takes a deep breath. It is hard to lay out a plan of deception; he had forgotten how much energy deceit requires.

Sayhran nudges the Eninac to get its big, comfortable body off the floor, and they file out of her bedroom. Leyashe is quiet, disappointed that it will be several days before returning to the rocks. Still, he is content that Bryzon and Sayhran seem excited to see his discovery. Sayhran pours a mug of Ellpa juice for everyone. Expectations of what the cavern may hold turn into fervent discussion in lowered voices.

Close to the midnight hour, Raine and Leyashe leave for home, but the day is not over for the siblings as they make their way to their cabin in the dark. Their pupils are aglow the moment they step into the dark and seek out the lights on the lanes of the colony. They hurry to avoid any encounters with colonists.

The moment they step through the door, Leyashe retrieves the two items they brought back from the cavern. He places the small metal box on the table. Raine sits down opposite her brother and sighs.

"This is absurd, Ash. We need to talk about why you are in my head," she tells him.

"You mean, why you are in my head, sister?" he tries to correct, his tone exhibiting his frustration with the whole situation.

"The cavern, the storm, something changed us. We are connected somehow. Turn off the lights," Raine tells him.

Leyashe looks confused, "But Rai?" he starts to say, but she insists.

"Turn it off, Leyashe!" the command makes him move faster. In the dark, two sets of green pupils stare at each other; it has not changed since they entered the cabin.

"See, nothing has changed since we were outside, Raine," Leyashe blurts out, sounding indignant.

"We will have to find a way of controlling this, this, this thing that is happening to us," she says, sounding desperate. "Our eyes... someone is going to find out. We cannot hide it forever, Ash," Raine pleads as if her brother has a solution. She paces in the small space available, her hands on her hips, a worried look on her face.

"Who is going to understand this?" Leyashe asks his sister, the roles now reversed. Raine cringes at the thought of having to explain it to Sayhran and Bryzon or the people of Noitibma.

"Ash, get something to open this box," she says, changing the subject. "There may be an explanation in there to explain why we are changed."

Raine is still thinking about their eyes when the little metal box snaps open by itself. The sound it makes is loud in their small cabin, and they both flinch.

They lean in to study the contents and discover metal strips, each with something etched on them. Raine lifts the pieces one by one, immediately noticing they are numbered. She lays down the pieces in order. The script is Earthling, not Drennan. Something else is embedded into the bottom of the box, something triangular. She tries to lift it with her fingers, but it is perfectly recessed and stuck. Reaching for her brother's now-infamous knife, Raine is about to pry the piece out when it pops out from its mould by itself. It is metal, and in the centre is a green stone that reflects in the light, much like their eyes in the dark. At each of its three points, the numbers 1, 2 and 3 are etched.

"I think it is the key, Ash," Raine whispers as she holds it to the light. Then she wonders why on Kearthat she is whispering.

She passes the strange object to her brother and begins to read aloud what the metal strips say.

The Code to Freedom

A message to the Selected –Those who are Rain and Ash

It must be your ambition that when the dawn comes, to leave this illogical life of oppression.

You must strive to reach the distant stars with the guidance of the unknown entity.

Use this energy, and reach a present as idyllic as the past.

The Selected and the many of Kearthat must agree and together strive to become one again, to be untroubled.

This trust will allow the path to a new destiny, a fate in a peaceful co-existence with the moons and stars of the universes.

Search for a planet that is not unlike your own; discover a world renewed.

Learn from the past and always rule with equality in this dominion.

Noitibma, Arorua, Rednos, Elbaffeni, Laeredis, Sigae, Noyclah,

Sedecca, Ytineres, Temsik, Ygyzys, Niamod

The last two lines simply list the names of all the colonies, making the message even more ambiguous. Raine looks at her brother, and in unison, they repeat the words, "They are those who are Rain and Ash."

Raine has also noticed the blunder in the text, where it references 'universes.' Whoever did the inscribing had made an error.

"Rai, am I dreaming? It sounds like it is reciting our names, our names, but not our names, if you understand what I am trying to say?" Leyashe corrects. "What is happening, Rai? Are we losing our minds? Are we awake, sister?" he asks.

"We will figure it out, Ash. I know we will," Raine tries to assure her brother. Exhausted, she suggests they go to bed. Then, a knock at the door almost stops their hearts from beating. Raine grabs a cloth and spreads it over the items on the table. She opens the door, making quite sure to step back into the light. She is surprised to find Kergann at such a late hour. The young boy's hair is more tousled than usual. He has undeniably been awakened from his sleep to deliver a message.

"Sorry t..to wake you, Rai…" he stutters, the l...leaders, th...they sent mmm... me tt.. to …, tell you that you m...m... must come bbb... before the… the council at fi...fi... first ligh... light."

After the boy leaves, Raine leans against the closed door with her back, then slides down to the floor into a sitting position. Closing her eyes, she shakes her head.

"We are in trouble, little brother," she says, "We need to get our story straight before going to our beds."

Chapter 34 - The Expedition

When Remek and Krom return to Noitibma, they are elated to find Bryzon home. Accompanying them from Rednos is Nedai, undeniably Marcus King's son, his light blue eyes giving him away immediately. The other young man accompanying them, Bryzon does not recognize him.

Greetings come with laughter and smiles, and family bonds are renewed, but Raine's attention is focused on the guest who has returned with her cousins. She knows who he is; his name is Rence, the son of Lesser Leader Dourok of Rednos Colony.

She had last seen Rence when they had competed against each other at the secret tournament held to determine Overseers for the colonies. Time has matured him; his jawline seems more distinct, and he appears taller than she recalls. He is a mixed-blood, and it suits him well. Highlighted by his Drennan skin tone, his light, nut-brown eyes dominate his face. His brown, wavey hair hanging below his shoulders frames the picture of a handsome young man. Raine catches herself looking at Rence a bit too long, and her brother notices her interest. Within moments, she hears him giggling in her head, and she feels the onslaught of heat coming to her cheeks.

"Stop that, Leyashe, please," she reprimands, scowling at him.

"Stop what, sister?" her brother asks, with a playful grin on his face. No one is aware of the silent conversation between the siblings, who have already become somewhat used to their new ability.

It is not long before Raine and Leyashe repeat their story to Rence and their cousins. Afterwards, Krom and Remek bombard them with questions about the cavern, many of which the siblings have no answers to.

Bryzon listens to the young people talking back and forth as they debate what the cavern may hold. He mulls over whether he should tell his family about his impending quest to find High It-Ha Layrrah.

When dinner is over, Bryzon raps his knuckles on the table, clears his throat, and tells them of his plans to find Layrrah. It is a pursuit he hopes will end in making the It-Ha bestow the gift of long life to all the colonists. However, he does not discuss his plans to fight another war against the Eslaf.

"This would mean that my mother and I will no longer grow old, while my father does not. It is what I have dreamed of all of my life. My father will have no words when I tell him of this. Thank you, Bryzon. You are truly the hero they all speak of," Rence gushes.

Caught off guard by Rence's hero comment, Bryzon almost chooses to ignore the praise. Instead, he nods awkwardly without comment.

"First, I must ask for tolerance. I have a concern that must be overcome before this can be a certainty. We cannot speak of our plans to anyone until I have settled this matter." Bryzon asks of everyone present.

"What troubles you, Bryzon?" Krom asks, his forehead wrinkling into a frown.

"The ritual of the gift of long life," Bryzon tells them, is in the hands of High It-Ha Layrrah, but success will rest upon support from Elder Moss," Bryzon divulges but does not elaborate.

"The It-Ha is the only one left who knows where the waters of the Cigam flow and where the Enoce trees grow. We need the waters that hold magic and the trees that will forfeit some of their roots for the elixir."

"Where do we find her, and would she want to be found? She was the one who chose to abandon the colonies. Perhaps she has passed? There is nowhere to hide on Kearthat, Bryzon," Sayhran rattles off.

"I always thought my father was losing his mind when he spoke to us of the It-Ha, his friend Layrrah who had vanished," Sayhran states, raising her eyebrows. "Then she returns when Nick is ill, and then, just like that, she disappears again. It is all so confusing," she complains.

"If she had such powerful magic, why did she not warn of the invasion?" Remek queries, as if it were that simple. Why has she not rid us of the Eslaf?

"It-Ha have always been known to move between many worlds, gifted with powers I do not understand. Why the It-Ha were unable to warn of the Eslaf coming to Kearthat is something I have never understood," Bryzon admits, sighing in answer to Remek's question.

"You are not from the old world, so I will tell you what I know to be the truth about the It-Ha of Kearthat. Perhaps you will better understand," Bryzon deciding that an impromptu lesson in Kearthatian history may answer some of his family's questions.

"A young girl was born to a simple Drennan family more than two thousand years ago. She was of pure heart with a gentle soul. It is written that the High Yraif, who lived somewhere on The High Mountains, chose her to be the very first mystic of Kearthat, the first High-It-Ha."

Bryzon pauses to sip water. The silence in the room is deafening, everyone is eager for him to continue.

"The first High It-Ha, named Solaarr, was one of three women chosen by the High Yraif. Second came It-Ha Layrrah, and then It-Ha Sihuun."

"Why would the High Yraif just give away a gift like that? If it is true the Yraif existed, why has it been excluded from our lessons," Leyashe fires away.

It is Sayhran who puts a stop to her nephew's interruptions. "Quiet boy, Bryzon is trying to tell us what he knows."

"Ash, it was Elder Moss who forbade the teachings that tell the true history of the Yraif. At the Evalc that dealt with the lessons for the children of the colonies, Moss was against recognizing the importance, his reasoning is unknown to the Xennes of the colonies.

"Yet later, it was Moss who began speaking of the Yraif. You know this," Bryzon comments as he looks around at the young people sitting in silence.

"He has sat many nights, and still does, I have heard, sharing stories of the Yraif with Noitibma's young ones. But Moss has deliberately chosen to confuse what is true and what is not. His reason is not known to me," Bryzon admits.

'The elder, it seemed, was a problem no matter what the subject,' Raine realizes for the first time.

"The Drennan thought there was no other life on Kearthat when they first arrived on this sphere. They only saw animals and birds and were unaware of the Yraif living in the mountains," Bryzon continues.

"One day, the Drennan son of Great Elder, Luvian of the Supreme Council of Kearthat went hunting in the mountains. The young man, looking for a place to lay his head for the night, came upon a stream as he gathered wood for his fire. Sitting at the edge of the water, he saw the most beautiful girl he had ever seen. She was washing her hair, surrounded by hundreds of Firemoths that lit up the dark for her."

"It was the first time a Drennan had seen a Yraif."

"The Yraif girl had long white hair and a pale, delicate face, so delicate that the young man was certain she had never seen any sunslight. Afraid that he would scare her away, he stayed quietly hidden."

"The Drennan had long ago begun to build Kearthat's two cities, Seccus and Kuldab, at this time. The young man told no one about the girl. He returned many times to the stream, sometimes waiting for several days, wishing only for another glimpse of her. Then, one night, there she was, and to his amazement, she spoke."

"Reveal yourself, outsider. I feel your presence," she said.

"You remember the exact words," Raine cuts in, smiling.

"As it was written in the book that we learned at our lessons when we were children," Bryzon tells her with a half smile. The memories of the huge library in the council building in Seccus, the voice of his mother reading the texts, flooded Bryzon's mind briefly.

"When the Yraif girl and the Drennan man laid eyes on each other for the first time, it is written they fell into a deep love for each other. The girl begged the young man to keep their love a secret. They did so for many seasons until Great Elder Luvian became suspicious of his son's many trips to The High Mountains."

"Were they discovered?' Remek asks, and Sayhran 'shushes' him immediately.

"Luvian's soldiers captured the Yraif girl. When the leader of the Yraif heard this, he was angered. He sent three thousand Yraif to descend on Seccus and Kuldab. Armed with bows and arrows, spears and great magic, Luvian was forced to surrender the girl or fight against powerful conjuring."

"The Leader of the Yraif and Elder Luvian came to an agreement. The Drennan were far more advanced in technology and possessed great weapons and spaceships, while the Yraif lived much simpler lives in the forest, but they had a potion that could give long life. Neither wanted war."

"The two young people were forbidden to ever see each other again, and the Yraif allowed the Drennan to remain on Kearthat. Elder Luvian made a pact with the Yraif that there would always be peace between the Yraif and the Kearthatians as long as time withstood."

"Oh, Bryzon, what a beautiful but sad story," Sayhran interrupts, shaking her head. "So... so sad," she echoes, breaking her own 'silence while Bryzon speaks rule.'

"To ensure the elder of the Drennan people would keep his word, the Yraif leader gave the Drennan access to the Cigam Spring and the Enoce trees through High It-Ha Solaarr. It would be a secret that she alone would bear and pass on. Luvian was a man who enjoyed power, and the Great Elder barred his son from going into the mountains ever again to make sure he had access to the potion and the fealty of the newly chosen It-Ha."

"The High Yraif was instructed to gift two more women of pure hearts the power of The Inmo, 'the eye that sees all.' As time passed, the It-Ha were given many other abilities, but it is written there was one gift the High Yraif withheld for herself, again something she would bear, and only she could pass on."

"The Yraif called Kearthat 'Lan~Igiro.' It has never been understood why they chose to share their home when they could easily have rid themselves of the Drennan. It was a curious decision. Later, Luvian chose his son to receive the gift of long life, but his son refused the potion, angry at his father for what he had done, angry for forbidding him to see the Yraif girl."

"Bryzon, do you remember the name of the Yraif girl?" Raine asks.

"The young Drennan man was called Jaenus; the Yraif girl went by the name Su~nev," he answers without hesitation.

"Oh no, how terrible they were torn from each other like that," Sayhran whispers as if her lowered voice excuses her interruption.

"Our records of history talked of many hundreds of years of peace between the Drennan and the Yraif who lived in the forests of the mountains. Then, one day, Ante Mountain erupted, and the Yraif were no more. The mountain was shortened for all time."

"Many stories since were written by our people to amuse the children. The stories argued that Jaenus disappeared, never to be seen again. One of the books my mother read to us told that Su~nev drowned herself in the stream where she first met Jaenus. There is no truth to these stories," Bryzon apprises his family with a smile. "Another claimed the Yraif leader was so distraught upon his daughter's death in the stream that he could not be comforted. Later he became so inflicted with a violent madness and the Yraif Assembly *nulled* him, taking away his title and his magic. The texts told that the humiliated Yraif leader returned to a planet where the Yraif of Kearthat originally hail."

"Oh, Bryzon, tell us more; the stories are wonderful," Sayhran implores her brother-in-law.

"Very well, sister, one more," Bryzon says, smiling.

"What of Jaenus? Do you think he died as a mortal? Leyashe asks.

"It was not recorded; it is a mystery," Bryzon laughs before telling them another story written of a spaceship that came and took Jaenus away so that his father could never find him again.

"And what of the other gift that was not passed onto the It-Ha by the High Yraif?" Raine asks, "You said the It-Ha of Kearthat received most of the powers the

Hight Yraif possessed, but for one," Rain queries, then answers the question for Bryzon.

"I think perhaps it was a last wish and that the High Yraif used it to save Jaenus and Su~nev from the Kearthquake, and they lived well after that day?" Raine offers a more romantic twist, a wink suggesting she is only joking.

"Oh, Bryzon, why did you not tell these stories before? That was wonderful," Sayhran says, smiling from ear to ear.

"It all sounds too unbelievable," Remek says, shaking his head from side to side.

"Remek, I pass on what I was taught in my lessons. Magic is beyond my understanding, and tales are for telling. Our chronicles were for believing," Bryzon confirms, laughing at his nephew's serious expression. "Do not bother your mind; there is no proof that it was indeed true, but the magic of the It-Ha is true. I have seen it many times," Bryzon says, his face serious.

"I must finish what I wish to say. It is getting late," Bryzon tells them as he abandons the pointless stories written so long ago.

"As time passed, the Drennan leaders decided who would be worthy to receive the ability of long life. This despicable practice has remained. Now it must change," Bryzon tells them, finally reaching the point he wanted to make.

"Everyone a Xennes, sounds good to me!" Remek agrees and pats his friend Rence on the back.

"It has angered me that those who were injured, became ill, or grew old perished in the colonies. In the years I have been in prison, I have lost many mortal friends. These unfortunates should have been allowed to receive the gift before our It-Ha chose to abandon us. May she regret her choice," Bryzon curses, his lips pursed, not hiding his displeasure at Layrrah.

"When we return from searching the cavern's contents, I will search for the It-Ha. I wish for Krom to accompany me, Sayhran. With your permission, of course," he asks, looking at his sister-in-joining.

"Keeland and Nowber will give their consent, of this I am certain?" Bryzon adds as an incentive for Sayhran to give her approval. Raine notices Bryzon has left out Elder Moss's name, and she gets the distinct impression that he has it in for the last elder of Kearthat.

"Of course, Bryzon, Krom may go if he wishes," Sayhran says without hesitation and Krom nods in agreement.

By the end of the evening, it has been quite noticeable that Rence has been unable to look away from Raine. He is clearly smitten, and Remek has a good idea of what is in store for his besotted friend.

Sleep is only moments away when Raine puts her head down. The last thing she remembers thinking is whether her brother could tell what she was dreaming, or would she hear his dreams.

Bryzon can feel the clarity of his mind returning. The freedom of breathing clean air is healing and his nightmares have lessened. He, however, spends a lot of his time thinking of Pateeo and the other men in the mines. Would they be released on the day promised by the Eslaf?

The next morning, Bryzon is about to exit his room at the Visitors Lodge when the familiar sound of an Eslaf craft makes its way to his ears. His heart begins to race. It is not a shuttle; he knows the sound well. It is an Eslaf transporter. He rushes to the nearest window overlooking the center of the colony.

The aliens display their usual lack of civility as they land their craft inside the settlement. Dust is stirred up, and things go flying off tables set up in the square where inter-colony trading takes place every fourteenth day. Things crash to the ground as the turbulence generated by the craft is expelled. It is mayhem.

Bryzon shakes his head at the idiocy of the Eslaf as he watches colonists scurry to save their precious hand-made wares. The chaos only ends when three aliens emerge from the craft, and the soldiers stride towards the centre of the market.

The Freelanders back away, giving the grey, menacing figures more than enough space. The children, witnessing the aliens from the day they are born, still cower at the sight of them.

Bryzon clenches his hands, forming tight fists as he tries to control the uncertainty he is feeling. A sentiment of dread overcomes him, 'Have they come to take me away?' he panics.

Keeland appears, and the red-suit steps forward to face the Noitibma leader. Bryzon's heartbeat slows as he keenly tries to follow the dialogue by looking at Keeland's actions and those of the Eslaf that towers over him. Having known Keeland all his life, Bryzon is sure he would know if the Xennes leader is distressed.

The discussion lasts for only a few minutes. The alien turns to leave, but Keeland remains standing in the same spot. The red-suit is about to step onto the craft's walkway when suddenly he turns back to speak to Keeland again. Once more, the conversation is short, and when the noisy craft leaves it inflicts chaos for the second time as it ascends into the clouds above the settlement and disappears.

Bryzon has to sit down. Relief washes over him, but at the same time, he feels as if he has betrayed his people.

"How am I supposed to save them when I am so easily frightened? I behaved as a child," he whispers. Disappointed, he wonders if the courage he thought he had, may have been lost after so many years spent in prison. A knock at the door comes, interrupting his self-deprecation.

"Greetings, my friend. The Eslaf enquired as to your whereabouts. I confirmed that you are here and will remain part of this colony. The repulsive creature started to walk with me to seek you out, but then, quite suddenly, he took my word. Of this, I am grateful. You have been spared facing the disgusting, foul-smelling creature," Keeland says, smiling at Bryzon as he pats his friend's arm.

"Thank you, Keeland, I am in your debt. Did you enquire as to the release of Peteeo and the others?" Bryzon asks.

"I did. The alien assured me they would be released on the day we agreed upon. I did not ask why you were sent home before your friends. I felt it best not to provoke; he is one I have not exchanged with before."

Bryzon takes pleasure in Keeland's remark about the Eslaf being repulsive, smelly creatures. It makes him smile after the nerve-wracking encounter.

"Yes," Keeland continues. "There is no need for concern. You can go about your day; there is no need to be anxious."

"Thank you, Keeland," Bryzon says, putting his fist to his heart to show his gratitude.

"Be at ease. I bid you well on your journey to Rednos. I will put my seal down, giving you all permission to travel without the Eslaf meddling. Raine has informed me that you will be visiting your family. Return safely, and convey my greetings to Marcus and his kind woman Zaviah."

When Keeland leaves, Bryzon feels a weight has been lifted from him. With the Eslaf satisfied he is living and working in Noitibma, he now had a clear path to execute his plans to speak to Marcus King about finding It-Ha Layrrah, and planning a full-on war against the aliens.

The following morning, Bryzon meets up with the group at Seyhran's cabin. He finds Krom and Remek negotiating who will carry Sayhran's bag. He feels great joy as he witnesses the boys' respect for their mother. A flat pebble, one side marked with an 'X', is flipped into the air by Remek. When it lands on the dirt, Krom shrugs, and without a word, reaches for his mother's belongings.

At the gate, the group lists their destination as Rednos Colony. To everyone's amusement, the Gatekeeper insists on asking Raine and Leyashe twice when they anticipate returning.

Rence, copying the gesture made earlier by Krom and Remek, offers to carry Raine's bag.

"No, thank you," Raine snaps, Rence's kind offer flatly rejected. The young man looks confused. How could his kindness be seen as an insult? Remek claps him on the back, and with eyebrows raised, his face delivering the 'I told you so' to his confused friend.

The suns are warm, the breeze slight, and the sky is a perfect soft pinkish-peach, displaying a scattering of small creamy-coloured clouds towards the South. Kearthat is promising another sweltering day, but Bryzon feels content. He finally has his family close. His concern for his friends at the Pishdrah mine has lessened somewhat with the knowledge that Pateeo and his men will soon be returning home.

They walk for an hour before they decide to quench their thirst. The suns are much higher now, and no one objects to taking a break. A patch of bright yellow Lido plants displaying large, orange, cup-shaped blooms offers shade. Leyashe reminds everyone to be careful not to bump the stems. Raine smiles at her brother's advice as he chooses instead to sit beneath two overlapping leaves, far from the flowers and their staining pollen.

The enormous waxy blooms hold sweet water that attracts birds and insects alike, making it a busy place. Remek tells of the many times his mother had sent him to gather the sweet syrup from the Lido growing near the colony. Seyhran listens as her ever-cheerful son describes in detail the freshly baked sweet cakes that were a reward for not spilling too much of the precious liquid on the way home.

Silly conversation followed by laughter among the young people is akin to a healing tonic for Bryzon. He closes his eyes and leans back, resting his head, he soaks up what he has been denied for so long.

Nedai comments that the bugs are becoming aggressive, convinced it has something to do with the intense heat of late. Then he tells them of an unusually large Tenlegs that he came across in the forest near Rednos Colony. "Bigger than I have ever seen," he shares with everyone as he stretches his arms wide to explain, while making a cringing kind of face to accompany his story.

Raine and Leyashe look at each other but remain silent about their encounter with the Tenlegs in the cavern.

Bryzon agrees silently with Nedai. The increase in shakes, the incessant heat, and now the massive storm. It was as if Kearthat was trying to speak.

Raine gets up and slings her pack over her shoulder. It is time to move on. Bryzon watches as Rence files in behind Raine when they set off.

"He is persistent," Bryzon says, directing his comment at Krom in a low voice.

"He is a brave man," Krom whispers, and chuckles.

As they enter the forest, they hear an Eslaf craft and Bryzon shouts, "Get down." They scramble to hide. Raine's heart beats fast as she crawls into the closest brush, listening to the two-man alien craft hovering. It does not linger, and within seconds, its sound fades.

"I am sure they did not see us. They were probably hovering for another reason. It is just a coincidence," Krom decides aloud.

They dust themselves off and continue walking. It is not long before they begin to enjoy the cooler temperature. Under normal circumstances, they would not have hidden from an Eslaf ship. Freelanders were free to travel within the marked zones with permission from their colony leaders. Somehow, today was different. They all felt as if they were doing something wrong.

A little while later, Raine sees the large tree that reminds her of her interaction with the Agnak. Remek starts whistling a tune, breaking the silence of the forest, making the encounter with the Eslaf craft and the Agnak a thing of the past. Raine unknowingly increases her stride, setting a faster pace for those behind her.

Leaving the forest, they walk alongside the river until they reach the log bridge. Remek scrambles up first and secures a rope around his waist. When he is ready, Krom helps his mother up, tying the other end of the rope around his mother's waist. Then he offers her his free hand and they begin crossing the Elin River.

"Do not look down, Mother," Krom instructs, shouting over the noise of the water. Raine, who crossed first, can see Sayhran finding the crossing challenging. When they reach the other side, she hears her aunt firmly declaring she will be crossing at the 'real bridge' on the way back.

Leyashe scampers up the smooth rocks to check the sky for drones and alien craft. When he comes back down, they stay silent to listen for any other unwelcome noises. All they hear is the buzzing of insects as they soak up the heat of the day.

Leyashe takes over and leads them through the brush towards the rock face. Her brother is in charge of his discovery and enjoying it. Raine smiles at Bryzon and nods as they share a moment that communicates their mutual delight at Leyashe's excitement.

The artificial rock entrance slowly begins to slide open, and Leyashe takes pleasure in everyone's reactions. One by one, they follow him through the opening.

Rence is the last one in. Leyashe pushes down on the lever, and the door groans to a close.

As their eyes become accustomed to the dark, the orange glow of the Firemoths begins to manifest. To this point, the siblings had purposely avoided facing the group, but the time had come. Before Raine lights a torch, she turns to face everyone, and her brother does the same. Sayhran lets out a gasp, pointing at Raine. She is speechless. Tiny little indescribable squeaky noises escape her mouth as she buries her face into Krom's chest.

"Your eyes, Raine, oh child, what has happened to you and Leyashe?" Sayhran asks sounding desperate for an answer.

"Do not be afraid, Sayhran," Raine begs as she lights the torch. We were fearful of telling you, afraid to tell anyone," she corrects.

It is Remek who changes the whole event into something else.

"That is amazing. It is the best trick I have ever, ever seen," he says with a huge grin on his face. "How do you do that?" he asks as if it is a magic trick.

Leyashe lights another torch. "Look, Sayhran, in the light, our eyes are normal. I…, we are sorry," he adds.

"We thought it too much to tell you all at once," Raine continues as she looks at the stunned members of her family and, of course, Rence. 'Rence, who probably finds her hideous now,' she tells herself.

"We did not know if you would be affected too. You can all leave if you wish. Rai and I could unpack the containers. You could wait for us at the Trigga tree Sayhran or go onto Rednos," Leyashe scrambles to save the moment.

"I am staying," Remek declares firmly. "Green glimmering pupils are great; I without doubt want them too," he adds, confident he would be overjoyed if it happened to him.

"No, we are here to stay. I am sorry that I was so afraid. If there is anything down here that will help to make our lives easier at the colonies, we must remain to find it," Sayhran decides as she looks at Bryzon, who nods.

"So where do we start?" she asks bravely. "Your eyes will probably clear up in no time," Sayhran adds as if the siblings are afflicted with something akin to a scratch.

Raine and Leyashe are relieved no one can hear their current conversation. They are discussing what will happen as all their secrets begin to come out, one by one. Raine walks over to Bryzon and hugs him. She is regretful; so many falsehoods have crept into their lives.

They follow Leyashe to the bigger cavern. Raine waits before she pulls down on the small lever above the second entrance. The door to the blue box clicks and swings open.

This impresses Bryzon, and for the first time, he is beginning to wonder if the cavern was used before the invasion by the Drennan. But why?

"How far does the cavern extend?" Bryzon asks Raine.

"It goes quite a distance to a solid wall of rock," she tells him but does not offer to show him. She is deliberately steering clear of the giant lifeless Tenlegs. "This way, Bryzon," she coaxes as she heads for the opening into the blue wall.

Raine is sure Rence has probably lost all interest in her now that she has these silly glimmering eyes. 'I cannot blame him,' she decides. Then she hears her brother giggle, she scowls at him and shakes her head.

"Incredible, so tidy and clean," Sayhran matching almost the exact words Leyashe had used.

"Wow," what do you think of this, brother?" Remek says, and Krom agrees, it is truly amazing.

Leyashe offers Sayhran the only chair in the room, then proceeds to unpack the earthling Enscriptor from his bag and puts it down on the table in front of her. He walks to the door and closes it. The secret of the dead Tenlegs was to remain as such for now.

"What is that?" Bryzon asks.

"It is a laptop; the earthlings brought it with them," Leyashe relays to keen ears.

Bryzon's immediate thought is, 'Why would the earthling have anything to do with the cavern?'

"Rai and I took it last time we were here. I have gone through all the books we have at the colony. I found earthling text that spoke of it," he tells them proudly. "It is much like the Enscriptors we use at our lessons," he clarifies. "I think this place contains things brought here by Grandfather Jon," Leyashe proclaims quite calmly. "They must have stored it down here to avoid the Eslaf from destroying it."

"There is no way the earthling survivors brought all of this here from the city after the invasion," Bryzon reasons. "It must have been done before the invasion," he says emphatically.

'Is it possible Jon knew the Eslaf were going to attack?' Bryzon thinks to himself. Shaking his head, suddenly mystified. His confused reaction goes unnoticed. Everyone's attention is locked on Leyashe's earthling discovery.

"My father would never have kept such knowledge from his family," Sayhran insists. "It does not make sense," she comments. "We must open the boxes; it was someone else," Sayhran insists, certain her father could never have been guilty of such deceit.

Raine watches Leyashe. He suddenly looks all grown up to her.

"I have not even told Rai yet," Leyashe says, turning his face to his sister he flashes an apologetic smile. "I was able to activate it just before dawn," he confesses, and they know Leyashe was up all night. A bit of giggling erupts, and it takes Remek to explain to Sayhran that they are laughing at the name of the earthling technology.

"Why on Kearthat would someone name a machine an Ass-us? How terribly foolish," Sayhran says, sounding a little offended.

"I am sure that it is pronounced 'Ay-sus', Sayhran," Raine corrects, putting a stop to the silliness for the second time.

Leyashe connects a small Zraphite pack. Raine notices how skillfully her brother has fashioned what is needed to bring the unfamiliar technology to life. But she knows it is a bigger piece of Zraphite than her brother spoke of originally. Leyashe had traded again.

"How many Tibbar did this cost you, brother?"

"Too many; I will be hunting until I am an old man," he admits to his sister. He smiles, lifts his eyes-brows and shakes his head at his latest quandary. He presses a button and the computer screen lights up. Krom and Nedai lean forward. They are fascinated.

"Cousin, I knew you would do great things one day," Remek praises.

It was true; Leyashe had an uncanny aptitude for electronics, sums, numbers and memorization. They wait for the loading sequence of the machine before it reveals a screen with multiple miniature pictures.

"I did not have time to go through all the choices," Leyashe confesses, "But it definitely contains information about the earthling ships. If only they still existed," he laments.

"There is information on the day-to-day running of their big spaceships and matters relating to many other things. I did not have time to read it all," he admits, stepping back from the small table as if to present his work, grinning from ear to ear. "What do you think, Bryzon?" Leyashe asks.

"I think," Bryzon said slowly. "If only we had those earthling ships, we could defeat the Eslaf in one day. We could make Kearthat our home once more."

"Do you truly believe that, Bryzon?" Nedai asks.

"I do," Bryzon says with conviction.

"Many years ago, I asked It-Ha Layrrah if they had destroyed the earthling ships as ordered by the elders. She assured me they had turned the ships to dust in the Barren Lands. I believed her to be sincere. Sayhran was right when she said there is nowhere to hide on Kearthat. If the spaceships had been left in The Nerrab's Barren Lands, they would surely have been found by the Eslaf by now?

"The three It-Ha together had great powers. Who knows how they might have used their conjuring?" Bryzon tells them in a voice that makes it sound like It-Ha were deceivers. "Layrrah must know more. If only the spaceships existed, we would have weapons, powerful weapons, and a chance to rid our sphere of the Eslaf," Bryzon fantasizes.

Sayhran takes Leyashe's hand. "If your parents were here now. They would be so proud of you, my clever boy. Ships or no spaceships, thank you for bringing me here," she says, looking up at her nephew with pride. Leyashe is noticeably embarrassed by her compliments, and his cheeks redden. Remek notices his cousin's predicament and breaks the awkward silence.

"Question, my dear cousin, how on Kearthat do you think this big box came to be in here? Not through that tiny opening," he questions, pointing in the direction of the exit.

"That is what I have been asking myself since the first time I saw it. Rai and I have talked about it, and we think the answer is below us."

"Why would you think that, Ash?" Bryzon is quick to ask.

"Two reasons. When you tap on the floor, it sounds hollow in some places. When Rai and I were trapped in here, a stream of water ran underneath it. The next morning it was dry. The water had to have gone somewhere. Perhaps the box was put into the cavern from a larger opening below it."

"You mean," Remek says, "that there is another opening below us big enough to bring this box up into this space?" he asks, puzzled. "What is below that, then? Is there a cavern with another entrance that we do not know of? Remek continues scrunching his face as he queries something he cannot imagine.

"Well, Leyashe, we are waiting. What else do you think you know, nephew," Bryzon asks, and everyone can see that Bryzon is genuinely interested in what his clever nephew is thinking.

"I think," he continues, "that if there is a place large enough underneath us, it may be a perfect place to hide even bigger things."

"Not possible," says Sayhran. "We would have known, the Rednos leaders, my father… he would have told us. Then she turns to read everyone's reaction. Smiles on their faces leave her confused for a few seconds until she realises what they are thinking.

"Well, if it is so," Sayhran huffs, "then let us discover this place beneath our feet."

Krom easily picks up a heavy box from one of the stacks. To their surprise, it opens easily. A gasp escapes Sayhran's mouth when she sees the layer upon layer of celestial charts.

Leyashe studies the first chart he takes out. He is quick to notice that it does not resemble the night sky that he knows so well. It is the universe as the people of Earth saw it.

The next container has everyone silent as they examine its contents. Pictures of earthlings can be seen through hundreds of sheer envelopes. The cover of each bears the name of the person and two dates, a date of birth and a date of death.

"So much sadness, a whole life in one tiny packet," Nedai comments.

Raine takes a few envelopes out of the box, thumbing through them. She can see that some have pictures in them. "These must have been the people who died during the journey to Kearthat. There are so many," she says, cupping her mouth with her right hand, expressing her dismay.

Then Bryzon spots a name he recognizes. The envelope could only have been added many years after the invasion. He says nothing at first as he goes through the contents and then hands them to Sayhran. She looks at the package, which is fuller than most. When she realizes the name, she puts it to her chest. Tears stream down her cheeks, but she does not make a sound. Shocked at their mother's reaction, Krom and Remek try to console her, but it takes time before Sayhran shares the contents.

The first picture she passes along is of a little girl standing next to a tall man with blonde, reddish hair. On the back of the photo is written 'my dad Rick Brand, me aged 5.' There is one of a young Jon King and Farron dressed in fine clothing. When Sayhran turns the picture over, it reads, 'Our wedding.' The young couple appear to be standing in front of small green trees, and Sayhran knows it is Earth she is looking at. It is Stal Settlement, a place that her mother and father spoke of endlessly to them when she, Caite and Nick were children.

Finally, Bryzon can put faces to people like Frederick King and Rick Brand, men whom Jon King had spoken of so many times with great praise and admiration,

"Can we take these with us?" Sayhran asks after everyone has studied the photographs.

"Keep them well hidden, Sayhran. I am sure Marcus will want to see them too," he tells her in a gentle voice. Bryzon has a great understanding of what his sister-in-joining must be feeling at this moment. 'Why had Jon and Farron King never shown these pictures to his children?' he wonders.

"When do you think someone was here last," Raine asks aloud.

"I think it was after your mother passed to the next world, Raine," Bryzon responds, as he finds an envelope marked Caite King. Raine takes the package from Bryzon. It has Caite's name, date of birth, and date of death; otherwise, it is empty, but for the metal ring Dayson forged for his bride before their joining. Raine looks at Bryzon as she slips the ring onto a finger on her right hand. He nods, and she puts the envelope back but keeps the memento. Leyashe smiles at her and pats her on the arm.

"My father may not have told me about this place, but I know Nick would have known, and he would have told Marcus," Sayhran insists, turning her sights on Nedai, who is still leafing through the many envelopes.

"Does your father know of this place, Nedai?" Sayhran asks earnestly, and all eyes turn to Marcus King's son.

Nedai throws his hands up in the air and firmly pronounces, "I did not know, and I wager my life that my father does not know. Father would have brought me here to learn of our ancestors if he knew. I am as surprised as you are, Sayhran," he defends. "You must believe me," Nedai pleads, sounding slightly nettled. "If he did know, he would have told all of us, his family," the young man insists, pointing to all of them in a sweeping gesture.

"We are not saying Marcus knows," Raine tells a now slightly dejected Nedai. "We were just hoping that there was someone in Rednos that might know of this place," she says gently.

"We are all together in this; let us try to find more evidence. The only way is to search further," Sayhran suggests, as she reaches for Nedai's hand and squeezes it, offering a silent apology to her nephew.

Several boxes contain photographs and other small items of those who perished. Nedai goes through many of them quietly. There is no envelope for Jon or Nick King. Raine is glad when they finally open a box that contains books, bringing the sadness to an end.

'Is it possible that the earthling leader kept his secret because of something far darker than anyone knew?' Bryzon finds himself thinking. 'Was he deceived first by Jon and then Nick King? But for what reason?'

Raine notices Bryzon shaking his head. Then he falls silent and it is apparent that he is struggling with the fact that he did not know his earthling friend that well after all. She admits to herself that she, too, feels a little confused about her grandfather's motives.

Books with beautiful houses and people, a single sun and moon in the sky, strange food, big buildings, and airships. All that their eyes see is unlike anything they could ever have imagined. The many different forms of transport have the boys passing books around to show each other what they have found, everyone gasping at this or that.

The books are nothing like the few earthling books that had mysteriously found their way to the leaders of Kearthat. Instead of science and sums, these show scenes of leisure, riches, and wonderful animals and places. But there are also scenes of great destruction, devastation, and hardship, all part of the visual education of what Earth was like, bombarding their senses.

Leyashe keeps one book out, the cover of which reads Leisure & Swimwear Issue#12, December 2026. It displays a young woman on the front cover. She is very pretty with long blonde hair, and she wears a ridiculously small red top and bottom, leaving most of her body exposed. She appears rather pale to Leyashe, but he thinks she is beautiful. In the background is a huge expanse of very blue water, and he comments that it must be the ocean on Earth. His face turns crimson when Remek teases him.

"Cousin, please share what you read about the ocean on Earth when you have had enough time to study it," he mocks. Remek winks at those following his little charade, and soon it brings a burst of laughter from all the boys. Bryzon finds it hard to keep a smile from turning the corners of his mouth.

A publication that Bryzon is paging through contains pictures of the animals of Earth, and he is fascinated by how small they all appear. He soon discovers a picture of an elephant. Turning the book around, he shares his discovery.

"Looks a bit like a Trungo but very small, but it has big teeth" he comments with a chuckle.

The next container they open offers different stories printed on large sheets of paper that fold in two and then into each other. They soon realise these are news reports. On the front of the first one they pick up, there is a faded picture of a hand-drawn spaceship soaring into the sky. The story reads, "Rumours of a secret Project! Fact or Fiction?" The date on the page is Earth year, August 2nd, 2037.

Raine notices a quiet Rence leafing through a book with strange means of transport. Some are large with many wheels; others look like they could carry only two people. The same book, she notices, contains a few attractive earthling women. When he asks Bryzon if it is ok to keep the magazine, he consents.

A strange feeling overcomes Raine, but she is quick to convince herself that it is not jealousy. 'That would be ridiculous; he can look at whomever he pleases. Then she quickly looks over at Leyashe, thankful to find that he seems oblivious of her thoughts.

The next box yields necklaces, earrings and other adornments of gold and silver, and sparkling stones. It took them only seconds to know that the items belonged to the many who had died.

"These must have all been very precious to the people who wore them," Sayhran comments as she picks up a chain of gold, then lets it slip through her fingers, watching it snake back into the box. Krom closes the lid, and the container finds space on top of a box of books.

"My mother wore a chain of earthling gold around her neck. Do you know what happened to it when she passed?" Raine asks Sayhran.

"It was the same necklace my mother wore when your grandmother passed?" Sayhran muses, her face displaying an expression of someone trying hard to recall something.

"Yes, I think she called it her Jayson. No, she called her necklace her friend Jaenus."

It is as if Sayhran has rung a loud bell.

"You mean to tell us that Grandmother Farron named a necklace? What a strange coincidence that the name is the same as in Bryzon's story," Raine says, a somewhat surprised look on her face.

"Yes, it is a curious, is it not?" Sayhran agrees.

"Do you know what happened to the necklace when my mother passed, Sayhran? Raine asks again.

"I do not know. I simply cannot remember," her aunt admits, looking confused. "I know Caite wore it every day. She was wearing it on the day she passed. I fear it was somehow lost," she declares with genuine puzzlement.

They spend a few hours opening container after container, coming across mostly personal items, many books, and news-related pages. However, the floor does not reveal an exit, just a solid base as far as they can tell. When they stop to stretch their legs and eat, there is a noise from the smaller cavern. Leyashe opens the door and Bryzon grabs a torch and races out of the room, Krom hot on his heels.

Leyashe notices that the Firemoths have left the cavern, signalling that the suns have set over The High Mountains. Bryzon steps on a rock lying in the centre of the doorway between the two caverns. He picks it up, quite sure it had not been there when they entered. They scan the area around them, Krom's short sword raised and ready.

Leyashe looks up and sees that the sheer force of the moths leaving the cavern is responsible for dislodging the tiny rock from the cavern roof. The moths had created the noise. He decides it may be time to tell the story of the Tenlegs that he and Raine killed.

Bryzon is surprised at yet another lie coming from Leyashe, but he does not show it. He quickly turns his slight disappointment into action. They light another torch and scour the two caves for any Tenlegs that may be lurking. When they come across the dead creatures, Bryzon cringes. "How is it possible they grow so big now," he comments, shaking his head.

Leyashe is pleased Bryzon knows about the creatures. It is one less secret.

Minutes later, Bryzon decides to restore the lie about the Tenlegs. Knowing Sayhran's feelings about the multi-legged crawling bugs, it would be best not to say anything.

Bryzon lifts Leyashe onto his shoulder to adjust the opening and make the hole where the Firemoths escaped just big enough to let them back in. Before he is done, there is a growl, and Leyashe feels a hot, foul breath only inches from his face. He bends his knees and drops down from Bryzon's shoulders. On the way down, he knocks the torch from Krom's hand. Bryzon tries to catch the torch; instead, he bumps into the wall and they all stumble.

It takes him only a few seconds to comprehend what has happened. He has just had his first encounter with a Night Creature, from way too close. Excited, Leyashe does not notice that his hearing and strength have increased considerably. In the dark, he can see Bryzon on his hands and knees, trying to find the torch that has gone out. Leyashe reaches to the left of Bryzon, picks it up and lights it. He starts chuckling.

"What is so funny, Ash?" Bryzon asks, thinking that Leyashe is laughing at him.

"It was a Night Creature, Bryzon. I, son of Dayson scared it. It has never seen a creature with eyes like mine. Rai and I are special. It was so scared that I could hear its cry as it ran away. This means that Rai and I can probably move around at night without fear of being attacked," he proclaims triumphantly.

They may have decided to keep the dead Tenlegs a secret, but Leyashe cannot wait to get back to the others to tell of his encounter with the Night Creature.

"Why is it that you can never see the danger you are in?" Raine asks her brother, then lands a playful tap on his head with a book revealing her treasure without intending to. She immediately slips it under her and sits on it so the boys cannot grab it.

The family eats while discussing their journey to Rednos, all aware they would have to leave by the mid-day hour on the next day to reach Rednos before nightfall. Raine jokingly adds, "But we need not be concerned about any danger. If we do not make the curfew, little brother and I will scare the Night Creatures all the way back to Ludinia if we have to," she jokes.

They all giggle at Leyashe's expense while he gives his sister an I-am-going-to-get-you look and you-wait-and-see smile.

They decide to continue unpacking boxes for a few hours before resting for the night. Raine wraps up the leftover food, storing it away for the following day. Before she hides her book, she scans the cover again, Fashion Update, October 1st, 2029. A woman with a beautiful yellow dress adorns the cover. The dress sparkles as if it has been covered with shiny dots. It reminds her of the water of the Elin River in bright sunslight. 'Earthlings must have had riches beyond imagination,' she thinks as she puts the magazine with her belongings.

The next container reveals books on the history of Earth, but on the very top is a handwritten copy of 'The Code to Freedom.' Bryzon reaches for it and begins to read it aloud.

Leyashe and Raine look at each other. Their astonishment does not go unnoticed by Bryzon, who immediately stops reading. "What else do the rest of us not know?" he asks, raising his eyebrows. Without a word, Leyashe gets up, goes to his bag, and takes out the small box.

Subsequent minutes are spent putting the metal strips into the correct order and matching them to the printed copy that Bryzon holds in his left hand. Then Raine takes the box, turns it upside down and the triangle key falls out.

"Right, of course, there is more," Bryzon says. "Is that all? Or would there be more secrets that we need to know?" he asks, shaking his head, his face not angry but rather more confused at the siblings.

"This is all, we promise," comes out of Raine's mouth before she can help herself. Leyashe and I think it is a key that must open something in this room, something we have missed," she confesses.

Bryzon starts reading the sheet in his hand from the beginning again. When he stops, all eyes are on Raine and Leyashe.

"Those who are Rain and Ash; sounds like it was written as a message for the two of you," Remek points out.

"Those who are Rain and Ash," Bryzon repeats, as if trying to discover the meaning of the cipher.

Sayhran bends down, her head disappearing under the little table where she sits. Raine looks at Bryzon, who shrugs his shoulders. She walks over, goes down on her knees and joins Sayhran. When their eyes meet under the table, she jokingly asks, "Anything we should know about, Aunt Sayhran?"

"Yes, my foot just touched something, and I felt it move. I hope it is not one of those big Tenlegs that Nedai was talking about."

Krom comes over, picks up the table, including its contents, and moves it away, exposing Sayhran and Raine on their hands and knees. His first instinct was also a Tenlegs, and he is grateful that there is no creature at his mother's feet. Instead, they discover a metal square embedded into the floor. It is virtually unnoticeable. Krom pulls on the latch in the center of the square, and a strip of metal slides open, revealing a hollow triangular space.

"I think we need this," Raine says, passing her cousin the gemstone key found embedded in the little box.

Krom inserts it into the space, but nothing happens. They all look at each other, then Raine notices numbers on the metal pad. She turns the key and matches the numbers up. The green jewel glows and the floor where the table stood moments earlier begins to slide open.

They jump back, but Raine is a little too slow. Her feet go out from under her and she slips into the opening. Krom reaches out in a flash and manages to catch her by the wrist, holding onto her arm while her body dangles into the gaping darkness below. Warm air rushes up into the room as she lets out a little whimper. Rence rushes over and reaches for her other arm. She looks up and grabs hold, and together, they pull her to safety.

"Thank you," she says breathlessly, "we found our way down, Sayhran," Raine announces and smiles.

Chapter 35 - The Descent

They peer down the dark hole but cannot determine how far it drops down or where it might lead.

"Hand me a torch, Remek," Bryzon asks, then leans in to see what the light might reveal. Raine and Sayhran lean forward, looking over Bryzon's shoulders.

"There are metal steps leading down to solid rock, and an opening to the left. It might be a passageway. Bryzon describes what he sees and quickly decides to climb down to investigate what lies beyond the steps.

Facing the ledge at the top, Bryzon discovers a rope tied to a large ring set into the rock. "This is useful," his voice echoes back, holding the rope above his head to show them.

When he reaches solid ground, he disappears from their sight, and Sayhran shouts down at him to be vigilant. The torchlight fades, leaving everyone nervous as they stare down into the black hole. A short time later, the hole becomes brighter and brighter. A hand holding a torch re-appears, followed by Bryzon smiling broadly.

"It is a passageway," he announces. "With steps that lead somewhere, and the opening is large enough to walk upright," he tells them as he climbs back up.

"Do you think we should take the chance to walk further than you did, to see where it leads?" Leyashe asks eagerly.

"Krom and I will go," Bryzon decides, looking at Sayhran for approval while a disappointed Leyashe looks on.

"Do you think there is anything to fear down there?" Sayhran questions. "What if the Night Creatures go down there, or a Tenlegs or a whole nest of Tenlegs?" she describes as she shivers at the thought.

"We cannot be sure of that, Sayhran, but if we do not explore, we will not know the answers we seek," Leyashe comments, and Sayhran nods.

Bryzon leads the way, Krom following closely, his short sword at his side. At first, the opening is quite narrow and starts with a steep slope, but they have no problem walking upright. Twenty stairs into the descent, they see the first of many oil lamps hanging on the wall to their right. Jars of Shiftaf oil are placed beneath in recesses carved into the rock. The oil reminds Krom of when he and Leyashe recently caught a huge Shiftaf in the Elin River, not for its oil, but for its tasty, soft, flaky flesh when cooked on an open fire.

They have not gone far when the passage widens considerably. There is a sharp left turn, after which the stairs continue at an ever-steeper descent. Bryzon can feel a warm breeze coming from somewhere below them, and his thoughts go to the men labouring in the depths of Pishdrah. Reaching level ground again, Krom and Bryzon instinctively feel a bigger space around them. To their right, there is another passageway. It appears to continue down another section of the tunnel at yet another decline.

Krom puts his finger to his lips, indicating that Bryzon must be quiet. He tilts his head slightly to isolate the sound that he thinks he heard. They remain like this for several seconds before Krom finally whispers. "I thought I heard something bang, something metal, but now all I can hear is water. There must be an underground river."

They decide to go a little further. The stairs continue down the passageway, and so do the oil lanterns. They reach what seems to be the end of the tunnel, and then they can both feel the enormity of the space that surrounds them.

When they light another torch, the light does not reach any walls except the one directly behind them. After a while, their eyes become accustomed to the darkness, and shapes begin to emerge. They can make out the outline of what could be trees in the distance, but this is by no means a normal scene.

A dim light comes from all around them from millions of sparkles. All the grass and small shrubs in their immediate area appear dead in the light. The plants are stark and white. Squinting, they force their eyes to look further outward, becoming accustomed to the low light, and they see something that astounds them. The vegetation is glistening in the dark, a display of beautiful luminous colours like nothing they have witnessed. It is the trees and shrubs that are creating the twinkles. Each leaf and branch comes alive in the dark as it glistens.

"They will not believe us when we get back," Krom says as he scans the cavern. "It is like looking up at the night sky, but with millions more stars," he describes.

Bryzon hears a noise nearby, something much closer than the sound of the water. Krom heard it too. They look at each other and slowly start backing away. With their weapons ready, they wait silently. The noise comes from a cluster of shrubs. They focus on the spot, not blinking. More rustling, branches and leaves shaking, something is definitely inside the plants. In the torchlight, the plants directly in front of them are ashen, their leaves white, their branches white.

"What is it?" Krom whispers. Before he can say anything else, a snow-white Tibbar hops past them, its four long ears flopping about as it disappears into the dark. They had both seen the animal only briefly. Still, it had been enough time to watch the creature turn from white into a display of shimmering colour when it entered the dark.

"A Tibbar," Krom announces, "And it looks exactly like the ones on the Freelands, but it was white. Was I dreaming, or did it change colour?" he asks, pointing into the distance with his short sword still in his hand.

"No, Krom, I saw it too. You are right. We will not have the words to describe what we are witnessing. Let us return; we shall all come again in the morning," Bryzon suggests as they begin to ascend the steep stairs.

Everyone speaks at once, but Bryzon raises his hand in a gesture that begs their patience.

When he is done relaying an account of what he and Krom saw, he can see that Leyashe is bursting to speak.

"I have read of this phenomenon," Leyashe says when he finally has a turn to talk.

"Well, are you going to share this wise knowledge you possess or not, cousin?" Nedai asks impatiently.

"It happens to fish and bugs, I know that, or that is what is written in our texts," Leyashe replies.

"What happens, Ash?" Raine asks.

"Well, it is evolution. If, for example, a fish is deprived of light for many thousands of years, the creature will lose its colour and lose its sight as they no longer need to see or be colourful," he tells them. "But the part where they change into colours in the dark is something I know nothing of," Leyashe admits.

"Poor little creatures in the dark, and blind so cruel." Sayhran comments. Remek laughs aloud at his mother while the rest of them stifle their amusement as best they can.

After some discussion, they decide that it is no good to wonder about what may exist below their feet. They agree with Bryzon. They will all continue the search into the cavern below them at first light. Remek comments that first light has no meaning where they are, but everyone is deeply cemented in their thoughts, and he does not get a reply to his attempt at some fun.

Bryzon quizzes Krom on how far down he thinks the stairs took them before reaching the bottom. His nephew decides that it is at least the height of the big Trigga tree outside. Bryzon silently decides that it may have been nearly twice the distance.

Krom re-inserts the key that opens the hole in the ground. As he pushes on the green gem, they watch the metal piece slide to close the gaping hole. Leyashe's curiosity as to how the secret doors operate is immediately aroused. His mind is going to be a busy place.

With too much to take in, Sayhran backs away and announces it is time to rest. "Until dawn," she announces, sighing when she realizes how hard the floor is beneath her thin blanket. It is not long before they all appear to be asleep, but in reality, most of them are wrapped up in their thoughts. An hour passes before snores can be heard coming from the boys, only then does Bryzon give into the night.

Raine and Leyashe go back and forth, asking and answering questions without uttering a word aloud. Their conversation continues until, finally, Leyashe's mind becomes quiet, and Raine knows that her brother has fallen asleep.

She is not quite certain of the time when she awakes. She pulls the lever to open the door, sure that the whirr will awaken everyone, but they are all still fast asleep when she looks back. Raine is careful not to step on anyone. Only Remek stirs, then settles back into sleep. She heads for the small cavern to search for a breath of morning air. It does not take her long to spot a dim, greyish light from the opening where the moths come in and out of the cavern. Her brother told her of the Tenlegs search the night before, and Raine feels secure that it is now safe to be out of the blue box.

The moths are back, confirming that dawn has come. Still hankering after the fresh morning air, she moves around the smaller cavern until she finds a spot where she can feel the air filtering in from above. She closes her eyes and takes a few deep breaths. When she hears her name being called in a whispered voice, her eyes snap open. She has been missed.

She returns to the second cavern and bumps into Leyashe. He scowls at her, "Where were you?" he asks. "I was troubled when I found the door open and you were gone."

Taken aback at her brother's adult-like attitude, she apologizes. He rolls his eyes and says, "Do not do that again," and walks away. For a moment, Raine is a little annoyed, but then she smiles.

"Yes, my leader," she salutes, muttering under her breath.

As they eat their morning meal, Bryzon lays down the rules. He explains that, to ensure their safety, they should always be no more than three feet apart.

"Check that you have your weapon ready in case you need to use it," he asserts.

Sayhran protests when given a short sword and pouch to attach to her belt.

"We do not know what is down there, Mother," Krom says in a stern voice, putting an end to her resistance.

"Everyone must be very careful, please," Raine blurts out, feeling relieved that she has shared some of her unease.

"Yes, Overseer of Noitibma Colony," Leyashe says, saluting his sister, a huge smile on his face, and she knows that he must have heard her leader comment earlier. But how had he known that she saluted, he had his back turned to her. 'Was it just a coincidence?' she asks herself.

Krom inserts the triangular key into the lock mechanism and presses the jewel. It clicks. Careful this time, they all stand well clear until the opening is fully ajar. Within minutes they are descending in a pre-arranged order.

Halfway down, they hear running water as it echoes into the passageway. When they reach the end of the stairs, everyone is silenced as they take their first look. They are astounded at what they see.

Bryzon decides to light the oil lanterns outside of the exit. As the extra light brightens the immediate area, he sees something he had not noticed the day before. Just a few feet away from the passage is a vent. It is hissing, but he cannot hear how loudly above the noise of the river.

The cavern floor is rocky at first. Then they encounter more brush, a type of short grass covers some of the ground. Outlines of glittering trees can be seen in the distance, but it is not clear how far away or how big they could be. The semi-dark, the many vibrant colours are altering everyone's perception of depth.

They are silent as they study the shrubbery around them; it is an amazing sight. White in the light, as if dead, but the very same vegetation dazzling with colour once in the dark. When the growth begins to thin out, they are standing on soft black sand, sand that looks and feels like it has been brought there from the ocean. An underground river comes into view, and again, the plants at the water's edge are white in the light. Yet they appear luminescent in the dark beyond the river, shimmering with miraculous colours.

The river flows fairly rapidly. Amazed at the clarity of the water, Leyashe estimates that it cannot be deeper than perhaps three to four feet at most. Rocks and sunken pieces of wood are visible at the bottom resting unmoving in the pristine water.

Hundreds of tiny white fish swim in shoals, twisting and weaving as if performing a choreographed water dance. When Raine spots some larger fish, she goes on her knees and leans forward. She gets a good look at them; they veer away when they spot her shadow. Leyashe was wrong about them being blind.

"You were right and wrong. The fish are white, but they can see," she says in her mind, "I wonder if there are more white animals, the same as the Tibbar Krom saw?" Leyashe answers back.

Raine watches as her brother stops and rips out a small plant. He proceeds to study the roots in the light of the torch, and then he tosses it aside. Smiling, she assumes that the small investigative exercise yielded no valuable clues.

She wishes that she could see the other side of the river, and within seconds, it is as if her eyes obey her request. She breathes in, shocked, when she grasps what has just happened. She walks back to where Leyashe is standing, looking into the distance.

He turns to look at her. "I know, sister, I can do it too. "The other side of the river is probably a hundred feet or more across," and this cavern goes far beyond the river," he approximates.

With control over their new eyes, they see that the cavern is larger than Noitibma Colony and the roof higher than Leyashe can calculate accurately. Leyashe informs his sister that they have been walking at a decline ever since they left the stairs. They were going deeper and deeper into the belly of Kearthat.

Then, the magic of their surroundings takes on a completely different spectacle as they see Flutterbugs. The white, gentle creatures fly dangerously close to the torches. When they fly back into the dark, they are a wondrous display of reds, yellows, and blues.

"Look, birds!" Nedai says, pointing.

A flock of birds appear as if out of nowhere. Sayhran loves birds, and much to Remek's frustration, his mother stops every few steps to watch them. The birds miss their amazed spectators by mere inches each time they swoop down. They appear harmless, using their natural instinct to guide their change of direction just in time to avoid crashing into anyone's head.

"Everything down here has lived in the dark for so many years that they have created their very own light," Leyashe decides. Little does he know that he could not be more wrong.

Raine tries to look discreetly at Rence, who has been noticeably quiet. He is probably trying to grasp his surroundings, she decides. Her glance in his direction is noticed, and she quickly pretends that she is just taking in the scenery. With her pupils going from blue to luminous green depending on the light, she must be a sight to behold, she concludes.

The air feels quite humid. The river's water is cool to the touch but does not seem to cool the air much. Soon they must shout to be heard above the din of small rapids further downstream. Bryzon motions for everyone to follow him as he lights another torch and passes it to Remek.

"From the prison to Noitibma, now here," he says, "It is all too much," but no one hears his comments over the noise of the running water as Bryzon keeps to the soft black sand on the river's edge.

The light from the torches remains the takers and givers of enchantment. Soon, they notice that the further they walk, the quieter it becomes. Grass and rock below their feet mean they are moving away from the water. A natural path seems to lead them to their left as they continue to an unknown destination. A while later, the trail takes them back to the rock wall, and the first oil lamp appears.

"It is a world below a world," Rence says, almost repeating word for word what Leyashe had told Raine earlier. "It is wonderful, Rence, hard to believe," Sayhran adds, agreeing with Lesser Leader Dourok's quiet son.

Suddenly it is easier to hear each other as the river snakes away from them. Leyashe can feel that the ground has begun to level out. The terrain, however, is difficult to navigate in some places. They must carefully negotiate smooth rocks with each step, some quite large. They stay close to the cavern wall to their left and make sure that they can still hear the river in the distance to their right.

What comes next has everyone sucking in their breath. There is a vast stretch of beach ahead, and the river is suddenly closer but is a lot quieter. They are quite stunned to find a huge boat tied up at the river's edge. The boat looks as if it will carry at least fifteen people, maybe more.

"It must have come from somewhere down the river," Bryzon says loudly, speaking over the sound of the rippling water. Everyone can see the opposite wall of the cavern for the first time in the distance. Narrowing from the bottom, the cavern above the river appears endless.

Ignoring the boat for the moment, Bryzon leads the group down a narrow pathway that is carved out along the wall. They continue in single file, clutching the rock to their left to avoid stepping into the water. Not long after, the oil lamps mounted to the cavern wall end, and so does the path.

"Stop!" Bryzon shouts, putting up his hand.

"Whatever lies beyond this point can only be reached by using the boat," he announces, "this path ends here." Silence ensues while they all wait for Bryzon's next instruction, but it is Raine who suggests the next move.

"Well, it looks like we are taking a boat trip. Does anyone know anything about boats?" she says with a smile. They turn around and start making their way back, with Krom leading them back to where the boat is moored.

Bryzon inspects the vessel and walks around it. Lying down on the sand, he lights up the bottom to study it while everyone watches. When he is satisfied, the men push the boat into the water; the current has quite a pull and they have to hold onto it.

"Wait!" Leyashe says.

"What is your concern, brother?" Raine asks above the sound of the water, looking around.

"The river runs opposite to the Elin; it is going towards The High Mountains. How can this be?" he queries.

"We cannot be sure that it is flowing towards the mountains, and brother, does it truly matter? Hurry, get in the boat, Ash," she tells him.

Leyashe is quiet as he watches Bryzon take his time, making sure that there are no leaks now that the boat is in the water. Satisfied it will stay afloat, Raine walks knee-deep into the water and hops in. Remek carries Sayhran, and she joins Raine, who is seated on the last bench at the back of the boat.

Six oars pull in unison, and with the natural flow of the river, the boat propels forward. It is not long before Bryzon shouts, "Oars in, brace yourselves!"

Krom shouts, "Hold on!" Knuckles turn white as the boat suddenly seems small against the force of the river. But the craziness is brief as they comfortably make it through some small rapids. The water becomes abruptly calmer, and the cavern opens considerably wider as the vessel slowly glides into a gentle drift. They push out the oars. There is an eerie quiet; the only sound is that of the oars and the rippling of the water beneath each oar's swish.

Rence comments that he had not heard the birds chirping. It was true. There were birds, but no birdsong.

A large animal catches Raine's eye to the right of her; it is a creature she has never seen before. It seems rooted to the spot, allowing Raine to get a good look at it. It is only slightly bigger than Regor; its coat is smooth. It has enormous dark eyes. Docile but unsure, Raine can see its fur quivering around its belly. The creature desperately twists and turns its ears to locate the new sounds before it sprints into the dark, becoming one with the glittering background.

Raine is suddenly struck by an idea. What if she and Leyashe could learn to project each other's thoughts into pictures? So much has changed in just a few days. Talking to her brother without speaking was a special gift; it added to their already extraordinary bond.

Remek whistles in the quiet. Raine knows this means he has seen something that impresses him. She focuses on where he is pointing. It is a large bay, and just beyond the trees, she can make out parts of a cabin's roof. The men row towards the beach. As they get closer, they see two bollards sticking out of the sand at the river's edge.

Bryzon jumps into the shallow water, and his nephews and Rence follow suit. Remek immediately offers his outstretched arms to his mother. Rence seizes the opportunity and holds out his arms to Raine, offering the same service. She shakes her head and jumps in the water beside him.

Sniggering can be heard coming from the young men after the boat is secured, and Bryzon knows they are teasing Rence about a second failed attempt at wooing Raine. He smiles, enjoying the simple things in his life, even if they are happening in a strange, mysterious dark world below his own.

"Come, stay together. Let us go and look at this place," Bryzon requests, saving Rence from his latest humiliation. They file into the same walking order as before, crossing the soft, black, sandy beach that appears larger than it did when they were on the river. The first thing Raine notices is that there are no footprints anywhere but their own.

As they reach the grass and brush, something moves up ahead. Leyashe is quick to pull out his knife. Crouching, he stops. Everyone is on high alert as they scan the area and wait for the culprit to show its face. Within seconds, they are rewarded; it is a large Tenlegs the size of the two in the cavern. The hairy, multi-legged bug makes a quick getaway by retreating into the brush behind it. When Sayhran asks what it is, Bryzon quickly tells her that it is a Tibbar. Only Leyashe, Bryzon, and Raine saw the creature, and they kept their creepy secret.

The cabin is much like the ones in the colonies. Leyashe is the first to step onto the small deck of the dwelling. There is a window to the left of the door. He peers in but only sees darkness inside. He tries the door, fully expecting it to be locked, but it turns freely. He inches it open while the rest of the group fan out behind him. When he steps inside, he blinks. It is as if he has to reaffirm what he is seeing.

"Wow, take a look at this," Remek says, whistling through his teeth as he squeezes past Leyashe. There are four beds lined up beside each other on one side of the room and a small table off to the side. An oil lamp and a jar of oil sit on a small table. Three sides of the room are stacked with metal containers from floor to ceiling. In some places, the containers are two deep and four high. They appear to be exactly the same as those in the blue box, only much bigger.

"Take a look at the floor where the beds are." "Faint footprints under a layer of dust. They certainly do not look recent," Raine comments as her keen eyes study the prints leading from the bed to the table, then to the door and back again. "We are not the only ones down here," she comments. 'The footprints are boots, but not the kind we wear. Who could have been living here?' she wonders to herself. Could it be the It-Ha perchance?

 Bryzon suggests that it is probably safer to be on the beach than in the shelter while they decide what to do. They walk back, sit on the soft black sand, and pass the leftover food around. Nedai is the only one with a timepiece and takes it upon himself to reveal that it is already two hours past midday. When they finish their meagre meal, they return to the cabin to explore the contents of the boxes. Raine hands out several Ellpa fruits that she has kept hidden until now, thankfully making her pack much lighter.

"Rai, you are my hero," Leyashe says as he takes the fruit handed to him.

"I thought I would save them as a surprise. You see, you should always be good to your sister," she jokes. "I noticed fruit on one of the trees when we walked towards the cabin." They look similar to Ellpa, but they are white like everything else down here. Do you think they would be safe to eat, brother?" she asks.

"As long as they taste good, I do not see why not," he answers her. "But I would like to taste them first," he quips as if now an authority on all things white. Raine and Bryzon look at each other. He winks at her, and she smiles as they enjoy her brother's newly gained confidence.

Safety becomes an issue, and Krom, Remek, and Sayhran volunteer to be the sentries. Nedai and Leyashe promise to swap places with their cousins shortly as they follow Bryzon, Raine, and Rence into the cabin. Raine whispers to Krom about the Tenlegs and he nods.

Leyashe lifts the first container, and when Rence tries to move the box closer, he is shocked that he does not have the strength to lift it alone, and Leyashe jumps in to help.

"This thing is heavy. I am sure it does not have books or charts in it," flexing his fingers to encourage the circulation back into them. "It is like there are rocks inside," Rence complains. You are really strong, Leyashe," he adds, a bit baffled.

Her brother's sudden strength does not go unnoticed by Raine.

"It is true, sister, my strength has increased. I think it is the cavern. Do you feel any different?" he 'mind-speaks' to her. "Maybe you are stronger too. You should lift something heavy, Rai," he suggests. Thankful that Rence could not hear the conversation between her and her brother, Raine decides to save her strength test for later.

They are unprepared for what they find when they lift the lid off the first container. Inside the box are at least twenty weapons. This time, it is Leyashe who lets out a long, whispered whistle. Bryzon studies the contents for a few seconds before slowly revealing his thoughts.

"Earthling weapons, why did Jon not tell us of this? So many dead; these weapons could have saved them and freed us from the Eslaf." Bryzon puts his hand to his chin, cupping it between his forefinger and thumb. He looks up at the roof and shakes his head, his eyes shiny. He quickly wipes away the tears for his twin brother, Dayson. 'Jon King deceived us all,' he thinks to himself.

"Maybe they do not work. Perhaps there is no ammunition, or something!" Nedai exclaims as his hands demonstrate that he is at a loss at what he is seeing, at the same time trying to justify his great grandfather's actions.

"I think not," Bryzon says, sounding angry as he lifts out one of the weapons. He tries to figure out how it works by turning it around in his hands and running his fingers over a row of buttons, careful not to press down on any of them.

"How did he manage to take it all off their ships before the It-Ha destroyed them?" Bryzon asks, confused, but he knows that only High It-Ha Layrrah can give him the answer he seeks. Then, in the quiet of the room, a row of buttons beep on the weapon in Bryzon's hands. The buttons on the long gun turn red in succession and then green. A soft scratching, then a soft whirring sound follows. Bryzon puts the cold weapon down immediately. He looks at it as if it is about to bite him. A few seconds later, the row of lights on the barrel turned red and then off.

"Right, ok," he says, clearing his throat. "What was that? Does the weapon know when it is being handled?" he asks. He gets no response. Everyone is as shocked as he is at what they have discovered.

Bryzon waits a minute while he thinks things through before picking up the weapon again. This time, it only takes a few seconds before he understands. It is being activated by the warmth of his hands, of that he is certain. Bryzon is unaware that the weapon, designed by Frederick King, will only read a human hand. He twists and turns the weapon, looking for a chamber for ammunition, but there is none that he can see.

Bryzon recalls a conversation with Jon about MagnoA. The energy source that Frederick King had developed operated everything on their spaceships. He is sure the weapons must work on the same principle. These guns had endless power.

"These weapons are far more advanced than the Eslaf Nobrac," Bryzon says under his breath. "The only difference is that the Eslaf weapon can kill Xennes."

They decide to call in Krom, Remek, and Sayhran. Now that they have guns, there is no need for anyone to guard the door.

"So, the power that makes these weapons fire is more capable than Zraphite?" Krom asks, sounding a bit confused.

"If I understood your great greatfather correctly, the answer is yes," Bryzon confirms as he stares at the killing machine in his hands.

Sayhran and Nedai seem to have teamed up as they discuss what might have stopped Jon King from sharing this huge secret with the Xennes leaders of the colonies. Nedai is finding it difficult to understand his great-grandfather's decisions.

Raine interrupts their conversation. "Our biggest question should be, who left the footprints? Whoever it was helped Grandfather Jon keep his secret."

Just as if someone hit him over the head, Bryzon suddenly knows the answer to one of the questions. "Nick King!" he says aloud.

Sayhran puts her palms to her cheeks. "Of course, that is it, Bry," she exclaims, her mind racing. She, too, knows exactly why everything has remained a secret for so long.

Bryzon paces up and down in the cabin, rubbing his forehead as if willing his mind to remember.

"I thought we would be able to speak to Nick the following morning, but he passed during the night," he says and clicks his tongue. His rambling is confusing the young people looking up at him. "I knew he had something to share. He was going to tell me about the cavern. I always thought he wanted only to bid me farewell," he rambles on before turning to look at everyone, his eyes wide. He has solved the mystery. The memory of Nick lying in his bed comes flooding back to him.

"If only I returned to Rednos sooner," Bryzon says, looking at Sayhran as he takes a large breath to relieve the tight feeling of regret that overwhelms him.

"We would have stood a chance during the uprising if we had these weapons," he repeats. "I should have left immediately. I should have walked," Bryzon keeps repeating, shaking his head in disbelief at what occurred all those years ago.

Bryzon thinks of It-Ha Layrrah. She was there; Nick King could have told her. Is it possible she knew of this place below Kearthat? Bryzon feels confused about his feelings towards Jon King and the only remaining High It-Ha. Did they just sit back and watch as people died after the invasion? There had to be an explanation.

"We are here now. We have solved some of the mystery and must continue our search," Raine suggests, trying to relieve the tension that seems to have taken over the room.

Remek takes out a weapon for each of them. No one objects as he hands them out. After carefully watching Bryzon earlier, he gives everyone an impromptu lesson on how to work the long guns.

"I think we should sleep here tonight," Nedai suggests and is pleased to find that no one objects.

Remek closes the lid on the box containing the weapons. He and Rence move it to the other end of the room as Krom reaches for the next one to open. The next twenty boxes reveal weapons of the same kind. A quick count comes from Leyashe. "There are about three hundred weapons so far, and who knows how many are in the unopened boxes? We can without doubt show the Eslaf who the masters of Kearthat are now," he boasts pointing his weapon towards the door while mimicking firing noises.

Raine watches her brother and sees the little boy with a wooden gun pretending to annihilate the Eslaf under their big Trigga tree. As if she is suddenly very cold, a shiver runs through Raine. Leyashe turns to look at his sister. He nods and so does she. They know their lives are about to change; they can feel it.

They keep opening containers until Sayhran protests; they all need sleep. The count is over six hundred weapons when they decide to split the group. Raine refuses Sayhran's offer to be part of sentry duty. They would take turns to sleep.

When Sayhran protests, Leyashe cuts in. "It is best never to disagree with Rai," Leyashe quips with a smile. Just do as the lady Overseer tells you," he jokes. Raine lunges at him, and he ducks, anticipating the playful strike from his sister, but she is too quick.

Bryzon, Raine, and Remek continue opening containers as quietly as possible, re-stacking the opened boxes against the wall on the other side of the room. They are almost at the end of the first wall of containers when they open one, which, to their surprise, contains handguns.

"There must be fifty in here," Remek comments with a quiet whistle.

"I still cannot believe these have been here all this time," Bryzon says, shaking his head again. Sighing, he paces up and down to stretch his legs while his mind goes back and forth about Jon. Never could he have dreamed that the earthling would ever deceive him.

It is evident to Raine that the hours have not quelled Bryzon's disappointment in her grandfather. 'Could he possibly have had a good enough reason to withhold this from the Drennan?' she wonders.

The next fifteen boxes uncover yet more handguns.

We have the weapons we need to kill them all," Raine says quietly, her statement hate-filled, the conviction in her voice very real.

The last six containers yield the biggest surprise. In them, they find round balls no bigger than the size of a small Ellpa fruit. Each of them has a pin through the middle, and each ball displays a tiny red tag that reads; EXPLOSIVE - DO NOT REMOVE PIN UNTIL READY – FOUR SECOND DELAY – THROW IMMEDIATELY AFTER WITHDRAWING PIN TO AVOID DEATH OR INJURY.

Remek carefully picks one up, "They are so heavy. They are balls of fire," he decides correctly. "It is their weight that will allow them to be accurate."

"You are right, Remek," Bryzon says, smiling at his nephew. "I remember Jon telling me about something similar. He said earthlings used them during their many wars. You pull the pin and then launch them towards the enemy, but it must be done quickly before it explodes in your hand."

"These will come in very handy," The wicked look of jovial revenge on Remek's face expresses what everyone is thinking. They all revel in the thought of their revenge against the Eslaf. Their final count on the fireballs ends with a tally of one thousand eight hundred.

"It is almost time to wake the sleeping heads," Remek says, yawning.

Nedai promises to keep track of time while Bryzon calls Leyashe to sit next to him. He tells his nephew what they have discovered and makes him promise that none of them will touch the grenades. As Bryzon closes his eyes, his mind shuts off and sleep overwhelms him.

Before Raine drifts into slumber, Leyashe enters Raine's mind and asks her if she is blown away yet by the discovery.

"Yes, brother, I am indeed blown away. Now leave me to rest." She hears him chuckle, and she cannot help but smile at her brother's playful revenge. 'I deserved this one,' she tells herself.

Chapter 36 - The Yraif

The cabin door opens with just a slight scraping noise, and Raine leaps to her feet, her short sword swiftly appearing in her hand. She had completely forgotten about the long-gun within an arm's reach. Bryzon is ripped from his slumber, but it takes him only a few moments to point a weapon towards the door.

 A slender man with a bow and arrow in his hands stands in the doorway. Although readied, the bow is lowered. His long, straight, white hair flows down well below his shoulders. He is dressed in a tunic made of fine fabric. His brown leather boots are knee-high, and he wears a cape that drapes from one shoulder. Holding the cape in place on one shoulder is a clasp depicting a gold moth. The moth glints as the flicker of the lamplight plays on the shiny bauble.

In mere seconds, Raine has assessed that the intruder's face shows no aggression. He is unusually pale, his eyes display an odd sparkle as he turns his head, and Raine finds the shimmer in his gaze distracting. Next, she tries to make out the mysterious symbols that are etched on his forehead. Then she notices that his boots have soft soles. She sucks in her breath. She and her family are the imposters.

The white-haired visitor lowers his bow further and smiles.

"Are you the greatson of Jon King, the son of Nick King?" he asks, as his eyes firmly lock onto Nedai's light blue eyes.

The epic silence that follows prompts Raine to poke her Rednos cousin on the arm, bringing him out of his apparent stupor.

"Nedai, he is talking to you," Raine says, nudging him again.

"Me? Yes," Nedai answers, sounding confused as he stumbles over his speech, making him appear simple-minded.

This reaction triggers the pale man to repeat his question, "Are you the greatson of Jon King?" This time, his voice is a little louder but not hostile.

"Yes... No, I am his great greatson," Nedai corrects, wide-eyed. The answer somehow has the required effect. The stranger immediately bends his one knee to put his bow and arrow on the floor beside him. While keeping his eyes on the group, he raises his hands in the air as a sign of surrender.

"No weapons, please. I welcome you to The Below descendants of Jon King. We have waited many years," he declares.

Bryzon looks around, lowering his weapon slowly, indicating to Krom and Remek to follow his example, but Remek appears hesitant.

"Please, if you are the family of Jon King, then I am your friend. You can put the weapons down; there is no danger," the man assures them in a soft, even voice.

Remek looks at Bryzon. Bryzon signals him to put down the gun and he obeys hesitantly.

"Thank you," the stranger says, sounding sincere.

"I am Nor~han, leader of the Yraif of Lan-igiro, he says, bowing his head. He gets no reaction; they are stunned into silence.

"You are a Yraif?" Bryzon finally manages.

"Yes, I am the leader of the Yraif, the strange man with the white hair confirms.

"We were taught that your people had all died thousands of years ago," Bryzon states, dumbfounded.

I am not alone. I have brought with me some of the men and women of the Yraif Assembly. The Yraif leader goes on to confess to the group that he and his contingent have been following Bryzon and his family since they first entered the cavern from what he calls The Above."

"We were waiting to understand your true intentions," Nor~han admits.

The white-haired man moves forward two steps, and four men and a female Yraif file into the room behind him. They all look similar, their faces young, their hair white and long, their eyes shimmering, their ears slightly pointed. The Yraif silently nod a greeting towards the group in perfect unison as they line up next to their leader.

Nor~han introduces his Assembly, and Raine knows immediately that they will have difficulty recalling the strange-sounding names.

"I present my brother Ju~neh, this is Ae~ranh...," and so Nor~han continues until all are presented. Bryzon follows by introducing his family and Rence. Then, an awkward silence ensues. This lull inspires Bryzon to break the silence by stating a fact already established.

"So you are the Yraif?" he foolishly utters.

Nor~han seems unfazed and answers just as if it were the first time he has been asked the question.

"We are. Only three-hundred and four remain of our people," he reveals, then asks if they may sit.

"It is your cabin," Bryzon says, not sure if his answer sounded as if he said, "Sit if you like, it is your cabin," or if he meant, "This is your cabin," again sounding a little foolish.

"Of course, why do we not all sit," Raine offers as she tries to put an end to the uncomfortable, almost comical situation. By the time a circle formed in the middle of the room, many male throats had been cleared, and Raine is sure that this moment is the strangest she has ever felt in all of her life

"We are happy you have recognized the imminent danger. We were not sure how long it would be before you came Below after Leyashe was led to the cavern," the conversation becoming more and more bizarre as the Yraif continues.

"When the great storm came so soon after the last shudder, we knew that talks would have to begin as a matter of urgency. Last night, I sent word to It-Ha Layrrah and our friend from The Above to advise them that our High Yraif had received a message from The Order to hasten our plans. We do not have long to prepare, ..." Nor~han begins to say, but Bryzon raises his hand and the Yraif stops in mid-sentence.

"I wish you to know that we do not understand what you are trying to tell us," Bryzon informs the man with the odd ears.

"We need to ask questions of you?" Bryzon sighs in between his words as he requests to be heard. "Why is it urgent that we leave Kearthat? We have the means to fight the Eslaf now; weapons that will win us back our freedom."

Nor~han raises his hands, palms towards Bryzon, and then he lowers them slowly. It is a gesture that implies that he understands, but Bryzon keeps talking.

"I am sure all of us are wondering who your friend is from the Freelands. Why has the It-Ha not shown her face? Where is she, and what is this order you speak of?" All of this we need to know first," Bryzon insists, almost breathless he huffs loudly.

"I will answer all that you query," the leader offers, his voice calm. Raine wonders if it is the Yraif's way to soothe Bryzon, whose voice has risen considerably.

While Raine has noticed the impatience on Bryzon's face, Sayhran sits quietly. Raine can see Sayhran is mesmerized by the Yraif man; she is fixated on Nor~han's face.

"The magma from deep below is making its way close to the surface, even here where we sit right now," the Yraif explains, pointing down to the cabin's floor. "The anger we thought to be asleep has been awakening for many years. When it breaks through, it will fill Kearthat with fire. Ante Mountain's fury will be unlike Lan~Igiro has ever known."

"The High Yraif foretells that all of Kearthat will be lost. All that exists will be destroyed." Nor~han inhales, his face sullen as he waits for a reaction. But there is none. Bryzon and his family are astounded at what they are hearing.

Leyashe and Raine look at each other as the Yraif tells them of the impending demise of Kearthat. It all sounds so surreal.

"In answer to your second question, Bryzon, you have indeed found the weapons that the earthling leader left for us to safeguard, but these weapons will not serve our purpose. Much must be prepared, and we will talk in great detail about this. We will all be leaving this sphere in a few weeks; there is no other way."

"How …?" Bryzon starts to say, but the Yraif asks him to be patient.

What Nor~han tells them next makes Bryzon feel as if he has been slapped hard across the face.

"We have been keeping the two earthling ships in good order as we waited for this day to come. It has been our honour, and now we extend this honour to The Selected."

"My grandfather's spaceships? Where are they?" Leyashe asks, sounding almost disrespectful.

"Yes, young Leyashe, greatson of Jon King, we have taken care of the earthling spaceships for many years. They are ready. The time to leave Lan~Igiro is upon us."

"This means that we will finally be free of the Eslaf?" Sayhran asks, seemingly the only one who understands what Nor~han is trying to convey.

"Our punishment has been great, woman of Keazan. We will fight for freedom if we must; we cannot allow the Eslaf to stop us from leaving. If we fail, we will perish in the great fire that is coming."

"You … knew Keazan?" Sayhran utters, adding to the list of silly questions asked thus far.

"No, gentle woman, it is the High It-Ha Layrrah who spoke many times to us of the brave men who died in the short war between the Eslaf and the Xennes men of Kearthat."

"There is much planning before we can escape to safety. Decisions must be made. It is time to proceed to Telmah. Our home is far. We must leave soon," the Yraif tells them without asking anyone if they want to accompany him to his home.

"So you are saying that the shakes will destroy Kearthat this time?" Remek echoes.

"Yes, that is what he is saying, Remek," Raine replies before Nor~han can answer. She shakes her head at her cousin and turns away, rolling her eyes as she recounts the total number of silly things asked by her family thus far. The score is four, 'but the day is young yet,' she thinks.

"When we reach Telmah, I will tell you everything you wish to know, but come, we must go now," Nor~han insists.

"So we have time to prepare before we must leave Kearthat?" Bryzon asks, looking at the Yraif.

"No, my friend, there is little time. We have less than fifty days."

Nor~han's comment is alarming. It is as if they are unable to comprehend it all. The whereabouts of the It-Ha' remains unanswered while the group mulls over the Yraif's words. There are suddenly too many things to occupy their minds.

'Is this a wonderful dream, or is it a nightmare' Raine asks herself?' Her brother hears her thoughts. They look at each other and Leyashe shrugs his shoulders.

"I need to ask the question that everyone has ignored, please," Nedai pleads when Nor~han stands to exit the room.

"You may speak, young Jon," but Nedai is quick to correct Nor~han.

"My name is Nedai, I have my own name," he says, trying to sound as polite as possible.

The Yraif repeats Nedai's name softly several times as if imprinting it on his tongue before he lets Nedai continue.

"Where are the ships kept?"

"They are where no one would look; they wait inside Ante Mountain," Nor~han answers, and Raine swears she notices just an inkling of a smile on the Yraif's face.

"Where have the Yraif been? So many years passed before the invasion. Why have you not shown yourselves?" Bryzon asks bluntly.

"I will go back to when the Drennan came to Lan-Igiro. Our people knew that the Mountain was angry. We hid across the ocean in your city of Kuldab when it showed its fury. With the help of your Supreme Council, many Yraif and Drennan survived." This bit of information confounds Bryzon. Why on Kearthat would his parents not have told him and Dayson that the Drennan had hidden the Yraif when Ante erupted? Their greatparents must have retold their story. There had to have been texts stored under the council building in Seccus. Why was it kept secret?

"After discovering that Ante Mountain's anger had created these caverns, our Ancient One made a cruel decision. Our leader, Ore~itna, chose that we would live underground. We will never understand his reasoning. When Ore~itna's powers were taken and he was banished from The Below, we had already built Telmah. We had become used to the ways of the caverns. We remained."

"Why was he banished?" Remek asks.

"It is a story for another time Remek, son of Keazan," the Yraif offers. To Raine it is obvious the Yraif leader finds her cousin's question irrelevant in the current situation, yet he had been courteous, almost gentle, when replying to Remek.

"Our elders, yours and mine decided to use the gift of long life unwisely, Bryzon. Our High-Yraif Laathria has felt your disillusionment. You are wise in your decision to correct the harm they have done. We, too, wish more than anything to be free of the darkness. We are people of the forest; we long to live that way again." Nor~han goes silent and sighs. To Raine, it appears as if the Yraif has just unloaded a burden he has carried for a long time and she too wonders why their leader of old was banished."

"Jon King and It-Ha Layrrah did not pick the locations of the colonies. They were instructed by us to build them near the entrances to The Below. The cavern that brought you here today is one of two. There was no good reason for us to reveal ourselves. We, and those of The Above, had much to lose, as you will soon learn."

"You mean to say there is another entrance?" Leyashe asks, shocked at this information. Raine's list grows as she adds Leyashe's name to the silly questions list.

"Yes, my young friend, you will soon learn where it is."

The surprises keep coming. The Yraif leader looks so young, but Raine is sure he is older by many decades or perhaps hundreds of years, and she is certain that he has many more secrets to divulge.

"We must proceed, Telmah is far, and time is dwindling. I have much to show you when we get there. Let us hurry."

At the beach, there are two boats moored. Nor~han walks over to Rain and Leyashe and places a hand on each of their shoulders.

"I give you my vow of friendship. My people and I are at your service. The earthling ships are now yours. You are The Selected." His palms emit an orange, pinkish glow, and for a moment, the siblings feel a surge of energy go through them.

"Thank you," is all Raine manages to stammer before Nor~han steps back. He bows his head and turns to give his assembly members orders, and soon the boats are in the water.

"Do you think we need the weapons?" Remek asks Bryzon, but it is Raine that answers the question.

"I think not. We have a man who possesses magic to take care of us," she says with a smile.

"We will pick some up on our way back," Bryzon suggests. The strange occurrence between Nor~han, Raine and Leyashe in all the rush remains a topic to be discussed later.

Suddenly, they hear a noise nearby that is familiar to Leyashe. It is Ae~ranh, the female Yraif, the youngest, or so Raine thinks. She is standing on the beach next to a beautiful white Inop.

 It looks in every way like those found on the Freelands, but for the fact it is white. The Inop's long mane almost touches the ground, the horns running down its forehead no longer straight, divulging that it had been an adult for some time.

"You came here on the Inop," Leyashe asks the Yraif girl.

"That is so," Ae~ranh confirms.

"It is a magnificent animal," Leyashe compliments as he pats the animal's smooth coat. Ae~ranh begins to unfasten the leather straps around the Inop's head and chest.

"You are letting him go free?" Rain asks.

"Do not be concerned, Es~Roh will find his way back to Telmah without me," the young girl assures her.

Brother and sister watch as Ae~rahn whispers something in Es-Roh's ear. The animal rears, neighs and then gallops into the dark. It's long mane waves in the wind that its speed creates. The Inop changes into thousands of beautiful sparkles as it enters the darkness. The magic of The Below does not cease to amaze.

Overwhelmed by the sights, everyone is mostly silent. The Below and its secrets have tired their racing minds as the group attempts to put the surreal world around them into perspective. Raine and Leyashe's eyes are no longer an oddity to their family as they flicker on and off. For now, the siblings forget they look different.

Raine notices that Leyashe glances in Ae-ranh's direction several times. She hopes her brother will consider that the young girl could be decades older than he may think.

A creature, once again remarkably like an Eninac, lays quite still between the shrubs on the riverside. It has black eyes and small, hornlike protrusions running from the top of its head down its back. It is so strange that it draws almost everyone's attention, but for the Yraif who keep rowing, obviously accustomed to the strange-looking creatures.

Later, when they encounter strange long-legged water birds, Leyashe notices the birds have no wings at all and he is enthralled. The large, flat beaks of the wingless birds make them look quite funny, and Remek laughs aloud as he points at the strange spectacle. Like most of the other creatures of The Below, the peculiar-looking birds show no fear as the boats glide past them.

Leyashe is intrigued when he notices white slithering creatures that are following alongside the boat. He points them out to Raine as he leans closer to the water to get a better look. A cross between a fish and the slithering Ekans found in the Elin River, they have long, feathery bits all along their spine making them unique.

Leyashe asks Nor~han whether they are dangerous.

"They cannot kill a man. We call them Rek~cus," he tells Leyashe. "They will follow the boat for a time but then return to their dark world. We have never discovered their reasoning," the Yraif reveals, returning to his rowing.

Leyashe puts his right hand into the water. Before Raine can tell him she does not think it is a good idea, a Rek~cus wraps itself around her brother's arm. Raine lets out a loud shout that has Nor~han dropping his oar into the boat and rushing to Leyashe's aid.

Just as he had done earlier, the Yraif puts his palms on the creature, which is tightly wrapped up to the top of Leyashe's armpit. This time, a red glow emanates from Nor~han's hands, and the Rek~cus drops back into the water and slither-swims away.

"Perhaps, greatson of Jon King, it is safer not to challenge the blood-sucking Rek~cus of the Nut~ca River."

"I agree," Leyashe says sheepishly, quickly adding, "Thank you."

There is silence while Leyashe checks his arm for damage. He finds he has escaped without much injury. There is a small trickle of blood where the creature started sucking on the soft skin of his inner upper arm. Leyashe wipes it off quickly as if to rid himself of his stupidity.

"Are you recovered, brother?" Raine asks, breaking the silence in her brother's head, and Leyashe nods.

"He did say they will not kill you, Ash. He just forgot that they harmlessly want to suck your blood for a little while." Raine giggles and her brother's cheeks redden.

"I always thought the Yraif were a myth. It is truly remarkable. Almost as if we will soon awaken from this dream," Raine tells her brother, feeling bad about teasing him and regretful that she has embarrassed him.

"I agree with you, sister," Leyashe answers, eager to forget the incident with the Rek~cus.

After about two hours, Bryzon leans forward and offers to take the oars from Ae~rahn, but the Yraif girl waves him away.

"Oops," Leyashe whispers, smiling at Bryzon. "I think you just offended her." Bryzon raises his eyebrows and shrugs his shoulders.

Three hours into the journey, it becomes considerably lighter, almost to the point that the torches can be extinguished. A few minutes later, Nor~han and his men stop rowing. The Yraif leader produces a large conch shell from a leather bag and blows on it several times.

"We have arrived at my home, my friends. We are now inside Ante Mountain. We will go and see the spaceships soon, but first, we will eat.

The Yraif expertly manoeuvre the boats to the shore, and as if out of nowhere, Yraif men, women, and children appear.

"How adorable the children are," Sayhran whispers to Raine.

Remek jumps into the few inches of water and stretches out his arms to Sayhran, carrying her to shore. Rence does not offer his arm to Raine this time, and she selfishly feels a little let down as she jumps into the shallow water, drenching her boots.

The people on the beach move back when they notice strangers. Nor~han holds his arms up in the air, silencing them. In the Yraif tongue, Nor~han talks to his people calmly. Jon King's name is heard several times as Nor~han points first to Nedai and then to the rest of them. It does not take long before the serious Yraif faces turn to smiles.

Nor~han and Bryzon walk side by side when they leave the beach, and Raine can hear him asking questions.

They follow a path that runs alongside the river.

Raine tries to think back to how long it has been since they left the blue box, but it is as if time itself has become distorted. She spots a young girl about her age who has been by her side since leaving the river. The girl smiles often, her eyes twinkling as she quietly studies Raine and Sayhran.

 When they exit the short walk through the trees, they find themselves in a cavern that Leyashe calculates to be the size of at least four colonies. To the left, a village is built into the side of the rock; to the right, fields of crops stretch as far as the eye can see. Beyond that, it is black with distant sparkles.

Remek whistles as he stares at the enormity of it all. The best is yet to be realized when they look up. A sliver of sky peeks through the top of the mountain. The natural light that meets their eyes runs the entire length of one side of the rim of Ante Mountain. An overhang from the eruption thousands of years ago has moulded the top of mountain so uniquely that it lets in the light from above without exposing the hollow expanse below.

Bryzon looks around, "How is this possible? At this angle, no one from above could ever see into the mountain, incredible,… unbelievable. Rai, we flew over The High Mountains many times? And from above, at any angle, the mountain appears solid. We believed that the hole where lava once escaped had closed itself," Bryzon tells his niece.

It was indeed an ideal place to hide from the outside world and keep secret the whereabouts of the earthling spaceships. A fine place to hide if you are the High It-Ha Layrrah!

"Jon King and Jean Bouchard were brave to bring the spaceships through the opening. It looks almost too small for such a large craft. Without the It-Ha, this would never have been possible," Nor~han expresses. "You see the dark beyond the fields? It is where the ships are. It is a long way to walk, so we shall return to the boats to use the river, but first, we eat. Come, follow me, my friends."

Everyone is enamoured by the village built precariously amongst the giant rock ledges. Minding their footing, they follow Nor~han. They cross narrow bridges and climb steep stairs carved out of the solid rock that lead up to where quaint houses with pointy roofs are nestled precariously. Some of the homes have small gardens, and a sensation of serenity overcomes Sayhran as she takes in the intricately carved wooden trellises surrounding each dwelling. Smiling faces greet them from doorways and windows as they follow Nor~han.

The higher they climb, the clearer the sound of rushing water.

"Where is the sound of the water coming from? Is it a waterfall?" Leyashe asks Nor~han.

"Beyond our village on the way to the spaceships, you will see it soon. The waterfall drops many hundreds of feet into the abyss. We will leave the river before we reach its edge," the Yraif reassures.

Leyashe is pleased that his first inclination, which is that the river of The Below ran in the opposite direction to the Elin River above, is correct. The waterfall had just confirmed this. His mind, however, dwells on what lies below the raging water. Where does the water go? A mystery he knows may never be explained.

The cottage is inviting when they reach their destination. A huge wooden table and several chairs take up the centre of the first room. Raine notices two doors leading off the main room and she steps forward to peek into one. There are several beds and a small table in each. The blankets and pillows are invitingly, and serenely colourful. The cosiness of it all has her imagining what it will feel like when she can finally rest.

"Jon lived here when they came to work and talk with It-Ha Layrrah. Sit, my friends, sit," the Yraif invites.

The words echo in Bryzon's head like a chiming bell as he tries to envision Jon sitting at this very table. Then, his thoughts go to the weapons left behind in the cabin beside the river. Would he ever be able to forgive the earthling?

"How was Grandfather Jon able to leave Rednos Colony without being caught by the Eslaf," Remek asks. "How come no one ever noticed his absence?"

"It-Ha Layrrah and the High Yraif Laathria cast the enchantment of The Veil. They came unnoticed, and many excuses were used for his absences from the colony," Nor~han says casually, as if lies were a common practice among the Yraif.

"But when your Greatmother Farron passed, it became more difficult to keep up with the deceit," Nor~han divulges.

Yraif men and women enter through the door; their arms are laden with bowls of food and fruit. The fragrant smell of thinly sliced fried Gip grabs everyone's attention. It is a feast compared to what they are used to.

"Eat, my friends," Nor~han quips. "When we are satisfied, we will go to see the spaceships."

The men and Ae~rahn of the Yraif Assembly arrive to join the group at the table. "We apologize we are late to the table," Ju~neh says, bowing his head to his leader.

"I will introduce you to the Assembly again and tell you their position," Nor~han announces. Raine knows that the Yraif leader had recognized their confusion earlier in the day. Now, he was skillfully disguising that he knew of their dilemma by feigning to reveal the positions of his Assembly. Nor~han was clever, something Raine added to her mental notes on the Yraif leader.

"My brother, Ju~neh, and one of my advisors," Nor~han begins.

Raine studies the fine-featured young man. Two thin braids adorn each side of his head while the rest of his hair hangs below his shoulders. He appears to be much younger than his brother. The colour of his eyes in the light is that of the ferocious large cat-like creature known as a Reggit on Kearthat; they are a pale yellow. When he moves his head, they shimmer as shadows pass over them.

"This is Va~had. He deals with matters related to Telmah's crops and many other affairs" Nor~han does not clarify what the other affairs may be. With a much sterner face, Va~had smiles but not for long, and Raine decides that he is perhaps the oldest in years of all of them.

"This is Ter~rok," he points to a young man who looks Remek's age, slight in build and by far the gentlest in appearance of all the men. The young man's status is not divulged, and no one asks. When Ter~rok smiles, Raine notices that he has two shiny stones embedded in his front teeth.

"This is Zoh~ren, my old friend. He is Guardian to the High Yraif Laathria." Raine notices a gold ring on Zoh~ren's left hand. On top of his hands are runes, the fine lines displaying half of a moth on each. Zoh~ren has unusual light-green eyes in the light. They remind her of the colour of the water in the Elin River. He is the only one who carries a dagger on his belt; its hilt is engraved with a pattern that she cannot discern from where she is sitting.

"And Ae~ranh, the youngest of our Assembly. She does not yet hold a title in the Assembly and will not until she is proven," the Yraif leader says, smiling. Ae-rahn's cheeks redden and Leyashe feels a little sorry for the girl without a title. His first Yraif friend who loves the white Inop of The Below.

"You like Ae~rahn," Raine says, cutting into Leyashe's thoughts.

"She likes Inop, and I like Inop," he insists matter-of-factly, and Raine smiles.

On cue, Sayhran whispers, "It is so difficult to tell how old they are."

"Yes, they seem almost too young to be in charge of anything," Raine agrees with Sayhran.

Conversations start and stop while they eat. The food is delicious. Empty bowls lead to excitement, the anticipation of seeing the homeships very evident, and Nor~han excuses his Assembly to ready the boats.

They sail past many fields with ripening crops. There are large grassy areas where animals are grazing. They see several creatures they have never seen before, but it is the small white animals with long coats that touch the ground that hold Leyashe's interest.

"What are the fur-covered small white animals?" he asks, looking at Nor~han.

"They are Pa~esh. We harvest their coats to weave our tunics and other items. They are also flavoursome," Nor~han says with the barest hint of a smile.

Leyashe's questions do not cease as he asks about the dirt in the cavern. The answer is astonishing as Nor~han explains that the Yraif has been bringing in dirt from The Above, little bits at a time, for close to two thousand years.

Sayhran's gentle compassion immediately comes to the fore as she takes the Yraif leader's hand, telling Nor~han how sorry she is to hear of their suffering and the sacrifice he and his people have endured.

"You are a kind woman with a pure heart, earthling daughter of Jon and Farron King; good will seek you out. You, too, shall have a special place in my heart, as your father did." Sayhran feels her cheeks flush with this praise, but the Yraif appears unaware of her awkwardness.

As they sail downriver, Leyashe studies the cavern wall up ahead. It is much darker than the other walls of Telmah. When they get closer, he realises it is not a wall at all. It is an opening that leads from the cavern they are in. The entrance to this space is many hundreds of feet high. It is enormous.

As the Yraif steer the boats onto a narrow shore Leyashe can hear the waterfall and make out a huge outcrop of rocks on both sides of the river where the water plunges into the dark chasm. There is no spray coming from the cataract. This alone indicates that the leap the water makes must be a great distance. 'Where does it lead?' Leyashe's mind nags. 'If only he had time to explore,' he wishes with all of his existence.

Raine, to her chagrin, notices that Rence chooses to help the Yraif moor the boats instead of joining the group as they get ready to walk the rest of the way to the spaceships. 'It is your own fault,' she reminds herself and sighs, then quickly looks over at Leyashe to see if he may have read her mind. But Leyashe's mind is filled with the mystery of where the river goes after it plunges into the abyss, and she is relieved.

As they enter the second cave, leaving the waterfall and the fields behind them, the dark returns and only Raine and Leyashe can see ahead of them. Or so they think. Nor~han orders the men and women who accompanied them to go ahead and light torches along the way.

Raine can hear Leyashe talking to Krom and Remek about the huge eruption of Ante Mountain thousands of years ago that created the underground caverns, forming a perfect place to hide the homeships. "Nerves of steel, to get the angle just right …." her brother's voice trails on, and Raine is astonished at the insight they have gained about their grandfather in the last few hours.

"It feels like a dream, Rai. Kick me. Am I awake?" Leyashe asks jokingly as he catches up to Raine a few minutes later.

"Do not tempt me, brother," she says, smiling, feigning a kick in Leyashe's direction, which he playfully dodges. They both laugh, and when their eyes meet, it is as if they know at that very moment that they are happy for the first time in their lives.

The outline of the first spaceship comes into view and everyone stops to take in the sight.

"This is the best thing that I will ever see in my whole life," Remek announces, whistling as he twirls on his heel in a circle to demonstrate his delight.

"I have to agree with you, my friend," Rence says, supporting Remek's excitement.

"My mother is the most excited and happiest I have seen her," Krom tells Bryzon. "I thank the galaxies that she can now discover the life she was supposed to have. She is deserving."

"You are right, nephew. Our dignity will be ours once more. We will teach the Eslaf of Ludinia a hard lesson."

Memories come flooding back as Bryzon lays his eyes on the first spaceship. He remembers the first glimpse of it in the sky over Seccus. It was a sight to behold.

Before they board the first homeship, Nor~han requests everyone sit at one of the several long benches erected by the Yraif at the bottom of the towering craft. The benches look old; they must have been put here in the time when her grandfather came to Telmah, Raine decides.

"Before we enter, I wish to speak to you of certain matters," the Yraif tells them.

From where they sit, they can only see one of the enormous stanchions that hold up the huge spaceship. The rest of the metal giant soars into the great height of the cavern and across to a wall they can barely make out. A strange quiet comes over everyone as they wait for the Yraif to gather his thoughts.

"I know you have many questions, so I will tell you what I know." Nor~han's expression is suddenly serious. The group is silent as they hanker after any kind of detail at this juncture as Nor~han begins by telling them of The Accord between the Yraif and the elders of Kearthat; a pact that still holds fast they will discover.

To their astonishment, they learn that enchantments were woven into the agreement two thousand years ago that granted the It-Ha their powers. However, the spells also gave the eldest elder of the Supreme Council of Kearthat ultimate power over the It-Ha. The binding spells they are told would shatter if an It-Ha ever went against the wishes of the dominant Great Elder. After the invasion, this responsibility fell to Elder Moss.

Shocked, Bryzon now understands Elder Moss's behaviour.

It-Ha Layrrah, Nor~han continues, was forced to answer to the remaining Elder. Layrrah knew, that should she ever break the accord, she would lose her magic. She would lose her connection with The Order of Lanrete, and then she would finally cease to exist in any form. She was compelled to follow direction from Elder Moss.

Raine immediately raises her hand.

"I know what you wish to ask Raine daughter of Caite. You desire to know of Lanrete," Nor~han assumes.

Raine shakes her head, "Yes, but first, is it not true that the It-Ha broke The Accord by helping my grandfather hide the ships? Yet you say It-Ha Layrrah was forced to be obedient to Elder Moss? Why has Elder Moss deliberately watched as his people suffered? If he knew of you, the Yraif, this place and It-Ha Layrrah?"

Bryzon looks at Raine and smiles. She is a clever girl; nothing escaped her.

"Daughter of Dayson, you are wise to ask this. The answer is simple: Solaarr and Sihuun gave their existence to save Jon King's spaceships. Solaarr chose It-Ha Layrrah to be the guardian after they gave their lives. Solaarr and Sihuun purposely went against The Accord.

"The story of Moss goes back a long time," he tells them.

"Elder Moss was spurned by the Elder Council. They thought him an imposter when he took his father's seat at the table after his father passed to the next world. Moss's heart became hardened, and when he became Great Elder, he showed his malevolence towards all who crossed his path. Moss remains a great disappointment to The Order. 'The one we do not speak of' has communicated his displeasure; the Elder's punishment is forthcoming."

"Lanrete is the true home of the Yraif; it is beyond this realm. This realm, or universe as you call it, is one of three that are connected. We, as Yraif, have always believed there to be more realms beyond ours, but we are still to discover this. A gateway opens only every one hundred and seven years to Kearthat, to this universe where we find ourselves. We were not abandoned when the Eslaf attacked. 'The one we do not speak of' was unable to send our great force to Kearthat to battle the Eslaf. The Ya~zeld, as we call this gateway, was closed; they could not travel to this realm." Nor~han explains to the silent faces, and even larger eyes staring at him.

Learning that there are gateways between a multiverse was indeed mind-bending. The Drennan had not even been aware of the other inhabited planets in their galaxy before Kearthat was invaded, and now learning of other realms was quite unsettling.

Raine is quickly reminded of the reference to 'universes' in The Code to Freedom. The mysterious were all beginning to reveal themselves, one by one.

Leyashe raises his hand to speak, but Nor~han waves it down.

"I must continue, young Leyashe. You may direct your question later."

"Jon King knew he had to bide his time when Elder Moss warned It-Ha Layrrah of her obedience to The Accord. Afraid that the old man would wield his power to destroy her, Jon King, and the Yraif of Telmah suffered silently, and It-Ha Layrrah remained dutiful to the agreement as she watched the suffering Above. It was a difficult decision to make, and she became hardened, but hardened against only one."

They also learn from Nor~han that it was Great Elder Moss who chose to withhold the gift of long-life from the colonists, his bitterness knowing no bounds. The Yraif telling them that the It-Ha had tried many times to reason with the elder, but he refused to listen.

A glint from the hilt of Zoh-ren's dagger catches Raine's eye. She can now make out the design. The previously hidden inlay is that of a gold moth. On either side is a circle with a small dot in the centre; beside it is a triangle, containing a solid circle completing the rune.

"It is time to act and stand together," Nor~han continues. "Before Jon passed to the next world, he gave us the Code to Freedom that Farron had received from her visions. The High-Yraif Laathria gave me instructions to place it in the blue box in the cavern for The Selected to find. The moment Raine and Leyashe entered the cave and found this text, they were given the powers that gave them their place as the leaders of their people. We can now go home now," Nor~han declares, smiling for the first time since they met him.

Finally, they knew the story behind the blue box and its contents. Raine and Leyashe can feel the mysterious forces at work; spells old and new seem to be part of their lives now. As for Elder Moss, he deserved what was coming to him. What remained was the strange quote from Nor~han's last words. Who was the being that the Yraif do not speak of?

"The Selected?" Leyashe interrupts, "why us?" he blurts out.

"I am forbidden to reveal the reason. All that was asked of the Yraif of The Below has been accomplished, my friends. You are here. The time has come. The Drennan of Kearthat, the earthlings, and the Yraif of this mountain have endured much cruelty. We will leave this sphere for another, where we will be safe, where we can heal and begin our lives again. All will be revealed in time, young Leyashe."

Nor~han's words sound like a proclamation rather than a plan, but Raine and Leyashe agree. If Kearthat was going to end in a fiery death, it was time to leave, and now they had the means. Their only obstacle, the Eslaf!

Then, as if struck by lightning, Bryzon knows where Layrrah is.

"I know where she is; she is hiding in Temsik Colony."

"Yes, my friend, Layrrah has been hiding among her people for some time now." the Yraif leader confirms.

Bryzon shakes his head. Why had he not put it together when he was in Temsik Colony? He can remember the strange feeling he had. It had been as if something did not quite fit. Now, he knows it was the magic of High It-Ha Layrrah.

"You must understand that It-Ha Layrrah is innocent of any wrongdoing, Bryzon. She was following the direction of the Great Elder; she had only good in her heart for the Freelanders. All these years, waiting for the time when we would leave this sphere, the It-Ha has become powerful. Her ability to use The Inmo, *the eye* that sees all has grown. It-Ha Solaarr and It-Ha Sihuun passed onto It-Ha Layrrah what they could before they departed this world. This has enabled her to become stronger, beyond what was gifted to her when Yraif Laathria chose her pure heart so long ago.

"I will reveal that It-Ha Layrrah is on her way to Noitibma Colony. She has been granted permission to cast the spell she and the High Yraif had conjured. This will make null the binding spell cast when The Accord was created. Permission was granted by The Order a few hours ago. Elder Moss will no longer have the power to control The Inmo. 'The one we do not speak of' has been angered; his anger will be assuaged."

This statement from the Yraif leader is good news; Moss had always been frustratingly hard to deal with, and at best, he could be only described as a very unpleasant old man. He had, for many years, caused much disagreement between the leaders in the colonies. The truth about him is known, and it is truly unforgivable.

The Yraif changes the subject by addressing Bryzon. "You are known for your courage, Bryzon. It took much bravery to fight an enemy against whom you knew there would be only a slight possibility of success." Nor~han reminds him.

We must deceive our enslavers to their deaths if we are to survive. Bryzon, you must set aside the revenge you planned for the aliens and think anew."

Nor~han narrows his older, wiser eyes as he continues. "If we fail, we all die. Tricking the aliens to their demise will be the vengeance we all seek, my friends. Revenge for those who lost their lives to the cruelty of these beasts, and for Bryzon, it will be sweet vengeance for the death of his brother and others he loved."

"Two questions, Nor~han," Bryzon asks, looking at the Yraif leader. "Of course, Bryzon, brother of Dayson."

"Why did Jon not tell me about the weapons? We could have used them in the uprising?" he asks quietly, and Raine can see Bryzon seems a little defeated at all that he has learned to this point.

"Bryzon, you must recognize that a difficult decision had to be made. The weapons would have killed many Eslaf, but the outcome would not have changed. The weapons alone were not enough to take back Kearthat from the Eslaf. Revealing the spaceships would have taken away the chance you see before us now. The Eslaf outnumbered us in every way. Now, we have Kearthat's demise on our side. Lan~Igiro will help us defeat these beasts. They took our planet, now our sphere will take them to their deaths," Nor~han explains, putting his hand on Bryzon's shoulder. "I feel your loss, I understand your loss, I feel your pain," the Yraif adds.

"What will become of Moss?" Bryzon asks as if changing the subject.

"That will be up to The Selected," the Yraif tells them as he looks at Raine and Leyashe.

And just like that, the siblings discover they have been handed their first official task. They were expected to be leaders, to be in charge, and it felt strange. Their first charge will weigh heavily on them until they make their decision. The old man had been a tyrant, but he was old, very old, and neither they nor the elder could change what had already transpired.

Nor~han manipulates some buttons on a keypad on the spaceship's stanchion; a large bay door opens on the first level high above them, a flood of light emanating from the gaping hole. Suddenly, the semi-dark of the cavern disappears as the light reaches into the darkest recesses behind them. Little sparkles of Zraphite can be seen everywhere.

A walkway makes its way down. They back away, giving the enormous piece of metal extending towards them enough space. When it stops, they step onto a conveyor system on the edge of the wide walkway that propels them upward.

At the top, Nor~han inserts something into the panel to open another door. Remek nudges Leyashe. The key is a replica of the one that opened the trap door leading them to The Below.

Nor~han seems secure in his confidence as he selects another set of buttons. The door opens. They are astounded at the earthling craft they had no idea existed mere hours before. A loud hiss fills the air as the door slides closed behind them.

The Yraif moves on. Another press of a button opens a sliding door and they find themselves in a small room. When the doors close, they can feel the space propelling them up at great speed. Raine and Sayhran grip the rails that surround the little room. The sensation is strange but, at the same time, quite exhilarating as they experience their first elevator ride.

Stepping out, they look over the railing. There is a huge open bay below them. Looking down over the rail there are several fighter spacecraft lined up, evenly spaced from one another. Bryzon spots the two transporter-craft that Nor~han had spoken of during their meal. There are many other land vehicles. Some look similar to a Traxid but are much smaller. In the very last row, he notices several mini-craft, one of which had transported Jon King down to Kearthat all those years ago.

There are blue and grey containers stacked two and three high on two sides of the bay, confirming to the group where their blue box at the Trigga tree entrance came from. They are all quiet at first, their senses overwhelmed, but soon, the questions fired at Nor~han seem endless.

Raine notices Sayhran has gone quiet. Her thoughts are of her parents, who had lived on this same ship so many years ago.

Nedai walks over and takes his aunt's hand. She looks up at the boy; "this is where our family lived. You must be feeling so excited to see it?

I am," Nedia says to his Aunt Sayhran.

"I am too, nephew. If you really think about it, it was their planet for so long." Then he notices her eyes gloss over. Nedai gives Sayhran a brief hug and makes his escape, leaving Raine to deal with her tears. No one notices Nedai quickly wipe his own tears before he rejoins his cousins.

They follow Nor~han onto another elevator that hurtles them off to a section of the ship that reveals two more rows of fighter craft. Huge lettering on the metal beams above the bay reads BAY#2.

Leyashe and his cousins immediately see themselves as spaceship pilots, and Bryzon is unable to keep up with the questions being asked. The count of fighter craft is nine in each bay, which means there are thirty-six and four transporter ships between the two spaceships. It is not the Starfleet of old Kearthat, but it will do nicely.

"We Yraif do not understand all of the technology, Bryzon. You and your men and women of the long-ago Starfleet will have only a short time to learn all you must," he forewarns. Bryzon does not answer. He understands it is going to take a miracle to learn the earthling technology and manoeuvre the spaceships out from under Ante Mountain's hidden caverns.

The next two hours are spent moving from deck to deck of the giant craft. It is an extraordinary spaceship, and Bryzon knows they are beyond adequate but perhaps beyond comprehension. The more he sees, the more he becomes concerned they will almost certainly die on Kearthat. Suddenly his shoulders feel heavy with the burden of what is to come.

There are living quarters, facilities for eating, recreation, and many other comforts. When Remek touches a large screen and then picks up a small, elongated object with buttons, Nor~han reprimands him.

"Remek, son of Keazan, it is better to be patient than to be regretful," he tells him, and Sayhran's son immediately puts down the remote he is holding in his hand, the episode an invitation for his cousins to tease him.

Bryzon recognises that learning everything about the earthling homeships poses an enormous challenge to him and the small group of ex-KSF pilots. Only one engineer among the Drennan had survived the invasion. He starts making mental notes. There had to be enough men and women capable of conquering at least some of the complexities of Frederick King's creations.

Nor~han takes them to see two sections of the ship that contain row upon row of upright preservation pods. Leyashe is fascinated, telling everyone that once they are all Xennes, the pods could be used to extend their already long lives when they begin their mission to find a habitable planet. Leyashe not considering the Yraif-dominated Lanrete permanent destination as yet.

They enter a space allocated to food production. Already, row upon row of colourful, healthy plants fill the enormous area. Leyashe looks up at the sign on the wall. It reads, TERRA BAY#1. The Yraif reiterates that this is where the strength of the Yraif people lies, informing the group that it would be his responsibility and the honour of his people to continue food production on the spaceships.

Raine wonders if Nor~han knowingly left out the words 'until we reach Lanrete,' in his offer.

Nor~han takes them to see row upon row of refrigeration units. The Yraif have been very busy, the units are well stocked; Frederick King's genius seems unending, and Jon King's foresight to pass on the knowledge to the Yraif is invaluable.

Leyashe has seen the words Hy-Ox on pipes that run all along the walls of the ship, and he asks Nor~han for an explanation. They learn that Frederick King had developed a means to make water on the spaceships. Hy-Ox is water. Bryzon is again astonished that the Nor~han knows so much more than Bryzon had initially thought. Jon had indeed instructed the Yraif and Nor~han well.

The command deck at the front of the craft has everyone wide-eyed with apprehension. It overwhelms Bryzon, his challenge growing tenfold in less than ten seconds. The Command Deck of the massive craft consists of panel upon panel of intimidating screens, levers, and buttons. It is hard to imagine they could even begin to learn all this in five years, let alone fifty days.

Bryzon's turmoil is lessened when Nor~han leads them to a large room adjoining the command centre. There, they find hundreds of rows of flat metal drawers. The drawers are marked alphabetically and numerically, beginning with Assemblies – Power Distribution Schematics DWR #1," continuing until the last drawer that reads, Zero Gravity Indicators DWR #5057." Bryzon pulls open the nearest one. It reveals the drawings of one of the many working parts of the spaceship. It was going to be challenging, he was sure, but at least now they had something to reference.

Everyone's attention shifts to Leyashe when he turns on one of the computers in the room, which initiates a series of beeps, and the many screens on the walls around them come to life revealing that all the spaceship's information is available at the press of a button. Bryzon smiles from ear to ear. This is more like it.

On their way out, Raine's eye catches a glimpse of a large room. She stops to read the sign above the door. It reads, ARC ROOM and she is drawn like a magnet. She surveys the space. In the middle is the biggest table she has ever seen in her life. Surrounded by what seems to be close to thirty or more chairs. The table is highly polished and reminds her of the shine of water on a still day. Many chairs line the two walls closest to the giant table.

"This place must be the room where they gathered to discuss matters of great importance," she whispers. "I can feel it."

At the far end of the room is an area where a few comfortable chairs and small tables are laid out in groups of two and three. Under a huge round window, the height of at least three of her, is a bench. On the bench is a cheerfully patterned cushion depicting tiny Flutterbugs, pillows in the same fabric arranged on it.

Raine picks up one of the cushions and puts it to her nose. It smells of Mura flowers and honey. She immediately puts it down. How is it possible it smells so familiar, and then she knows? It is the smell of her mother's hair.

'Did Grandmother Farron teach her daughter Caite, her mother, to grind the Mura blooms, add a small amount of the oils of the Trigga tree leaves, and then mix it in with a small amount of freshly churned honey? Tears fill Raine's eyes as she feels the all too familiar burn in her chest. It was the hurt she felt each time she thought of her family, who had not lived long enough for her to get to know them.

Looking through the enormous window, she can only make out the dark grain of the cavern wall. It does not matter. Soon, they will be flying high up into the sky. From here, Raine will see what lies beyond Kearthat. The Arc Room feels like home. This is where she will come to contemplate, she decides. Here is where she will feel as if she has wings.

The door opens, so engrossed in her thoughts, Raine flinches. It is Leyashe, and his face is twisted into an annoyed scowl.

"Rai, what are you doing? You have everyone looking for you. Come, sister, we are going to the second spaceship. Hurry!" he says before turning on his heel.

They exit the gigantic spacecraft, leaving by the same means. As the group covers the distance, Bryzon turns to Rain, "Our people are not going to believe it to be real until they see it," he tells her, smiling at his niece.

Many things were falling into place. Raine and Leyashe had discovered they could block each other from their minds and do a kind of 'mind-knock' if they wanted to speak to each other. They can now also control their eyes in the dark, turning them off and on as they wish. They were learning to manipulate their abilities to their advantage. After trying only a few times to share visions, they are astonished. The 'mind-pictures,' as Leyashe decided to name them, were possible. The consequences were not that attractive, though, as each time they sent a vision, their pupils flickered back and forth from green to blue. The day was turning into one that was utterly spectacular.

PART III

Chapter 37 - The Liberators

The exit slides open, and a bright, sunny afternoon greets them. There is silence among the group as their eyes take time to adjust, their minds scattered after more than two days underground. To Raine, it suddenly feels like they have awoken from a very long dream.

Bryzon looks around, assessing the world above The Below, wondering what the next few weeks will hold. He feels his body tingling as it regenerates, and within minutes, he feels strong again. However, he is painfully aware that his family, including Rence, can feel the adverse effects of being underground.

Ignoring the sounds of birds, the buzzing of insects and their breathing, they listen and scan the sky in silence for the well-known sounds of Idlers and Eslaf craft. It is two hours after midday, and there is a slight breeze, but it neglects to cool the heat of the day.

Lack of sleep is affecting Sayhran, and she feels slightly disorientated.

"Did we dream it all?" Krom asks. He gets no answer to his question; everyone is engrossed in their thoughts and feelings.

"It is a good dream," Rence comments and Remek is the first to agree, his eyes bright, the ever-present smile on his face implying his glee at the adventure that awaits them.

Nedai expresses his concern about the late hour. They need to hurry, Rednos Colony is a long walk. They pick up their packs that hide the four weapons they decided to bring along. Against their better judgment, they had all voted in favour of taking the risk of sneaking the hand-guns into the colony. Nedai takes the lead, and in single file, they begin their journey. Soon, his father Marcus King, would learn of a place he would never have thought possible.

It does not take long for them to work up a thirst. The heat and the fast pace set by Nedai's stride are wearing on them and there are requests for a short break.

"We cannot rest for long. If we are late for the gate, we will be spending the night with the Night Creatures." No one comments on Nedai's words of warning. The strictly enforced laws imposed in the colonies are general knowledge. When the suns go down, the gates are locked.

Five minutes later, Nedai stands and picks up his pack. There is no objection.

On their way back from Telmah, Rence and the family had discussed what strategy would be best to relay what they had learned from Nor~han. Telling the people of Kearthat their home was about to become an inferno was going to be complicated.

Reaching the outer fields of crops near Rednos the weary group is met with a spectacular sight. Bright yellow Otatop root are in full bloom, and the round bright orange root vegetable under the ground will soon be ready for harvest. It is picture-perfect as the last rays of the suns prepare to leave for the night.

Then, the sound of a drone reaches their ears, and Bryzon shouts for everyone to fall to their knees. They scramble to hide their packs under the lush growth of the crop. Kneeling, they shuffle along, spreading out along the mounds of plants. Feigning work, they busy themselves by adding dirt to prop up the root vegetables. They are silent.

All they can hear are the inner workings of the Eslaf droid's mechanisms as it hovers above them.

Rence can feel his heart race as he slowly turns his head towards Raine. She looks at him, her eyes wide with uncertainty. The Idler dips down low and lingers. It feels like the minutes become hours as it watches their every move.

Sayhran feels dizzy, she breathes deeply, but the warm air does nothing for her anxiety. Her heart is pounding in her chest, and a sick feeling comes over her in waves. She does her best not to pass out. The Idler moves again, this time hovering directly above Raine. The whirring noises from the machine are intimidating as the airborne droid scans their movements.

Is it about to shoot them? Can it detect the weapons? Raine wonders in panic. She closes her left eye as the perspiration runs down her forehead into her eye. It burns, but she is afraid to wipe it away. Without warning, the Idler shoots away at great speed. In hardly any time at all, it disappears over the trees to the right. It is gone; they are safe.

When they dare stand, everything happens quickly. They retrieve their packs as several Otatop plants suffer irreparable damage underfoot they make a run for the colony gate.

Rence is told by Bryzon to return home. The confused young man is about to say something, but Bryzon interrupts.

"Tomorrow, at first light, you will accompany your father and leader, Kadez, when we gather on the matters that lay ahead of us. I ask that you keep what you know from your family for this one night. You will be part of what we plan, Rence," Bryzon promises.

"Of course, Bryzon, my word is true," Rence assures him before heading in the direction of his home. Raine is left disappointed. Rence had not made eye contact with her before he left. She is certain that he has lost interest in her.

It is getting dark now, and Raine wonders what her cousin Marcus will make of what they have to tell of The Below. What will his reaction be when he hears of the spaceships and the fiery death of Kearthat predicted by the High Yraif Laathria? The existence of the spaceships that brought their grandparents to Kearthat will most assuredly come as a huge shock. Discovering that there is truth in the existence of a multiverse, the Yraif, the Ya~zeld, the matter of Elder Moss, the list is as long as it is challenging.

Remek remarks they should think of a name to describe the group. "We are a sort of freedom force," he jokes keeping his voice low. "What about 'The Liberators'? Yes, The Liberators, that sounds fearless," he suggests, chuckling.

Raine takes the bait and plays along.

"From this moment forward, my dear Remek, we will be known as The Liberators." Raine jokes, placing her fist on her heart. Deepening her voice, she mocks her cousin's silliness by pledging her allegiance as she watches a Firemoth flying just above their heads. It flutters for a while and then flies off.

When Raine points out the Firemoth, she is puzzled to learn that no one but her and Leyashe saw it. Nedai laughs at Raine, "how is it possible, Raine," he says. "The suns are not yet down." It was true. Had they imagined it?

The spontaneous fun ends when they reach Marcus King's cabin.

Nedai calls out to his father. A male voice responds. Bryzon recognizes Marcus instantly but waits for father and son to embrace before he steps forward. Marcus stares at Bryzon for a few seconds. An enormous smile takes over his face, his arms opening wide to greet a man he has great respect for.

"Welcome back, Bryzon. Finally, you are rid of those creatures. My heart is gladdened by the sight of you."

After requesting a gathering with Marcus and his Lesser Leaders for the next morning, the group leave to overnight in the Visitor's Lodge. They are exhausted, but

Bryzon did notice how Marcus had not even asked for a hint of why they would gather so early.

The night passes quickly.

Bryzon, Raine and Leyashe are surprised to discover they are the last to arrive at the Council Lodge the next morning, although it is not quite dawn yet.

 More people seem to fill the room than Bryzon anticipated. To his amazement, Ohre is among them. The big, burly man makes his way towards him, smiling as he blocks the view of everyone behind him. When, finally, Bryzon is set free of Ohre's huge arms, the voices in the room begin to muffle and retreat into the distance. Bryzon feels disoriented, almost dizzy, as he recognises the woman in the dark purple robe. It is High It-Ha Layrrah.

"At last, we meet again. Welcome back to Rednos," she says. Her long hair is as black as Bryzon recollects; her face has not aged a day since he last saw her at Nick King's bedside. The It-Ha's smooth skin and well-formed lips remain unblemished. She has not changed in any way.

Layrrah reaches for Bryzon's hands, and looks deep into his eyes. He notices her pupils are dark green, almost black. She has indeed become powerful; the last time he saw the It-Ha, her eyes were a tranquil shade of green.

"Bryzon, I have missed you. "I promised you I would return when the time was right. That time has come." The expression on her face is hard to read. Bryzon greets her willingly but is still not sure if he can fully trust the High It-Ha.

Layrrah's voice has the same soft, slightly husky tone he remembers. It is the same voice that bestowed the gift of long life on he and Dayson all those years ago. As Layrrah's voice trails on, Bryzon sees a Firemoth materialise from nowhere and flutter just above her left shoulder.

Ohre's boisterous voice calls out his name. He is asking Bryzon to come sit next to him at the large council table. He looks away for only a second, and when he looks back, the Firemoth fades and dissolves into nothing. The It-Ha has managed to pass her message on to Bryzon. She has returned as promised, and she brings with her powerful magic.

"I know you are surprised to find me here, my friend," Ohre bellows. Layrrah commanded my presence, so I am here!" he laughs and winks as Bryzon takes a seat next to him. Bryzon hesitates before he smiles at his friend. It is very odd that Ohre would use the It-Ha's name without her title, very unusual indeed.

It-Ha Layrrah stops in front of Raine and Leyashe. Her eyes fill to the brim with tears. The It-Ha does not change her expression as two big tears roll down her cheeks. Leaning forward slightly, she is quick to catch them before they escape her chin. She rubs the tears into her palms, then she places her hands over those of Raine and Leyashe. They immediately feel a warmth, followed by a strange vibration passing through their bodies. It lasts only a few seconds, then it is gone.

"Welcome, Raine and Leyashe. I have been waiting for you," the It-Ha greets as she releases their hands, leaving them dumbfounded at the strange greeting. Speechless, they only manage a nod as a greeting.

"What was that?" Leyashe asks while stumbling over Raine's same query to him.

"What on Kearthat did she do?" Raine repeats. Leyashe shrugs and shakes his head from side to side as they take their seats. The siblings are aware that it is the second time they have felt magic surge through them in the past few days, and it leaves them with a distinct feeling that there is more to be revealed. The Above was fast becoming as strange as The Below.

As soon as everyone is seated at the table, Bryzon rises to speak.

"Marcus, I can see that you are aware of what we are about to tell you. The presence of It-Ha Layrrah and Ohre suggests that you knew of our arrival," he says, looking at Marcus.

Before Marcus can answer, a female voice calls out to Marcus and the council room door opens. Everyone's attention is diverted as Marcus's wife, Zaviah, appears. She stops dead in her tracks, quite startled to see the many faces.

"I have interrupted your gathering. My regrets, I will leave you," Zaviah apologises, smiling while making a funny little wave towards Sayhran.

The odd greeting to his mother mimics a quacking Ikud, a water bird of Kearthat, and Remek giggles, finding it amusing. The sideshow ends abruptly as Krom gives Remek a light swipe to the back of the head.

Marcus is quick to stop his wife from exiting the room. Gently guiding her by the elbow, he steers her to Bryzon. Bryzon studies the attractive woman whose slim figure is hidden under a loosely fitting green tunic, the colour of the tunic giving away that she is a healer.

"Do you recall greatfather's friend Bouchard, Bryzon?" Marcus asks. "Zaviah is of Jean Bouchard's family," he reveals, smiling.

Bryzon bows, Zaviah walks over and reaches for his hands and smiles, her small hands barely covering his. "We are in your debt, Bryzon, my heart is gladdened that you have been returned to us by those savage creatures, welcome to Rednos." Her kind words surprise Bryzon. He has so far only received warm welcomes from everyone he meets in the colonies. It was something he could never have imagined.

Marcus walks with his wife to the door, Bryzon takes the opportunity to get reacquainted with the two ex-Starfleet men whom he worked with before the invasion, Dourok and Kadez. They are extremely happy to see their old commander free again, or so to speak. After greetings filled with laughter and talk of the men who will soon be returning from the Eslaf prison, they take their seats and Marcus reconvenes the gathering.

Many questions and expressions of disbelief follow as Dourok and Kadez are brought up to date on the fate of Kearthat, and the numerous other surprises. Rence smiles occasionally, nodding as he reaffirms facts to his father, reliving what he saw in The Below.

The four Xennes of old Kearthat start drumming their knuckles on the table. A new generation witnessing a Kearthat Starfleet tradition that they have never seen before. The men now have a reason to revive something they never imagined they would ever do again. When the knuckle rapping stops, the men stand and say something that the young people around the table do not understand. It is in old Kearthatian, before the Drennan language became what it is. The saying they learn means, 'We are one, we are fearless, we shall triumph.'

Raine can tell from the first uttering out of It-Ha's mouth that it will be an interesting day.

"Jon King flew a transporter craft through the tunnels on many occasions. He drew charts that show each of the caverns and their paths," the It-Ha reveals.

The mention of his grandfather flying a spacecraft in the tunnels makes Leyashe careless, and Raine hears him thinking, 'I am going to be the first to do that.'

Nedai whispers something to his father, but Raine cannot hear what he is saying. After the short conversation, she sees Marcus shake his head from side to side. She knows that Nedai has asked his father if he knew of the cavern at the smooth rocks. She could tell from the look on her cousin Marcus's face that the answer had been an emphatic no!

"When I heard that you had all entered the cavern, I knew the wait was over," Layrrah continues. She gets up from her seat. To everyone's slight annoyance, they find themselves waiting for her to disrobe. The heavily hooded item of clothing removed reveals that she is wearing a long tunic hanging to the floor. The dark fabric is delicate, and its flow is almost regal as she moves.

When she finally settles back into her chair, the first thing Raine notices is the It-Ha's forehead. With the hood of her robe no longer hiding most of her face, her brow reveals a delicate rune. It had not been there earlier.

There is no need to mind-speak; Leyashe's face reveals to his sister that he is also perplexed at what he sees. The rune on Layrrah's forehead comprises a small, delicate, light brown outline of a moth, its wings separated, its body split in half. On either side of each wing is a circle with a small dot in the centre. Beside the circle is a triangle and a solid dot that completes the design.

"We have, that is the Yraif and I, been waiting for many years for this day to come," Layrrah continues... but Raine and Leyashe are distracted. Looking around the room, the siblings know that they alone can see the runes. They are the same symbols that Raine saw on the hilt of Zoh-ren's dagger. It was also the moth that Sayhran described on her mother's necklace. This was no coincidence; it had to have meaning, some connection.

Raine and Leyashe watch as the runes on Layrrah's forehead begin to fade until they are completely gone. She looks over at her brother; he stretches his eyes at her, indicating that he also saw it. Raine blinks her eyes several times, stretches her neck, then does a few circles with her head and sighs. 'It is all just too much,' she tells herself.

"Now that High Yraif Laathria has confirmed what is to befall us, the Code to Freedom urges us to act quickly. We must plan immediately," Layrrah goes on to say.

"Why?" Bryzon asks, interrupting. "Why wait for Leyashe to discover the cavern? He folds his arms across his chest and waits for Layrrah to answer.

"If you knew all along what would happen to us, the entrances to The Below, the Yraif and the earthling spaceships, why did you not approach us before?" Bryzon insists.

"Bryzon, my friend, you have not listened well," Layrrah answers in a firm tone.

Krom immediately recognizes that the mystic might not win this battle. He knows Bryzon. He will not be inclined to accept her stance. Layrrah is speaking to Bryzon as if he were a small child. Her somewhat forceful tone will not go down well with him."

Bryzon's face reddens. He unfolds his arms, clenches his fists into tight balls and stares directly into the It-Ha's dark green eyes. He is challenging her, and the group at the table is waiting, holding their breaths to hear what the mystic's answer will be.

"We waited for a signal. We waited for Raine and Leyashe. Many things were in our way. The Order of Lanrete..., the Ya~zeld was closed, and Moss." Layrrah stammers but then recovers as she changes her wording.

"We followed the pronouncement. The decisions were not mine to make, Bryzon, this Nor~han has explained to you," she says firmly, looking straight into his eyes. She does not look away until he does. The silence in the room is akin to that of a dead man's resting place before Layrrah speaks again.

" If Jon were here now, he would say that 'the stars had to align.' This you know to be true," Layrrah insists, raising her left eyebrow in a questioning expression, talking in a softer, kinder tone than moments before.

"I beg your understanding, Bryzon. Do you truly believe that I would have watched as our people died if I could have prevented the suffering?" the High It-Ha asks. Her pupils flicker from dark green to yellow before she takes a deep breath to get her emotions under control.

She was telling the truth. Bryzon relaxes, unclenching his hands as he shifts in his chair. He clears his throat but does not say anything. The challenge was good; he knows he and the It-Ha now understand each other.

Bryzon remembers well Jon King's many sayings that embellished different situations. Adages that had to be explained to Bryzon each time Jon produced a new one. 'There are forces at work in the universe that will never be fully explained or understood' comes to mind. Bryzon can almost hear his old friend repeating this dictum, and at that moment, he knows that he has forgiven his old friend Jon King. He misses his earthling friend.

When Raine interrupts by passing a pitcher of fruit juice around the table, Bryzon thinks of the High Yraif Laathria in Telmah. He remembers back to when they were in The Below, the first time he set his eyes on her. Bryzon knew then that he would never forget what he was witnessing. She was taller than most of the women in Telmah, and the staff she held flickered as if it were alive. Her hair was white, reaching well below her waist, strands of hair had danced about her face as if manipulated by some mysterious breeze surrounding her head.

Laathria was beautiful, but her voice was hard to explain. She had worn a long flowing dress of tranquil colours, the hues so slight that the shades were barely discernible. When she waved her hand in a gesture for the group to sit, the already dim light in the room dimmed a little more. Bryzon could have sworn that the Yraif mystic was floating a few inches off the ground. She just seemed to glide.

"Welcome to The Below. My name is Laathria," she had said, and it was as if her voice was coming from all directions in the room. As her phrases floated through the air, Bryzon felt as if he were in a dream within a dream.

"The time has come for the people of Lan~Igiro to again escape the anger that lies below the mountains," Laathria told them. They were mesmerized by her. "Raine and Leyashe carry within them the knowledge that will restore us she decreed. When you take your leave of Telmah, you must plan. Many lives depend on your cunning. Take heed of the visions of High It-Ha Layrrah and follow the leadership of The

Selected. Be mindful of the alien fortress and the strength of the Eslaf. Go in unity, and may my conjuring aid us when the time comes," she promised.

A silence fell in the room after Laathria had pledged her magic to them. They watched as her staff gave off a green mist that encircled everyone and everything. When the wisps of mist had wound their way back to the silent High Yraif, it formed a circle. The sound of collective breaths being taken could be heard in the silence as the circle changed to the shape of a moth before it completely dissipated. At the same time, Laathria grew fainter and fainter as she retreated into the background. Eventually, there was nothing where she had just stood. When the dim light in the room brightened on its own, she had simply evaporated.

Bryzon brings his attention back to the present when Layrrah, who is looking down at her hands speaks, her tone is muted.

"My visions did not show me the death and suffering of our people before the Eslaf came to Kearthat. This I vow to you all," she announces, making certain that her eyes meet with everyone around the table.

"There was a disturbance, a kind of interference between the realms. It started many days before the attack. Laathria and I could not communicate with 'the one we do not speak of.' The Order did not answer our *Seeking*. Layrrah's use of these bizarre expressions has everyone looking at each other, and Bryzon flagrantly shakes his head, not caring who sees his reaction.

Layrrah's pupils flash a deep-yellow as she speaks of her innocence. To everyone present, it is interesting that she should choose this moment in time to exonerate herself of something she had no control over from almost six decades prior. Perhaps it had something to do with the challenge from Bryzon that prompted her to deviate.

"My visions before the disturbance may not have shown me an attack on Kearthat, but it did show me the birth of two children. Children who would one day save us from something worse than we could ever have imagined," It-Ha Layrrah tells them.

"Many years after the invasion, Farron King told me of her dreams, and I finally understood. Farron found it difficult to believe her dreams when she first set her feet on our sphere. Her visions were burdened with war, cruelty, and creatures who were so unbelievable to her. She ignored the warnings. But she, too, was not to blame. She understood them to be nightmares. Bad dreams that stopped at the same time as my Seeking was not being answered by The Order," she reiterates.

"Grandmother was forewarned of the Eslaf attack on Kearthat?" Raine asks, half standing up before she settles back into her seat. "She had visions... visions, magic? Raine repeats as she closes her eyes and shakes her head as if trying to wake herself from a stupor.

"Not magic Raine, daughter of Caite, your greatmother was, as her mother before her, and the many before her, only a messenger. The earthlings finding their way to Kearthat was your greatmother's charge; leaving Kearthat is yours, yours and Leyashe's," she proclaims, looking at the siblings. "Fated more than two thousand years ago, the message it bears will soon be delivered. All will be revealed in time. You must remain patient," Layrrah promises Raine.

Raine rises as if she is going to speak, but Layrrah waves her down.

"After the invasion, I doubted some of my visions. It was inconceivable to me that we would survive the Eslaf cruelty. Visions that came to me seemed pointless," she tells them, raising her eyebrows and shrugging her shoulders, expressing the helplessness she felt at the time. I felt alone without Solaarr and Sihuun. They had given their lives to hide Jon King's spaceships, and I was left without a means to help our people. Unexpectedly, one day, my daily Seeking of The Order was answered; the disturbance was gone, but it was too late."

"When the aliens ordered us to build the settlements, Laathria, Nor~han, and I had guidance. We knew what we had to do. We chose to build the colonies around the two entrances to The Below. It was clear we had been tasked to wait for our leaders to be born and grow to adulthood. Meanwhile, we continued to wait for the Ya~zeld to open."

Bryzon and Raine's eyes meet; the mention of the multiverse is still hard to digest.

"When Caite and Dayson named Raine and Leyashe, I knew they were the children in my visions. They were the ones who would inherit The Code to Freedom."

Our wait is over, my friends. Our time has come," Layrrah says, smiling as if the mere existence of Raine and Leyashe vindicates all the bad that has happened since the Eslaf invaded Kearthat for its Zraphite all those years ago.

Raine is suddenly aware that The Order and 'the one they do not speak of' might be more cruel than the Eslaf. For the first time, she feels afraid of what is to come. If Layrrah and Laathria could not fully explain The Order of Lanrete and this mysterious being, one who wielded such great power, could they trust him or her? When would they actually know what it really was all about, and would it be too late by then?

Remek whispers something to Rence, Rence's cheeks flush and Raine wonders what her cousin is up to, but ignores it. Rence feels her eyes on him and looks her way, but Raine quickly changes her gaze towards Dourok, who is sitting opposite her.

"We knew that earthlings had a short physical existence. Jon had only a short time to teach the Yraif what was needed to preserve the earthling spaceships and prepare for this very day." Layrrah stops talking and looks at Remek. She raises her left eyebrow slightly at him, and Remek's cheeks turn crimson. He leans back in his chair as if to show Layrrah that he will not utter another sound.

"After the aliens invaded, the High Yraif and I were alone. The Veil Laathria and I conjured so frequently to transport Jon to Telmah was at times weak. It was a dangerous time for Jon, but the Yraif needed to learn all they could about the spaceships under Ante Mountain. Discovery by the Eslaf was beyond imagining. It took many years, but Jon succeeded before he died. He taught the Yraif much; this you have now seen for yourselves," Layrrah says, then leans forward to sip her fruit juice.

Nedai raises his hand, "It-Ha Layrrah, did grandfather doubt the ability of the Xennes? Could they not have learned to fly the spaceships?"

Layrrah takes a few seconds before she answers. Raine watches closely as the It-Ha considers her response carefully.

"Nedai, son of Marcus, for decades, the Eslaf forces on Kearthat have been greater than the strength we could have assembled against them, even now it is so. But, the Eslaf have become complacent. They underestimate us; to them, we are farmers, ignorant fools. The impending fury of what is boiling to the surface will make us a greater force." There is silence as the room digests the It-Ha's explanation. It was true, and no one challenges Layrrah's answer to Nedai's question.

"The High Yraif spoke with Jon many times. As time passed, he began to understand that he and Farron had been brought here to save what was left of the earthlings, Drennan and Yraif. The bond between our spheres is a mystery that can only be revealed by 'the one we do not speak of," the It-Ha admits to them. She does not tell them that Jon and Farron refused the gift of long-life, but she is sure the question would soon be asked of her.

"Will the Order of Lanrete give us protection... a place to ....? Nedai begins to say, but Layrrah cuts him off.

"I must continue; it is best not to interrupt again. Our time is not enough to question what we do not yet know," she tells the dismayed young man.

To Raine, it becomes evident that for now, the question of the mysterious leader of the Yraif, The Order, or Lanrete was a subject Layrrah was not going to discuss at length with anyone.

"I have much to share," Layrrah tells them sighing, sounding as if time has suddenly sped up.

"The secret of Ante Mountain and the existence of the Yraif have always only been known to the It-Ha and the two oldest elders of the old Kearthat Supreme Council, as recorded in The Accord."

"I never knew of this," Bryzon says aloud, and everyone notices how utterly surprised he is to find this out. "My mother, my father, they never told Dayson or me about this… this." Bryzon stutters, trying to find the words.

"The secret of the Yraif has always only been passed on to the next Great Elder. Your mother and father did not know because it was not their place to know Bryzon," the It-Ha tells Bryzon quite flatly.

"I had to go into hiding shortly after the colonies were established. Yraif Laathria instructed me not to risk death by the deadly Eslaf weapon. I was to remain alive at all cost," she continues.

This statement has Bryzon rethinking his outbursts in the past, and he is woeful of some of the anger he directed towards Layrrah.

"I owe much to Ohre, who protected me. Many times he patiently travelled with an old woman," Layrrah praises, with a slight smile as she looks towards him.

"Without Ohre's years of steadfast spirit, it would not have been possible for me to remain unseen," she attests. Layrrah respectfully bowing her head in the direction of her accomplice. For a moment, her pupils flicker deep-yellow." Ohre nods and grins, his large moustache following the lines of his broad smile.

Now they all knew who the friend was from The Above that Nor~han had talked about.

"Unfortunately, in my absence, Elder Moss overruled many unanimous decisions made by the Xennes leaders of the settlements. This power that Moss wields over our people has been halted. I was granted permission by The Order to break The Accord. Moss is no longer an elder. He no longer wields power." The announcement cementing what everyone in the room had been waiting to hear from Layrrah herself.

"Moss knew of the Yraif after the invasion. I watched as he chose not to share this knowledge. When we awaited our fate in the empty fields of the Freelands, not knowing if we would live another day, the elder refused Nor~han's offer to take us Below. Moss forbade me to speak of the Yraif, yet he amused the children of Noitibma Colony by telling twisted stories of the Yraif. As an It-Ha I had to abide by The Accord of the ancients, but this I do no longer. I trust that The Selected will choose to banish Moss to the Barren Lands," she declares with a scowl.

Lesser Leader Dourok is so angry he begins to speak in Drennan. Infuriated Kadez adds something to the conversation. Soon, there are heated discussions between the Xennes men at the table. Men who were once subservient to the Elders of the

Supreme Council of Kearthat and their strict rules now speak their truth openly against Moss.

The lights dim in the room, and the table starts to shake, upsetting several cups. Layrrah's pupils flicker deep-yellow for a few seconds. The men become silent, the shaking stops, and the lights brighten. Layrrah sighs. Order has returned, and she had restored it.

"You are angry, Dourok, that is fair. But The Selected alone have been tasked to render the punishment of the last elder of Kearthat," the It-Ha conveys sternly.

Layrrah turns to the siblings. "Raine, Leyashe, I shall turn him to dust in the Barren Lands if you so wish. Shall we vote on this matter?" her expression harsh with anger at Moss.

They ask if there might be an alternative punishment for the old man, and much to Leyashe and Raine's shock, the It-Ha suggests Moss be left behind on Kearthat.

To those around the table, it looks as if Raine and Leyashe are just quietly staring at each other. No one realises that they are speaking back and forth, frantically trying to solve the problem of Moss and his future.

Leyashe and I wish for the old man to remain with us as a common man. And there it was, Moss had gone full circle.

"So be it. I will inform him of the decision of his fate when we visit Noitibma Colony," the It-Ha sounding utterly disappointed.

"Well," Leyashe says, breaking the lull that has permeated the room. "There is one thing I am certain of, that is there are at least three of us that can see in the dark," referring to the It-Ha's glimmering pupils.

"Oh yes, and we know it scares the darkness right out of the Night Creatures," Nedai adds, keeping the lightheartedness going as he gives his cousin a friendly pat on the back. There is light laughter as the jokes continue between the boys, and Leyashe is pleased to see things return to normal, if only for a short while.

"Raine and Leyashe, you are quite different now. Do you and Leyashe wish to share anything?" the It-Ha asks.

Leyashe's eyes widen. The It-Ha is forcing them to speak about their little secret. They realize that they have solved the mystery of Layrrah's tearful greeting. It comes with abilities yet to become their new reality.

Leyashe clears his throat, "Raine and I have been waiting for the right time …" but before he can finish, Bryzon cuts in.

"Here it comes, Sayhran. I told you they were hiding something. I could feel it." Bryzon sits back in his chair and cups his chin, his pointing finger over his lips as if to shush himself while he waits to hear of the latest secret that his niece and nephew must reveal.

Raine interrupts her brother just as Leyashe draws a deep breath to continue.

"It has been difficult to tell you… to tell anyone. We were not sure what was happening to us," Raine confesses. She looks at her brother, whose expression shows he is grateful for her intrusion.

"Well, what is it? Out with it," Bryzon insists, with a hint of a smile on his lips as he feigns annoyance.

"Go ahead, child," It-Ha Layrrah commands, swooping her hand to mimic a queen giving her subject permission to speak.

Instead, Leyashe takes over again, talking fast as if he cannot hold the secret any longer.

"We can talk to each other without using our voices. It is like mind-speaking." He says breathlessly.

"So, you can read our minds?" Sayhran says, sounding a little silly and confused.

"No, no it is not like that Sayhran, we can talk to each other with our minds," Leyashe corrects as he points his finger first to his sister and then back to himself.

"And there is more," Raine interjects.

"Indeed, there is more" Bryzon remarks as he pushes away from the table and stands. He knits his hands together at the back of his head and arches his back. Raine continues explaining her and Leyashe's vision sharing.

Remek giggles inwardly as he watches Bryzon. His jesting nature painting a picture of Bryzon straightening his posture to help the new information sink in.

"The men born to Kearthat will once again be pilots," Krom says, smiling with obvious joy, saving his cousins from more questions about their newly found abilities.

"Perhaps our men, and women, will be pilots, Raine corrects him and she rolls her eyes.

Bryzon contemplates the enormous foresight of the It-Ha. Layrrah has spent her many years in hiding planning far ahead. Ohre was chosen by her as her protector because he was a man of great honour, a man who could keep a secret. He was highly respected by all the Drennen, Xennes men and women. Ohre's word was known by all to be true. The mystic had indeed chosen well.

Marcus calls for a break. The group splits up and go in different directions, their intention to return to the Council Lodge in an hour.

Before they leave Layrrah makes it clear that no one other than The Liberators are to know of Raine and Leyashe's ability to communicate. Her use of the word Liberators takes everyone by surprise. How on Kearthat did the It-Ha know about Remek's silly bantering, Raine wonders.

Chapter 38 - Bryzon's Plan

All eyes are focused on Bryzon as he takes over from Layrrah after the short recess.

"What I am about to say, you may not yet have considered," he begins, talking slowly as if stalling, putting his words in order.

"The Korak at the mines are blameless, like us they have been treated cruelly. They were brought here against their will. I feel it our responsibility to save them," he declares. The reaction is exactly what he expected. It is very noticeable from the expressions around the table that everyone had completely forgotten about the unfortunate Korak prisoners. The room goes from silent to multiple people speaking at the same time, but it is Dourok's deep voice that prevails.

"Bryzon, this may not be possible," Rence's father expresses and the room begins to rumble with voices.

"Stop! Please!" Marcus implores, putting his hands in the air to silence everyone. "Let Dourok speak his mind."

"Bryzon, how will we achieve this?" the lesser leader queries. "We could be sacrificing our own people to save them. They are innocent, this we understand. Leaving them to die is unspeakable, but how? There are many Korak at the mines."

"There are more than three thousand Korak at the prison," Bryzon confirms, putting a number to the aliens toiling below ground each day. "And yes, it will take courage and planning. Would you have it rest on your conscience if we ignored the Korak?" Bryzon asks. He looks at the faces around him and can feel everyone's unease.

Raine is momentarily paralyzed by the thought. Having three thousand gangly olive beings fighting with them against an organized enemy such as the Eslaf seems almost unattainable. What would they do with three thousand Korak on the spaceships for a long period? But how could they not try and save them?

"I know that this has come as a further burden. The Korak have been slaves to the Ludinians for as long as we have. We must not, and cannot forget, that as Drennan and as earthlings we are unlike those who hold us prisoner. If we ignore the Korak," Bryzon insists, then we can no longer call ourselves innocent. Would you wish to carry dishonour in your heart?" he begs, trying to make them understand.

One could drop a Torrap's feather and hear it, it has become so silent in the large room. Everyone's mind mulling over this new dilemma.

"It is so," Ohre says sighing, breaking the awkward silence.

"There would be much to overcome for us to achieve this," Marcus cuts in. Looking at Bryzon whose face pleads understanding to his quandary. Marcus suggests they revisit the matter after speaking to the other colony leaders.

"Are you in agreement, Bryzon, my friend?"

To everyone's surprise, Leyashe pushes his chair back, the noise diverting everyone's attention.

"The Korak in the colonies speak our language, they attended our classes, their hate for the Eslaf is as great as ours. It is my opinion that they are as much part of Kearthat as you or I. Leyashe looks at Raine and she nods her head, agreeing with her brother.

"If we accept those who were born on our sphere, grew up working, and living among us in the colonies why is it so hard to imagine that the rest of them at the prison are any different?" he questions.

Leyashe waits, measuring the silence as he looks enquiringly from one member of the group to the next.

Marcus saves the awkward moment. "Before we close on this matter, would anyone like to add anything more about the Korak prisoners?

"I have given it much consideration over the many hard years as I laboured with the Korak by my side," Bryzon says, using the open invitation to speak. "I wish to send Krom and Remek to visit with Pateeo. They could use the opportunity to talk with a female Korak that I consider to be my friend. She goes by the name of Namow, she knows our tongue well enough. Namow and another called Nam could ready their kind, they will battle with us, this I know," Bryzon reiterates. "But this visit must take place soon. Our men will leave the prison to return home on the date agreed upon. It is important that Remek and Krom go to the mine now, to avoid suspicion." Bryzon looks around taking a deep breath, hopeful that his fears are understood.

"Once our men are home there will be no need for our people to go to the prison as visitors. Our opportunity to talk to Namow will be lost. If we are going to ask the

Korak to be ready to leave Kearthat and fight, then it is important that we do this now, tomorrow if possible," Bryzon insists.

"Bryzon is correct, I would ask that anyone who has objection make their judgment known," the It-Ha asks in a stern voice as she backs up Bryzon's plan.

"We should be as one on all of the decisions that are made at this table. There should be no regret. It is my opinion that we vote on the matter without delay," the It-Ha presses. Then she adds, "If The Selected so choose?"

Bryzon's eyes follow each arm that is raised around the table as he counts and holds his breath. Then, it is over, all votes are in favour, and the Korak will have a chance of escaping a fiery death. The how, and where to, no one knows as yet.

Raine notices the relief on Bryzon's face after the unanimous decision, at least one of the burdens Bryzon has been carrying with him since Telmah has finally been lifted from his shoulders.

Leyashe sits, not saying a word, he knows that his intervention has pushed everyone to search their hearts on the matter, and for the first time he feels like he is contributing. Raine smiles and winks at her brother, acknowledging his achievement.

"It has been a long day, but I have left a most important matter for last," Layrrah tells the group as she casts her eyes down, her lashes making little shadows on her cheeks.

"I had a vision, of Ante Mountain filling with red, boiling lava, it spilled over and ran down the mountains towards the Freelands. I was standing in one of the earthling ships."

Her voice softening the It-Ha tells them that the ripening crops burned. She saw Eslaf soldiers drown in the city, the molten liquid swirling everywhere. Rocks flew through the sky as the mountain exploded, and black clouds formed while lightning danced across Kearthat's purpling sky. When the rain stopped the wind blew ash that covered everything."

"Kearthat looked as I never could have imagined. Our sphere was black and grey, it was no longer Lan~Igiro. The Below again became one with The Above, it was a place I no longer recognized," Layrrah recites.

"We do not have many days before our sphere is lost to us, my vision warned that we must use our time wisely." As Layrrah speaks her pupils flicker between normal and luminescent yellow. The It-Ha seems exhausted after sharing her story, she takes a sip from the cup in front of her.

The room is silent.

'How is it going to be possible to prepare what we must before time runs out?' Sayhran asks, her face distorted into a worried expression. No one answers her question.

The silence prompts Marcus to suggest that they meet again in the morning.

On this night there will be restless sleep for all.

The next morning Bryzon readies to leave his room when there is a knock at the door and he is astonished to find Raine and Leyashe carrying with them three plates of food.

"Leyashe and I thought we could all eat together before we gather," Raine says, smiling. Bryzon waves them in, Raine needs no invitation to sit in the only chair, leaving her brother to find a space next to Bryzon on the bed.

"Does it not feel strange to you ?" Leyashe asks. "It is like living inside a very long dream, I keep thinking I am about to awaken." Raine cuts in and assures her brother that it is all very real, but Bryzon does not hear this part of the conversation.

Before they leave Bryzon tells the siblings that he is ready to bring up the matter of long life as soon as Marcus convenes the meeting.

Sayhran is already waiting when they arrive at the Council Lodge. Seated next to her are Ohre and Layrrah. Dourok, Rence and Kadez make their appearance a few minutes later. Marcus and Nedai join them within a minute of their arrival, the only faces missing are Krom and Remek.

Raine can feel a sense of urgency has replaced Marcus's usual calm demeanour, as he gestures for everyone to sit, there would be no time to engage in idle conversation on this day. Today they would lay out the plans as to how they will leave Kearthat.

Leyashe asks if anyone has seen Krom and Remek. Sayhran starts to answer him but is interrupted by Layrrah. "I have sent them on an important undertaking," she says dismissively. Leyashe looks at Bryzon as if expecting an answer, but he shrugs his shoulders.

Decisions are made on how to approach the other leaders, and how to prepare the colonists for the end of daily life as they know it on Kearthat. Bryzon shares many ideas, some are agreed upon, while others remain matters proposed for a later date. He remains silent about his request for long-life for the colonists. Raine tries to remind him to speak of the matter, but he whispers, "Not now," she nods, but the sudden change of heart leaves her a little confused.

Marcus, Dourok and Kadez discuss how the leaders might keep up the appearance of normality within the settlements once the colonists know of their plans and many begin to go Below to accomplish tasks on the homeships.

A list starts to form of undertakings to be accomplished immediately. It is decided who will travel where and when. To avoid coming across the same Eslaf soldiers too many times while journeying from one colony to the next, they decide to make use of both the daily shuttles and Traxid transport.

Several hours later, Marcus leans back and smiles.

"So, we are ready to proceed with our mission, we will hold a meeting with the people of Rednos tonight. I will send word that everyone is to return from the fields as soon as the last alien shuttle leaves the colony. When it is safe and the gate is locked, our people will gather here in the Council Lodge for the announcement. I will ask that some of the women of the colony cover the windows so we can avoid curious Idlers."

"I will darken the windows, Marcus," the It-Ha says, "no need for the tired women coming from the fields to do so," she adds.

Marcus concludes the first half of the gathering by waiting for a show of hands to confirm approval of all that was decided to this point. Then he asks the question that everyone has been waiting for.

"Layrrah, it is the midday hour, where are Krom and Remek, why the secrecy?

"Just a little while longer Marcus," she says. "All will be clear soon, please be patient my friend. We have one more matter to discuss before we take leave for our mid-day meal," Layrrah announces unexpectedly. Marcus looks a little surprised but patiently sits down again, waiting for the It-Ha to tell them what is on her mind.

"Bryzon, the time has come for you to speak on the matter that has been on your heart for many years. The one you wished to address earlier, but did not," she prompts.

"How did you know…?" Bryzon begins to ask, stopping in mid-sentence. The It-Ha raises her eyebrows. "The Inmo sees all, and the eye of the High It-Ha prevails," Layrrah informs him without so much as a blink.

"I wish to speak on an issue that I have dwelled upon since I became a slave in the mine," Bryzon admitting for the first time how paltry he had felt as a prisoner.

"I am asking that the gift of long life be granted to all of our people before we leave Kearthat."

"And I agree with Bryzon," Layrrah says before anyone can comment. "And now I will explain the absence of Krom and Remek. I have sent them to meet with the Yraif. Nor~han has procured water from the Cigam Spring and root from the Enoce tree. It will be delivered to Sayhran's boys at the Trigga tree cavern, the brothers will return with it soon."

"It is not only Bryzon's wish but that of Raine and Leyashe that we tell our people the good news as soon as possible. I know it was you Bryzon who came back from the mines with this intention. Now it is the 'The Selected,' who command that this be so," the High It-Ha declares looking at Raine and Leyashe.

"It looks like the decision was made for us, brother," Raine mind-speaks, Leyashe smiles. Finally, there was good news. The siblings recognize the It-Ha's candour, but she would soon have to understand that they can make decisions on their own.

"It-Ha Layrrah is correct, this is our wish, it will ensure the survival of our people," Raine cuts in. "Being Xennes will give us the advantage we need on our journey to find a new home."

The vote to bestow long life on all the people of the colonies takes less than a minute to deliver a unanimous vote.

After the vote Ohre stands, pushes his chair back, and bows to Raine and Leyashe. "To The Selected," he says, raising his right arm high as he makes a fist. He thumps his chest twice with his clenched hand, repeating the chest tap, and the rest of the group follow Ohre's gesture of respect.

It is a vastly different alliance that takes their leave from the Council Lodge, leaving Raine and Leyashe to process what just happened to them.

Chapter 39 - The Tiro

After the mid-day break, they discover that Krom and Remek have returned.

High It-Ha Layrrah raises her hand. "I wish to speak of the potion ceremonies," It-Ha Layrrah begins, and immediately Dourok interrupts.

"Are we to assume that all the leaders of the colonies will be agreed?"

"They would never go against The Selected or their High It-Ha," Layrrah fires back sternly. "The time for that is long past." Her lips drawn tightly, pupils flickering deep-yellow for a few seconds affirming her impatience with the lesser leader's question.

"I agree," Marcus interjects, stopping the It-Ha from perpetuating her tirade. Marcus can feel that the It-Ha feels Moss's punishment is far less than he deserved, her patience severely shortened by it.

"We need to proceed as quickly as possible. We have no time to waste, we have voted, it is done," Marcus insists as he backs up the High It-Ha.

The matter is drawn to a quick close leaving Dourok smiling within as he contemplates the long life he and his family will share. As for the High It-Ha, he was angered by her temper but for now, he is willing to forgive her behaviour. It was an exchange, long-life for his wife Treival, and his son Rence, and his understanding of her conduct.

"I shall continue," Layrrah says sighing, seemingly spent after the effort she had to expend to defend the inevitable.

"It is the judgment of the High Yraif that we choose an It-Ha," she announces.

Frowning faces greet her before her words grow cold, and Layrrah is quick to reassure everyone that she has no plans to depart in any shape or form.

"It is time for us to rebuild the strength of the It-Ha as it was before. My burden has been heavy and I have grown weary," she tells everyone.

"The High Yraif Laathria has chosen the one who will serve beside me."

"She will be the first to become Xennes, the first since the old world to receive the gift of long life. She will be the next It-Ha, if the sanction stone sees a true, pure heart within her."

"I would ask that Sayhran be my Tiro?

Layrrah can see the stunned look on Sayhran's face and quickly adds, "You do not have to accept Sayhran, it is your choice."

The young people who have only ever thought of Sayhran as a mother or an aunt find themselves silenced by what is taking place.

"What is a Tiro?" Nedai whispers, leaning over to Bryzon.

"A kind of a fledgling It-Ha, I think," Bryzon guesses.

Sayhran slowly rises from her chair, looking around at everyone, all of them waiting for her answer to the It-Ha's question.

"I am …, I... I would be honoured," the only surviving child of Jon and Farron King from Planet Earth stutters.

"Then you must come forward, woman," Layrrah encourages, ushering her with her hand as if slightly impatient.

Sayhran crosses the room. Facing the It-Ha as she watches the Layrrah reach down into a sack made from the fibres of the Enoce tree. She takes from it a smooth, flat stone. In the light, the round sanction stone is so black that it reflects a deep blue glint. Next, she brings out a small wooden cup and a jar from which she removes the stopper and pours a brown liquid, but not before she waves her hand over the neck of the jar, as if casting a secret, mysterious spell on it.

Krom looks at Bryzon, they can almost read each others' minds. The size of the sack and the number of items it yields does not add up. It is inconceivable that a bag so small can hold that many items. They are witnessing magic at play.

"Drink of the waters of the Cigam and the root of the Enoce," Layrrah commands in a low poetic voice as she hands Sayhran the cup.

Sayhran blinks several times after swallowing the contents in one gulp. It appears that she is experiencing something, but she does not say anything, while Bryzon knows exactly what his sister-in-law is feeling at that moment.

It-Ha Layrrah asks Sayhran to put her hands out in front of her, then she places the sanction stone on Sayhran's palms. The light in the room dims and Raine sees Remek look up for a second.

Slowly the stone illuminates as it turns light pink. It begins to pulsate and shimmer, as if a thousand stars live within it. Sayhran's eyes close without being told, the room darkens even more. This change highlights Sayhran's face in the glow of the pulsing object. The High It-Ha puts her hands on Sayhran's shoulders and begins to chant. Soon they are both reciting strange words over and over. Out of nowhere a large Firemoth appears and settles on Sayhran's left shoulder. Pink wispy clouds emanate from the stone encircling the It-Ha and Sayhran, it twirls and weaves in and out of their hair and their bodies. When the twisting haze that has filled the room begins to fade the light comes back slowly. Layrrah and Sayhran stop their chanting. The sanction stone begins to darken and the last wisps of floating pink streaks fade, and with it the Firemoth.

Raine gasps in shock before she can stop herself. Her appearance is startlingly different.

Sayhran's hair, is as black and straight as that of a true Drennan, strands of grey distinguish her as being older, but from this moment forward Raine knew her Aunt would never age.

When finally Sayhran turns towards the group her eyes say it all, they are a tranquil green, she has the mark of an It-Ha.

Layrrah reaches into the bag and withdraws a short dagger. The blade of the dagger gleams in the light and Raine notices the moth etched into the hilt. Without asking, she reaches out for Sayhran's hand. The newest It-Ha pulls back slightly before relenting.

"Look into my eyes, Tiro," Layrrah commands her as she deftly slices into Sayhran's palm. Sayhran winces; her eyes grow big, and she stares at the injury oozing blood.

Remek stands up, he looks at his mother in horror but before he can find words to express his shock at what Layrrah has done, the It-Ha grabs her Tiro's hand and wipes away the blood. The injury has simply disappeared, and with it the pain.

High It-Ha Layrrah addresses It-Ha Sayhran while giving Remek a look that has him immediately sitting down.

"It-Ha Sayhran, you are chosen, you hold The Inmo within you, 'The eye that sees all' will be with you always, prove yourself worthy. In time the High Yraif will gift you the ability to see what we never speak of, you will receive this last gift when you have completed your Tiro~pedah, your time of insight."

Raine can see from the smile on It-Ha Layrrah's face that she is genuinely happy. But she is not alone in wondering yet again what on Kearthat it could be that the It-Ha, and also Nor~han insisted they cannot speak of?

The extraordinary day endures as Layrrah proceeds to pull a second bag from the first. She fills it with the items that she took from the first. To everyone's amazement there on the table where seconds earlier was only one sanction stone, a second stone has materialized, she adds one of the stones to the second bag and then hands it to It-Ha Sayhran. Either Layrrah does not notice the perplexed faces around the table or she chooses to ignore them.

Hugs in abundance come Sayhran's way. When it is Raine's turn, her tears flow freely. She whispers her love for the woman who, in all truth, is her second mother, but she knows their relationship has been forever changed.

When Layrrah clears her throat, it is a sign for everyone to settle down again.

"Marcus, I ask your permission to use the room adjoining the Council Lodge to ensure our privacy for the preparation of the potion and other matters."

"Of course, Layrrah, whatever you and Sayhran need, It-Ha Sayhran, he corrects."

"Then it will be so," High It-Ha Layrrah confirms, smiling at her Tiro, seemingly enthralled to have a companion at last.

Bryzon requests to speak, then proceeds to take a small note from his pocket. He unfolds it and smooths the edges, laying it on the table in front of him.

"I need consensus on a matter of importance," he begins.

"I think we should send two men to Telmah as soon as possible. It is imperative they immediately begin to study the ships. We need to train our pilots to fly the transporter craft, fighter craft, and spaceships. We must begin to learn the earthling technology as soon as possible," Bryzon reiterates.

It sounds surreal to be discussing spaceships when, only a few days ago, everyone concerned themselves with what the storm had done to the crops. The expectation of leaving Kearthat is suddenly all too real. At the same time, it feels like an impossible undertaking.

Bryzon's list yields a decision that he and Layrrah will travel to each of the colonies to convey the message of their impending departure from Kearthat to the colony leaders, and to administer the potion. They also decide who will be best to send to Telmah without the aliens noticing that they are missing from their colonies.

Nedai raises his arm to speak, but Bryzon waves him down. A look of disappointment comes over the young man's face, but he lowers his arm.

"Now that we know that Jon King flew craft through the tunnels, his drawings will make it easier for us to navigate The Below. This will be our way to move back and forth to Telmah, but we can only achieve this if we send some of our most capable men and women to Telmah without delay," Bryzon urges again.

"Do we have consensus?" Marcus asks, looking about the room.

For the first time, Bryzon feels that things are beginning to fall into place, as arms shoot into the air.

Questions continue to be asked and answered and the decisions noted by Layrrah, as the day begins to dwindle.

"It-Ha Layrrah, is it possible that we can keep Nor~han advised as we reach conclusions on our many matters," Bryzon asks. It seems that you have no difficulty in this regard," he says, smiling at the It-Ha, winking at those around the table who are looking at him.

"Your messages will be sent without delay Bryzon brother of Dayson," Layrrah answers, her voice sounding tired as she ignores Bryzon's attempt at making light of her mysterious ability to *Seek* the Yraif.

Bryzon notices Nedai's impatience. The young man has been wringing his hands since he had spoken of the transporter and fighter craft. Unfortunately, he would have to wait a little while longer.

"Ash and Xandr from Laeredis Colony will go to Telmah. Xandr is the best man to learn these ships. He was once the commander of starship training in Seccus. Leyashe has a mind that can store numbers and can memorise well. Those of us who know him will understand my choice."

"Is everyone in agreement that Leyashe and Xandr make the journey to Telmah?" Bryzon enquires, and a round of raised hands settles the matter.

"So it shall be," Layrrah repeats. "Leader Xandr does not know it yet, but he is going Below."

All this time, Remek has been watching the It-Ha as she makes notes, but each time Layrrah writes down a name, it immediately vanishes into the paper, leaving no trace. She notices Remek's curiosity, leans over to him and whispers. "Remek, son of Keazan, you are observant. One day, you too will be a leader," she tells him, leaving the young man confused but enormously pleased that she has finally paid him a compliment instead of a reprimand.

"Leyashe, you must follow all carefully the instructions given to you by Xandr. I will not allow disobedience. All of our lives are in your hands," Bryzon tells his nephew with a most serious expression.

Leyashe is a little stunned at Bryzon's trust in him and his promise of reprimand if he does not obey his requests. He is beyond excited, forgetting that he is one of The Selected, and without noticing he has accepted Bryzon as his guardian.

"I swear that I will learn everything and more. Thank you, Bryzon, for your trust," Leyashe answers, bowing his head, a broad smile failing to hide his joy.

Leyashe's cousins are glad for his good fortune. They know his ability with numbers and his keen memory. For now, they hide their disappointment, certain that their part in the mission will be according to their merit.

Nedai does not raise his hand again, Raine notices, and she feels bad for her cousin. She makes a mental note to include him in something important as soon as she is able.

Layrrah leans over to Bryzon and whispers something to him. He listens diligently and when she is done, he tells everyone that the High It-Ha wishes Ohre to join Leyashe and Xandr, but only after he returns from completing a task that she had requested of him. She does not elaborate and no one will question her. Raised hands confirm that the request made by the It-Ha is acknowledged and accepted by all.

"The Liberators will next come together as one in Noitibma before we move our people Below?" Bryzon says. Using the words The Liberators for the first time since Layrrah mysteriously knew of Remek's jesting. Several smiles appear around the table. Raine winks at Remek and she can see how proud he is of his contribution.

Last on Bryzon's list is the matter of leader Ameka, of Laeredis Colony.

"She is a good engineer, our only engineer," Bryzon corrects. "She is highly skilled. There is little she cannot master," he reaffirms.

"Perhaps she should accompany Xandr, Leyashe and Ohre," Dourok suggests.

"Our strategy, and our path to victory will be to stop the Eslaf from getting their fighter craft off the ground. It will take much planning, I am of the thinking that Ameka can help us in that regard, how I do not know, but I trust in her judgement," Bryzon states, raising his eyebrows as he speaks.

"I am of the same opinion as Bryzon," Kadez agrees, joining the conversation. "We cannot be drawn into a fight with the Eslaf."

"What of the men returning from the prison? There are many capable men among them. Would they be asked to go Below?" Leyashe asks.

"We will wait for their return to make this judgment. I fear our time is short. Once they return, we will better know if we have enough days to train all those who we know are capable," Bryzon replies, taking a deep breath.

He rubs his chin. "To send the men being released from prison to The Below to enter the darkness immediately after their release could be a mistake," Bryzon queries, sounding desperate to figure out what is best.

"When our people return from prison, it may also attract more Eslaf to the colonies for the first while. The aliens inquired about my whereabouts shortly after I came home to Noitibma," Bryzon shares, relaying his encounter.

"This means that the men returning from prison must, for now, remain at the colonies until we are certain that the Eslaf are complacent," Raine insists.

"If the aliens become suspicious, they will send more to watch over our every move," Leyashe adds.

"What if Pateeo and the other men are not released in time?" Krom enquires, posing a question that brings a sudden silence to the room.

"We must not let ourselves be distracted; we can only hope that the aliens abide by what they agreed to," It-Ha Layrrah comments, determined to put a stop to the speculating.

"So what happens when all of this is done?" Rence asks next, changing the conversation. "Once we have everyone 'potioned up' and we are ready to move our people Below, how do we plan this without the Eslaf noticing? he asks.

"We do it during 'the darkening that will be upon us close to the time that the High Yraif Laathria predicts Ante Mountain's ire," Bryzon tells him.

"When all is ready," Raine cuts in smiling, "We will get everyone onto the ships and away from Kearthat without losing even one life."

Without any prompting from Raine, Leyashe reaches to hold his sister's hand. Their pupils glow as they seem to be transported into a different world. Everyone is stunned as the siblings turn to statues. Seconds later, Raine begins to slide off her chair, as if she is fainting. Leyashe lets go of his sister's hand, and for a moment, he seems confused. Rence leaps from his seat to catch Raine before she falls to the floor.

"What happened? Are you whole?" Raine talk to me? Rence panics, shaking Raine by the arm. Her eyes open and she sits upright. "I am fine," Raine tells him, but her face is filled with sadness. Her eyes shine as tears begin to fill them.

"It was just a shock to see it," she says, wiping her eyes with her sleeve as she gets up from the floor.

"See what, Rai?" Bryzon asks gently.

"We … Ash and I saw Ante Mountain. Lava was spewing from it, spilling over and running down The High Mountains. It was a vision of what was to come. It was going to be horrible. We cannot fail." Raine begs, her face full of dread.

"We must not fail," Leyashe agrees. "If we do, our deaths are unthinkable," he says, shaking his head.

It is decided they will all take a short break. Hardly out of the door, they hear an Eslaf craft approach.

Raine and Leyashe are on their way to the Visitor's Lodge when the alien transporter hovers above the colony. The siblings are frantic, noticing two field rakes they begin raking the dirt beside one of the cabins where someone has planted several rows of Otatop.

Out of the corner of Raine's eye, she can see some of the group split up and walk in different directions of the colony. At first, the Eslaf craft seems to be deciding where it must land, but it is as if, by some miracle, it decides instead to shoot away. It disappears over the trees to the west of Rednos; the panic is over.

"What do you think that was all about?" Raine asks her brother.

"It was very strange. I am glad they did not land. An inspection of the colony is not good for us at this time, sister. The thought of them finding the handguns has me awake at night. It scares me, Rai" Leyashe admits.

"I feel so different now, Rai," her brother tells her after the panic is over.

"I know, Ash. We are different now," she tells her brother.

"I can feel that we are supposed to take charge of something, but what? And how?" Leyashe admits to her.

"Bryzon and the It-Ha have planned everything so far. They know the men and woman of old Kearthat. They know who is best to serve our purpose and we are left doing nothing," Leyashe grumbles.

"You mean as the new supposed leaders of the people, Ash?" Raine asks, smiling as she gently claps her brother on the back, making light of his concern, and their new status.

Away from the colony and well hidden, they enjoy the shade of the tall red stalks of a Ylock crop, each of them in their thoughts.

Raine notices that the crop is recovering well after the storm. She reaches and breaks off a cob of Ylock from its stalk. After peeling off the leaves that protect its bounty, she sits and picks off the almost hardened kernels one by one, watching as they fall onto the dirt.

"Will the Freelands still be here when this crop is ready to be harvested?" Raine asks her brother.

"Will there still be a Kearthat?" Leyashe questions. "What do you think of all the plans so far, Rai?" Leyashe asks, changing the subject.

"There is something important that evades us, Ash. Something is missing. I can feel it."

"What do you think it can be? And if we are supposed to be 'The Selected', why does it feel as if we are not contributing? Raine adds, and Leyashe sighs.

Raine takes her brother's hands. Their pupils, projecting green in the sunslight are a spectacular sight, but only the Ylock witnesses it. They remain like this for several minutes. When they release their hold on each other, they jump to their feet.

"We have to tell them, Rai."

Leyashe takes off at a run, ploughing through the Ylock's tall stalks. Raine finds it difficult to keep up with her brother as she darts through the crop and heads for the colony's gate.

Chapter 40 - The Beast

Raine knocks on the Council Lodge door, and Ohre lets the two out-of-breath siblings in.

"Back so soon, that was short," he comments.

"We have something very important to share," Raine tells the big Xennes man. To their surprise, they find everyone except It-Ha Sayhran accounted for.

"We must find Sayhran and bring her here," Raine requests breathlessly, momentarily forgetting to address her aunt as It-Ha Sayhran.

"Leyashe, you go," she asks her brother.

"No need, she will be here soon. I have summoned the It-Ha," Layrrah says as she puts her hand on Leyashe's shoulder to stop him from leaving.

Moments later, Sayhran walks through the door. Raine notices that she is dressed like Layrrah in a long flowing tunic of beautiful fabric, but now is not the time to comment.

It-Ha Sayhran takes one look at Raine and Leyashe and she knows immediately something is weighing heavily on their minds.

"What is it, Raine, what has happened?"

"It is the Eslaf, Bryzon was right. We already know for certain that they are not all of flesh. We were wrong about how many of them are machines."

Without warning, Leyashe reaches for his sister's hand. Their pupils aglow they seem to retreat into another world. Rence moves closer to Raine as if half expecting her to fall to the floor again.

As the siblings communicate, they can feel Layrrah attempting to enter their thoughts. The High It-Ha's eyes light up and go dull repeatedly as she tries and fails.

The silence is broken as Raine and Leyashe release their hands and their eyes return to normal.

"Sorry, but Ash and I had to be certain of something," Raine apologizes as if what everyone just witnessed is quite normal.

Layrrah's slight annoyance is something that only Marcus notices. He had watched the It-Ha as she tried to share in his cousin's visions, but Raine and Leyashe had quickly put a stop to it when they felt her interference.

It was obvious that the gifts The Selected had acquired were increasing in power. What no one, except perhaps Marcus, saw was that they were establishing dominance, something It-Ha Layrrah may not have anticipated.

"You tell them, Ash," Raine says, looking at her brother.

"The Eslaf have little holes just below the left ear," he says, looking at the group.

"Yes, they have those ridges like the gills of a Shiftaf," Ohre says and chuckles at his description of the markings.

"They all have them," Bryzon adds, frowning, not understanding.

"Yes, but the real Eslaf have four on each side," Raine explains. "The Androids have four on the right and three on the left. I always thought it peculiar. Leyashe and I are sure that it was an oversight in the design of the droids. There are more Androids than Eslaf of flesh on Kearthat. If we can stop the machines, we will have the advantage we are looking for."

"With help from the engineer, this Leader Ameka that you speak of, we might find a way to stop them," Leyashe speculates, his heart racing.

"For so long, I have been looking forward to this day," Bryzon exclaims, smiling. The thought of disabling hundreds of Eslaf droids with the push of a button could change everything.

"If Ameka and Leyashe find a way to turn off the Idlers and the droids, it would be the shortest war the Eslaf have ever fought and lost. They would not know what hit them," Ohre remarks, laughing as he bangs on the table with a fisted right hand that makes the cups bounce.

"At last, we will prevail. The Selected have given us what we have been waiting for," Layrrah declares. "Our patience has been rewarded, thank the galaxies," she says, smiling at the siblings.

"The Eslaf have become content. They think us weak. Underestimating us will be their end. Our attack will be satisfying," Dourok adds fervently as he and Kadez elbow bump, yet another Xennes practice revived.

"This will delay me from going to Telmah," Leyashe suddenly realises, his eyes pleading with Bryzon, his heart plainly torn.

"Disabled soldiers cannot fight and they cannot fly craft. If you and Ameka can find a solution, our people will have a better chance," Bryzon says, looking at the disappointed young man.

"Tonight, we will capture a Night Creature to find out what makes them what they are. Leyashe and I believe that this will help us," Raine announces.

A short silence follows.

"Leyashe and I think that the Night Creatures could be droids. If they are, they are sure to operate with the same technology as that of the Idlers and the Eslaf Androids themselves. If this is true, then we have found another weakness.

Marcus watches Raine as she talks, and he knows that The Selected have found their place. The Xennes leaders of Kearthat are no longer in charge.

"After the meeting with the people of the colony tonight, we will find out whether Night Creatures are beast or machine. I would like Bryzon, Rence and Nedai to accompany us," she asks. Raine looks over to Marcus, then to Dourok and waits. The two men look at each other, and then nod their consent for their sons to be part of the hunt.

Raine has fulfilled her promise, Nedai is to be a part of something very important.

The ever-jovial Remek smiles. He knows that his friend Rence is over the moons regardless of the dangers involved in the hunt, as long as the event includes Raine.

Leyashe's original plans quickly begin to unravel as priorities change. He knows it will not be long before one of his cousins approaches Bryzon to take his place with Xandr in Telmah.

As they leave the lodge, Bryzon rushes to catch up to Raine and Leyashe.

"I knew it," Bryzon says, smiling. "I knew that someday we would profit from your observation of the creatures. I am curious, how did you two know of the marks if your writings are in Noi?" Bryzon asks his forehead wrinkled into a questioning frown.

"I could read them in my mind. I shared my vision with Leyashe: we did it together." The moment Raine finishes her sentence, she can see Bryzon's dismay. She gets the feeling that his smiling face is hiding the fact that in the mayhem of magic, enchantments and abilities, he feels a little left out somehow.

Later that evening, the citizens of Rednos are ready, seated and waiting for their leaders to speak.

Marcus clears his throat.

"Good people of Rednos, I have called you all together to tell you that we will soon be leaving Kearthat." A low rumble of voices quivers through the crowd, but silence quickly returns when Dourok waves his hands, gesturing for them to quieten.

"I know that we … you, have been talking about the big storm we suffered recently. There are those of you who speak often of the many tremors and the heat. There is a reason, my friends. Ante Mountain has awoken and threatens our very survival." This statement generates a reaction. Marcus is forced to raise his hands to hush the crowd.

"Ante Mountain will soon unleash its anger. The destruction will be worse than the explosion that befell Kearthat thousands of years ago. This time, it will destroy our sphere."

The crowd is stunned into silence for a few seconds before loud talking takes over the room. Marcus raises his voice to no avail. He decides to sit until his people are silent. When quiet returns, a lone male voice from out of the crowd shouts out a question.

"How will we escape this? The Eslaf will flee on their spaceships and leave us to die. There is nothing we can do. We have no spaceships to carry us away. We will be left to …"

Before the man can continue, Dourok is on his feet next to Marcus, asking the Freelander to sit and listen to their leader without interruption.

"Some of you may have noticed that old friends have returned to us. If you are Xennes, then you know Bryzon and High It-Ha Layrrah. There is a low murmur, but Marcus continues to speak. They have come to share what we must do to save ourselves from the fury of the mountain. I want you to know that Ohre has sworn that all that Bryzon tells you is true. Be patient, my friends. Give Bryzon a chance to tell you of our plan before you ask questions of him."

The crowd breaks out in a spontaneous chant of Ohre, Ohre, Ohre…, and it takes a while before decorum is achieved.

"People of Rednos, my friends…," Bryzon begins. "The answer is yes. Yes, we do have spaceships to take us away from Kearthat."

The crowd is attentive. They hang on to each word as they hear that the Yraif still exist and that the earthling ships are safely stored in a surreal world below their feet. The colonists learn that The Selected have been chosen to guide them all to a place of safety, a place of peace and dignity.

Bryzon, however, does not share the information about the Eslaf Androids and the imminent Night Creature hunt. When the plan to offer the gift of long-life to all is divulged, there is pandemonium.

Bryzon looks towards where Raine, Leyashe and the rest of The Liberators are watching the proceedings from the back of the room. This is their cue, and they join the colony leaders and Bryzon on the platform.

"For us to be successful, the pretence that nothing has changed must prevail. The Eslaf cannot know our plan," Bryzon requests from the people before him. "Strict rules must be followed, this you must swear. If the Eslaf suspects our plans, it will assuredly bring our deaths before that of Kearthat."

Bryzon, having concluded his part, motions for Raine and Leyashe to step forward.

The siblings raise their fisted right arms high, tap their chests twice, and then repeat the action. Five hundred Freelander fists sound like a drum beating as they interrupt the warm, quiet Kearthat night.

It has begun.

Sayhran can see many tears of happiness in the crowd. She knows that her tears, however, are for Keazan, Dayson, her sister Caite, her brother Nick, and her parents, Farron and Jon King, who never lived long enough to see this day.

When the last person leaves the building and the group is alone again, Bryzon shakes his head and says, "There is no turning back now." Although the thought is scary, he cannot stop the smile on his face.

"Time to rest. I wish you well on the hunt. I left instructions that you are free to come and go at any hour; the Gatekeeper has been sworn to secrecy. Success, my friends," and with that said, Marcus and Zaviah leave the room hand in hand.

"Marcus is tired," Raine comments. "Talking to his people took a great deal of courage. Now, it is our turn to show our daring. Come, we have a beast to kill."

It-Ha Sayhran sighs, "Are you sure you want to hunt these dangerous creatures tonight, Raine?"

Leyashe answers his aunt with a grin, "It-Ha Sayhran, you must get some rest. We need our It-Ha tomorrow. You have a very important potion to prepare."

"Young Leyashe, I am still your guardian; never forget that," she tells him sternly. And he knows that he has overstepped the line, but all is forgiven as she winks at Raine and hugs them both.

"It-Ha do not need their slumber and seldom become weary. Look out for each other and return whole," she implores, as her light green eyes flicker for just a split second.

The rest of them wish the hunting party well, and Dourok stops in front of Rence. "Until we meet again," he tells his son.

"I know I am of no use to you in this matter, so until dawn, my young friends, be vigilant," and with that, Layrrah exits without protest. It is obvious from her parting comments that any animosity she may have held against Raine and Leyashe earlier in the day is now forgiven.

The five of them are alone at last and jump straight into hunting mode as they begin discussing their strategy before heading in different directions to ready themselves.

Within an hour, Leyashe, Nedai, Rence and Bryzon head to the gate. When they get there, Raine is already waiting. In the bag over her shoulder are the four weapons they brought from The Below. The Gatekeeper opens the gate only far enough for them to squeeze through.

"Come, what are we waiting for?" Raine whispers. They turn their backs on the safety of the colony, moving quickly towards the fields ahead of them. They hear the bolts on the gate click into place. The metal, loud in the still of the night delivers the message that they are now at the mercy of the Night Creatures and Idlers.

The first growl does not reach their ears until almost an hour into their quest.

"Time to turn on your eyes," Bryzon whispers to Raine and Leyashe.

No one except Raine sees the excitement on her brother's face as they wait for the creature to make its move. When it growls, it sounds like it is practically on top of them. Its red eyes are fixed on Raine and Leyashe.

"He is right in front of us," Raine whispers.

"Get behind me. I will shoot as soon as he is close enough. I will not fail," she promises. The growl comes again. Raine can see the creature's exposed teeth, its front legs bent ever so slightly, readying itself to leap.

She aims for the space between its chest, and in these split seconds, she can hear her heart pounding in her ears. The weapon feels strange to her as she takes aim. The creature leaps as she pulls the trigger. An enormous weight crashes down onto Rain's small frame, knocking her to the ground.

Leyashe screams his sister's name. He runs forward, leaving Bryzon, Nedai, and Rence exposed.

A second growl causes Bryzon to spin around. He pushes Nedai against Rence with such force that they bump into Leyashe, who is still trying to help his sister. Bryzon has no time to aim as he pulls the trigger and fires in the darkness in front of him. A loud crash follows, something swipes his cheek, it stings and he can feel warm blood trickle down his face, and then there is silence, but for the night bugs frequenting The Freelands.

Leyashe and Rence help Raine out from under the dead animal.

"Rai, are you ok?" her brother begs, his voice loud in the dark, quiet night. "I am whole brother," she says breathlessly as she rushes towards Bryzon who is still on the ground.

"Are you harmed, Bryzon?" Raine shouts, her voice shaky as she goes down on her knees beside him. "Your face is bleeding," she tells him.

"I am whole. We must get back to safety. With all this noise, there could be more, and it could bring Idlers. My face has healed, so do not be concerned." Bryzon pats the dust from his tunic and goes to the Night Creature that knocked him down. He picks the animal up and hoists it over his shoulders behind his head. Rence watches and then follows Bryzon's method to transport the second lifeless animal. Leyashe gathers up the weapons, and Nedai readies the torch. The adrenalin pumping through their veins makes for a hasty retreat.

Out of breath, they can make out the safety of Rednos Colony. Nedai lights the torch. The gate opens and they slip through. The Gatekeeper's eyes widen when he sees the carcasses. "Now I believe that things are going to change," he whispers, keeping his distance.

The hunters cautiously make their way through the quiet streets, using the shadows of the buildings as cover. The hunt of the Night Creatures must remain a secret for now.

Bryzon turns to Nedai and asks him to wake Zaviah. He looks at Bryzon and raises an eyebrow.

"Your mother made me swear I would wake her if we returned with a beast."

As Raine closes the door of the Healer's Lodge, she can hear Nedai's feet pounding on the ground, and then they fade away. She looks at Bryzon, then at the exit. She walks over and slides the bolt on the door into place.

"Secrecy," she says and sighs loudly.

Bryzon and Rence are breathing heavily. They sit down and wait for Zaviah and Nedai to return.

Where the Night Creature's paw struck Bryzon in the face, the wound has healed completely, leaving no scar. Only a small trickle of blood remains as proof of the injury.

Leyashe spreads the animal's limbs out on the two large tables he has pushed together to accommodate the additional Night Creature. Even in death, they look menacing. He avoids their mouths as he runs his hands over their smooth bodies. Bryzon's shot had gone through the creature's head, and Raine had hit the other animal dead center in the chest exactly where the heart was positioned.

They are as black as the night that they stalk, with ears small for the size of their enormous heads. Their tails, Leyashe notices, are no more than the length of his thumb. With long, slender bodies, they are made for speed. Their paws are huge, their long claws perfect for leaping. The creature's tongues hang from their mouths, exposing rows of yellow teeth. Bryzon gets up and pulls the jaws apart on the closest animal. This displays a ferocious mouth. When he pushes the animal's jaws together, its closed mouth reveals four long fangs that extend far outside of its cheeks.

"These teeth would kill a man with the first bite," Rence comments, shaking his head in awe of the animal's size and strength.

Leyashe decides to climb onto the table, lying down beside the dead Night Creature. The Night Creature is longer by several inches.

Zaviah and Nedai are back and she gasps when she sees the creatures.

"They are so big, and quite beautiful," she says, circling the two tables where the creatures lie spread out. Zaviah runs her hands over the animals just as Leyashe had done earlier.

"Two beasts, how unexpected. You have done well. Let us not waste time. We must proceed immediately; there is little of this night left."

Zaviah brings over a tray of narrow sharp knives. They watch as the Rednos healer deftly cuts into the belly of the first beast. It does not take long for them to see two things they did not expect. The animal's stomach is so small that the beast cannot eat anything bigger than an Ellpa fruit, and its blood is as black as the beast itself.

"How can it maintain its stamina and strength?" Zaviah frowns as she queries the size of the animal's stomach. She gets no reply from her onlookers.

Rence opens a window slightly, commenting that they need fresh air. Raine notices he looks a little pale. It is only when Zaviah starts cutting into individual organs of the animal that Rence excuses himself, heading for the door. Raine follows less than a minute later. Bryzon smiles and winks at Leyashe.

She finds Rence sitting on the steps leading down from the lodge.

"Are you not well?" Raine asks, her voice concerned.

"I am now that I have some fresh air in my lungs," Rence admits, smiling at Raine. "I had to get away from the smell of its blood," he confesses. "I have hunted since I was a boy, skinned all my kills, but this animal smells different. It does not smell right," he says, shaking his head.

They sit in silence for a few minutes. Rence offers his hand, and she willingly takes it. His touch is comforting, and Raine does not let go until they are inside again. The sign of affection does not go unnoticed by Leyashe, who opens the door for them.

It is close to dawn when Zaviah cuts into the animal's head.

Bryzon takes a step forward, unsure if his eyes are deceiving him. The beast's head is more machine than animal. Leyashe smiles. He and Raine were right; the Night Creatures are part Android.

"Nedai, go wake your father and then get to your bed. The rest of you will do the same. We will wake you in four hours," Zaviah adds. "Sorry, Bryzon, I did not propose that you go to your bed," she says, smiling with an apology.

"Yes, mother," Nedai says playfully, rolling his eyes backwards into their sockets.

"But I would like to stay Zaviah, if I may I …?" Leyashe starts pleading, but a stern look from her stops him mid-sentence.

"It will all be here, young Leyashe, when you have rested," Zaviah insists, and he has no choice but to obey.

Zaviah asks Bryzon to bolt the door once the room is cleared and proceeds to remove the electronics from the animal's flesh, her hands black with its blood.

Marcus arrives with Dourok and Kadez. They are astonished at what they see.

"My compliments, Bryzon, I must ask forgiveness of you. I doubted you would bring back a Night Creature, killing two is truly remarkable!" Marcus adds with a little bow of his head.

"I only shot one; Raine killed the other," Bryzon praises. It would take a fool not to notice how proud Bryzon is of his brother's firstborn.

When Marcus sees the mechanism taken from the Night Creature's skull, he is stunned. Leyashe and Raine had been right. It was time to send for Ameka.

"Bryzon, do you not fear that the Eslaf will discover the loss of the two Night Creatures? If tonight we bring down an Idler, would it not raise even more suspicion?" Marcus's forehead is deeply frowned, Bryzon knows he must at all costs allay his concerns.

"It is a risk we must take. I strongly believe that the Eslaf no longer knows the number of colonists, their beasts, or Idlers. Keeland assures me that it has been many years since they marked the number of Freelanders in the colonies. They have become careless," Bryzon insists, reassuring Marcus.

"It-Ha Layrrah has assured me she will use the conjuring of The Veil if we need it. Our plan to discard the bodies of the creatures is a good one, Marcus. The Eslaf will find nothing in Rednos, if they come looking."

"Leyashe has proposed a solution for the Idler that we capture. We plan to return it to where we find it. We will do this before the dawn greets the new day. It will appear damaged due to its own failure," Bryzon replies.

The consequences of the Eslaf finding out they have destroyed not only two Night Creatures but also an Idler would be catastrophic, but Bryzon knows if they pull it off and find a solution to the Eslaf Androids, they will have the upper hand when the time comes to flee Kearthat.

Dourok sends a message with the first Traxid that leaves for Laeredis Colony. The excuse is a sudden Ylock and Nusflower seed exchange between the colonies. The Traxid's return journey ensures that Ameka will be in Rednos the following day.

Bryzon ambles off to the Visitor's Ledge to clean up and eat. He lies down on the bed, his mind trying to analyze the events of the last few hours, but exhaustion takes over and he falls asleep.

Raine has to shake Bryzon several times before his eyes snap open.

"What is wrong? What has happened?" Bryzon panics as he tries to focus on her face.

"Everything is going well. There is nothing wrong. You asked Kadez that you be woken in four hours, remember?"

"The It-Ha are readying the potion. Are you eager to go Idler hunting?" she asks, smiling. Raine is the happiest he has seen her. The role of leader suits her, Bryzon thinks to himself.

"Now that we are alone, Rai, do you think it wise that Ash takes the potion now? Also, Remek and Nedai. They are all so young?"

"But why not ?" she asks, looking at him a little confused. "Why would you ask this?"

"Leyashe is still so young. It will be years before ..." Bryzon begins to say, then asks, "Would it not be wise for them all to wait for perhaps their twentieth year?"

"I fear for their lives," Raine answers, clearly disappointed at Bryzon's thinking.

"I must insist that Leyashe take the potion. We cannot chance that we could lose him. He is different now. High Yraif Laathria promised me ...," she begins to say but is interrupted by a knock at the door.

Bryzon calls out for the visitor to enter. The door opens an inch at a time before fingers creep around the door's edge. It is Marcus who finally peeks into the room.

"Good, you have awoken," he says. "I am leaving. The shuttle should be taking off in a short while. I will see you tomorrow, Bryzon. I wish you both well with the hunt tonight. May you be as successful as you were last night. I will take part in the potion ceremony with the colonists in Elbaffeni Colony. I look forward to seeing you and the It-Ha soon."

Marcus bows to Bryzon and hugs Raine. "Until we meet again, young liberator, Selected leader of our people!" he tells her smiling.

When Raine and Bryzon find Leyashe, he is sitting in the Council Lodge. He seems utterly engrossed in drawings he has made of the Night Creature's electronic brain. Leyashe does not seem to hear them, but just as Bryzon is about to call out, Leyashe speaks.

"Greetings, Bryzon, are you rested? I have figured what we must use to bring down the drone. I have given the Rednos forger the exact specifications, and he assures me that it will done before the light fades."

Bryzon and Raine noticed that Leyashe had not turned around when they entered the room but somehow sensed they were there. She smiles and walks up to her brother, folds her arms around him and hugs him. Leyashe squirms to get out of her grip.

"Why do you do that, Rai?" Leyashe asks his sister indignantly, shaking his head, his face giving her the 'ugh' look.

"I do this, brother, because I love you. I do it because you are so clever and far older than your years," she says, winking at Bryzon. Bryzon knows Raine has just told him that she has no intention of withholding the potion from her brother, Remek or Nedai.

"And what is this amazing discovery, Ash? Will it allow us to take down the Idler without danger?" Then she leans her head back and looks her brother up and down. "Why on Kearthat are you wearing so many tunics?"

Raine begins tugging at the layers around Leyashe's neck while counting aloud. One... two ... three ...before he interrupts her.

"I, Leyashe The Liberator, have spent the last hour in the ice-box in the Healer's Lodge cutting into the Night Creature's paws. I nearly froze to death, Rai," he protests, as he proceeds to peel off one tunic after another until he is left with one, passing his sister the discarded items as he undresses.

"What am I supposed to do with these?" she asks, holding them up in the air.

"They belong to your beloved, Rence" he says and laughs, immediately moving a few steps away from his sister's reach. She goes after him, but he is slow getting out of her way, and she manages to smack him playfully on the head. She throws the bundle of clothing in his direction. Leyashe manages to catch some while other pieces fall to the ground.

"Terrible catch, brother, and he is not my beloved," she insists.

"Enough, you two, we do not have time on our side. Tell me what you have found, nephew?" Bryzon asks, putting a stop to their fun.

"Under the left back paw of both beasts is a small implant in the bone. It confirms that they go somewhere to 'dock.' Once there, they must receive what sustains their bodies. Zaviah is doing further investigation to confirm my..." Leyashe is interrupted when the door opens; it is Krom and Remek.

"I hear we are going Idler hunting tonight, Rai?" Remek smiles, then picks Raine up by the waist, twirling her around as if she is a child's doll.

"Stop Remek, please," Raine begs. "Leyashe has found something really important, there is no time for this now."

When her cousin settles down, Krom goes over and gives his brother a light tap on the back of his head. He also says something to him, but Bryzon does not hear what it is. Remek's silliness ceases immediately.

Darkness has come, and the group steps out into the night. The bolts on the colony gate click into place and they find themselves outside for the second night in a row.

This time, seven of them leave the colony, and Bryzon, Rence, and Nedai are armed with guns. The rest of them each carry a specifically modified bow; each has two arrows fitted with heavier concave tips made to Leyashe's specific instructions.

"Our charge is to escape the Night Creatures and draw an Idler to us. We must be vigilant, not daring," Bryzon whispers, pleading sensibility for the dangerous mission.

Walking in silence, they head in the direction of the open grassland, everyone listening for an Idler. When they reach an area with a large Trigga tree and open grassland, they choose it as their spot. Bryzon, Rence and Nedai kneel at the tree's base, where they are well hidden in the dark shadow of the overhanging branches.

The rest of the team remains in the open, quite visible to any Idler who may pass overhead and very much in danger of being seen by the Night Creatures. Vulnerable but brave, they wait as they scan the sky.

The men under the tree squint into the darkness, listening, watching and waiting for any sign of Night Creatures, their weapons at the ready. Two hours pass before an Idler can be heard heading their way. The four cousins stand back-to-back so that they will have a three-hundred-and-sixty-degree view.

Leyashe and Raine stand out, their luminous pupils staring upwards from the huddled group. The Idler hovers. When the droid is within range, they all point their arrows at the hovering machine. They can hear its constant 'zinging' as it tries to focus on Leyashe and Raine. It backs away, then moves closer and hovers again. It does this three times. The Idler is uncertain what it is looking at; its programming does not have such creatures in its database.

"It thinks we are Night Creatures, but it is not sure," Leyashe whispers to Raine.

"It is not certain if it has the situation under control. Get ready to fire," Raine whispers back. "Three, two, one ... now!" They release their arrows in unison.

The weighted projectiles hit the Idler on only one side as planned. It tilts, obviously damaged, struggling to find its balance. It weaves from side to side, flying lower and lower, finally dropping to the ground.

The men rush out from under the tree. They grab hold of the noisy machine, covering it with a large, dark sheet of fabric provided by Zaviah. They can hear the Idler's mechanisms turning from inside the cloth. It is trapped; the machine is confused in the dark. Without a target to identify and lock onto, it cannot fire. Krom picks up a rock, smashes the Idler's visible camera, and it goes quiet. Leyashe's prediction that the Idlers were not that clever after their encounter with the one in the Otatop field proves that he was right.

They erase their footprints. Using branches, they sweep as they back away from the area and head for the colony. The Idler starts up again but quickly goes silent. The sounds the droid makes are loud in the still of the night, and everyone is a little nervous. Ignoring it, they move as fast as they can; the awkward round machine is difficult to handle. They keep swapping hands, places and positions as they try to carry the Idler and its protruding features. Just before they reach the gate, Nedai lights another torch. At almost the same time, they hear a growl coming from the left.

They stop.

"Put out the torches, Nedai. Now!" Bryzon whispers urgently.

"Move to the back," Raine tells Nedai quietly.

"Time to find out if they are truly scared of us, brother," Raine challenges, looking at Leyashe.

"We do not want to kill another one, but you must fire if it approaches you," Bryzon whispers as he passes his weapon to Raine.

They move back slowly, forming a tight group. Leyashe and Raine face the area out towards the expanse of the Freelands where the growl is coming from.

The growl gets closer. Raine and Leyashe can see the red eyes of the black snarling beast. They are thirty feet from the gate, but the Night Creature keeps advancing. Raine watches as its legs bend, ready to pounce, but it hesitates. It stares at them, snarling. Its prominent yellow canines are threatening, glistening with froth.

"Pick up the Idler," Raine whispers. "Start moving to the gate slowly," she orders, only run when I tell you to."

A few seconds later, Raine screams, "Run!" as she breaks away from the formation and rushes in the opposite direction towards the creature. She shouts at the animal and waves her arms. Leyashe, not knowing what Raine is up to, screams her name several times. Ignored, he mimics Raine's shouts and charges towards the creature. The animal moves back so fast that its front legs catch up to its hind legs, and it almost topples over backwards, trying to get away from them. Then, it gives a strange, ominous yelp as it turns and runs into the night.

"Run, Ash," Raine shouts, and they dash for the gate, the rest of them still moving awkwardly, struggling with the weight of the Idler. Nedai waves a lit torch, shouting for the Gatekeeper to open up.

Every second waiting for the heavy gate to move seems endless. When they are all inside the colony walls, Raine turns around, pointing her weapon towards the closing gate.

The Gatekeeper stares at the group once the craziness subsides, shaking his head.

" I am happy you are back and you are safe. If you want to go out again before the dawn breaks, you are half-witted, but I will be here," the young man tells them, a wry smile of pity on his face for the crazy people standing in front of him, his eyes locked onto the gun in Raine's hand.

They head for the Healer's Lodge. Once inside, they bolt the door. Leyashe opens up the Idler carefully. It is motionless as they move it onto the metal table where the Night Creatures lay the previous night.

Chapter 41 - The Gift

Nedai looks at his timepiece and then at Raine, his expression indicating that time is not on their side.

"Please tell your brother to hasten, Raine," Nedai whispers.

"How much longer before the Idler is assembled, brother?" she asks gently.

"Do not fret, sister. I have almost completed the task," Leyashe insists as he lets out a bit of a 'huff' sound. The silence in the room is beginning to play on everyone's nerves. A huge sigh coming from Bryzon adds to the tension.

Leyashe's hands fly over the bits and pieces and fifteen minutes later, the Idler looks like it did before he took it apart, but for one small piece, a tiny square with circuitry imbedded in it.

"Let us go; we have an Idler to return," he declares to everyone's relief.

When they get to the gate, they find that they must wake the Gatekeeper.

"Open up, Kristoh," Nedai nudges the sleepy young man. The embarrassment is easy to read on the Gatekeeper's face as he hurriedly goes to turn the lever that will open up space enough for them to get through.

"Do not go back to sleep, Kristoh. Watch the dark for our torches our lives are in your hands," Nedai tells him firmly.

"I will be here. I will be awake. I swear this to you, Nedai," Kristoh promises. "Please do not tell your father," he pleads.

It is almost three hours past midnight. Time is running out. Staying close together, they move as fast as they can. The bulky droid is difficult to manoeuvre between the brush, but they persevere as fast as they can. At the edge of the grasslands, they veer left towards the spot where they took down the machine.

Raine stops dead in her tracks, and they all crash into one another.

"What is it?" Krom whispers.

A slow deliberate, "Sssshh" comes from Raine.

They hold their positions in silence.

Raine and Leyashe watch as a Reggit slowly emerges from the shrubs. It is a female with a cub. They can all hear the low growl; it is a warning. The animal sniffs the air while staring at them intently, her long tail swaying slowly from side to side. The Reggit has her eyes locked onto Raine and Leyashe. The two sets of glowing pupils staring back at the creature confuse it as it tries to interpret them. Her sensibility prevails, and she decides to turn away. She steers the cub into the darkness and Raine is glad of the animal's decision.

"It is gone," Raine whispers. "We must move."

"What was it?" Remek asks.

"It was a Reggit with a cub," Leyashe answers.

"Wow, it just walked away! I must get myself a pair of eyes like yours. I will talk to my mother. Perhaps she can help me out now that she is an It-Ha," Remek remarks, gathering a few smiles from his family in the dark.

Leyashe is the one with the urgency in his voice now, "We must move faster," he whispers.

Once there, they place the Idler near some large rocks. Leyashe goes over and smashes the side of the Idler where he took out the circuit board, just to be sure that it cannot be identified.

They work quickly. They scatter leaves and small branches as they back away from the scene of the crime. They drop pebbles and bigger stones randomly, recreating an undisturbed landscape.

A short while later, they slide through the gate, and Kristoh closes it behind them.

"We did it. Now we can only hope that the Eslaf consider that it fell from the sky because its parts were failing," Leyashe contends.

"Well, that was easy, until dawn liberators of Kearthat," Remek greets, then walks away whistling softly to himself.

"See you in a minute, Ash," Raine tells her brother.

Raine waits for Leyashe and Bryzon to round the corner before she takes Rence's hand in hers. In the dark, she looks into his eyes, eyes that have begun to melt her heart. A rush of heat reaches her cheeks, and she is grateful for the dim light protecting her.

"Thank you, Rence," she says, looking up at him.

"My feelings for you grow more and more each day, Raine, daughter of Dayson," he confesses, touching her cheek gently, his expression soft and caring. He tugs on the strands of her hair that have escaped, tucking them behind her ears, and brings his face close to hers. For just a moment, she hesitates, but when his lips touch hers, she gives in to his gentle kiss and a wonderful dizzy feeling cloaks her. His strong arms encircle her narrow waist and she feels safe, her tough veneer melting in that moment.

"There will be much time for this after we defeat the Eslaf," she says, mustering the courage to gently push him away.

"Do not give up on me, Rence, son of Dourok. Try not to get yourself killed, or I will never speak to you again!" she says, smiling.

"I will stay alive just for you," he whispers into the humid breeze that is blowing over Kearthat. Rence watches her as she sprints away in the direction of the Visitor's Lodge before he heads for his home, his heart filled with love for her, his stubborn Raine.

It is dawn and Bryzon, Leyashe, and Raine head out to meet the group at the Healer's Lodge. When they get there, they find only Nedai and Rence. Raine looks at Rence and she can feel her face flush: the It-Ha arrive and it saves her. A few minutes later, Krom and Remek knock and are let in.

"Dourok and Kadez will be here shortly, with Ameka," Krom informs everyone.

They hear a noise in the back room. All the time they have been talking, they have not been alone. Raine moves slowly to where the noise comes from. She takes out her short sword. The others follow close on her heels. Suddenly, the silence is broken by a cheerful Zaviah, causing them near heart failure as she steps out of the room where the Night creatures are being stored on ice.

"Oh, I thought I heard something. I was looking at the feet," she tells the surprised group, who are now all huddled together in the short walkway, causing a jam. Then she laughs and clarifies her comment, "I mean the beast's feet, of course."

"I am not practised on knowing all about paws, but I can tell you these animals have been cruelly treated. It was painful for them to go through these changes," Zaviah shares, shaking her head in pity for the animals as she follows everyone back to the main room.

"And I agree with Leyashe. It is a docking mechanism that is implanted in the paw. I also found something else. Hidden in the natural cavity between the front legs and chest is a small hole, and below it a metal implant. This is where the feeding tube goes directly into the vein. These creatures were programmed to attach themselves to a feeding machine."

"Very cruel, very cruel," Zaviah says under her breath. "Oh yes," she adds, "and they shortened their tails. I am not sure why? It could be that they got in the way of the feeding tubes, or perhaps they were docking issues," she adds as an afterthought.

There is a knock and Nedai peeks to see who it is.

Ameka enters first, followed by Dourok and Kadez. Tall and slim, her black hair drawn back from her pleasant features, she looks exactly as Bryzon remembers her.

Dourok introduces her; she smiles and bows, then walks straight to Bryzon, her arms outstretched.

"My brave friend," she greets Bryzon with a hug. "I have thought of you many times in the past years. I am happy to see you."

"It gives me much joy to see you," Bryzon retorts as he embraces her.

Ameka had fought bravely when the Eslaf attacked the City of Seccus, and Bryzon recalls something that he had not thought of until the moment he saw her again. She was there when the tunnels under the city were sealed up.

"At first, it was hard to believe what I now know is true. I am sad for the loss of Kearthat, but happy for our people. I will welcome freedom after so many years of living in the old ages," Ameka admits with a wry smile. "Where are the beasts? Let us get to work, Leyashe," she says, looking over at the boy who is eager to learn from the Xennes engineer of old Kearthat.

It is decided that before the It-Ha proceeds to administer the potion, spotters should be positioned to look out for Idlers and Eslaf craft. The Gatekeeper receives instructions to ring the big bell used to call the colonists from the field at day's end to warn them if they spot anything near the colony.

Later, Bryzon returns to the Healer's Lodge, his impatience getting the better of him.

"Do you have anything to report, nephew?" he asks the moment Leyashe opens the door.

"We cannot tell if the Night Creatures and the Idler have the same mechanisms," he informs Bryzon.

"We do not have the tools to do what we must, Bryzon," Ameka pleads. "But Leyashe tells me that the ships in Telmah have such means. If we are to find a solution we must proceed to The Below," she requests.

"Then you must go to Telmah," Bryzon says without hesitation.

A half hour later Kadez and Dourok bring a cart to the back door of the Healer's Lodge. The bodies of the Night Creatures leave under the cover of freshly harvested Ylock. In the middle of a Ylock field not far from the colony a deep hole dug shortly after dawn awaits the dead beasts.

For some reason, no Eslaf had ever been seen to venture into a field filled with crops. This fact had been in a report Raine had presented to Keeland many seasons past. Leyashe deduced that their boots, or more likely their suits were not well suited to venturing into the soft soil, or perhaps the dust affected their armour. It was the perfect hiding place.

Bryzon leaves Leyashe and Ameka to find Krom and Remek. He must speak with them before they leave on the afternoon shuttle that will take them to the prison camp to see Pateeo and Namow. The brothers are attentive as Bryzon gives them advice on how to go about the task ahead of them. Their mission will either save or destroy the Korak's chances of survival, and perhaps their own.

Later, there is news to share among the group. Nor~han has sent a message to It-Ha Layrrah. The Yraif navigated the cavern that leads all the way underground where an opening near the city gate can be created. Bryzon is over the moons, this takes care of how they will enter the old council gardens unseen. From there they will go into the tunnel that will lead them to the old Starfleet base in the city.

"I think there is a good chance they have never discovered the underground walkways, my friend," Kadez says confidently assuring Bryzon.

"What were all the walkways used for in Seccus?" Raine asks.

"They were used to minimize the air-shuttle crowding above the city," Bryzon explains. But the tunnel that we speak of was used by the Xennes who were permitted to enjoy the beautiful garden. Leaving the garden outside of the wall that the Eslaf built around the city is another mistake they have made. It is an incredible stroke of luck," Bryzon tells her using his old friend Jon King's expression." Raine smiles, it is good news, and she is happy to hear him use her grandfather's sayings. It means that Bryzon has forgiven him.

"In the garden there is a secret entrance that we covered well during the invasion, it became one with the garden. It will be overgrown now, from there a staircase will take us into the passage, the other end is sealed. When we break through we will be in the base," Bryzon explains.

First in the group to receive the potion are Krom and Remek, their faces beaming when they emerge, followed by Rence and Nedai.

"Rence my friend, now you have a thousand years to convince my cousin to love you," Remek teases. Raine blushes as she watches a scuffle when Rence playfully wrestles Remek to the ground.

Raine and Leyashe are the last to receive the potion.

The windows in the lodge are covered. In the semi-dark several candles on the long council table cast shadows against the wooden walls. A dozen or more small wooden cups are neatly lined up next to a jar of potion right next to the mysterious black sanction stone.

"You and Ash kneel here," Sayhran requests.

For a moment Raine wonders what the potion will taste like, but she is distracted by the It-Ha as they move about.

The chanting begins.

"Neraz mazeiz livoz, Neraz mazeiz livoz," the It-Ha repeat.

The sanction stone turns pink, the light it emits seems to twinkle, millions of dancing silvery speckles float around them, while pink wisps of mist travel in twirling circles, moving throughout the whole room.

When the wispy clouds encircle Leyashe and Raine the wooden cups float towards them. High It-Ha Layrrah pours the potion into the cups when they come to a halt.

"Drink of the waters of the Cigan and become Xennes," It-Ha Layrrah declares, her voice a hollow-sounding echo.

The siblings swallow the liquid in one go and immediately feel its effect. An incredible heat courses through their veins. It takes their breath away and they gasp, it is like nothing they have ever felt. Just when they think it is intolerable, the heat is quickly replaced with an icy cold feeling that lasts for what feels like forever. Then all is normal again, the wisps of pink begin to fade, and the sanction stone darkens taking with it the beautiful speckles that filled the room. It is done.

"You can stand now," Layrrah tells the siblings, her voice quite normal again. "You now have long-life. Your body will regenerate when you are hurt, you will live for many, many years. Accept this gift and do good in your life, remember who you are always. You are Xennes.

Unable to hold back tears of joy, Sayhran hugs them both. At that moment she is not an It-Ha, she is just their aunt.

Then all chaos ensues. The bell at the gate rings out three times, it stops for a few seconds and then rings out again. The Gatekeeper has spotted danger.

Three Eslaf craft land just outside Rednos Colony. Eslaf soldiers pour out heading for the colony.

Suddenly everything on the table slides into two bags, the covers on the windows vanish and light streams back into the Council Lodge. The It-Ha Layrrah opens a trap door under the council table where the earthling guns are hidden and stores the potion. Marcus's Eninac gets up from where he is lying and repositions himself on the trap door covering the entire area. Layrrah casts a spell, and the bags vanish into thin air.

The siblings slip out the door and head for the crop sorting area in the colony. They quickly find a seat and begin shucking a pile of Ylock. Everyone is silent. Out of the corner of her eye Raine spots Remek and Nedai, they are busily sewing sacks of vegetables that are ready to be transported to the prison. The aliens flood the buildings. They are searching for something.

It is not long before Raine can see Dourok waving his arms about as he speaks to a red-suit. She cannot hear what he is telling the ugly alien that towers over him, but she can see Kadez first nodding his head, then he shakes it from side to side as if denying something.

Aliens accompanied by another red-suit come around the corner toward the tables where Raine and Leyashe are helping with the sorting of fruit and vegetables.

The Eslaf soldier growls, "Move, you move."

A man seated next to Raine is slow to move and the alien pushes him roughly out of the way. The man falls and hits his head on the edge of a bench, when he manages to stand he has blood streaming down his face. Raine rushes forward to help him but the Eslaf shouts something at her, she stops dead in her tracks when he points his weapon at her head.

The alien soldiers kicks over some sacks and seed spills everywhere, another pushes the tables over to see if anything is being hidden under it. All the while Raine is watching as the wound on the injured man's forehead begins to close, leaving only the blood on his face. She raises her hand to her forehead and looks directly into his eyes, it takes a few seconds before he realises that Raine is prompting him to place his hand over his forehead where the wound used to be.

When they are satisfied that nothing is out of the ordinary, the Eslaf stomp away, their heavy-booted alien feet crunching down on the dry dirt kicking up puffs of dust.

Bryzon had slipped over the wall where he had been pretending to toil in a nearby Otatop field with other Freelanders.

The aliens leave behind chaos, but the colony has not yielded what they were searching for. Eventually, the alien craft take off in the direction of the city.

The Liberators instinctively head for the Council building. They must regroup.

Dourok explains that the Eslaf are puzzled by the droid that has fallen from the sky so close to Rednos Colony.

"They do not know that we killed the beasts yet!" Kadez adds. "If they did, they would still be here searching, and there would be blood spilled. Our blood, he emphasizes."

"Our freedom is in danger so soon," Leyashe says sounding a little dejected. Suddenly he is afraid they will be caught out by the Eslaf before completing their mission.

Their discussions go nowhere, for now all they can do is proceed with their plans. There was nothing to be done.

"Ash and I have reached a decision," Raine says, changing the conversation.

"We wish you to take a message to all the leaders and the Freelanders as you travel to the colonies. We have decided that we are no longer Drennan, or Earthling. It is time for us to become one. We have chosen to be known as The Xennes. Our decision excludes the Yraif, of course," she says with a smile.

"The Selected have spoken. It is done. The leaders will accept. Raine and Leyashe have chosen well, come Bryzon, we must ready ourselves to leave for Elbaffeni Colony,"

Layrrah says firmly as she pushes her chair back. And so it was that the Drennan and earthlings of Kearthat were solidly melded together forever in a matter of seconds.

"It-Ha Sayhran, please extend my greetings to the two leaders of Noitibma Colony. I wish you well my Tiro," Layrrah says smiling, and everyone picks up on the greeting that excludes the now-obsolete Elder Moss.

It is up to the newest It-Ha to extend long-life to all of Noitibma's people, but Sayhran is ready, she has magic, and The Inmo, she is an It-Ha now.

The afternoon shuttle travelling to the Western Colonies arrives. Bryzon and Layrrah are ready, waiting to head down to Elbaffeni Colony where Marcus is expecting them.

Raine and It-Ha Sayhran will go in the opposite direction, returning to Noitibma when the same shuttle returns. Krom and Remek will continue to the prison to visit Pateeo.

Ameka and Leyashe will proceed to the cavern at the big Trigga tree where Nor~han's men await them. Preparations to leave Kearthat have begun in earnest.

The Eslaf guards take no notice of Bryzon or the other passengers heading for the Elbaffeni. When the craft ascends he manages a glimpse of the clearing where they returned the Idler. There is an alien spotter craft at the site. He has only seconds to take in the picture of two Eslaf soldiers beside the damaged drone, then his view is blocked.

The shuttle sets down outside of Elbaffeni Colony. Bryzon recognises Leader Udo directing men as they offload the shuttle but Bryzon does not linger, he heads for the colony gate. He is tempted to look back but resists the impulse.

Layrrah in her guise as a Freelander winks at the man giving the orders. She deliberately focuses her gaze on two sacks sewn closed with double rows of stitching. Udo instructs a young boy with an empty cart to load the special cargo.

"Take those to the seed master now. They need to go out with the work crew first thing tomorrow. Hurry boy, the suns are low," he bellows so that the Eslaf soldier nearby can hear him.

When Layrrah enters the gate followed by the young boy pulling the cart relief washes over Bryzon. They have managed to bring the potion with them without incident. 'A few more trips like this are all we need,' he thinks as they head for the Council Lodge in silence. The It-Ha miraculously dressed in her flowing dress and cape has Bryzon wondering how he had not noticed when this change occurred. He shakes his head, he would have to accept to all the magic around him now.

"At last, Bryzon my friend, you are home," Leader Dehrazz greets his old commander. He bows to Layrrah, then takes her hands in his, "Welcome It-Ha Layrrah, we have been eagerly awaiting your arrival."

Kearthat starts to shake beneath their feet. Shouts can be heard from outside as the shuttle flies overhead adding to the confusion. They scramble in under the table as items tumble off it around them. Bryzon does his best to shield Layrrah by holding his big hands over her head as she lies face down. The shaking does not last long.

Bryzon holds out his hand to the It-Ha and she takes up the offer. She dusts off her cape and dress while Marcus rights empty cups that lay overturned on the table. Strangely a jug of fruit juice sits upright, not a drop spilled.

"Marcus has told us that soon it will be as in the old days when we were our own masters," Udo says, smiling as he enters the lodge to join them.

"I hope so, I hope so Udo." Bryzon agrees, moving forward to greet his old friend. Before they begin their meeting Udo tells Bryzon that he had joined with a woman from Rednos not long after Bryzon went to prison. "I waited for the most lovely woman on Kearthat, my friend," Udo boasts, his face lighting up as he talks about his wife referring to her as 'my beautiful Zari.'

Bryzon remembers Zari's grandparents clearly, their complexion much darker than that of the Drennan intrigued him. Jon King had praised the couple for their brilliance. Together, with Frederick King, Zari's grandparents had engineered the technology that propelled the earthling homeships at an incredible speed they called DIPPS. After the invasion sadly only Zari's mother remained. She later joined with a Drennan mortal.

The rest of the day and the next day proceed as planned. By the time Bryzon, Marcus and Layrrah leave the colony there are six hundred and three new Xennes in Elbaffeni, the count includes Marcus King. Two of the three leaders of Elbaffeni, once Starfleet men, are requested to join Nor~han in Telmah. A Xennes woman from the colony named Elfradah joins the men as the first woman pilot to go Below.

The shuttle ascends as Bryzon and Layrrah journey to the next colony, the potion destined for Laeredis safely stored in sacks of Ylock kernels. Bryzon finally decides to ask Layrrah why they have to transport the potion instead of concealing it with her magic, and he learns that the liquid can be manipulated by magic, but cannot be concealed by magic. And just like that, Bryzon learns more about magic as he accompanies the High It-Ha.

When they arrive at Laeredis Bryzon walks directly to the entrance. Marcus stays on the shuttle bound for Rednos Colony. Layrrah lingers only long enough to see the special sacks of seed loaded onto a cart before she makes her way to the colony gate. The three pilots chosen to go to Telmah sit scattered among the dishevelled-looking group of workers going to various colonies, they too will disembark at Rednos.

The scene plays out in Laeredis Colony much as it had in Elbaffeni. Xandr is asked to make his way to Rednos Colony, from there he will be taken to the Trigga tree entrance, then by boat to Telmah. He will be joined by others as Bryzon selects more men and women for the mission. The following afternoon four-hundred-and-nineteen Laeredis colonists become Xennes.

Layrrah and Bryzon travel to Noyclah Colony next, they choose to go by Traxid to avoid running into the same Eslaf on the shuttles. At this stop only the Leader of Noyclah is asked to go to Telmah. Four-hundred-and-twenty-six Freelanders of Noyclah Colony become gifted Xennes. Next, Layrrah and Bryzon head for Sedecca Colony, again choosing to use the Traxid transport available. On this trip two Eslaf escort the Traxid.

"Do not be anxious, as soon as we reach Sedecca the aliens will re-join their shuttle," Layrrah reassures Bryzon.

Each time they have travelled the It-Ha has changed her appearance, it is something Bryzon cannot get used to as he looks at the ordinary young girl sitting next to him with Layrrah's voice.

Halfway through the journey Bryzon can see for himself that the Eslaf have become complacent. The guards stare ahead of them, all the way to the settlement. They do not bother to check the load on the vehicle. Time has indeed made them negligent of their duties and Bryzon is certain that the two aliens were those of flesh.

Layrrah sighs softly as she considers the dream that she had the night before. In her dream the potion seeped out into Otatop sacks. The same sacks that she carefully prepared for carrying the potion to Sedecca Colony. The Eslaf unknowingly eat the soaked Otatop, turning them into Xennes, and they are invincible. When she awoke from the dream she knew that it had not been a vision, it had to have been a nightmare. Mystified, she had decided it best to ignore the dream but her mind insists on analysing it.

A small child clambers over from the seat in front of her and comes to sit next to Layrrah, she touches The It-Ha's hand and Layrrah is stirred away from questioning her nightmare. The child is holding a doll.

"Her name is Untru," the little girl tells Layrrah. The doll is made of dry Ylock leaves cleverly woven to create the toy, its eyes painted light brown like that of the child. The doll's mouth is sewn into a curl of perpetual contentment.

"Untru," Layrrah says softly and smiles. The little girl was there to bring a message, her nightmare must not be taken seriously. Layrrah looks up from the doll, closes her eyes and smiles. When she opens her eyes the little girl is nowhere to be seen. Looking down on her lap the doll is gone.

Leader Sanew of Sedecca Colony, once a scientist in old Kearthat meets the shuttle. He and his lesser leaders, Divaad and Nedwon are overwhelmed by what they are told. Discussions with Bryzon and Layrrah extend well into the night. The following morning the High It-Ha administers potion to the smallest colony on the Freelands long before the first daily shuttle arrives. Bryzon and Layrrah leave behind three-hundred-and-five gifted with long-life.

Leaders Nedwon and Divaad board the shuttle for Rednos Colony. Layrrah and Bryzon, seated apart, remain on the Eslaf craft when they reach Rednos where the two men leave the shuttle. Their next stop, their home colony, Noitibma.

Bryzon has to admire Layrrah, she had thought everything through very well. Having Ohre go to the colonies ahead of them to assure the validity of what he and the It-Ha had to convey made everything proceed smoothly, and far quicker than he had imagined.

When the shuttle lands outside of Noitibma, Bryzon and It-ha Layrrah walk the short distance from the ICS Station to the big gate. The suns are just about to disappear behind the mountain range. Hardly inside the colony they hear the shuttle leave, the sound of it fading as it heads for the city completing its round trip for the day.

The bolts on the colony gate clang into place. The silence is deafening. Layrrah changes from an old lady into herself. Bryzon notices they have not seen anyone since arriving. The further they walk, the more they frown at each other. What on Kearthat is happening? Where is everyone?

Halfway down the lane that will take them to the center of the colony, Bryzon is bothered by the quiet. When they round the corner at the Healer's Lodge they are shocked to see all of Noitibma's citizens waiting in silence.

Keeland steps out of the crowd, followed by Lesser Leader Nowber. Raine and Sayhran join them as they form a line in front of the people of the colony. Elder Moss is not in the lineup. They raise their right arms and clench their fists, every Freelander behind them follows their example. In the hush, the swish of tunics can be heard as the many arms go up into the air.

Bryzon is overwhelmed, he shakes his head at the bravery in front of him.

The citizens of Noitibma tap their chests twice, then repeat the action. The sound of that many fists hitting chest bone is loud in the quiet dusk hour.

Then an eruption of cheers fills the air.

Tears sting Bryzon's eyes causing him to take in a deep breath to clear the burning lump in his throat. 'I cannot let them see any weakness now,' he thinks, 'The Liberators must show strength.'

Later when they open the door to Sayhran's cabin they are astonished to find a table laden with food.

Sayhran's dinner table is quiet without all the young voices it has enjoyed of late. To Raine it feels strange not having her brother close, but she understands the importance of his journey Below.

"We have never been apart," Raine shares as they sit to eat the feast prepared by kind women of the colony. Bryzon pats her on the arm, "Soon, Raine, soon we will all be together," he reassures her.

The subject of The Below and the visits to the Western Colonies dominate the conversation. Raine learns that the visited colonies were without question all in favour of being known as the Xennes who hail from Kearthat.

"Leyashe will be pleased to hear that many are joining him and Ameka in Telmah," Raine quips, reaching for a piece of fruit in the bowl in front of her.

While Layrrah and Bryzon plan for their journey to the Eastern colonies, Raine lets her mind drift to thoughts of Rence. She has begun to have deep feelings for the man with the light brown eyes. She reminds herself that they are both Xennes now and as such they will have many years to spend together if they can avoid the deadly alien Nobrac, and escape a fiery Kearthat.

After dinner Bryzon and Raine bid everyone a good night. They are halfway to Raine's cabin when the ground begins to move under their feet. Raine loses her balance and Bryzon leaps towards her, scooping her up as he dashes for an open area in the colony. The violent shaking persists for several seconds before stopping. The second shake does not last long before the still night returns.

The knowledge of impending disaster fresh on everyone's mind, Bryzon is sure there will be wakeful hours on this night.

"Two in the last few days Bryzon, it is really happening. Do you think the Eslaf know that there is danger?" Raine asks him.

"They imagine that it has always been this way on Kearthat. Their love for Zraphite will be their ruin," Bryzon comments smiling. But in his thoughts he is hoping that, he, is the one planning their ruin.

When she closes the door to her small bedroom Raine feels surprisingly tired for a Xennes. She spends a few minutes looking at the picture of her parents, making a mental note that she must not leave Kearthat without it. She turns off her small lamp and snuggles under the cover. It does not take long before she drifts into sleep.

"Raine, can you hear me? Raine, are you there?"

Raine stirs, and a few seconds later she bolts upright.

"Leyashe," she says aloud. "You are dreaming, Raine," she whispers, lays down and immediately drifts off again.

Then, clear as a bell the voice is back and she is wide awake.

"Raine, can you hear me?"

"Leyashe, is that you?" she asks in her head, answering her brother.

"Who else would it be sister? He giggles.

"Ash, this is wonderful. I did think I was dreaming, brother," she replies, chuckling.

"We can speak from this distance; that is amazing,"

"Are the plans in Telmah going well?"

"I was really hungry when we were done for the day. The food here is like no other," her brother tells her, and Raine smiles in the dark of her room at his comments.

"In the morning we go to the ships. Ameka and I have decided that it makes good sense for our group from Above to live aboard the first ship. We have given the homeships numbers until you join me," he tells her. Raine can hear in her brother that he has changed. He now considers the two of them as one.

"Together we will decide the new names for the homeships."

"That is good brother, we will find strong names," she answers.

"I spoke to Nor~han today, I am hoping you will agree Raine," Leyashe prompts. "We think that we should begin moving his people onto the spaceships too. The Yraif have been very busy cultivating the gardens on ship number two, but it would go faster if they worked in shifts."

"Brother, you must decide what is best until we can make such decisions together," Raine agrees. She knows that given the freedom to make choices will only encourage Leyashe to do his best,

"I wish you were here, Rai, it is so different. I sometimes find it hard to understand the reality of what is happening," he confesses to her.

"We are expecting Ohre in two days. Nor~han told us he is soon to complete his mission for the It-Ha. He will be entering through the waterfall near Sigae, Leyashe apprises her.

"Can you imagine, all this time there has been an entrance behind a waterfall,? he continues excitedly.

"Suddenly, there is silence and Raine asks, "Are you still there, brother?"

"I saved the finest news for last, Rai," suddenly Layashe sounds much like he did the night when he withheld the secret of the cavern from her.

"Speak brother, do not keep me in this uncertainty, what is it that you have done?"

"Xandr and I have already flown a transporter ship through the tunnels. It was incredible. He is a master Rai, he is truly a great pilot. We are going to amaze Ohre. We plan to be there with the transporter when he enters the cavern."

As Raine listens to her brother she can picture him being attentive to Xandr, quickly mastering the earthling technology. Her brother's love for numbers and the technology of old Kearthat had paid off, Leyashe's talent for memorising had always been a mystery to Raine, but now it was invaluable.

"That is outstanding brother, Bryzon will be gratified that Xandr has mastered the ways of the earthling ships." It was happening, they were beginning to conquer their biggest obstacle.

"Xandr is extremely practised," Leyashe trails on with obvious admiration for his tutor.

"How are the preparations above?" he asks when he realizes Raine is silent.

"One-thousand eight-hundred and Five Xennes at last count," she verifies proudly.

"Did you feel the quake earlier?" she asks changing the subject.

"Yes, I dread that we will not have enough time to achieve our plans," he answers sounding a tinge uncertain.

"Brother, you must be strong. You are Xennes now, you are a leader of your people. You must not doubt. The It-Ha has confided to me that her judgement will prevail.

"I will let you go back to your rest, Rai. We will talk again tomorrow. My greetings to Bryzon and ... It-Ha Sayhran," he corrects. "Tell them we have achieved much in a short time in Telmah."

"And Raine, do we call Sayhran by her name or It-Ha Sayhran?" it is unclear to me.

"I think that when we are truly alone with her, she is Sayhran, but when we are with others we should refer to her as It-Ha Sayhran."

"Until dawn brother."

"Until dawn, Rai, I love you."

"I love you too Ash, take good care of yourself brother, and before you go" she adds, "Rence is waiting with four more people at the beach Below."

"Xandr and I picked them up earlier, they were shaken when they saw the transporter," he tells her and she knows that he is grinning with pride.

Suddenly her head is empty, Leyashe is gone.

Raine is quite renewed after the communication and decides to tell Bryzon immediately of the successes in Telmah.

Bryzon does not dream of the mine and hardship on this night, instead, his dreams are filled with a place that is lush with green forests and clear streams.

Raine dreams of a Firemoth with a confusing message. The following morning, her dream fades fast and by the time they sit for their morning meal, she cannot recall any of it to tell Bryzon.

"You look troubled, do you wish to talk about it?" he presses.

"I cannot. Not really, and not because I do not wish to" she answers. "I had a dream of a Firemoth speaking to me. I know in my dream that I was upset," Raine says, her face expressing her desire to remember. "But I cannot remember why."

"Perhaps you were not meant to remember."

"You are right Bryzon," she says sighing, but still wishing she could remember.

Chapter 42 - The Visit

At the main gate, Krom tells the Korak guard that he and Remek are there to visit prisoner number two-zero-two-three.

Krom hands over his short sword and Remek surrenders his bow and several arrows. They pass through the body scanner to confirm that they do not have any other weapons. The bag they brought with them is snatched out of Remek's hands by a green-suit. It contains their two blankets and a letter to Pateeo, written by Bryzon sending his greetings.

The Eslaf soldier carefully examines the items then throws them back at Remek. Krom signs the register. Nothing has changed at the prison since Bryzon left and Krom and Remek are kept waiting as always. They take a seat just inside the entrance to the prison, they remain silent.

A few female colonists arrive to visit their men, Krom recognizes them, they are all from the Western Colonies. He is certain they are here to share their news, he knows this because none greet Remek or himself. The fealty to secrecy is working.

When the suns sink in behind The High Mountains a guard appears. He points his weapon in the direction of the small group that has gathered. In single file they are led on a short walk that takes them to the fenced-off section adjacent to the main prison camp. Here they will be within little more than an arm's reach from the prisoners on the other side of the electrified chain fence. Locked in for their own protection from the Night Creatures. They scan the prison camp for Pateeo but it is Namow who recognizes them before they can find him amongst the thousands of prisoners. She smiles as broadly as her small alien mouth allows.

"You come see Peti, yes?"

"Yes, Namow, how are you?" Krom asks the gentle alien woman.

"Namow still heere, Namow good," she says, tilting her head, her large sad eyes speaking of her sad life in the prison.

"Brizo is good?" she asks.

"Yes, Bryzon is well, thank you," Krom answers.

"Namow, you must find Pateeo, please, and you too must come and sit with us tonight," Krom tells her.

"We have an important message from Bryzon," Remek adds.

They can see that Namow is surprised at the request. She nods and disappears into the masses to find Pateeo.

It is not long before she appears with Bryzon's Xennes friend.

"You have no idea how happy I am to see you," Peteeo greets with a huge smile on his face. "I am honoured that you have come to visit. Tell me of my friend Bryzon?" he immediately asks. "He is not in trouble?" he enquires, the smile on his face vanishing in anticipation of what could perhaps be bad news.

"Bryzon is doing well, Pateeo, thank you, but he has sent us on an urgent matter," Krom continues and passes Pateeo the letter from Bryzon.

Peteeo opens the now unsealed note and scans the words.

My friend, I hope my letter finds that you are doing well, and that the men are heartened that they will soon be returning to their families. Ohre sends his Honour, and so do all at the colonies. Your Trusted friend, Bryzon.

When Pateo is finished reading the note, he puts it in his pocket.

"We have much to tell you and Namow, but first we will tell you Pateeo, the Eslaf have confirmed they will keep their word, you will be released on the date arranged by my cousin and Leader Keeland."

"It is good news," Pateeo says, and Krom can see the relief on his face.

"Speak of the message you bring, what is this urgent news? I am impatient to hear Bryzon's communication," Pateeo asks. I see it comes with the seal of Ohre's trust, and my friend's honour.

"Remek and I ask that you listen carefully to what we are about to tell you and Namow," Krom requests as he looks at Namow.

Pateeo's eyes narrow as if a little confused, but he does not say anything.

"There will be grave consequences for our people if this is not kept secret. Perhaps it is best that you do not ask questions until you know all of what we have come to share," Krom whispers.

Pateeo's happy face is suddenly replaced with a look of concern. He moves in a little closer, gesturing for Namow to get closer to the fence.

This matter that we wish to talk of affects all the people of Kearthat," Remek states, adding "including the Korak."

The siren interrupts, as it announces that the fence will be electrified and Remek flinches.

"You are a little anxious today, brother," Krom mocks his younger sibling and chuckles. A sigh escapes Remek's lips as he rolls his eyes at his brother.

Krom begins to tell the story of Lan~Igiro and its Yraif and the predicted end of Kearthat. An hour later a stunned Pateeo and a very confused Namow have been made aware that their lives will soon be quite different. But they are not given time to question the story that Bryzon's nephews bring, as the ground under them begins to shake.

Namow and Pateeo rise to their feet, moving away from the fence. Krom and Remek are immediately on their feet too as they attempt to steady themselves from the violent shaking, avoiding the electrified fence at all cost.

It does not last long before all is calm again. The aliens turn on all the tower lights and scan the prison and its perimeter. After several minutes they douse the lights and the prisoners and visitors alike settle down again.

"Returning to the mine tomorrow will not be so difficult," Pateeo says, knowing he and the other Xennes men are now almost guaranteed to be released soon and that total freedom is within reach.

"Namow no understan all you mans tock," she says softly, her eyes pleading for a better grasp of the discussions.

"We have time Namow, you can ask and we will explain it to you," Krom reassures her.

The hours pass quickly, every question that Pateeo and Namow ask is answered as well as Sayhran's sons are able. They have difficulty explaining to Namow of the existence of the Yraif and who they are, but finally she makes a comment that draws a laugh from Remek.

"The raiff they liv dark place, this cleva hide from uggla ezlaaf," she finally tells them, and it is hard not to laugh out loud.

"So you are also telling me that the visitors that are here now, talking to their family, are telling them they are Xennes and that Kearthat will soon be no more," Pateeo echoes, as if still unable to grasp the enormity of what he has just learned.

Remek looks around to make sure there are no Eslaf guards nearby. He tugs at a leather string around his neck. Pateeo recognizes the medallion, it is one of two that Keazan had made for his boys when they were little.

Remek uses the thin metal adornment to cut a short line into his palm. He winces as the blood begins to ooze from the wound.

Namow's already large eyes grow even bigger, "You crazi boy Remy, why you cutta," she exclaims in a whisper, horrified at what is happening. But her words are barely spoken when right before her eyes the wound begins to close. When Remek wipes away the blood, his hand is healed. The action prompts Namow to speak in Korak, then she smiles, "Namow trus Brizo, Remy you no hev cuta to show."

Peteeo slowly turns his head, looking to his left and right where several men are huddled too close to the dangerous fence. He can see the joy on the faces of the men even in the dim light.

"You have not rested, Pateeo," Krom points out when the light begins to change in the sky and dawn is about to greet them.

"Namow and I will have much to think of during our day in the mine. It will help to keep us awake," Pateeo assures the concerned young man.

"Secrecy is everything now," Pateeo tells the boys who are very aware of the refrain by now.

Time has almost run out for the visitors and Pateeo hurriedly tells Krom and Remek that the day before, the Eslaf had brought in a large number of Korak prisoners from the city.

"There must have been two hundred or more," he surmises.

"Peti it kuz you mans leave u go you house," Namow says.

Pateeo looks at Namow, his forehead suddenly creased in a questioning frown.

"Why did you not tell me?" he questions.

"Namow sad," the Korak woman admits, putting her large palm to her chest, her big eyes glistening with alien tears.

"Remy, Krum, you tell Brizo, Korak fight for be free agan, you tell Namow say tank you, Brizo good man, when Peti and mans go you home, we ready, we look sky," she tells them, her head tilted up as she looks at the sky.

"We will try to save all the prisoners when the darkening comes. On that day the Eslaf will drop to the ground like bugs. Bryzon gives you his word," Krom whispers, his face filled with undiluted hatred for the Eslaf.

Namow walks into the crowd, then turns back, puts her large fist to her chest and taps it twice. Bryzon has managed to teach the alien woman more than they ever could have imagined. The boys return the gesture. She smiles and Krom can swear he notices a little spring to her stride before she melts into the throng.

The sharp sound of the siren that wakes the prisoners every morning fills the air, it is time for another day of gruelling, endless digging in the Pishdrah Zraphite Mine. Time to leave Pateeo behind.

"There will be much confusion when we strike. The Korak have to put all their trust in us, they must follow only our direction. If what Namow told us about the new prisoners arriving from the city is true, you and the men will be home soon Pateeo, my heart is gladdened," Krom hurriedly conveys.

"Until we meet again my young friends," Pateeo taps his fist to his chest and then hurries away into the scurrying crowd of prisoners. The brothers echo the greeting and wave. The visit is over.

They line up and wait. The Eslaf guard finally arrives to lead the visitors out. Krom and Remek pick up their weapons as they exit the prison and head straight for the shuttle station. They arrive a few minutes before the first shuttle makes its appearance, just enough time to put their names down as travelling back to Noitibma Colony.

Remek steps onto the walkway to board the craft, but an Eslaf shouts at him to stop. The soldier puts his weapon sideways across Remek's chest, blocking him from boarding.

"You stay," the creature commands.

"Why?" Remek blurts out, his eyes wide, he searches his brother's face for help. Before Krom can reassure his brother another Eslaf soldier strides towards them. A red-suit, and Bryzon's words jump into Krom's head. "If they are not armed, and wear a red body shell, they are in charge."

"You visit two-zero-two-three?" the unarmed Eslaf enquires in a deep grinding voice.

"Yes, he is a friend of my uncle and a friend of ours," Krom answers as confidently as he can muster.

"Explain?" the Eslaf asks bluntly.

"We brought news of family and we bring wishes from the families who cannot travel," Krom justifies, his pulse racing as never before. He concentrates, he must not show his fear as it could be interpreted as guilt.

The alien turns, rumbling off several orders to the armed Eslaf soldier in the Eslaf tongue as he strides away. The Eslaf soldier blocking Remek waves his weapon, motioning that the brothers are now free to board the shuttle.

The siblings waste no time getting settled into their seats, while routine procedures seem to take forever. The walkway begins to retract, but then stops. There is a commotion among the Eslaf who work the transporter as the hatch reopens. Krom and Remek watch in panic as the same Eslaf in red, heads towards them.

"You talk to Korak woman, explain?" he demands, before Krom can say anything the Eslaf shouts "Speak!"

His foul, hot breath reaches the siblings where they are seated. Krom stands up, putting one hand on Remek's shoulder, he squeezes, hoping that his brother will recognize it as a signal not to say anything.

"She worked with my uncle for many years," he sent his good wishes. "We let her sit; she is a friend to Pateeo, and they work on the same shift," Krom spells out for the creature. The alien stares at Krom for what seems an eternity and Remek can tell that it is trying to ascertain if his brother is telling the truth. Finally the Eslaf seems satisfied. He grunts and stomps off the ship.

When the craft takes off for the colonies Krom slides down in his seat putting his hands over his face. It takes a while before he removes them and sits back up.

"Brother, I fear trying to save the Korak, will bring our deaths," he whispers to Remek. "Perhaps Bryzon was mistaken in his decision, so much can go wrong," he adds, shaking his head.

Krom stares out of the small window at the Freelands for a long time, not speaking. Remek leaves his brother to his thoughts. It was not often that Krom was shaken by anything, perhaps the decision to include the unfortunate Korak prisoners was the wrong choice. When they ascend leaving Temsik Colony behind them, Remek notices that Krom seems to have returned to his thoughts, a while later he sits upright.

"I have considered what we should do." It-Ha Layrrah and Bryzon should be in Ytineres Colony tomorrow or the next day," he whispers. "I think it best that you leave the ship when we stop there. You will wait to speak with the High It-Ha and Bryzon about what happened today, while I continue to Noitibma as planned."

"But what good would that do, brother?" Remek asks.

"We must warn them, it is better we say something now. I do not want to live with regret" Krom insists. "You know how Bryzon feels about secrets? We must tell him what happened," he says firmly, to make sure that Remek understands his reasoning.

Chapter 43 - The Tunnel

It is a quiet morning in Noitibma Colony; dawn is about to break. Those present in the Council Lodge for the Evalc are Keeland, Nowber, Raine, the two It-Ha and Bryzon. They are eager to start the gathering, and all have seemingly endless lists with queries to be resolved during the short while they have.

"Let us begin," Leader Keeland announces, but before he can read out the first item on the agenda, Layrrah rises from her seat.

The chair scrapes loudly over the floor and tiny echoes fill the mostly empty room. "I had a vision," she declares. This has everyone's attention focused intently on her as they wait in anticipation for what she has to reveal.

"In my dream, the Firemoth showed me three ships leaving Kearthat. This peculiar declaration has everyone attentive.

The swishing of the It-Ha's long robe is loud in the quiet of the largely empty room. Layrrah wanders a few steps towards a window and looks out fleetingly. Then she turns back, walks over to her chair, her hands gripping the back of her seat she faces the group sitting at the long council table.

This action of Layrrah's, Bryzon has seen before. The It-Ha is about to declare something very important.

There was a strange ship in my vision last night," she tells them, "It is to be found in the City of Etah, in my dream it was very different from the Eslaf homeships. My vision did not show me to whom this ship belongs," she admits, looking down for a moment as if distraught at the lack of this knowledge. "However, I have reflected on the matter. I deem the ship to be Korak."

Bryzon raises his hand to speak immediately after Layrrah's remark. "How could that be possible, no Korak ships came to Kearthat, the Korak were brought by the Eslaf?" he states.

"The Inmo can only speak of what it sees and what it feels Bryzon," the It-Ha states as she takes her seat.

"My apologies, It-Ha Layrrah, I did not imply that it was impossible, merely that the possibility was small," Bryzon decides to add.

"I accept what you tell me, Bryzon, I will wait for the Firemoth to enlighten me," Please continue she sighs.

"I was in contact with Leyashe last night," Raine says, breaking the short silence that follows the It-Ha's expose of her vision.

"Ah! A morning full of surprises," Keeland exclaims. "Just the way I like to start my day." The comment raises some light laughter from around the table, breaking the seriousness of the It-Ha's earlier announcement. Raine smiles at the man who has always been there for her and Leyashe.

"How is that possible, Raine, when your brother is Below?" Nowber asks, the lesser leader perplexed at Raine's statement.

"We spoke through our..," she begins, then hesitates and lowers her lashes, "our gift," she tells him, but does not elaborate.

"The first group of men and woman that have gone down to Telmah are moving onto the ships," Raine relays to everyone. "The Yraif have begun cultivating crops on the second ship. I will be contacting Leyashe after our meeting today to update him on any changes we are to make today," she adds.

When Raine continues, she tells them of the transporter that Xandr and Leyashe are already flying through the tunnels there is a spontaneous bout of knuckle rapping.

"I knew this was going to be a good day." Keeland reaffirms smiling broadly.

By the time Raine stops speaking Bryzon can see on the faces of Keeland and Nowber that they now grasp that Raine and Leyashe are firmly in control.

To this point, no one has mentioned Moss, and his chair next to Nowber remains empty.

"Thank you Raine for the update. We have to get our fighters ready and we have to plan who else from Noitibma will be joining Xandr in Telmah," Bryzon reminds those present.

"Well then my friends," Keeland comments. "I will leave for Telmah via Rednos later today where I will wait for Rence to take me Below." Bryzon nods and smiles, his friend knew he was going to choose him.

"What of the Korak ship?" Bryzon asks, looking at a suddenly quiet It-Ha Layrrah.

"If it is one of their spaceships that you saw in your vision," Bryzon hesitates and smiles, "would it not be perfect if it were the Korak's own weapons that slaughter

Eslaf at the prison?" Bryzon laughs aloud. "The vision of this in my mind brings me great joy," he adds.

Again a round of knuckle tapping demonstrates enthusiasm for Bryzon's reference, Raine giving in to the revived tradition of old Kearthats Xennes by joining them.

When Bryzon contains his obvious amusement, silence returns, and he continues.

"I am expecting Remek and Krom will bring us good news. It will be of great interest to hear what they have to tell of their visit with Pateeo and Namow."

"If there is a Korak pilot that made it to Kearthat, and if he or she has survived the mines, then perhaps,..." Bryzon says, rubbing his chin, "Perhaps they could return to their sphere on such a craft if it exists, but... no...no it is too impossible to... no we must, for the moment consider this is not an option," he decides.

There is a knock at the door of the Council Lodge. Raine being the closest to the door leaves her seat to open it. To her surprise it is Ohre.

"I have returned my friends, the Eastern colonies await It-Ha Layrrah and Bryzon," he announces. "The arrangements for the special containers are made and the leaders look forward to learn of what we have to tell," he affirms. He does not wait for an invitation, Ohre walks over and sits next to Nowber filling Moss's old seat, no one comments and the group continues their discussions.

The matters raised are mostly from the list that Layrrah and Bryzon put together during the time they spent going from one Western Colony to the next.

Layrrah confirms she had been in contact with Nor~han earlier and that she had spoken with him regarding the exit tunnel to the surface near the old Council Gardens.

"A good place to dig a path to the surface has been found," she relays. Removing the rock has been slow, but it will be done in time."

At this news, Bryzon's face lights up. It is the confirmation that he had waited for. Bryzon's fear that an exit to the surface may not be possible through the lava tube dissipates in an instant, and his lips give in to a smile.

It comes as no surprise when Raine motions to speak, and announces she should be part of a team that will enter the city from the tunnels to fight the Eslaf.

"No, Raine, that cannot be allowed. It is too dangerous," is the immediate reaction from Bryzon then reinforced by Sayhran.

"Bryzon, It-Ha Sayhran, your concern for me shows that you both care a great deal for me. I will, out of respect for you and the memory of my mother and father, always take guidance from you, but this time I must insist," Raine says with a clear authoritative tone.

"It is my destiny, I know that I have to be there, this is meant to be. You must allow yourselves to trust me," she repeats. "I am sorry if it displeases you, but I will be going."

Raine does not stop there. She continues her protest.

"I will, at this time, go ahead and communicate that it is my brother's destiny to be one of the pilots on the fighter craft that will attack the city."

Noticing the look of shock on Bryzon's face, she continues before he can get a word in.

"Leyashe and I were chosen for this purpose, you must learn to accept this." Silence follows and in this silence the roof above them creaks, the wind leaning into the wooden building blowing even hotter than it did on the day before.

Bryzon clears his throat after an awkward few seconds, "Of course, Raine."

Layrrah notes the decision, and Remek notices that the entry still does not exhibit any visible writings as the It-Ha dips her Torrap quill into the red ink forfeited by the unfortunate beetles that create the high-pitched screech on the grasslands on a hot day.

Raine smiles at Bryzon, he returns the smile with a nod. The exchange between uncle and niece serves as a truce. They have great affection for each other, and that has not changed. What has changed is that Raine and Leyashe are making decisions now.

"How is it possible that Nor~han did not talk to us of this tunnel when we were in Telmah?" Raine asks.

"There was much to discuss," Layrrah answers, protecting her Yraif friend from any wrongdoing. "He may not have recognised its great importance at the time," she insists.

"That is true, there was so much happening," Raine says sighing.

"Providence abides us Bryzon," Oreh says. "I feel our strength returning my friend. The aliens will soon feel our anger, we will destroy those bugs, they will not see us coming."

"Layrrah and I leave for the eastern colonies later today," Bryzon tells everyone, as if in a hurry now. "We will attempt to complete our work in few days. When we return Raine and I will join you in Telmah," Bryzon confirms with Ohre, who will be making his way to Elbaffeni on the morning shuttle, and then by foot to the waterfall entrance.

"There will be much discussion to be held before we can go forward with the attack from the walkways," Bryzon adds as he blows air softly through his teeth.

Ohre knows his friend's mannerisms well. He can see that the long list of undecided issues are worrisome to Bryzon. He is a man with a very orderly, strategic mind. Bryzon was the kind of man who planned carefully and took his time to guarantee success for every action taken.

"As for the Korak spaceship," Bryzon begins saying, then adds, "If it does exist, and we have no one to fly it, it will be of no use to anyone."

The subject of the Korak in Noitibma is raised next. Keeland gets up to open the door and calls Kergann's name and the boy emerges as if out of thin air. "Go boy, tell the Korak to come to the Council building. Hurry, we must conclude this evalc before the shuttle arrives," he orders the child with the tousled hair.

Ten minutes later the Korak file in and sit down, their nervousness is obvious. Then several much older Korak follow, taking a seat behind the younger group. It is a Korak male in the front row who raises his hand immediately after they sit.

"May I speak freely, leader Keeland?" he asks.

"Of course, go ahead, Dessas."

"Are we being sent to the mines?" the alien asks. "Since our old ones have been returned to Noitibma from the other colonies over the past few days we have been afraid," he says.

"Oh no, this is not so Dessas, you are not going anywhere near that dreaded place," Keeland reassures the nervous young Korak.

"Why is it then that we have been kept away from the many gatherings? We know there is something strange happening in Noi," Dessas pleads. "We have been like prisoners kept away from everyone for days now. No one wants to tell us what is happening," Dessas adds looking dejected. "And we were also excluded from the gathering of the people in the square yesterday. We heard the silence, then the cheering."

Raine feels sad to see the large pleading eyes and the genuine trepidation Dessas has.

"We have all missed our work detail several times now, we are very troubled," the Korak admits, and continues, "Please, we need to know what we have done to deserve your distrust."

"Raine, I think you and Bryzon will best deliver this information to them," Layrrah says.

"I will, if you do not mind," Raine insists, looking over at Bryzon.

She takes a deep breath before sharing the story of the impending danger to Kearthat with the Korak she and Leyashe grew up with. Both the younger and older Korak sit listening intently without interrupting. When Raine is done, the Korak are rendered speechless for a while before one of them stands to speak.

"Yes, Bailea, ask us anything you want," Raine smiles reassuringly at the young Korak female.

"What about the people at the mines? Are they to be saved, too?"

"We are working on that," Bryzon cuts in. "But right now, we have something else to tell you," and he looks at Raine.

Sitting motionless and silent at first, as if not understanding what Raine has just told them the Korak seem to be finding it hard to comprehend.

"But we are part of the colony. Why can we not have this gift of long life," Bailea asks.

"Yes, I know, my friends," Raine tells her. "You are very much part of our colony and of our people, but we do not know if your bodies will accept the potion. What if the potion …," Raine begins to say, then decides to put it bluntly, "What if it kills you?"

"We did not want to take the chance that we could harm you," Keeland adds, backing up what Raine has told the young aliens.

Finally, Raine says, "Leyashe and I promise you that we will do everything we can to get as many of your kind from the mines to the safety of our spaceships."

Raine looks over at Layrrah and she nods in the affirmative.

"We just heard today there is a possibility that a Korak spaceship exists in Etah. If this is so, we will fight to bring it out of the city. If someone in the prison can fly this craft you will all be able to return to your sphere."

"They trust Remek and Krom. We should ask them to speak to the Korak when they return from Pishdrah," Raine whispers to Keeland.

Bryzon hears Raine's suggestion and agrees.

"Bryzon spoke of your safety in the very first meetings we held with leader Marcus King at Rednos and with all the leaders they have met with since," Raine continues. "Preparations are being made to get all of us off Kearthat safely. You must believe us. We will not leave you to die on this sphere."

The Korak appear to be more at ease after Raine's statement. It is only when Bryzon tells them that Krom and Remek will be returning soon to answer any questions they still have, that they seem content. Their fealty to secrecy is requested, and before the Korak leave the building, they are asked to raise their right arms in loyalty to the leaders and The Selected.

Brought here as babies, growing up in the ways of the Drennan, they show the respect they have learned. They bow as they file out of the Council building while Dessas comes to thank Raine on behalf of all of them.

Bryzon finds his thoughts wandering to Namow. It saddens him to think of her still toiling in the mine next to Pateeo. Then, there is a knock at the door.

"What now?" Keeland says, sounding a little irritated.

Raine again jumps up and is surprised to find Dessas, and with him an older Korak male.

"Raine, I have come to talk for my group," Dessas says. "This man, as you know, has been with Sedecca Colony for some time now. From what we can understand from his limited words, he was the pilot on the Korak ship, the one in Etah," the younger alien tells them.

Ohre brings his fist down hard on the table, causing everyone to flinch. "This is surely another sign," he bellows.

"We would like to volunteer," Dessas continues. "No, we insist that all of us be included to fight the Eslaf," his face is serious as he stares at the men and women gathered around the table.

"They turned our people into slaves. We are ready to fight and die; we were born here, we know no other home," Dessas says, pleading his case.

"We, the Korak of Noitibma, know no other way of life. We do not know the Korak tongue. Those of us who survive this war with the Eslaf do not want to return to our sphere. We wish to remain with the Xennes," he tells them.

Raine puts her hand on Dessas's arm. "We know you are one of us. We do not look at you any differently from our own," she says, looking up at the tall being. "I  promise you that we will make use of every warrior. You will be part of this battle," she reassures him. "You will have the choice to journey with us on the spaceships that will find a new home for us," Raine reassures Dessas. "You do not have to go back to your planet; tell all the Korak who grew up in the colonies that they are our people."

"What is your name?" Raine asks the older Korak.

"Name Mehtevas, you say Evas," he tells Raine, with a slight nod of his head.

"Can you fly your ship back to your home?" she asks.

"I want," he answers firmly.

"Will you come with me to Telmah and go with our ship through the tunnel to Etah?"

"Evas come, Korak go home," he confirms without hesitation.

Mehtevas taps Dessas on the shoulder, then leans his head sideway to the younger alien in a gesture only Bryzon understands. The gesture means, 'you tell.'

"What is it, Dessas? What do you have to tell us?" Bryzon asks.

"Well, from what I can understand," Dessas says, "This Namow of whom you speak is the daughter of a Korak leader. He is a sort of ruler or something," Dessas says and Raine has to smile.

"Namow is the ruler's daughter?" Bryzon repeats, shaking his head. He had known all along that she was important to her people.

"You know Namow well?" Bryzon asks Evas.

"Namow my fada dawta," Evas tells them.

"I believe him," Bryzon says, leaning forward and looking up and down the long table. "Namow told me years ago that her brother had been taken away. She thought he was sent to Etah."

Bryzon proceeds to speak to the man in his own tongue and everyone is taken aback at his ability to communicate with the alien. Evas smiles at Bryzon and tells him that the Korak ship has weapons and they will fight if the weapons have not been removed from their craft by the Eslaf.

"Well, one thing we are certain of," It-Ha Layrrah says.

"What is that?" Sayhran asks.

"We know the Korak can keep a secret," and even Dessas laughs at the comment Layrrah makes.

"Go and be at peace and know that you are all included, Dessas," Raine says, smiling at him. Dessas respectfully bows, but instead of turning to leave, he leans forward and gently folds his long arms around Raine and hugs her small frame.

"Thank you, Rai, thank you," he says before releasing her.

"Evas," Bryzon says to the older Korak man, "You will go to Rednos tomorrow on the first Traxid. From there you will go with Keeland to Telmah. I know you can understand more than you speak, so I will tell you that Namow does not yet know of the ship. We will today be sending a messenger to the prison to tell her. We will also inform her that you are alive and well."

"Go now, and think only of your days as a pilot. You have a very short time to remember how to fly your spaceship before we attack," Bryzon tells Namow's brother.

"Evas know, no forget," Namow's sibling tells them, pointing a long alien finger to his large cranium.

Bryzon studies the Korak as he speaks, deciding he can trust Namow's brother implicitly without ever learning to know him. It is obvious from the long scar on the Korak's face that he is a fighter. The old injury stretches from Methevas's forehead, over the bridge of the alien's small nose, diagonally down to his chin. The wound must have come from fighting the Eslaf, Bryzon decides.

"Tank you," Evas says before leaving the gathering. Suddenly, all their planning is changed, but this time for the better.

Chapter 44 - The Xennes

Bryzon and Layrrah head off to catch the shuttle that will leave Noitibma for Ygyzys Colony. They arrive just in time to board the craft. From the moment they sit down, they are uneasy. It feels as if they are under scrutiny. The shuttle has seven Eslaf soldiers aboard, more than double the regular complement. Only two are of flesh, Bryzon decides, but he is not sure.

Bryzon stares out of the window as they take off, stretching his legs out in front of him, trying to look as relaxed as possible. Halfway through the journey, the soldiers are still sitting close together at the exit, but they seem to be ignoring the passengers as the constant loud talking between the two of them grinds on in their usual deep garbled alien tone.

The Eslaf soldiers sitting staring ahead of them, Bryzon determines, must be droids. They do not speak or acknowledge each other, and soon, it is as if Bryzon can almost hear the circuitry inside of them. He looks over to where Layrrah is seated. Her eyes are closed, and she looks asleep. Today, she is a young boy dressed in a slightly dirty tunic. She looks perfectly suited as a passenger sent to work in Ygyzys. Her permission note from Leader Keeland states that the boy has a time-off.

Bryzon decides to take his mind off the many Eslaf on the craft as he mulls over the current progress. He thinks of Keeland, Evas and Ohre heading in different directions as they make their way to Telmah. New developments carried to remaining leaders are delivered through the men and women who travel through colonies on their way to The Below. So far, things have been going well.

"There is no turning back," he says under his breath, but no one hears this whispered declaration in the noise of the craft as it levels out.

Every so often, soft chatter among the passengers reaches Bryzon's ears. He feels almost peaceful. This time, the potion is carefully stored inside a sack of Torrak root.

He falls in behind a young girl in the lineup heading for the hatch. He bows his head slightly in Layrrah's direction. Their eyes meet for a few seconds, then he slowly closes and opens them. Layrrah returns the exchange. The simple gesture has become the acknowledgement to each other that all is still well. But Bryzon remains slightly concerned at the number of Eslaf on the shuttle.

Three of the armed aliens disembark and head to a waiting Traxid. Bryzon starts walking towards the colony, leaving the shuttle station behind him. He does not linger or look back as Layrrah waits to board the Traxid.

When he is an acceptable distance away from the shuttle, Bryzon turns his head only slightly to look back. Forgetting for a moment that he should be looking for a young boy, he shakes his head. He spots the sacks of Torrak containing the potion directly behind Layrrah, where the three Eslaf soldiers sit, menacingly close to her and the potion. Bryzon continues his walk towards the main gate. When he hears the worm start up, he increases his stride and calculates the distance he has to cover to make sure that he arrives before the vehicle.

The Traxid roars into the colony, stirring up a cloud of dust. The passengers jump off and start removing items that belong to them, while colonists offload goods sent from the Western Colonies. Bryzon sees a familiar face. It is Learridy, once a highly respected commander on one of the deep-space exploration craft of old Kearthat. He watches as she gives instructions to the young boy offloading the sacks containing the potion. Layrrah has blended in well.

Learridy's face changes when one of the three Eslaf soldiers grabs a young Freelander and throws him to the ground. The alien hits the young man with the back of his weapon. The man screams, "I am innocent," but the soldier grabs the bag slung over the colonist's shoulder and turns it inside out. Several items fall to the ground. It appears they do not find what they are looking for and proceed to stomp on the personal belongings lying scattered in the dust. Layrrah hurriedly pulled the cart with the sacks containing the potion a short distance away from the commotion.

Bryzon watches as the Eslaf instructs the man to remove his tunic. It takes only seconds before he stands naked, cupping his hands to hide what he can. One of the soldiers picks up his tunic and shakes it as if there might be something hidden. This, too, yields nothing. The disgusted creature throws the clothing back at the terrified, naked young man.

The two soldiers head for the Traxid, and Learridy walks up to the vicious creature that caused the mayhem and says something to him. It is obvious from her gestures that she is not happy with what just took place. The alien looks at the colony leader for a few seconds, then turns away to join his cohorts. The Eslaf's facial appendages swing wildly as they make their way to the vehicle. The worm starts up and makes a wide turn in the colony before it heads for the gate to drop the Eslaf soldiers off at their waiting shuttle.

It-Ha Layrrah, who has slowly made her way over towards Bryzon, is suddenly herself again. Bryzon sighs with relief. The It-Ha closes her eyes for a few seconds in silent agreement with his sigh. They head for the Council Lodge, Bryzon pulling the cart with the sack of Torrak root with them.

Layrrah is quiet as they walk, and only the sound of the crunching of dry sand afoot can be heard, as can the sounds of distant voices. It is quiet on the lane that takes them to the Council Lodge. The silence echoes what Bryzon is feeling as they both imagine the consequences if they were caught conspiring against the Eslaf. When they reach their destination, it is the smiling Leader Naylor that welcomes them. The tall, muscular man has not changed much since their days in the Starfleet.

"My friend, it has been a long time," the leader greets.

"Far too long, I hope I find you well and strong," Bryzon enquires.

"I am better now that I see that the creatures did not take away your soul," Naylor quips, smiling. The Xennes man that Bryzon has known since his days as commander in the Starfleet does not look much different except for his simple tunic. The tidy man with a good sense of humour who served under him is heartening to meet again.

When the door opens next, Learridy enters. Bryzon takes in the vision of the woman he has not seen up close in many years. Her long, black straight hair is tied back in one tail, accentuating her high cheekbones. Her eyes reflecting the light coming in the window behind him. He had forgotten how attractive Learridy was. His heart flutters, colour fills his cheeks. The tall, slender woman has caught Bryzon off guard. His behaviour is unexpected, but fortunately, she does not notice his weak moment as she enthusiastically greets the man she once worked with.

Leader Oznay comes forward to greet Bryzon. Only then does Bryzon let go of Learridy's hand.

"Finally, the beasts let you go. I am gladdened," Oznay says, making Bryzon feel welcome.

Oznay was a quiet man, a man of high principles. He looks much as he did seventeen years ago, his shoulder-length black hair a little untidy and his black beard in need of trimming. But Bryzon knows this no longer matters; too many years have passed since the Kearthat Starfleet and its regulations.

Learridy shares the encounter she had with the Eslaf with the other leaders of the colony. She discloses that the aliens seemed convinced the young man was guilty of something. She tells them that she had pressed the Eslaf soldier to divulge what it was that they were searching for, but the alien refused.

"One of the colony Overseers asked the man what he was guilty of, and he swore on his oath that he did not know what they wanted. I believe the boy, I know his mother well" Learridy says with conviction. "The aliens are all dim-witted," she adds, waves her hands in an 'I give up' gesture, and sighs. They all snigger at her accusation of the dim-witted aliens. But little does Learridy know that her statement could be more true than she can imagine.

Layrrah looks at Bryzon, and without saying a word, he knows she is concerned about the incident. Bryzon is suddenly worried about Krom and Remek. He feels a little uneasy. Had his nephews accomplished their mission, and were they safe?

Suspicious behaviour from the Eslaf was worrisome, but all the surmising about the unfortunate incident is abandoned for the time being as they settle down around the council table. When the sound of the shuttle fades into the distance, Bryzon relays why he and Layrrah requested an Evalc with the leaders. A little over an hour later, the tale of the impending loss of Kearthat and the anger Ante Mountain holds within it has been told again.

Leader Naylor looks as if he is doubtful; his questions make the It-Ha see a man who is having trouble grasping the reality of what they have conveyed.

"I have a message from Ohre," the It-Ha says as she lays a shiny emblem on the table. "He told me that you would know the message it brings."

Naylor picks up The Medal of Truth and Honor, rubbing the smooth, rounded metal encrusted with a yellow jewel between his thumb and forefinger.

"Then I doubt no more," Naylor says, handing the medal back to the It-Ha.

"You say that your nephew and niece are going to lead us to a new home, Bryzon?" Naylor asks, smiling, all scepticism dispersed.

"They are our destiny, beyond any question. They are The Selected as it is written. When you meet with them you will have no uncertainty of this," Bryzon assures Naylor.

"The suns will be behind the mountains soon; our people are returning from the fields as we speak," Oznay cuts in. "I will send the runner. We will meet with our people when the suns go behind the mountains."

It is decided that Learridy and Naylor will join The Below team, leaving Oznay to remain as leader at the colony. When the shuttle takes off the following morning, there are four hundred and two more Xennes than the previous day. Bryzon is pleased to note a different shuttle is on the line when they take off. This shuttle has a regular number of Eslaf guards. Two of the three that accompany the craft are Android.

Layrrah is seated away from him during the short flight. She has chosen to be an old lady for the journey. Assured they will be safe on the trip, Bryzon's mind drifts to thoughts of Learridy. She had warmly embraced him when he left. He can still smell the mixture of sweet flowers coming from her hair. The gentle look in her eyes and the feel of the unhurried, soft kiss she had placed on his mouth. He could sense it. It held within it an unspoken promise for the future. The twinge in Bryzon's stomach is strange, something he has not felt since the first time he saw Meirah. It is the feeling you get when you meet someone you know you want to spend more time with and Bryzon is very aware of it. A small smile tries to creep to his lips, but he knows it will look silly so he suppresses it.

The arrival in Ytineres Colony goes well as greetings bring old friends back together. Bryzon and Layrrah again find themselves in a familiar position, across the table from three leaders of yet another colony. The potion, safely stored in a sack of Ylock kernels, sits waiting patiently on a small cart in the corner of the Council Lodge. It-Ha Layrrah transforms into herself as soon as they reach the safety of the colony.

Bryzon looks around the table and recalls the roles that the Xennes leaders played in old Kearthat. Adarra had once been a controller at the base docking station in Seccus. He had always admired her. She was older than him, a kind woman, but she was different. She had been born with one dark brown eye and the other green. This made her special, as none on Kearthat had ever had that mysterious condition. Some said that she would one day become an It-Ha because of her green eye.

"We have been eagerly waiting to hear what you have to tell us, Bryzon. Ohre declared that every word you speak will be true," Leader Ashok says heartily.

Bryzon has known Ashok for a long time. They had worked together for many years in the City of Seccus, and their bond was formed on the day they received their Xennes status. He was a slender man but strong, his height making up for his lack of girth. His long black hair, partly braided into several thin plaits, hanging interspersed with the rest of his loose hair.

To Bryzon it seems an unusual way to wear one's hair, but the feathers plucked from an unfortunate Torrap tied into Ashok's braids bring a smile to Bryzon's face.

There is a knock and Adarra gets up to find out who it is. Remek's voice is unmistakable, and Layrrah quickly waves to Adarra to allow him in. Bryzon is a little shaken by the sight of his nephew. He only briefly greets Auwzen, the third leader of the colony and then excuses himself.

"We need to speak," Remek whispers.

Bryzon turns to Layrrah, "Will you continue, It-Ha Layrrah, I must speak with Remek outside."

There are benches under the shady branches of several big trees and Bryzon and Remek find a seat.

"Where is Krom?" Bryzon asks, desperate for a quick answer.

"He should be in Noi by now. Krom instructed me to wait for you and the It-Ha," Remek says, still whispering.

"What went wrong?" Bryzon questions, keeping his voice low.

"We were stopped by the Eslaf."

"Was this at the prison gate? Did you see Pateeo? Did you talk with Namow? Was it before or after your visit, nephew?" Bryzon asks anxiously.

"They stopped us just before we boarded the shuttle to come home after our visit." Remek's answer has Bryzon taking in a deep breath of relief. What did they want?" Bryzon asks wrinkling his troubled forehead.

"They asked us why we were at the prison. I was worried, Bryzon, I thought all had been discovered," Remek admits, as he recounts what took place.

"Krom thinks it is because we spoke to Pateeo and Namow until dawn. It could have looked suspicious," he sums up, looking down at the ground, rolling a small rock back and forth under his right foot he continues. "Krom spoke to the red-suit. He told him we were just visiting Pateeo to bring greetings from home," Remek repeats.

"Did Krom say anything else, Remek? Think carefully; tell me every word," Bryzon requests, rubbing his chin as if in thought.

"No, that was all. We acted as if we were dim-witted," he comments with a semi-smile as he tries to lighten the moment.

Bryzon thinks about what he has learned for a few seconds, then pats his nephew on the back. We will have to be more careful," he assures Remek.

"Go to the Visitors Lodge and rest. The It-Ha and I will wake you when our work is done. We will eat together before we gather with the colonists tonight."

"Bryzon, you do not seem concerned?"

"I do not believe for one moment that the Eslaf would have let you go if they suspected that we were conspiring against them. You would not be here, and Krom would not be back in Noitibma. Rest easy Remek, son of Keazan, you chose well to tell me of the matter."

Bryzon knocks on the door and Adarra lets him in. Even with the door closed behind him, he can hear Remek whistling a familiar tune as it fades into the distance. It is a simple song that Sayhran and Caite sang to the children when they were still young. The song was about a magic dragon that was described to Bryzon as a fire-breathing mythical creature. Bryzon laughed when he was explained the meaning of the song.

"How is it that earthlings would scare their babies to sleep by singing a song about a creature that could blow fire from its mouth?," he had once asked Caite. To which his brother's wife had simply answered, "But it is a baby dragon, Bryzon." That day he learned never to question the logic of a female of the earthling species.

"Is everything in order?" Layrrah asks, as Bryzon takes his seat next to her.

"I did not move ahead we waited for you," she tells Bryzon.

"The boys were questioned at the ICSS after the visit to the prison," he tells her, whispering. "But all is well. Krom has returned to Noitibma, Remek will remain for the night. He will journey on the worm that goes to Ytineres Colony tomorrow and the shuttle the following day to get back to Noi."

"I apologize for the interruption," Bryzon says, looking up at the patient leaders awaiting the story that is about to change their lives. Curious eyes face him and Bryzon feels the need to elaborate about the interruption.

"It was my nephew, nothing serious, but we will enlighten you shortly," he assures everyone. "Auwzen my friend, I am happy to see you," Bryzon greets.

It-Ha Layrrah and Bryzon tell their tale again, this time they have a shocked audience.

Auwzen is the most accepting of what he has heard. The promise of freedom has him asking many questions.

Auwzen was the only Xennes who survived the invasion with his wife Caradoi. But not long after the survivors had established the colonies, an Eslaf soldier shot her and no one has ever known why. She was found barely breathing near a field of Otatop opposite the Temsik Colony gate shortly after the afternoon shuttle craft had taken off. She had a gaping wound in her back inflicted by the alien weapon. Caradoi was too weak to tell Auwzen what had happened before she passed to the next world. She just kept repeating the word 'Eslaf' over and over until she succumbed.

Auwzen had relocated to Ytineres Colony after some months to ease the memory of her loss but his anger had never diminished. When the men volunteered to join the rebel force it was Dayson who refused to have Auwzen join, as he felt Auwzen's anger at the time would be dangerous to their mission. The angry Auwzen was instead elected to serve the colony as a leader, while the Xennes men left to battle in the short-lived uprising.

Bryzon does not notice any lingering animosity towards him. Auwzen instead portrays the look of a man who has become content, but how can he be sure the man does not bear a grudge?

"Shall we take a few minutes to stretch our legs and breathe the night air?" Bryzon suggests. Everyone agrees and Layrrah is surprised when Bryzon takes her elbow lightly and steers her out of the building in the direction of the trees where the benches are.

"You have a weight on your mind, my friend?" she says after looking into his face.

"I do," then he keeps silent for a few seconds.

"You wish me to wait until I am ashes?" It-Ha Layrrah pushes Bryzon somewhat impatiently.

"I am not sure we can trust Auwzen," he tells her.

"Why?" Layrrah asks with a confused look on her face.

Bryzon quickly tells her the story of the leader and his wife, and why an angry Auwzen had been excluded from the rebel force.

"I know this," Bryzon. "You forget I was there, even when I was not," she remarks with the slightest hint of irritation. "I am aware of all of this, but his anger is no longer. The Inmo sees all," she insists.

Bryzon sighs loudly and asks, "I implore you to use the sanction stone to be sure he has no thought of revenge?"

"As the High It-Ha, I must think on this Bryzon. Leave me, I will walk a while to ponder what you ask of me." Layrrah shakes her head, sighing as she walks away, leaving a frowning Bryzon sitting on the bench.

He is deep in thought regarding Pateeo and the Korak Namow, when suddenly Layrrah is back, and she sits down.

"I will do your bidding, but never ask this of me again, Bryzon," she tells him firmly.

"Thank you," he says, as he suffers the emotions of a young child who has just been scolded by his mother.

The Evalc progresses well, many questions are answered and Remek's sudden appearance is explained. It is Ohre's medallion that once again cements Layrrah and Bryzon's quest. Ashok is overjoyed to be going Below but Auwzen is somewhat quiet.

"Do you wish to go Below? Perhaps you would wish to join the men and woman who will attack Etah using the old tunnels?" Layrrah asks Auwzen. "We have been asking all the leaders and all Xennes of old Kearthat what they wish to contribute. You may choose," she says, clarifying her point.

The silence grows to the point where Adarra and Ashok are also looking at Auwzen for a reply.

"Would my request be denied if I chose another task?" he asks, looking only at Bryzon. "We would never deny you," the It-Ha insists, sounding slightly indignant. "We are at the mercy of the few Xennes that remain from the Kearthat we once knew," she adds, trying to encourage the innocence of her request towards Auwzen.

"Without charge from all our leaders and other Xennes of the old days, we cannot leave this sphere." The High It-Ha is quite firm as she leans slightly forward, looking directly at Auwzen. "We cannot endure without the support of every Drennan man and woman, and the Yraif and Korak," Layrrah reassures, as if Auwzen had not understood her.

Auwzen looks over at Adarra. "For the memory of Caradoi, I choose to remain and make sure that all our people reach The Below and the ships safely. With the help of someone very special to me," Auwzen says, looking at Adarra, then to Layrrah.

"I wish for you to know that Adarra and I have become one," the lesser leader announces to everyone's surprise, including the feathered Ashok. "We wish to be joined as soon as it can be arranged. It would be our honour to have you, Bryzon and It-Ha Layrrah, to witness our bond."

Only Layrrah sees the fine pink wisps of mist weaving in and out between Adarra and Auwzen. Laughter and congratulations among the leaders give the It-Ha time to whisper, "he is honest."

"I had to be sure," Bryzon whispers back. The It-Ha shakes her head at Bryzon.

The next morning, Bryzon notices that every step he and Layrrah take kicks up a small dry, tiny cloud of dust that feels different for some reason. He looks up at the sky, it is a clear light pink day. Another hot day.

The center of Ytineres Colony is busy, it is market day. The settlement is a hub of activity. The Freelanders hide their excitement well. Today they will be called to the Council Lodge in small groups to participate in the most important ceremony they will ever attend. Their lives are about to change significantly.

The Xennes count has increased by four hundred and eight when Bryzon and Layrrah board the shuttle. Having attended the ceremony that saw the joining of Adarra and Auwzen, the It-Ha is touched by how love subsists, even amidst chaos.

Once on the shuttle It-Ha Layrrah sits on her own, her thoughts dwelling on how lonely her life has been. Bryzon thinks of Learridy's big eyes and the gentle kiss he still feels when he closes his eyes. As they ascend into the sky above the colony his mind turns to Remek who is on his journey to Noitibma. Everything is still going well, but it could all break apart with just one little mistake.

The hatch opens and passengers leave the shuttle. It is the mid-day hour the searing heat is stifling, the warm breeze blowing Bryzon's long hair in all directions. His eyes scan to seek out Layrrah. When he sees her they make eye contact, she closes then opens her dark green eyes giving him the sign that everything appears to be in order.

Bryzon looks around to see if he recognizes anyone. After a few minutes he finds he is speaking softly under his breath, "Where are they?" A tap on his shoulder makes him spin around. It is Leader Sontarr, a tall well-built man. He greets Bryzon in a low whisper, barely moving his mouth. "Welcome, my friend, I will take care of the It-Ha. Enter the gate."

Then in a loud voice Sontarr bellows, "Move along, move along" while he looks at Bryzon and winks. The Eslaf soldiers stand guard as the shuttle is offloaded, everyone pays attention to the leader's forceful voice while Bryzon heads for the colony gate. The Eslaf craft lifts off, it's run for the day done.

The light is fading fast. Somewhere, the Night Creatures will soon wander the dark, their growls travelling on the wind throughout the Freelands. Bryzon waits for Layrrah. A few minutes later she appears, pulling a cart. Inside the sack of seed the potion is safe once more.

"For a moment, I thought there was no one to meet us," Bryzon whispers.

"I saw your eyes searching, Bryzon. I will not tell Ohre of your doubt," she laughs as she changes from a young ordinary-looking woman into herself in a split second. The It-Ha's attempt at humour does not cease as she quickly rambles off three things that she has on her friend.

"I told you the It-Ha sees all. Do you think your emotions for Learridy went unnoticed, Bryzon brother of Dayson? You were proven wrong about Auwzen, now your doubt concerning Ohre's abilities to arrange matters, Bryzon my friend your transgressions grow like the Lattgrass on the Freelands," she tells him. The It-Ha laughs as Bryzon looks away for a second to digest his quandary. But he knows she is joking, and smiles.

When they reach the Council Lodge, Sontarr comes striding around the corner, almost running Layrrah over.

"My apologies, It-Ha Layrrah," he says with a small bow before he turns his attention to Bryzon. The two men embrace, Sontarr steps back, his hands on Bryzon's shoulders, looking at the face of the man who was once his Commander.

"You survived the ugly grey creatures. It makes me happy Bryzon," he remarks.

"It-Ha Layrrah, please, the others are waiting," Sontarr says, graciously extending his welcome as he holds the door open for her.

Sontarr had worked with Bryzon at the Starfleet base where so many women through the years had behaved quite foolishly when they met him. Now, so many years later, Bryzon notices that his friend's handsome features have endured.

Sitting at the council table Bryzon knows both of the other leaders of well. Kahldeh, from his brother Dayson's fleet of old Kearthat stands when he sets eyes on Bryzon. The leader greets Bryzon warmly, he studies Bryzon's face for a few seconds before he says, "I still miss him, as must you, Bryzon my friend." Bryzon knows it is difficult for some of the Xennes who knew his twin. When they see Bryzon they are immediately reminded of Dayson.

Next to him sits Ethlah. She reaches over the table to extend a forearm greeting with Bryzon's while her other hand holds back her loose cascading straight black hair. The light from the window next to her reveals the same woman he had seen the last time he had visited Niamod Colony many years ago.

"You have not aged a day, Ethlah," Bryzon compliments the woman he has always known to have the spirit of a warrior and a pure heart. A woman who had been extremely upset at Elder Moss's decision not to allow her to join the rebel forces during the uprising.

"I thought I would never see you again after I heard the ugly ones had taken you all away to that terrible place. "But here you are, and soon I hear the others will also be leaving that dark place. My heart is gladdened by the thought," Ethlah adds, smiling.

"Ohre told us that you have urgent matters to discuss?" Kahldeh comments. "We have waited on your arrival with great curiosity. But I am uneasy, only matters of grave consequence require an It-Ha's attendance." Kahldeh spreads his large hands, palms down on the table. Sighing, he straightens his body against the back of his chair. His demeanour is that of a man who is ready to hear what he deems to be bad news.

Bryzon begins the story that he has so well rehearsed over the past few days. When he stops talking, his audience is unexpectedly quiet. It has him uncertain for a few seconds. Then Sontarr claps his hands together so loudly that Layrrah flinches.

"Bryzon, we shall carry the earthling weapons and show the aliens that we have not forgotten where we come from. A round of knuckle rapping brings an enormous smile to Ethlah's face. Bryzon knows that she has revenge planned for her husband and her daughter's lives that the Eslaf so viciously took from her.

"We will call our people to gather," Kahldeh announces.

When Bryzon takes out his list to announce who will be travelling to Telmah. The It-Ha beats him to it. Ethlah is to remain as leader for now she informs Bryzon.

It is clear to Bryzon that these three leaders are ready for anything that is asked of them. A few hours later the colonists are informed of the impending change in their lives. It-Ha Layrrah administers the gift of long life to all but those under the age of eighteen. Raine had set a precedent.

At dawn, Bryzon and It-Ha Layrrah leave on the Traxid bound for Arorua Colony. They are seated next to each other this time, the potion carefully folded into a bale of Lattgrass. With no Eslaf accompanying the Traxid they feel good about their journey. Layrrah is dressed in a tunic fit for a labourer in the fields, but the rest of her appearance is that of her own.

"How many were gifted at Niamod Colony?" Bryzon asks, as the worm bumps over the Freelands.

"Four-hundred-and-fifty-one," she says smiling. "We are close to accomplishing our charge, my friend." Layrrah looks content as the morning suns shine over Kearthat, their mission is going well. They would soon be returning to Noitibma. All too soon the day will arrive when everyone will journey to Telmah.

"How many children do you think are to be left unprotected? I think less than one hundred when we are done," the It-Ha estimates. Bryzon goes quiet, she knows he is thinking of the low number of young ones and the responsibility that rests on the shoulders of The Liberators to keep them safe at all costs.

"We are righting the wrongs, Bryzon," Layrrah expresses, trying to reassure him. "When we reach a new home our people will be free to have families once again. Our numbers will grow. We will be a great people again," she tries to encourage.

"You see this for us in your visions?" Bryzon asks her.

"No, my friend, I see this in my heart," the It-Ha states, smiling.

"There is still much to accomplish, so much to overcome before we can journey away from Kearthat," Bryzon thinks quietly. The It-Ha's positive remarks still do not allay his fear of making another mistake, just as he had done in the uprising against the aliens.

"Together, we shall overcome all that stands before us," the It-Ha reassures Bryzon, and for a second, he wonders if she can hear what he is thinking, but he knows this is not possible, or is it? Magic was everywhere now, it seems.

'How long before we find our place among the stars?' Bryzon wonders, his mind dwelling on Layrrah and her magic. And, how can the High It-Ha still insist she cannot see the outcome of their fleeing Kearthat?

Bryzon puts his hand on Layrrah's arm. "Thank you, It-Ha Layrrah, for surviving the Eslaf. You were wise in choosing to protect Jon and Farron so that others may now have hope. And also for choosing Sayhran as your Tiro; she is a good woman."

Layrrah does not comment on Bryzon's praise; instead, she tells him that Sayhran will be a great High It-Ha when her time comes, and she predicts that there will be another It-Ha soon.

Bryzon considers her words. Nor~han was right; Layrrah is a good woman. He had been wrong about her. He would have to find a way to show his remorse.

The next few days pass much like the previous gatherings with colony leaders. The Leaders and Freelanders alike are joyous at the news. Each time Bryzon and Layrrah board the shuttles and Traxid transports, they hold their breath until the potion is safely transported and administered.

Leaders Idna and Annrev of Arorua Colony leave for Telmah, while leader Nemzah remains. After they depart Sigae Colony, Lesser Leader Toakez takes the shuttle to Rednos to join the next team heading Below, and then they finally enter the gate of the last eastern settlement.

When the Traxid stops at Temsik Colony Bryzon is overjoyed that this part of their quest is almost complete. His thoughts go back to the first night he spent here, free of the prison walls. The memories seem to be years in the past but in reality, they have been very recent.

Bryzon can see on the It-Ha's face that she is relieved their journeys and endeavours to keep the potion safe have ended. She has a huge smile on her face. The meeting with leaders Senrah, Nezray and Nedyar proceeds swiftly, it is a little after the midnight hour when the last colonists have been gifted with long life.

The shuttle arrives earlier than usual on the following morning. They are exasperated when they discover that it will stop at each colony on the way back to Noitibma, they would have to be patient. With no potion aboard the craft they are content to wait out the time.

When they eventually walk through the safety of the big gate at Noitibma, the suns are rapidly making their descent, many days have passed, and time is running out.

Once inside, away from the prying eyes of the Eslaf soldiers, to Layrrah's surprise, Bryzon stops, faces her and bows.

"High It-Ha of The Xennes people of Kearthat, I show my gratitude," he tells her, going down on one knee in front of her, he lowers his lashes looking down at the ground.

"You are a brave man, Bryzon brother of Dayson, commander of our brave warriors," she says reaching for his hand. "Please, never kneel before me again, those days are no longer. Come let us be with our people, tonight even the It-Ha will find it satisfying to drink a large cup of Reeb."

They walk the rest of the way to It-Ha Sayhran's cabin in silence. The Eslaf transporter rises into the air behind them and turns for the City of Etah.

The alien craft's sound disappears into the distant purpling sky leaving a stillness in its stead. A soft whispering wind blows and Bryzon can hear the leaves rusting softly in the trees in the colony. Unseen, to the West of Noitibma the Firemoths fly out of their hiding places by the hundreds to feed on the Lattgrass of the Freelands. Kearthat seems changed, it is almost serene. It occurs to Bryzon that the planet is preparing to die, 'the quiet before the storm' is how his old friend Jon King would have described it.

It is leader Nezray from Temsik and It-Ha Layrrah who join the family at Sayhran's home for the evening meal. Krom and Remek are in Telmah taking instruction from Ohre. The conversation remains on issues of the impending escape from Kearthat.

Bryzon updates Raine on he and Layrrah's journey to the Eastern Colonies. She in turn updates Bryzon of the progress Below. It is late when Bryzon finally lays his head down to rest on Leyashe's bed below the kitchen table.

The following day Nezray, Raine and Bryzon enter the cavern on their way to Telmah and Layrrah returns to Rednos Colony to meet with Marcus to update the Western Colony Leaders.

Chapter 45 - The Veil

Raine looks around her, nothing has changed. She listens to the sound of the river as her eyes take in The Below. The dark beyond is aglow, a world shimmering with colour. At her feet where there is light everything still appears white and dead.

A very quiet Nedyar follows as they make their way to the rendezvous point where the transporter will meet them to take them to Telmah.

Leyashe and Xandr are sitting on the walkway of the craft. It is a sight that has Bryzon ecstatic. The two men are dressed in uniforms that were once worn by the earthlings that came to Kearthat. The scene that greets him validates they are no longer farmers.

The big transporter craft emphasises the enormity of the cavern as it looks small against the expanse around it. The smile on Leyashe's face is all Raine sees. Leyashe jumps to his feet and strides hurriedly to greet his sister.

"It is so good to see you sister. Nor~han informed us this morning that all of our people are now gifted, that is good news," he expresses, then releases her from the huge hug. Raine steps back and takes a look at her brother. In uniform it confirms her decision for him to take the potion, he is indeed a man now.

"Bryzon, greetings my friend, while you have been planning on the Freelands we have made great progress. We will be a force that the Eslaf will curse when the day comes," Xandr says, unquestionably a happy man, and seemingly unscathed by The Below. 'The strong men and women of the Kearthat Starfleet he once knew are re-emerging,' he thinks to himself while trying to keep his emotions under control.

Xandr steps towards the newcomer to The Below, "Nedyar, my friend, welcome. We have not seen each other in a long time. Soon, old friendships will be renewed when we speak for many hours of our victory over the aliens," he tells his friend and laughs loudly.

"Each of the transporters can hold at least three hundred. It will be easy once our people start arriving from the colonies to bring them to Telmah," Leyashe informs Bryzon, his mathematical brain once again in full bloom.

They board the craft and Leyashe immediately takes the controls with Xandr looking on. Raine watches how he deftly her brother manipulates the transporter. Her eyes fill with tears, she wipes them away but she knows that she just experienced an emotion of the very best kind.

Telmah comes into sight. When they enter the craft bay on homeship number one Raine is astonished at the progress. It is a hive of activity. Nor~han appears as if out of thin air and after salutations are shared he takes them to their allocated accommodations.

Raine looks around the spacious room. It does not feel real, and then she spots something on the bed, a note and a copy of the Code to Freedom.

Sister, I know you have been trying to cypher the reason for the colony names in the Code to Freedom. Go to a mirror, hold it up and read the names Grandfather Jon wrote at the bottom in his own hand.

Let me know if it blows your mind.

Raine smiles when she notices that her brother has signed the note as 'your clever brother.'

She enters the washroom in her quarters. Standing at the mirror she positions the piece of paper so that she can read the colony names. Then she chuckles. Her clever brother is indeed blowing her mind.

Noitibma reads as Ambition, Arorua reads as Aurora and Rednos reads as Sonder. The mirror reveals Ytineres to be Serenity. Going down the list Raine cannot believe it, 'why had no one ever realised the reflection of the colony names,' Raine queries to herself.

Leyashe has given her a clue as to the names they should choose for the ships. 'Ambition and Sonder,' she decides as she leaves to join Bryzon. But neither have yet discovered the riddle of the Code to Freedom in full. This would come to them much later on.

Raine and Bryzon are keen to inspect the progress as they follow Nor~han to the Command Deck where they find Ameka, Dourok and Ohre studying a paper schematic. The overwhelming number of buttons, levers and screens makes Raine glad that she does not have to deal with that. 'But one day I will know all', she tells herself.

"Finally you join us," Ohre says, smiling when he sees Bryzon and Raine. "We will be ready," he assures them. "The equipment and the ships are excellent, Jon King's people built them well," he praises as he folds his arms across his large chest. Ohre looks like the man Bryzon knew before Seccus fell to the aliens, the uniform and a clean-shaven face has resurrected the man Bryzon once shared command with, in old Kearthat, all traces of Temsik Colony and farming erased.

Many of the screens on the consoles are lit up displaying the spaceship's numerous functions. Bryzon walks around the deck looking at what they have managed to achieve. At last, the homeship has come alive. Bryzon claps Ohre on the back, elbow bumps Kadez, and then embraces Ameka. "This pleases me greatly my friends, thank you," he tells them smiling from ear to ear.

Leaving the Command Deck they follow Ameka to a lower deck where she and Leyashe have been spending many hours working on the devices to take down the Eslaf Androids and Idlers.

Bryzon looks down on the flight deck below and it is a hive of activity. The men are learning and he can see familiar faces listening intently to Xandr. It looks busy and it gives Bryzon hope that they will succeed.

"The device is complete but we must test it Bryzon" Ameka insists as she picks up a small round unassuming device. Raine looks around the fairly large room, there are row upon row of shelves and drawers. There are several computer screens lit up and she is sure her brother must have had something to do with that.

"I see you looking around this place Raine," Ameka says. "It has everything we would ever need to repair the technology of this craft. Your greatfather and his friend did good."

Leyashe arrives on a small two-man vehicle that is used to cover the large distances on the spaceship. Wondering what the whining sound is, Raine takes a peek out of the door. What she sees makes her smile.

"Do you not love this, Rai?" Leyashe asks as he jumps off the funny-looking three-wheeled vehicle. "Without these we would never get anything done here," he tells her, pointing to a small metal insert on the transport with the words 'Freddy's GoTrike' engraved on it. No one yet realises that there are different names on several of these small units. They will discover in time that there is one that reads 'Rick's GoTrike', 'Jon's GoTrike' and 'Dr. Jean's GoTrike' and so on.

Bryzon looks at Ameka and winks, they both know Leyashe is unaware that the Kearthat Starfleet had similar transport. They say nothing, leaving the young man to enjoy his moment with his sister.

Nor~han arrives after having excused himself earlier to deal with a matter on the ship. "I was informed that you were here. I wish to join you if that is acceptable," he asks, bowing.

"Of course Nor~han, we welcome your ideas, please sit," Raine invites. "We were discussing how we would go about testing the devices," Raine says smiling, bringing the Yraif man into the conversation.

Raine and Leyashe talk about the names of the ships while Bryzon and Nor~han speak about the progress in the Terra Bay. When Bryzon hears the names the siblings have chosen for the homeships he thinks them to be strong names. For now, The Selected keep their secret as to where they came upon them.

When Bryzon feels pangs of hunger he questions what time it might be. Nor~han informs them it is past the midnight hour. They decide to postpone their discussion on the testing of the device until morning when everyone has had time to think about how they were going to achieve this.

"It is difficult to keep track of the hour of the day down here," Bryzon apologizes to everyone.

"It is of no matter Bryzon, we Yraif do not tire easily and there is much to fill the day and night, but you and Raine must eat and find rest," he tells them.

Their meal is interrupted when Raine's pupils light up. Bryzon is quite taken aback at first but then notices that Raine is nodding her head, as if she is listening. When the event ends he can tell by Raine's expression there is something wrong.

"Bryzon, we have to leave The Below," Raine declares.

"Why, what is wrong?" he asks, suddenly afraid that their plans have been discovered as he feels panic rise in his throat.

"The Eslaf were in Noi looking for you."

"They are checking up on me again?" Bryzon is shocked.

"Yes, Nowber told them that you and I went hunting and were expected to stay with family in Rednos for the night. They will be returning tomorrow. It-Ha Layrrah is back in Noi, she asks that we return immediately, she suggests that Keeland, Krom and Remek accompany us. We will all hunt at first light," she adds.

The rock exit slides open and they step into the dawn. Once they have crossed the river Krom and Remek go ahead of them. Raine, Bryzon and Keeland manage to hunt two Tibbar.

When they reach the edge of the forest nearing Noitibma they hear the familiar sound of Remek's whistle.

Remek emerges from a thick clump of brush. "Krom has returned to Noi ahead of me, here are two Tibbar and a young Sixa," he tells them, smiling as he pulls the dead animals out from under the vegetation. "A good hunt for the morning would you not agree Bryzon?" he boasts playfully.

"We must leave now, see you in Noi," Keeland says and joins Remek. They take off sprinting towards the colony, hoping to beat the return of the Eslaf.

Raine carries two Tibbar and Bryzon lifts the Sixa over his shoulders, its tongue hanging out from its small mouth. The animal's short horns, and narrow stripes on its fur give away that the creature is still quite young. Holding a Tibbar in each hand Bryzon and

Raine set off. It is not long before their nerves calm while they get their stories straight for any questions the Eslaf might ask.

When they arrive at the gate the colony looks normal, everyone is getting on with their daily chores. Activities illustrate the Freelanders are hard at work as the colonists play their part and barely acknowledge Raine and Bryzon. There are Freelanders out in the nearby fields harvesting Otatop and no sign of Eslaf as yet.

The serenity is short-lived, within a few minutes of setting down the kills and starting to skin the Xiso they hear a 'four-alien' spotter craft hover above the colony. A huge cloud of dust follows the touchdown as scurrying colonists try to save their wares being propelled in all directions. When the hatch on the ship slides open three Eslaf emerge. Two of them exit carrying Nobrac, the other wearing red body armour walks ahead of the green-suits.

Nowber strides over to meet the Eslaf in charge while Keeland hangs back. Bryzon and Raine watch from around the corner. Words are exchanged but it is too far for them to hear what is being said by the alien. The big Eslaf in the red suit steps forward, he pushes Nowber hard on the chest and the leader falls back onto the ground into a sitting position. Keeland moves forward, then stops, Bryzon is sure Nowber has indicated for him to stay put. Keeland's presence however is yet another reassurance to the red-suit that all at the colony is just as it presents itself.

Nowber does not stay down long before he stands. The Eslaf in red reaches for his long hair, pulling him close. The Eslaf's loud, deep voice demands to know where Bryzon is.

Raine, standing next to Bryzon is watching what is taking place. She clenches her small hands into fists and threatens to confront the alien. Bryzon puts his finger to his lips and shows her to be quiet. The Eslaf follow Nowber who is pointing in the direction of Raine's cabin.

"The men know what they are doing, Rai, be calm," Bryzon reassures his niece as they scurry to get back to the carcasses and continue skinning the animals. It takes little time for the aliens to reach the cabin where Bryzon has the kills laid out on a table in the suns.

"I told you they have just returned from the hunt, now you see for yourself," Nowber says to the Eslaf who releases his hold on the leader's hair, shoving him aside.

"Good hunting across the river yesterday and this morning," Bryzon says with a loud voice, smiling, and making sure the Eslaf in red can hear him.

"There is no need to treat our leader with disrespect," Raine says, moving forward. "Our leader spoke the truth, we were hunting for meat," she states, her hands on her hips.

"Last night we were in Rednos with family, to escape the Night Creatures," Bryzon cuts in gently pushing Raine back with his hand. "But we have returned," he continues bravely while his heart thumps loud enough for him to hear it in his head. He begins pulling out the guts of one of the dead Tibbar to calm himself.

The alien walks forward and looks down at the dead animals lying on the tables. Then he turns to Bryzon.

"You work for Eslaf, not hunt meat for you for two days," he growls and kicks at the leg of the table, the small table does not withstand the onslaught and it topples over taking the fresh kills with it into the dust.

"I understand. Sorry, our mistake," Bryzon tells the disgusting grey creature, his hands dripping in blood as he does an exaggerated bow towards the alien creature.

"You prisoner, you work for Eslaf," the alien repeats at a distance of about two inches from Bryzon's face. The delivery of the alien's message is in a voice so deep it hurts Bryzon's ears. The alien's facial appendages swing from side to side as it bellows at him, foul alien breath burning the inside of Bryzon's nostrils. The alien makes some additional disgusted sounds in his own alien language before he turns away, striding with his long legs towards their waiting craft. Minutes later the spotter craft shoots into the air and the Eslaf are gone.

"Nowber my friend, are you whole?" Bryzon asks, concerned.

"I have healed, thank you," he insists. "I will take my leave now, there are appearances of normality to deal with." The lesser leader walks away, his pride damaged, the Eslaf red-suit has left Nowber angered.

"Why do you think they came back to check again?" Raine asks Bryzon after Nowber leaves.

"I think I know," Bryzon says. "The men at the prison have been released," he tells her. "If so then we can expect to see Pateeo and the others soon. This is good news Rai, but the Eslaf are being more vigilant than I imagined, it is obvious they do not trust us."

"Raine, you must talk with It-Ha Layrrah, ask her if she knows if the men are coming home. And you must contact Ash, I promised him I would remind you to update him on the matter of the Eslaf." Raine washes her blood-covered hands. She is only a few steps away when Bryzon reminds her, "Leyashe will be concerned for our well-being, talk to him soon Rai." She turns, smiles and gives him a thumbs-up.

Bryzon watches his niece walk away. He is proud of her but she had scared him when she stood up to the Eslaf earlier. He is however overjoyed at the thought that his friends will finally be free. He bends down and resurrects the table and puts down the next animal to skin, the Xiso and Tibbar lying in the dirt mostly unsalvageable.

"Our time has come," Bryzon says under his breath. His face filled with hatred for the Eslaf, his teeth bared like that of an ancient warrior. He picks up an axe and starts chopping, hard but accurately as he dissects the dead animal in front of him.

"Where is It-Ha Layrrah?" Raine asks, looking at Nowber who is speaking to a man about the crop of Torrak root that is being harvested.

"She and Sayhran come and go," Nowber answers, shrugging his shoulders. "It is the strangest thing," he adds. "They seem to be everywhere, but nowhere," he tells her with a puzzled look on his face and Raine has to smile at his comment.

She eventually discovers the It-Ha in the Council Lodge, they are sitting opposite each other at the long table.

"We watched with great concern," Sayhran says, standing to hug her niece. Raine feels it in the air when Sayhran releases her. She knows that the It-Ha had been very busy, she can feel the magic all around her.

"Could you have protected us?" Raine asks.

"Yes, but it would not have been good for our plans," Sayhran says in a stern voice.

"Bryzon handled the situation well, but you, young leader, came dangerously close to compromising what has been accomplished thus far," she chides.

"You are my leader, Raine," Layrrah says, looking at the young girl. "You are our leader," she repeats. "You have to command, and sometimes it means that you must control your emotions, no matter how difficult. Sayhran and I will always protect you, but you must help us. "You cannot be hasty in your decisions," she cautions.

Raine flops down next to Sayhran, running her hands through her long black hair, she lets out a funny-sounding little grunt. "I was so afraid," she admits to the two women. "I feel as if I am the wrong choice to be a leader," she adds softly. "What if Ash and I fail our people?" she rattles on as she puts her hands on her face and rubs her cheeks pulling her eyelids down into a funny face, expelling a long sigh.

Raine nearly falls off her chair as suddenly the room dims, the windows darken and the bolt in the door slides shut with a loud clang. As if out of a dream, Laathria appears, floating only a few feet from where they are seated. Raine jumps to her feet, but the High Yraif remains unmoving.

"Never fear me, Raine, daughter of Caite," High Yraif Laathria says calmly.

"Are you really here?" Raine asks the High Yraif, and then regrets saying such a silly thing.

"No child, I am but I am not. I felt your doubt, it is strong. It has been written that you and Leyashe will come to meet many obstacles, but you will not fail your people," the High Yraif communicates in a low voice. "You must follow your heart and your senses, and so must your brother. You must not challenge the Eslaf of Ludinia until the time comes. They are dangerous," she emphasizes.

"If you did not have fears, you would not be who we know you to be, but you must use caution" the Yraif mystic shares. "Trust in your feelings, believe in your decisions, hear the suggestions of those who uphold their belief in The Selected, consider the thoughts from those who surround you and love you. Consider well the guidance offered and you and Leyashe will succeed."

Raine cannot help but notice again how beautiful this Yraif woman is, her long white hair, mesmerizing voice and the calm she exudes. Her very presence makes Raine feel renewed.

"You will prevail," are the last words she hears Laathria say as the Yraif turns her back to them and begins to fade into the background of the room. The windows lighten and the sunsshine is allowed back in. The latch on the door slides open with a squeak as the metal pieces rub against each other in the silence that Laathria has left behind.

"Do you feel better now?" Sayhran asks, smiling at Raine.

"I do, but sometimes it all feels like a dream. It is almost as if I need to force myself to understand that so much has changed and keeps changing," Raine admits to the It-Ha.

"Pateeo and Bryzon's men have been released; several are on their way to Noi, while others have already returned to their colonies in the east. Those going West have crossed over the bridge at Elbaffeni earlier today," Layrrah says, confirming Bryzon's prediction. "They are free. Now my guilt can be less," she sighs. For the first time since meeting Layrrah, Raine can see tears form in the mystic woman's large green eyes and somehow, she feels her sadness.

"I must tell Bryzon immediately," Raine says, heading for the door, but something makes her turn back. She walks over to Layrrah and hugs the stunned It-Ha and then hugs Sayhran.

When Raine is gone, Sayhran can see on Layrrah's face she is confused at the show of affection from Raine, and at the same time she swears she can see just a hint of a smile on the woman's face.

Chapter 46 - The Spaceships

It is past the midnight hour when Bryzon and Raine lay their heads down to sleep. Fortunately, being Xennes will cheat their bodies of any weariness by morning.

The first shuttle of the day arrives, and Pateeo and forty-five men, originally from Noitibma Colony, are on it. They are home.

On the same shuttle is Leader Ethlah of Accedes Colony. Bryzon and Raine discover that the woman has been summoned by It-Ha Layrrah.

Raine and Bryzon call a gathering of the free Xennes men as soon as they have been given a chance to meet with family and have a meal.

The men are eager to exact their revenge on the Eslaf. They implore Bryzon to take them to Telmah, but to no avail. Raine insists they remain at the colony. This is when Pateeo and his friends realize that The Selected make the final decisions now.

When the shuttle leaves the area for the day, Bryzon, Keeland, Raine, Krom, and Remek make their way to the cavern for their trip back to The Below before the suns set.

Back in Telmah, they find that the diligent work has continued, and many tasks on the homeships are complete. It has been twenty-three days since the first encounter with Nor~han. A total of nineteen men and women are becoming more and more competent at flying the fighter craft. To Raine's amazement, the word Ambition has appeared in gigantic letters on ship number one. On ship number two, there is a similar change; the word Sonder is emblazoned on it in white.

Ohre and Xandr request that Bryzon consider bringing more men capable of learning how to fly the fighter craft. Ohre offers to go East while Xandr will recruit from the Western Colonies.

After much discussion it becomes clear they need some of the men who have just returned from prison, Raine relents giving her permission to bring whomever

Bryzon considers most experienced. Anyone not chosen will fill in where leaders have been summoned to Telmah.

Bryzon wants to see the waterfall exit at Sigae at the same time as dropping off Ohre and Xandr. Leyashe pilots the transporter craft, Nor~han joins them as they set off to see the waterfall from inside the mountain.

When the transporter reaches the area where the stairs lead to the cavern from the Trigga tree entrance, Raine recognizes it immediately. Bryzon taps her on the shoulder and points to something on the cavern floor. She squints to make sure that what she is looking at is real. Standing quite still below them are two Trungo. They stare up at the craft, Raine cannot help but feel great pity for these magnificent animals that have so little time left to live.

Leyashe knocks to cut into Raine's thoughts, "Rai, did you see that? Those were Trungo."

"Yes brother, thank you, Bryzon pointed them out to me. So amazing Ash, but so sad," she adds. Leyashe does not answer, she knows his heart too aches for the losses that are to come.

After seeing the veil of water cascading from the upper river from inside the cavern for the first time, Bryzon and Raine know it will be the perfect exit for the fighter craft.

Raine understands now how the Nut~Ca River below gets its water. Where the waterfall cascades down from The Above, half of the torrent is caught up in a natural rock formation, not unlike a funnel it guides the gushing streams of water feeding into The Below. Assisted by the natural slope of the terrain, it is transported swiftly in the opposite direction towards Telmah. The creation of the underground river is indeed remarkable, but its secret has been discovered.

"When the time comes we will be on the grey bugs within minutes, they will not know what hit them," Ohre comments, his hefty laugh and the joy in his eyes infectious to those around him. Bryzon and Ohre seal their mutual anticipation of crushing the Eslaf with a forearm grasp that seals their shared agreement, Raine glimpsing yet another old Xennes gesture.

Leyashe looks down to find a suitable landing spot. Ohre bids them farewell promising qualified men and women on his return. They do not linger after Ohre disappears down a narrow rock formation that will take him through the veil of cascading water to the surface.

They take off and head in the opposite direction. When Xandr leaves the craft Raine spots Rence waiting patiently. He looks up at the big transporter and waves, she waves back and puts her palm to her mouth to blow a kiss. Rence's face lights up, then it is over as Leyashe deftly flies them back towards Telmah.

Raine Seeks It-Ha Layrrah's mind to let her know the next phase of the mission is underway. It is clear to Bryzon that the gift Leyashe and Raine have is growing stronger as time passes. The Selected now easily send vital information back and forth to Layrrah, and Nor~han.

In the days waiting for more men to come Below Nor~han and his people, Bryzon and Raine are kept busy moving the metal containers from the blue box at the Trigga entrance and the containers of weapons from the cabin to the homeships. This is when Raine and Bryzon discover that Nor~han had completely forgotten to show them the armoury on the two craft.

Hidden in the most unlikely place behind a room that houses cleaning materials, many dust-collecting droids called a *Spaceba*, brushes, buckets, brooms and the like, there is an entrance to a large armoury on each spaceship. They are astounded to find not only hundreds more long guns, handguns and grenades, but rocket launchers and a seemingly endless supply of munitions for their newly discovered element of war. Bryzon immediately notices that these new weapons are too large for an attack using the underground tunnels. For now, he puts the new weapons out of his mind. It was good to know they were available, just in case.

The four days pass and Xandr and Ohre are back with their new trainees, they also bring with them news from the leaders remaining Above. The information is good, the aliens have not noticed any changes, but Bryzon's anxiety remains heightened. He knows that if the Eslaf were to do a count of the Freelanders at the colonies their plans would disintegrate. The constant agonising brings back his nightmares, his sleep disturbed each time he lays his head down to rest.

Everyone is surprised when the Yraif decide to split their people between the two ships, with the Yraif Assembly choosing to live on Sonder with Nor~han. Fulfilling her promise to Raine, the High Yraif Laathria has chosen to remain with the It-Ha on Ambition. The village at Telmah is finally eerily empty as it awaits its fiery end. And the abyss of the underground waterfall forgotten for the moment by Leyashe.

The days pass, filled with endless planning while those already living on the spaceships adjust to their new life. Daily reports from Layrrah and Sayhran leave Bryzon more worried than the day before. Life Above seems to proceed without the Eslaf noticing anything different, while life Below is bustling with activity.

The waiting is getting to Bryzon and he finds himself drawn to seek out Nor~han, Raine and Leyashe several times a day, asking they contact Sayhran and Layrrah for updates.

Finally, tunics are discarded by those charged to fly the homeships and the fighter craft, and others who will form part of the new Xennes Space Force, the uniforms are in good taste, the confidence it instils manifestly evident.

When Raine comes to meet Bryzon on the main control deck of Ambition he is taken aback. She is dressed in a uniform, the suit immediately portrays the look of a leader. Strapped to her waist belt Bryzon sees a handgun in a leather pouch. Raine's ever-present short sword has been discarded, her bow and arrows replaced by a new future.

"Why the strange look?" Raine asks, as she notices Bryzon staring.

"You look so much like Caite," is all he says, a slight crack in his voice. She understands it is best not to ask anything further, instead giving him a moment to recover.

"Are you ready to join Dourok and Ameka?"

"Yes, let us go and find out how they plan to fly these spaceships out of this difficult place." As they are about to leave, Leyashe enters the deck. His nephew is dressed much like Raine, he looks so different out of his pilot's outfit. Startled by the change in Leyashe's appearance Bryzon finds that he cannot speak. Leyashe notices Bryzon's uncomfortable moment and breaks the silence by teasing his sister.

"So Rai, as 'The Selected, are you Selected number one or number two?" he asks, trying to keep a straight face.

"Number one, brother," she answers without the slightest hesitation, raising one of her eyebrows. "Without a doubt, I am the older," she further clarifies for her brother.

"But I am the smarter, am I not? What do you think, Bryzon?" Leyashe persists, jesting. Finally, unable to withhold a giggle, Raine knows her brother is just winding her up.

"Bryzon please hit him for me, I am afraid I will hurt him," Raine says as she puts her hands on her hips, raising her head slightly playfully imitating her so-called status.

"I think you are looking for trouble, Ash," Bryzon manages to say, winking at his nephew.

"Well, now that the matter is cleared up, Number One, I will take my leave to do my duties in the humble belly of this ship. I will see you later, my leader," he says, smiling, then adds a swift salute.

"Happy to be your superior, Number Two," Raine shouts after him.

"He is in high spirits," Raine comments and laughs. "He deserves it, we all do, but we are not yet free of the Eslaf. There is much yet to overcome," Raine adds and Bryzon nods in agreement. There was much to accomplish.

Many hours are spent pouring over instruments on the main flight deck of Ambition. The schematics and instructional information are comprehensive, but there are no instructions on how to squeeze the homeships out of the caverns. Maneuvering them from their encased positions is going to take remarkable accuracy.

"Ameka and I wondered who you would appoint as commanders on Sonder?" Dourok asks, looking at Raine and Bryzon.

"If you agree Raine," Bryzon interrupts, looking at his niece. "I would recommend that we ask Ashok to be commander and Learridy to be his second-in-command," Bryzon proposes. "We will, of course, select many more to run the homeships after we leave Kearthat," Bryzon implies.

"If that is what you think is best, Bryzon, then I will stand by your decision," Raine agrees with him without question.

Raine can feel that the thinking on the ships has changed. In their minds they are thinking ahead to life after Kearthat, but it still sounds somewhat surreal to her.

Later that evening the strange 'bing, bong, bong' sound originating from the entrance to his living area has Bryzon confused for a split second. When he opens the door the vision that meets his eyes makes his heartbeat quicken immediately. It is Learridy.

"Welcome," Bryzon manages. She declines his offer of refreshment, instead, she drops down on the chair where he had been sitting earlier, and he is forced to sit opposite her at his desk.

"Raine sent a message that you wanted to see us? Ashok and I that is," she clarifies, breaking the awkward silence.

"We will wait for him then before I speak of the reason, if .. if that is in order?" Bryzon sort of stutters before the door thankfully sounds again. Ashok is in uniform, his hair tied back, with no trace of a single feather. He is the vision of a perfect officer of the new fleet, and Bryzon has to smile at the man's good sense.

Both are happy with the news they have been chosen to command Sonder. When they leave Bryzon sits down on the seat that Learridy had so cheekily stolen from him. He puts his head in his hands and sighs. He knows he has intentionally chosen Learridy; she was more than capable of the task, but he had done it to ensure her safety.

"High It-Ha Layrrah will have her comment on this," he says aloud, then shakes his head again. His list of secrets and indiscretions kept by the It-Ha keeps growing.

Time races and the day of the gathering draws near. All too soon it is time to leave The Below for the last evalc. Leyashe flies Bryzon and Raine to the Trigga tree exit.

Arriving at Noitibma Colony, Bryzon and Raine are greeted with great enthusiasm. Sayhran and Layrrah had gone ahead and informed the colonists that the time to leave was drawing near. The many smiling faces around them tell the story.

But there is news that Bryzon and Raine were not expecting.

The It-Ha tells Bryzon of an incident two days before. One of the Noitibma Korak stumbled and fell carrying a sack of Otatop, the roots spilled and some fell at the feet of an Eslaf soldier. The Eslaf shoved the Korak and hit him several times about the head, and on instinct Dessas reacted by stepping forward to confront the Eslaf. The soldier had shot Dessas through the upper leg.

"Nowber managed to calm the Eslaf. After they left, we quickly moved Dessas to the Healer's Cabin. He was bleeding badly, Bryzon," It-Ha Layrrah retells.

"I could feel his life was beginning to leave him, so I did the unthinkable. I administered the potion, and it worked. I have since bestowed long-life to all the Korak in Noitibma. The consequences of my actions will be known when The Order hears of my insolence. I fear it may be my undoing," she admits.

Raine is over the moons that Dessas has recovered, and that the Noitibma Korak are now protected, but she can see that it may come at a price for Layrrah. 'The one they do not speak of,' may be less than impressed.

"There is one, Raine, who would not take the potion. He told us he is going back with Namow and her people, and I respected his wishes," Sayhran tells them.

With the Eslaf's complacency still intact, Bryzon feels content for now. However, at the same time, he remains nervous after hearing what took place but does not share his fears with anyone.

The colonies are rotating tasks at break-neck speed, which gives the sense of busy colonies while produce levels are met and deliveries to the prison and city remain at the correct levels. Layrrah passes on to Bryzon and Raine that the pace is beginning to wear on the colonists.

"How long do we have, It-Ha Layrrah?" Raine asks, looking at the mystic.

"The Firemoth came to me. We have eight days until the day of the darkening," Layrrah divulges. "My vision has been confirmed by the High Yraif Laathria. We agree that the lava beneath the mountain is bubbling close to the surface. It will be close."

The late afternoon Traxid brings Marcus and Rence from Rednos and Leader Brann of Elbaffeni. The last shuttle of the day delivers the Western Colony Leaders Mezka and scientist Sanew. A second Traxid brings leaders from the Eastern Colonies, all under the guise of a 'crop-planning' meeting of the leaders of the colonies.

After greetings and gestures of welcome, they all meet at the Council Lodge where a meal is laid out for the group. It is not surprising to Bryzon that Rence and  Raine eat rather quickly, then ask to be excused, promising to return shortly.

Raine leads Rence to the West corner where Noitibma included a small forested area in the colony when it was built. They do not speak until they reach a large fallen log to sit on. The warm wind blows Rence's long, brown, wavy hair about, and he quickly sweeps some together forming a hasty knot on his head while some of his hair hangs freely to his shoulders.

"I have missed you, my leader," he says to Raine, smiling and then leans forward to place a light kiss on her lips.

"I thought of you too," Raine says, almost shyly. "A lot," she adds.

There is a noise in the brush, both Raine and Rence jump up expecting to see someone from the colony. They laugh when they realize that Regor has followed them. Afraid of being shooed away, the Eninac finds a spot nearby and quickly settles down. Very protective of Raine since it was a pup, the Eninac rarely leaves her side when she is in Noitibma Colony.

Rence holds Raine's hand, he looks into her eyes and then kisses her. He has missed her.

All too soon they know it is time to return to the lodge. A last passionate embrace has both young people hopelessly in love. It takes all of Raine's courage to tell Rence that they need to get back. He squeezes her hand tightly.

"I promise to be a good boy and stay alive if you promise me you will," he tells her, smiling.

Before they leave, Raine's expression changes.

"I am appointing you to a very important position," she tells him.

"I want to fly, Raine," Rence pleads.

"You will, but right now I need someone who can help our fighters on Ambition when we attack the city. I want you with Marcus and Nedai on the Command Deck.

This is a position of great importance," she insists. "When all of this is over I swear I will appoint you to the fleet. I give you my word," she promises.

"The first of the colonists will start going to the ships in the next two to three days. I need someone I can continue to trust with the lives of our people."

"I accept," Rence says after her many explanations.

"But now you owe me another kiss," he adds, he picks her up placing her feet on the log so that her face is level with his.

"If I knew that all it took was another kiss instead of a long discussion, I would have kissed you before I begged you," Raine responds, shaking her head. As they hold each other all their concerns melt away for a few seconds before she gently pushes him away. Serious matters await Raine's attention.

The gathering goes well into the night, and it is decided they will begin moving some colonists to Telmah starting in three days. Raine announces that Rence will be co-coordinating the Western Colonies. She casually divulges that she and Leyashe thought it pertinent that Rence assist Marcus and Nedai on Ambition during the battle. Bryzon recognizes he is not alone in his deceit, Raine has chosen to keep Rence safe, just as he had done with Learridy.

Auwzen is charged with moving the youngest and oldest colonists to the waterfall entrance for Ytineres and Ygyzys Colony first. Adarra is tasked to then oversee doing the same with Arorua, Sigae and Temsik Colony.

"We have brought with us the devices to stop the Night Creatures, the Idlers and hopefully the Eslaf droids," Bryzon says, holding up Ameka and Leyashe's creation.

"The device remains untested," he tells them.

"Before dawn, Raine and I will test one on a Night Creature. If we are lucky we will do so with an Idler this very night, but still we will not know if it will stop the Eslaf droids. This we will only discover on the day we attack the city," he tells them, and a low murmur can be heard among those gathered. Bryzon's audience remains quiet as he explains how the gadgets work. It briefly crosses his mind that some of the leaders may be feeling a little anxious about using the untested device against the Androids.

"If Raine and I manage to successfully stop a creature, each of you will go back to your colonies with one of these," he says, holding up one of Ameka and Leyashe's inventions. You will need it when you move our people to The Below.

"What if it does not stop the Eslaf Androids?" Auwzen asks.

"If it does not work," Bryzon says, looking at the many faces around him, "Then we will have to fight our way off Kearthat, but the aliens will soon have the fury of the mountain biting their backsides, and we will take pleasure in that my friends."

Raine hushes the laughter after Bryzon's comment.

"We have thirty-six fighter pilots that will be trained and ready. We have four transport ships that have been armed, thanks to Ohre. We have many long guns that will fire endlessly. And we have hundreds of handguns, hundreds of fireballs and a new weapon we call a rocket launcher. If we cannot fight and win our way off Kearthat, we are poor soldiers. I am not ready to die here, are you? Raine asks.

"We must prevail," Raine insists, her voice slightly raised, her pupils flickering for all to see. "Would you not fight with less if you knew the consequences of remaining on Kearthat? Fear is no longer an option," she declares and The Xennes present are astounded at her courage and shocked at her sudden change of appearance.

"Our fighter craft are far more advanced than those of our enemy," Raine continues as her eyes survey everyone around her before she smiles. "We are going to kill every last one of them," she states adamantly before she goes silent, and you can hear a Torrap feather drop in the large room before resounding knuckle rapping takes its place.

"If the droids fall, it will make our burden easier," Bryzon states after silence returns.

"Our main objective is to prevent the Eslaf ships from taking off. If they do get to their ships, our men will fight overhead while we deal with the creatures on the ground. This war, my friends, could take many lives, but we must be fierce to prevent the bugs from reaching their craft."

"Once we have reached the base at Etah, Evas will fly the Korak ship to the prison. We expect the battle there to be short, but loading the prisoners will take time. The Korak have only the Eslaf ground forces to resist at the prison. We are almost one hundred percent sure that two-thirds of the soldiers at the prison are Android. If they are disabled, we will have achieved our goal easily; the fighter craft will take care of the rest," Bryzon maintains.

Most of the leaders present are stunned when Bryzon tells them that several men who had served their sentences at the mines had volunteered to assist in getting the Korak onto their ship safely. It is past midnight when Raine stands to make a final announcement.

"My brother and I have decided to appoint Marcus King as head of a new Council that will be formed when we are free of the Eslaf," she announces.

"The other members who will serve under Marcus will be selected by our people, not by Leyashe, myself, or any other." Raine looks over at Marcus, who seems quite startled at the announcement.

"It will be the people who decide who the council members will be to hold positions. The It-Ha will continue to protect us each day, and they will remain in our highest regard. The mystics are our greatest asset," Raine tells everyone present. "But they too serve the people, not a council. The old ways can never be repeated." Raine remains quiet for a few seconds as she looks around the table, her eyes meeting each glance. This prompts everyone to stand, and a show of raised hands and fists to the chest comes as acceptance and respect of Raine's declaration.

After the Evalc ends, Raine calls Marcus to one side, "All of this has been made possible by our grandparents, Marcus. Accept your status with a good heart. Our forefathers made many sacrifices and have given us a way to leave Kearthat before it meets its end. You deserve to be a leader. Grandfather Jon and Grandmother Farron would have wanted it that way," she whispers and pats him on the arm.

Once outside the gate, Raine's eyes light up, and she scans the area around her. As they move away from the colony, Bryzon stays within two feet of his niece, a handgun at the ready. The device to bring down a Night Creature is securely fastened to his belt. It takes twenty minutes before Raine stops and whispers for Bryzon to stand still as she stares at a snarling beast just a few feet away.

"He is just looking at me, Bryzon. He is not sure what I am. Now, Bryzon, she shouts as the creature pounces. The animal leaps, then in mid-air it comes crashing down like a sack of Otatop right next to Raine.

"It works, it really works," Raine laughs, hugging Bryzon.

"Well done, Ameka and Ash," Bryzon cheers the absent designers of the technology he holds in his hand.

"What is the size of the area that it will be effective?" Raine asks.

"About a hundred and fifty feet, but that is more than enough distance to keep our people safe. Come, we must find a place to bury the beast. Bryzon lifts the creature over his shoulders and they head to the nearest field where a Ylock crop is ripening and ready to accommodate a guest.

They only manage three hours of sleep, but both feel amazingly refreshed when they meet at dawn with the men and woman who will be returning to their colonies. Unfortunately, an Idler does not make an appearance and the device remains untested on the drones. A quick lesson from Bryzon on how to work the device to stop the Night Creatures is welcomed. Everyone is more at ease knowing that it works. The small mechanism is easily hidden in various clever ways as they prepare to leave Noitibma.

That night, the over six hundred colonists in Noitibma are divided into four groups. A small group of the youngest children, the oldest men and women and one mother with a baby is chosen to return at nightfall with Bryson and Raine. The group also includes the Korak, Dessas and Bailea.

As soon as the last shuttle leaves the colony, they set off, armed with the Night Creature disabling device. It is slow-going as most of the youngest have to be carried. Layrrah communicates with Nor~han, while Raine contacts Leyashe to update him on Raine's decision to bring colonists on board the transporter.

They manage to enter the forest before any Idlers can be heard. Luck remains with them for the walk through the intimidating dark. Finally, they cross the river and arrive at the cavern. It has taken many hours and dawn is fast approaching.

As the cavern door begins to slide closed, Raine hears an Idler. She reaches for the lever on the rock wall and stops the door. Everyone remains as if they are statues, silent in the dark cavern. Bryzon hands Raine the device. They wait, and the Idler hovers as if it knows something is wrong. Raine presses the button. The flying droid drops from the sky and crashes with a thump.

"Bryzon, what shall we do?" Raine panics, but at the same time, she is elated they have managed to test the device and that it works. "It is so close to the cavern, I was not thinking," she adds, her eyes pleading for a solution from Bryzon.

"You must continue to the transporter; Leyashe will be waiting. Dessas and Bailea will help me offer the Idler to the waterfall. The force of the water will carry it away from here. With luck it will end up on the beach, which will divert suspicion from the colonies."

Bryzon and the two young Korak pick up the Idler. They make their way back to the log crossing, where they toss the disabled machine into the churning froth. They wait until they can see a sign of it bobbing about, as it flows quickly with the water heading to the black beaches of Kearthat before they turn and make a run for the cavern.

Chapter 47 - The Escape

The days come and go as more children and elderly Freelanders are cautiously transported to Telmah at night. There is a frantic flurry of desperate last-minute preparation on the homeships. The Xennes race against time to ready their strategies against the Eslaf.

It is day seven since the gathering in Noitibma with the remaining colony leaders. It is also the day the last shuttle on the Elbaffeni route retires in the City of Etah.

The day of the darkening is coming.

It-Ha Layrrah's daily reports have confirmed the colonists continue to be brave. As the numbers dwindled, working in shifts from sunrise to sunset has kept up the appearance of greater numbers in the settlements while having ensured the food supply levels to the mining prison had not deviated. The plan was an enormous success, and it was close to being done with.

With the superstitious Eslaf hiding in the city during the eclipse, the Xennes will get the opportunity to launch their assault, but would it work? They were largely outnumbered.

The after-dark excursions had so far progressed with almost no incidents, and only one near occurrence with a Night Creature was reported. They can only hope that bringing the last of the Freelanders to Telmah will be uneventful. The enormous fear of being caught in the act of moving people to the cavern had weighed heavily on the minds of all of The Liberators, and it was not over yet.

"Raine, why on Kearthat have you called for a gathering at this time?" Leyashe questions his sister when he enters the Arc Room. "We should wait," he insists.

"Brother, many of our people are here, and they need to be reassured. The time of battle is nearing. They will inform the last of those to arrive of what we are about to tell them," she assures him, as Bryzon enters the room.

"You asked for me, Raine?" he says with an enquiring look. "Has something happened? Is it serious?" Bryzon asks, concern written all over his face.

"Raine wants to call a gathering outside of the ships of everyone on the spaceships. She feels they need encouragement and that they need to put their feet on Kearthat one last time," Leyashe says, sounding somewhat apprehensive of his sister's intention, as he lifts his brows and sighs.

"Good, then it is nothing serious," Bryzon answers, sounding relieved. "If I am not needed for anything else, Rai, I have much to accomplish. Let Ameka know what time you wish to call the gathering." Bryzon does not linger. He leaves and Leyashe shakes his head.

Raine hands Leyashe the notes she has made. He does not comment, instead, he sits down and begins to read. When he is done, he hands them back to her and hugs her.

The message goes out on the com for everyone to gather in the large space between the two homeships.

There is whispering among the crowd as they wait. To Bryzon, it seems like a lifetime ago that he was down in the mine at Pishdrah, taking orders from the aliens. When Raine stands up to speak, more than half of the people stand in an attempt to raise their right hand in the air, but she waves them down.

"Soon, we strike our enemy and leave behind the only home we have known," she begins. "Leyashe and I want to thank you for your bravery, commitment to secrecy and willingness to do whatever has been asked of you. We need you to be brave for a little longer.

Raine speaks of the loss of Kearthat and the possible loss of life. For the first time, the people from all the colonies are getting to know her.

Leyashe is next. Holding a copy of The 'Code to Freedom in his hands, he begins to read. The crowd is silent as they listen to the words that Jon and Farron King were instructed to record by Farron's mysterious dream companion Jaenus.

When the last word is spoken, a loud cheer erupts. This time they do not wait for Raine's permission. The crowd raise their right arms into the air and then tap their chests twice. The sound of bravery echoes through the cavern.

After the gathering, Raine, Leyashe and Bryzon sit to discuss who will return to Noitibma Colony. Later, two transporters leave to pick up the last of those from the settlements. Ohre and Sahdmar make their way to the waterfall entrance near Sigae. Leyashe transports Bryzon and Raine to the Trigga tree entrance. Bryzon makes sure they are well-armed. He activates the Night Creature device the moment they step into the dark after emerging from the cavern. Two of the three moons are bright on this night, helping them navigate the darkness as they walk at a brisk pace.

Arriving at the colony, they are surprised to find the last group at Noi, including Sayhran and Layrrah, waiting quietly in the dark as the gate opens. No time is wasted, Raine excuses herself and heads toward her cabin.

Bryzon points the device at the Traxid and presses the button, he listens for the faint click that disengages it from reporting its movements to the Eslaf at the base in Etah. Only then does he start the vehicle. It works; the device has turned off the tracking mechanism. The colonists bunch together to fill the trailers attached to the Traxid. When Raine returns, she hops into the seat next to Bryzon. He notices she has something tied to her back, but in the dark, it is difficult to determine what it is.

They reach the forest. Bryzon drives the vehicle deep into thick brush, pushing over small trees and other vegetation. The men in the group hastily cut branches from nearby trees to hide the vehicle.

Raine leads the group, Bryzon following at the rear. The trip is slow in the dark, but words of encouragement from Raine's lips never stop as they walk. Crossing the river has some of the women fearful, but with patience they eventually reach the other side.

When the last person files through the entrance of the cavern and the door slides closed, Raine feels elated, and at the same time, sad. She knows she will never return to this place again. The discovery her brother made mere weeks before now feels like years ago. Leaving their beloved Trigga tree behind feels surreal to her.

When they step into the dark world below, Bryzon lights more torches. The silence is deafening as those from The Above are mesmerized by The Below. It takes several minutes before they talk amongst themselves. Comments reach Bryzon's ears. He and Raine smile at each other as they relive the first time they had seen The Below through the eyes of those following them.

This time, Learridy and Pateeo greet them.

Sitting outside the craft are colonists from the other settlements waiting to be transported to Telmah. Laughter can be heard among the people of Kearthat as they begin to understand their freedom may be close.

"Who is still to arrive?" Bryzon asks.

"We await only the last from Rednos Colony," Learridy informs him.

Bryzon is quiet. He picks up a pebble and rolls it between his fingers. Raine can see that he remains concerned, the waiting is getting to him.

'With the twelve colonies deserted and completely silent, Bryzon wonders if the Idlers will perhaps sense that something is not right,' then shakes his head. He is sure Leyashe would have mentioned it if it were so. The boy was too smart to make a mistake like that.

Raine is about to ask Bryzon what concerns him when she sees a light coming from several torches in the distance. Excited, muffled voices confirm the last group making their way towards the transporter. Raine's heart starts to race when she sets eyes on Rence, he is safe.

When everyone is seated on the transporter, Bryzon goes to the front and takes the seat next to Learridy.

"I thought there would be no harm in surprising you, Bryzon," she says in a soft voice. "It will give me time to inform you of what progress has been made to fly the homeships out of the mountain."

They talk for a short while, and then Bryzon squeezes her hand lightly, thanking her for the update. When their eyes meet, his stomach feels like it is filled with Flutterbugs.

Bryzon moves to the back of the craft to speak to the rest of Noitibma's Korak, who are seated together.

"Are you ready to fight?" he asks them.

"We are ready, Bryzon," they eagerly confirm, their small mouths forming smiles.

"When we land, I will send Ohre to escort you to the fighter craft bay, there you will meet Krom and Remek, Dessas, and Bailea, who will show you around and take you to see where you will be living on homeship number two, it is called Sonder."

"Which of you will not return with Namow?" Bryzon asks, and a young male lifts his hand, it is Hadvah.

"Thank you, we feel honoured that we have been chosen to fight alongside the men and women of Kearthat," Hadvah tells Bryzon. You can be certain that the anger we have against the Eslaf will be well applied," he adds as the rest echo his sentiment. Bryzon looks at the olive young Korak and he knows that he has done the right thing. He had grown to understand and respect the Korak of Dirha, and they had a fighting chance now to return to their home planet.

The final transporter flies into the flight deck, bringing the remaining Freelanders from the Eastern Colonies.

Bryzon volunteers to escort Marcus and Zaviah to their quarters.

"I listened to Nedai as he explained it all to me," Marcus tells Bryzon, "But I never could have dreamed how big these spaceships are, and The Below is...," Marcus begins to say, but hesitates and smiles. "You know there are no words to describe this world, and the Yraif Nor~han is not what I could have pictured, he is ..., it is overwhelming Bryzon," Marcus says instead.

"Jon, and his father Frederick King were men of great vision. We are indeed fortunate that your people chose Kearthat as their home. If not for them we would be facing certain death," Bryzon adds, and pats Marcus on the arm.

"Come, Marcus, we must not linger, my friend. You have much to learn before we depart," Bryzon adds, smiling as they leave for the Command Deck where Dourok and Ameka are waiting to teach the ex-Rednos leader, his son and Rence their new responsibilities.

Bryzon heads straight to his quarters intending to sleep for a few hours. When he rounds the corner he finds Learridy sitting on the floor in front of the door. He is surprised and somewhat concerned when sees her.

"Is something wrong?" he asks.

"Yes" she whispers, "Can I come in?" Bryzon frowns, putting his palm on the identifier pad at the door, and Learridy steps through.

"Sit please, tell me what troubles you, is it to do with moving Sonder?" Bryzon asks his face deeply serious.

"Well, I have great fear in my heart that we may die tomorrow," Learridy tells him.

"Do not speak of such things," he answers almost sternly. "We are going to crush the Eslaf, they will die while we watch," Bryzon declares trying to allay her fears as he reaches for her hand, holding it in his he looks into her eyes, but strangely he sees no fear at all.

"But just in case, I was thinking maybe we should kiss just once more," she tells him. She is putting on a show for him, Bryzon finally realizes and chuckles as he pulls her towards him and kisses her softly on the mouth.

"Like that?" he asks.

Learridy smiles and leans in closer, "Mmmm… perhaps, should we try again to make sure."

When Bryzon awakes from the sound of his door 'bing bonging' four hours later, he looks next to him on the bed, but Learridy is gone.

It is Raine. She has brought him a tray of food.

"Are you going to sleep all day ?" she teases. "It is time to prepare for our victory," she says and plops down on the edge of the bed.

I have called for a meeting of The Liberators to go over the final details, the darkening is imminent, Nor~han reports that the scouts have not seen any movement from the aliens, they remain in the city fearing the darkening," Raine says giggling. "The Eslaf and their foolish beliefs, it will be their ruin."

Raine leaves Bryzon to prepare for the final meeting. His mind mulls over the short time he and Learridy spent together. His pulse races at the thought of her beautiful slender body, her warm embrace and gentle kisses. Then he shakes his head, "You have many important matters to deal with Bryzon, brother of Dayson," he reprimands himself, squeezing Learridy out of his mind for time being.

Heading for the Arc Room Raine decides she needs a quiet place to prepare her mind for what is about to happen. She sits at the big round window staring at the cavern wall through the thick glass, her mind flitting from one thing to the next. Then she notices something she has not seen before. To the left of the window is an engraving. She puts her fingers to the recessed letters and numbers and reads it out aloud "ALUSIL56MM." She wonders what it could have meant to the earthlings who put it there, and why is it etched in this way? 'Another mystery to be solved', she thinks to herself.

As those called to attend the meeting arrive, Raine notices that Nor~han sits with the pilots. She waves for him to take a seat at the top end of the table, he bows his head towards her and moves.

Suddenly the room comes alive as the It-Ha Layrrah and Sayhran waft in, accompanying them is the High Yraif Laathria. The lights seem to dim just slightly when the beautiful Yraif mystic glides through the entrance.

Leyashe cannot help but take a few seconds to scan the room a little more thoroughly. His gaze goes to the additional chairs placed side by side against the walls where the pilots have taken up seats. He quickly counts the number of chairs around the table and gets a total of thirty-six. He is about to continue counting the chairs along the wall when Raine interrupts his thoughts.

"Ash, assemble your mind, brother! We are here on the most important matters." He looks in her direction and nods. He knows she is right to take him away from this silly exercise. He has always, since he can remember, counted and calculated, but now was not the time.

Bryzon takes over from Raine after she has welcomed everyone to the gathering.

"The time is here, my friends," he begins. Then he lays out their plans for the last time. Ohre listens to Bryzon, his old commander is back, Bryzon has thought of everything.

They are ready.

"Thirty-two-fighter craft are eager to go to the city, four will remain with the homeships to protect them and guide them out of the mountain. Marcus, you, Nedai and Rence will track the movements of all the craft for each second of the battle. To succeed we must be as one," Bryzon says, conveying the need to be flawless in their execution of the battle to come.

"The extraction of the Korak at the prison," Bryzon continues. "the time we spend loading the prisoners will be of great importance, the longer the Korak take, the more lives will be lost."

The devices to disable the Eslaf droids and the Idlers are divided among the tunnel team leaders, several go to Evas and his team. Bryzon's list spent, he hands over to Ohre to continue.

"Evas," Ohre says, as he speaks directly to the Korak pilot. "Our fighters will take out the towers overlooking the prison yard. It is up to you and your team to get your people onto your Korak ship as quickly as possible. As Bryzon has already said, extracting three thousand will take time, the Korak prisoners must make haste."

"Evas know fight, know Korak ship, Korak kill Ezlaaf sure," the alien pilot says, his alien emotions hard to read but the belief in his people steadfast.

"After we crush the Eslaf, Evas will be escorted by the fighter craft to rendezvous with Ambition and Sonder," Ohre adds completing his list of instructions.

The two homeships, everyone learns, will be waiting far beyond the Jagged Mountains where the Nerrab begins its endless desert. Here the Korak craft will be stocked with supplies for their journey back to Dirha.

Bryzon turns back to look at It-Ha Layrrah who seems quite relaxed. She smiles at him when he gestures for her to speak. But to everyone's amazement, it is the High Yraif Laathria who rises.

"For those who do not know me, I am Laathria. I am from those who were the first of the Lan~Igiro Yraif, that you know as Kearthat," she says in her silky voice. "I am here to tell you that we, the It-Ha will use The Veil to help you conquer the Eslaf that stand in the way of your safe return to the homeships." The room is silent, everyone mesmerized by this tall, beautiful woman with white hair.

"We will protect the homeships while we await your return from the battle, It-Ha Layrrah, It-Ha Sayhran, and I wish you, The Xennes, Korak and Yraif strength and courage. Slay those who took so much from us and return whole," she tells a wide-eyed audience as wisps of green mist emanate from seemingly nowhere to encircle everyone after her profound statement.

'A show of magic from the High Yraif to encourage strength among those in the room, a wise move by the ancient mystic,' Raine thinks to herself.

Next, Ameka describes how those commanding the homeships plan to manoeuvre the ships from The Below. "The last thing we need is for a ship to hit the cavern walls. A rock fall would be disastrous," Ameka warns as she widens her eyes as if to mimic the unthinkable.

Ohre's adds to the final plans. "On Ambition, Remek and Krom will be directing the fighter craft on take-off, and on their return. On Sonder, Nowber and Auwzen will do the same. They are there to protect, you know their voices, listen to them. Follow their instructions; we do not want any misfortunes," he implores as he looks at the pilots in the Arc Room.

More questions follow and The Liberators are kept busy answering them. When eventually more than an hour later all matters are dealt with Bryzon raises his right arm, his hand in a tight fist, "Until we meet again!" then as if speaking in one voice, the words, "Until we meet again!" reverberate through the room.

Raine notices that the chair where the High Yraif had been sitting is empty. Whispers in the room confirm that no one had noticed her vanish.

Bryzon feels a moment of enormous pride as he looks at the faces of the warriors before him and cannot help but smile broadly.

As the meeting concludes a lot of good wishes are extended, everyone seems to be ready for the battle.

Tears flow freely from Sayhran's eyes as she comes over to embrace Bryzon, Raine and Leyashe.

"If only," she whispers. And Bryzon whispers back, "I know, I know," as he hugs his sister-in-joining who is now confusingly, also his It-Ha. "I will see you soon, sister," he tells her in a whispered voice.

Before It-Ha Layrrah leaves the room she hands Bryzon a letter.

Leyashe in his battle suit is a sight Bryzon wishes Dayson could have seen. The boy looks every bit a grown man, shoulder and chest armour giving him a larger-than-life appearance. The belt around his waist supports a handgun and a pouch that holds the earthling knife given to him by Bryzon, his grandfather Jon's knife. In Leyashe's left hand he carries a long gun that he will take with him on the fighter craft, a precaution in the event that he has to land on the surface.

The time has come. It is T-minus twenty-five minutes before the tunnel teams depart for the exit. As they sit at the ready in the transporter, waiting for the time to pass before taking off, Bryzon hands out the fireballs, each soldier taking several. Raine pictures the very same thing happening in the other transporter.

Bryzon pats his pocket where he has carefully stored the sealed letter that Layrrah had passed to him. On the outside it reads, To my friend Bryzon. He assumes it contains words of encouragement from the It-Ha.

At first, Bryzon cannot believe what he is looking at. He closes his eyes for a few seconds to come to terms with what he is holding before he begins to read.

My dear Bryzon,

If you are reading this then I am long passed, and you have readied to destroy the creatures that shattered our lives. I trust that my words will be the strength you need to defeat the Eslaf.

I will not be long-winded, my dear friend. Know that my heart was with you as I thought of this day. As I write this I will assume that you are all Xennes. I hope in my heart that it came in time for my Nick, Caite, and Sayhran and their families.

It may not be all smooth sailing for you or Dayson, and for those who go on this journey with you, but take heart my friend and you will be victorious.

I do believe, that in time you will find what you are looking for out there in our wonderful universe, or universes as you may have discovered by now. Follow your hearts, and the guidance of The Selected.

I want you to know that for many years I thought of Earth as being no more. My Farron thought otherwise. She believed that when all the humans had perished, Earth would heal. She made me promise I would convey this to you.

Tell my children and my grandchildren, whoever they may be that I love them. Thank you from the depths of my heart for being there for Farron and I when we needed you the most.

Convey to It-Ha Layrrah that my descendants owe her a great debt. She is a good woman. Fight well my friend. Be brave. Your friend, Jon King.

Bryzon folds the page back into its original form carefully storing it in the inside pocket of his heavily armed battle suit. The breast protection covering his heart protecting a letter that he knows he will read many times in the years to come, if he survives today.

Suddenly Bryzon feels Ambition move below them, Ameka calls for the transporters to leave for the tunnels immediately. It has begun.

Chapter 48 - Fire, Rain & Ash

At first, it feels only like a slight movement of the homeship, but It-Ha Layrrah, Sayhran and High Yraif Laathria can sense that it is a Kearthquake.

The High Yraif Seeks Nor~han, Raine and Leyashe, her face no longer serene as she realises the severity of the situation. She warns them that the situation is about to change drastically.

The homeship's communication system clicks on and gives the order to disengage all locks. There is a distinct vibration as all the bays begin to slide open simultaneously, and Ambition rocks from side to side.

The women turn to each other, holding hands as they start chanting, the shaking gets worse, things topple from surfaces in the room as the quake hits again. The rocking stops but the com keeps on giving instructions.

First, the transporter ships are called to prepare for takeoff, then Ameka's voice can be heard telling everyone to stay in their quarters if they are not directly involved in running the spaceship.

"All standby," Ameka's voice announces, "Fighter craft to the waterfall, go, go, go!" A brief silence follows, next the now familiar voice echoes, "Transporters go, go, go!"

A short time after, they hear, "Transporter ships away," followed by a short silence before Ameka confirms, "All fighters away."

Once again there is silence, another shudder under their feet as Ambition moves slightly from side to side, the It-Ha steady themselves, Sayhran goes to a small window and looks out from the ship. "I cannot see a thing," she says, sounding desperate to know what is going on.

"Calm yourself, Tiro," Laathria says in a composed voice. "Come, we must hold hands," she motions to Sayhran. Sayhran settles next to the Yraif on the floor as all movements subside for the moment. "Use your gift, It-Ha Sayhran! Let us join so that The Inmo can prevail."

Between the concentration on her breathing and focusing on The Inmo within her, Sayhran can feel the ship moving gently under her as the minds of her fellow It-Ha Seek to *join her to them*, and she can finally hear Laathria's voice without her speaking.

"Transporters assisting Ambition, stand by!" the voice on the com announces. This time it is the voice of Marcus King and somehow, Sayhran makes space in her thoughts for the pride she feels.

The It-Ha see in their vision the advancing danger within The Below. Sayhran sucks in her breath as her new gift allows her to observe from somewhere above the river. Plumes of steam begin to rise, the water is starting to boil.

The It-Ha scan the tunnels, each letting their minds roam in different directions. When their eyes clear it is Layrrah who expresses her horror without words being spoken, her eyes wide, tears streaming down her cheeks. The lava is fast pushing its way through the bedrock below. It is finding a path up through the river and many other cracks. It is making its way into The Below in enormous bulging bubbles forced to the surface by thousands of years of pent-up pressurised wrath.

They stop the chant and sit quietly, waiting for confirmation that they have exited Ante Mountain. Soon the mystics will gather their collective energy to maintain The Veil that will protect the homeships.

Layrrah talks to Nor~han and instructs him to convey to the Command Deck on Ambition what is taking place under the mountain.

The race is on, will Ante Mountain wait for them to exit safely?

The last thing Sayhran hears before she drifts into a dimension that only the It-Ha know and understand is Marcus's voice saying, "Ambition clear, we are clear!" Faintly in the distance Sayhran hears, "Fighters ready!" then nothing. As she enters a world she has never seen before. She feels herself drawn into a tunnel where swirling light lets her mind float freely. An amazing energy runs through her, every nerve in her body is as if it becomes one with the realms.

The shaking does not return, and everything is quiet until another command fills the air: "Fighter craft prepare to assist Sonder!"

Time seems to stand still before the system clicks, and Ameka's voice is back. The words "Sonder away!" are like birdsong to Sayhran's ears.

On Sonder, Ashok and Learridy guide their homeship to the Barren Landscape of The Nerrab. They keep the ship proceeding at a steady pace flying low and as quickly as possible, the craft transforming from a dark grey metal to a light brown to mimic the desert sand the moment it left Ante Mountain. Soon The Veil will take care of their presence altogether making Ambition and Sonder invisible.

 Leyashe and the other fighter craft wait patiently, they can see the ground shaking beneath them. Hovering at the waterfall exit Leyashe and the fleet mark time, waiting for the signal to battle the Eslaf. Below them, they can see plumes of steam rising from the cavern floor. Lava is starting to flow bright red as it oozes to the surface, visibility is half of what it was when the fighter craft left the homeships.

Bryzon wonders if the Eslaf are noticing that the shakes are behaving differently. He is hoping they will remain complacent. The darkening has begun, The Xennes have that on their side, he can only trust the aliens will assume the shakes will subside as they wait out the eclipse that unnerves them so.

Raine begs Leyashe to leave the caverns, suggesting they wait out the time beyond The High Mountains.

"The moment we are in any danger Rai, Xandr and I will give the signal to leave the tunnels for the city," he promises, "Be safe, sister, I love you."

"Your danger is greater than mine, brother," she manages to say before Leyashe cuts off communication. Raine is left to tell Marcus and the commanders that her stubborn brother will not leave the tunnel exit as yet.

The ascent of the tunnel teams becomes a matter of urgency. The transporters must leave the tunnels soon, it has reached a critical point, the lava is rising fast.

The members of the tunnel team scamper up the side of the transporters on recently modified ladders to the top of the craft, once there, they pull themselves through the hole that Nor~han's crews excavated to The Above. When they reach the open air, the sky is dark, the darkening has come. They in turn must keep their eyes open for Night Creatures.

They run for cover to the forest area near the overgrown, barely recognisable council gardens of old Kearthat. Here they wait for the last person to leave the transporters. They can only hope the pilots have enough time to make their way back down the tunnel and exit Ante Mountain.

Several men linger at the rock where Dayson's body lies, not far into the dark forest, in respect for their friend they bend a knee before moving on. Raine and Bryzon are left to privately mourn the death of her father this one last time. When Raine finally turns to leave her father's burial place she knows her revenge will be sweeter, she can almost taste her hate for the Eslaf.

 "Brother, today I avenge your death," Bryzon whispers as he clears the long grass around the rock marking the spot where Dayson is buried. "I will kill many of the creatures before Kearthat takes its revenge on these beasts," he promises. He wipes his tears and puts his hand on the marker. "Farewell brother, I love you, I will never forget you, Dayson." He does not look back as he moves forward to join the men and women waiting at the edge of the forest in the dark. His heart is heavy after bidding a final goodbye to his brother, his chest feels as if it is about to explode with anger and sorrow.

When Bryzon rejoins Raine she has good news, the transporters have exited Ante Mountain.

Stealthily the teams move towards the clearing where the largest Trigga tree on Kearthat stands majestically. Ohre and the Korak watch the sky, listening for Idlers and Night Creatures as two of Bryzon's team begin clearing the overgrown metal cover that hides the secret stairway. They use metal rods to pry at the cover hiding the underground tunnel. Finally, it relents and snaps open loudly into the night. The noise travels and they all hold their breath, listening for anything that may have been alerted.

Suddenly out of nowhere two Idlers can be heard heading their way, everyone halts. They wait for the droids for a few seconds then Bryzon presses the button on the device tied to his belt and the droids crash into the ground not far from them. They can only hope there was no time for communication between the Idlers and the Eslaf base. If so, they will soon meet their deaths.

By the time the large contingent of men and women have made their way down to the passageway Bryzon can feel the tension in his chest. The metal cover is placed in position and fastened. They are locked inside.

If the Eslaf know they are coming there is nothing they can do about it now, they must move forward, and hope they have remained undetected.

The hollow pathway echoes. The men and women in the tunnel reach a certain pace and after a while the rattling of weapons joins the rhythm of their boots.

Bryzon puts up his arm and makes a fist. Everyone stops and total silence ensues as he turns to Raine who is a few paces behind him. Still under communications silence with the homeships he asks Raine to contact Leyashe and give him the signal for the fighter craft to move towards the city.

She closes her eyes and mind speaks to her brother, his voice enters her head immediately. "Now Ash, now!" she says, adding "I love you."

"On our way Rai. Be careful!" is all he says, then she no longer feels him in her mind.

Ohre comes over to Raine with an enquiring look, "What are we waiting for?"

"I just sent a message to the fighter craft. We have seven minutes," Raine tells him in a whisper.

To Raine's amazement Bryzon reaches up above him. She watches as he fiddles with something behind a pipe running along the walkway where they are standing. The wall adjacent to them slides open revealing a short stairway to another door.

"Secrets of old Kearthat," he says smiling.

They follow the surprise entrance as it leads them up to a wide set of stairs, then into a large room. In the wall ahead of them Raine can see where a doorway once was. The outline of the sealant is visible. It is wide, and she knows that once it is open they will be able to pass through it quickly.

"What is behind this?" she asks Bryzon.

"It leads into the men's showers, we placed shelves to hide the marks where we sealed it from the other side, it was our secret exit, a shortcut to the gardens for the fleet.

"And what of the female fighters?" Raine asks without thinking.

"They had their own exit to the tunnels, in their shower room," he tells her. "This one is closer to where we want to be," Bryzon tells his niece, and Raine nods her approval with a tiny smile of silent thanks that old Kearthat recognized the value of women as equals.

"Time," Ohre asks looking back at Raine from where two men are frantically working at unsealing the entrance.

"Four minutes," she answers, as she feels her heart flutter at the prospect of being in a gun battle. She is not sure if it is excitement or fear.

"Ohre, we are running out of time," Bryzon says. Then adds, "We can only hope that the Eslaf have not suddenly become devoted to cleanliness," his voice now sounding breathless with anticipation of what will be facing them when the opening is clear.

"Ready the devices!" Bryzon commands as the men with the metal prying tools seem to have conquered the opening. The message is sent down the line and the fighters behind Raine and Bryzon begin to ready their weapons.

It all happens at once, the sealed entrance falls away and Bryzon gives the command.

"Coms on!" he shouts. "Devices armed."

They file eight and nine abreast into the next room.

There are no Eslaf in sight. When they exit the large area filled with rows and rows of showers Bryzon and Ohre move into position ahead of Raine. They act as a shield hiding her small frame. The shelves that hid the opening to the secret passage from inside the shower now lay broken to one side, the items it once held scattered everywhere.

Then they see the first Eslaf soldiers. The aliens look confused, the devices have executed their job as hoped, there are many Eslaf down on the ground. The live Eslaf struggling to get past the downed Androids causing mayhem for the alien soldiers in their bulky armour. The Xennes fire and several Eslaf soldiers go down before they get a chance to figure out who is attacking them. Frederick King's weapons are quiet and they do not alert the Eslaf who are out of earshot.

It does not take long for Bryzon's ground force to spread out as they begin to make their way to the open area of the base. Androids lay strewn everywhere, the base is in a state of confusion as the Eslaf are unable to grasp they are under attack. They seem to be having difficulty identifying their attackers.

A group of Eslaf are spotted trying to figure out why their droids have simply fallen over. When they spot The Xennes force coming their way the real Eslaf dive for weapons and some manage to open fire. Men and aliens alike scatter, hiding behind whatever they can find closest to them.

"Grenades, grenades!" Bryzon reminds those who can hear him.

Mehtevas stays glued to his new Xennes friend's side as he and Ohre try to get further into the base to find the Korak homeship, with the group of unarmed young Korak from Noitibma not far behind.

Silence ensues as the Eslaf try to make sense of what is happening, but the hush is short-lived. Deep alien voices give instructions over the loudspeaker that serves the base and Bryzon knows that it means there will be more forces coming from the city. The aliens have realised what is taking place, they know that their enemy is blocking them from getting to their craft.

Leyashe and his fighters appear overhead. They fire at the Eslaf ships where they are neatly positioned on the West side of the base. The aliens are now left to clear the wide-open space between the explosions to try and reach their ships before they are destroyed. The Xennes are relentless as they fire on any aliens who dare make a run to an alien craft but some Eslaf make it through to the tens of ships that are lined up as far as the eye can see.

Many Eslaf, caught off guard, start firing up into the sky when they realize that the craft above them are not their own and that their spaceships are being attacked.

Evas indicates to Ohre that he has spotted the large Korak homeship, and no one even notices that the Korak's English is just as good as theirs. It-Ha Layrrah has again shown the power of her magic. Ohre hurriedly relays the description and position of the Korak spaceship to protect it from their own onslaught on the many craft surrounding it on the base.

Bryzon is stunned when he glimpses the Kearthat Starfleet fighter ships lined up to their left. His brain finds it hard to fathom why there would be craft from old Kearthat seemingly unharmed, just sitting there. It hits him that time would not have affected their fighter craft, Zraphite did not deteriorate for hundreds of years. As long as the Zraphite blocks were still in the ships they would fly. He points to the craft and Ohre waves back, he had also spotted them. Several other men comment over the coms, wondering if they will be of any use?

Bryzon turns to Raine and explains what he has just seen and directs her to tell Leyashe they must not fire on the old Kearthat fighter craft on the East end of the base.

"Do you think they will fly Bryzon?" Ohre asks Bryzon.

"This I do not know," Bryzon answers honestly, "I would say perhaps we have a good chance but who knows what the aliens may have done to them."

The Eslaf go down one after the other as they stupidly try to reach the far side of the base. They seem to have the same mentality as bugs when they are without direction from a red-suit. Hundreds seem to be pouring in from the city, but only some stay upright. Raine finds it mesmerizing to watch as the Androids fall to the ground, causing a barrier for the real Eslaf to navigate before they are able to retaliate. This alone gives The Xennes fighters a huge advantage to take them down as the barrier of downed droids begins to grow higher and higher.

The fighters above their heads battle the few Eslaf that have managed to get into the air. But then the Eslaf realize while they are so busy firing on the fighter craft they are ignoring the ground force killing those coming into the base in droves. The Xennes are well organized and already the Eslaf have suffered large losses.

Bryzon and Ohre shout to Raine to follow as they sprint towards where two Eslaf are trying to make it onto a transporter, while more aliens are heading for the unarmed shuttles. Ohre stops and pulls the pin on a grenade and flings it in the direction of the shuttles. At the same time Bryzon and Raine open fire as the aliens jump on the walkway that is almost fully extended.

Raine watches as the grenade that Ohre throws easily makes its way towards the target. Just as the Eslaf are close to closing the hatch of the craft the fireball explodes. The ship lifts several feet into the air before it comes crashing down, then bursts into flames. When the debris cloud settles a little there are no Eslaf to be seen, she knows they are now just part of the rubble.

Raine can see The Xennes firing continuously from above, and there are hundreds of Eslaf dying in their bid to get to a spaceship by any means possible. On the ground the earthling weapons deliver nonstop, deadly-accurate firepower, but the aliens just keep coming and Raine wonders how long they will have to battle the creatures. How many are there? She sighs as she opens fire on two Eslaf that suddenly appear from behind a drum of some kind right in front of her. They go down, their eyes wide as they recognise their killer as the Overseer of Noitibma Colony.

Evas runs next to Ohre, the troupe of young Korak hot on their heels as they head to the Korak craft now only a short distance from them. The Korak ship is slightly smaller, compared to the earthling homeships but still towers over everything else surrounding it.

Bryzon can be heard talking to Ambition as he updates the situation, then he speaks to the transporters and instructs them to be ready to evacuate the men at the base when he gives the word. He is thankful when he hears both transporters respond, they are still safe.

Raine talks to Leyashe and explains what is about to take place. "The transporters will need cover," she tells him, "and Evas will need protection," she conveys.

"Yes Rai, we are doing our best," she gets from an overwhelmed-sounding Leyashe. Raine remains in her brother's mind and he does not notice, his voice is clear as he communicates back and forth with the men and women in his squadron as he takes guidance from Sahdmar and Xandr.

"More strikes towards the city. We must stop them from coming into the area," she hears Leyashe thinking before she feels him cut her off.

The Korak Dessas appears from behind Raine. He kneels next to her.

"Until we meet again, Raine," he tells her hurriedly. Before Raine has time to answer Dessas, he and his troupe have moved towards Ohre and Evas, getting ready to make a final short run for the Korak ship.

They reach the Korak ship, and Raine can see Evas frantically pushing buttons on a panel outside one of the ship's huge stanchions. A walkway starts to emerge, making its way down to the ground. He runs up, and the Korak team follows. Ohre stops and crouches, firing at several Eslaf who are trying to stop the Korak from boarding their spaceship. When they are all inside, Raine watches Ohre run back down the walkway before it begins to retract. Hundreds of lights appear on the Korak ship. It is good to see it operational.

"Tell Leyashe to release the craft that will protect the Korak ship," Bryzon tells Raine.

Raine and Bryzon tuck themselves in behind a wall of metal containers as they hide from the dangers of the Korak ship taking off. Raine shuts her eyes and cuts out the noise around her as she contacts Leyashe.

"Sneaky, sister, what now?" he says to her.

"Sorry, brother, but I had to know that you were safe," she tells him, then quickly follows with the message from Bryzon. "Please stay safe, brother," is all she manages and Leyashe is gone from her mind.

The Korak ship begins its ascent as Raine and Bryzon cover their heads. The force of the ship rising above them causes everything without much weight to fly into the air. The giant craft weaves from side to side for a bit then shoots straight up. In only a few seconds it is hardly visible, several fighter craft leave the battle and join the Korak ship.

Bryzon can't believe his eyes when the departing Korak spaceship is joined by four more craft.

"Raine, tell Leyashe what is happening, and fast!" Bryzon shouts as he watches as more men in the tunnel team run the gauntlet of fire towards the waiting old Starfleet craft. The bravery of these men has not diminished during their years of toiling in the soil of Kearthat. It has become a one-sided war. The Kearthat Starfleet has been revived today, the Eslaf had made yet another mistake by keeping the Drennan fighter craft that were not destroyed in the invasion on the base.

Leyashe enters Raine's mind before she can relay Bryzon's instructions.

"Sister, the old Kearthat Starfleet spacecraft, do they still fly?" he asks jubilantly as he watches the sleek craft around him.

"Yes, Ash. Our grandfather's saying is coming true. 'The stars have truly aligned in our favour," Raine shares with Leyashe as she laughs aloud.

Now and again the sound of an alien Nobrac can be heard, the firing is sporadic and Bryzon knows the fight has turned the corner. Raine is sure there must be losses on their side but she wonders if they could have been so lucky and no one has lost their lives. She follows Bryzon weaving in and out of hiding spots to reach the only large open space available for their transporters to land. Bryzon scans the area for debris before he decides it is a good spot, then he nods at Raine.

"This will be where our transporters will have to set down!" Bryzon shouts over rapid fire coming from behind them. "We must keep up the charge to stop Eslaf soldiers from picking off our men when they board the transporter," Bryzon tells her. Raine knows it is her task to contact Leyashe. Bryzon calls for the transporter craft to head to the base, and orders the troops to be ready for evacuation.

A group of men appear in the open as they make a run for the clearing towards Bryzon and Raine are huddled. They are carrying fighters over their shoulders, and others are being assisted to walk. Suddenly a handful of aliens appear in the opening and start firing on the men. Two men go down, one dropping the person he is carrying over his shoulders.

Raine screams at the aliens. Breaking clear, she fires. She is exposed but does not stop firing until the last alien hits the ground.

"Raine, you are going to get yourself killed," Bryzon shouts at her breathlessly.

"Bryzon, they shot men who were carrying the wounded. I hate them," she screams. "I hate them," tears streaming down her face. Raine had reached her breaking point with the Eslaf.

The fight above their heads seems to have moved as Bryzon and Raine can hear the noises of the battle in the distance now. Several old Kearthat fighter craft hover above them, they stand guard awaiting the arrival of the transporters. Raine and Bryzon wait behind a small metal structure while many hide behind what they can find in the near vicinity.

Raine has not said much to Bryzon. She feels bad that she again let her emotions rule the moment. It had happened before she could think, it was going to disappoint Laathria when she heard of her actions.

"I think all the Eslaf that managed to take off in spotters and fighter craft were being instructed to head for the prison. They finally realised that the Korak ship would be heading there" Raine says after a brief time.

"That is so, stay close Raine, we must be ready to leave," Bryzon tells her, his manner much calmer.

There are at least twenty old KSF fighter craft lingering. Occasionally they open fire in one or the other direction as they protect those boarding the craft that will take them back to the homeships.

One of the old Starfleet craft breaks away from the formation and lands a few hundred feet from where Bryzon and Raine are. It is Ohre running towards them. He has a brief conversation with Bryson but Raine cannot hear what is being said. Then Ohre runs back to the craft and soon he is back hovering above them.

Bryzon signals two men to cover Raine as they run to the waiting ship. They weave their way there, Raine can see the old Starfleet craft open fire on Eslaf in the distance that are aiming their weapons towards them. Ohre has taken on one singular task. It is to protect Raine, no matter what.

The noise is confusing and relentless. Once she is inside there is silence and her ears begin to ring. She looks through the small window towards where she last saw Bryzon. To her horror Raine can see Bryzon running the gauntlet towards the ship, behind him Eslaf prepare to fire on him. She runs to the hatch and opens fire. The Eslaf go down and firing from above ensures they do not get back up.

Bryzon looks back to where the Eslaf lie in tatters. He focuses on the open hatch, he knows Raine just saved his life and that Ohre had made sure it stayed that way.

Once everyone is on the transporter craft, they take off.

"Transporter Two?" Bryzon calls over the com, "Report" he commands.

"We are whole," Dehrazz answers.

"What is the count, Transporter One?" Bryzon requests.

"We are whole, but for nine and six wounded." There is silence on both ships as the reality sinks in that there are nine *gifted* that are dead. Eight brave men and one brave woman. Bryzon is saddened to find that Idah is the one woman who has given her life, the men still unidentified.

"Head for the homeships," Bryzon shouts over the craft's shuddering as they lift off. It is not long before the base and city look small as they climb higher, further from the scene of the battle.

The men and women on board are silent as the reality of what just took place sinks in. The loss of life has them thanking the galaxies that the old Starfleet craft were available and still in good condition. They know the losses could have been far greater without the assistance of Ohre and the brave men who followed him onto the fighter craft of old Kearthat.

Bryzon informs Krom and Remek they may have up to twenty additional craft to accommodate between Ambition and Sonder, and quickly explains why. Bryzon smiles inwardly as he can hear laughter coming from both young men, as they enjoy the irony of the situation.

The silence on the ship is broken when suddenly Ante Mountain can be seen bubbling over in the distance. Red rivers of lava flow down its sides. The giant mountain releasing plumes of smoke and steam. There are bright red and orange explosions groping into the night sky as the mountain seems responsible for spitting out streaks of lightning that reach out for miles. Clouds of ash grow bigger and bigger, the scene is surreal.

Raine looks in the direction of the city. Fires are raging everywhere, the enormous city is a scene of chaos. When they had taken off from the base she could see the destruction in the light cast from the towering flames coming from the alien ships that now lay crippled. Some Eslaf craft, she knows had found a way to take off, she assumes they have all taken their fight to the prison. From a distance she can see the damage their air strikes metered out, the city was fast becoming a giant orange glow in the dark as they get further and further away. Raine feels sad for those Korak who were slaves in the city but she knows they did what they could to try and save the Korak.

"I want to talk to the fighter craft," Bryzon tells the pilot who hands him a hand-held com. "Ash, update me?" he shouts above the noise.

"Bryzon, good to hear your voice, where is Raine?" Raine hears her brother's concern and Bryzon quickly responds.

"She is whole, sitting right next to me," he assures his nephew.

"Bryzon, Ohre and his men were of great assistance but I am sad to report that I did see two old Starfleet craft get hit," Leyashe reports. The aliens are fast, they came up behind us in a manoeuvre that we must study. In the background, Bryzon can hear the sounds of the battle still raging on. "We are in the area of the refinery. They had craft stationed there. I cannot  say how many. We have managed to bring some down and there are Eslaf craft burning everywhere, the Dexim Refinery is burning."

Bryzon's heart aches as he realizes that no matter who the men are who have gone down in the old Starfleet fighter craft, he has known them all his life.

Just then, things change a little as the darkening starts going the other way. It is going to be light soon.

"It is a miracle, I cannot believe that the Eslaf left Kearthat's old ships unharmed. Now that we have more fighters in the air, we can assist those fighting at the prison. Send those that you can spare, Ash, the light is upon us" Raine tells her brother.

"When you feel it is under control, break away and head for the homeships, it is Kearthat's war now," Raine adds, and Bryzon nods approving of her strategy and orders.

"I have sent two fighter craft to search if anyone survived on our craft that went down, then we will head back," and with that Leyashe's voice goes silent.

There is a blinding flash of light and rain comes pouring down. The eruption has caused a huge storm over the mountains. By the time the blinking lights of the homeships bays opening come into view they have managed to outrun the rainstorm, now the sky is raining ash.

Raine pats her pockets, pulls out the picture of her parents and studies their faces. She puts the portrait to her chest. Bryzon can see tears run down her cheeks but she quickly wipes them away.

Chapter 49 - Victory

When Rence sees Raine he runs over. He holds her tight before he gently puts a single quick kiss on her forehead.

"Thank you for coming back safely," he whispers.

"I promised, remember, and I always keep my promises," she says, smiling, but the greeting is brief as she turns to Marcus.

"What news from the prison?" she asks.

Raine and Bryzon listen intently as Marcus, Nedai and Rence explain that the resistance at the prison had been more difficult than Pateeo and his fighters had anticipated.

"He reports that the Eslaf Androids and the Idlers went down the moment they were in range of the devices," Marcus conveys. "But they have been taking continuous fire from the soldiers on the ground as the Korak are making their way onto the homeship. The additional firepower from Ohre and his fighter craft has helped but it has been tough."

"There are many Korak down, Raine. The task we accomplished in small groups is now being attempted for thousands," Nedai tries to explain, shaking his head. "It has been difficult; there will be many dead, of that I am sure."

"I am expecting an update soon from the team leaders who are still out there. We heard from Leyashe that the Eslaf managed to get some transport shuttles off the ground, and the men that went down are safe. The demented Eslaf have tried to crash into our fighters in the air. They are crazy, they have no regard for their own lives," Marcus reiterates, making a face as he translates the madness of the Eslaf's intellect.

"The Eslaf used some colony shuttles to drop off many soldiers near the prison but more than half were droids," Marcus continues with a slight smile.

"Those of flesh could not fathom why the droids dropped like bugs as they left the shuttles, it has been reported that there are Eslaf scattered beside the prison that keep striking back. They seem to be attacking, then withdrawing, hitting the Korak and our forces again and again from the treed area outside the prison."

When Raine hears that, she asks Bryzon if there is a way to set the treed area alight or if it would affect the prisoner extraction. They discuss it quickly and decide it is too unpredictable and abandon the idea.

Rence confirms that Pateeo fears there will be large losses of life among the Korak. "But he did not say anything about any fighters that may have been ..." he begins to say, then stops as Pateeo's voice cuts in.

"We are leaving the prison now," is all he says and firing can be heard in the background, then some screaming, then silence as the com goes quiet.

They wait for what seems to be an eternity before they hear from anyone again.

"We are five minutes away," Pateeo informs the Command Deck, and Marcus instructs Krom and Remek on Ambition and Sonder to open the bay doors to take on the fighters accompanying the Korak ship.

Marcus speaks to Learridy and can hear her say, "Bay doors opening," before the com shuts off.

The Korak ship approaches, landing not far from the two Xennes homeships. A short while later the fighters return to their homeships. By this time Raine has rushed down to watch the ships return.

Raine recognizes Leyashe's ship by its number. Fighter #7 is coming in fast, then suddenly slows before it settles into a spot just a short distance from where she is waiting impatiently. It is the first time Raine notices the name painted on the front of the craft, it reads Firemoth.

It is a tight fit as the additional craft coming in have to cram up against each other in the two bays, which now seem to have shrunk considerably.

Bryzon joins Raine and watches the jubilant faces of the men leave the old Starfleet fighter craft. His heart beats faster as he blinks to make sure he is not dreaming.

Leyashe smiles broadly the moment he sees Raine. A huge embrace and words of pride are exchanged.

"We did it, Rai, we obliged, they never saw us coming" Leyashe shares enthusiastically. Then his demeanour changes and he is serious again.

"I must go, we are waiting to see if they dare follow," he turns and waves, the smile still there, he shouts "We will celebrate soon, sister!" Raine knows that Leyashe wants to share their success with his new brothers, men who have accepted him into a small, exceptional group of warriors.

When the smaller recon craft from the Korak ship enters the bay on Ambition Bryzon feels his heart skip a beat. Has Namow survived the battle at the prison? The hatch of the strange dull-coloured transporter slides open. Namow steps out and takes a look around before she slowly walks down the short walkway. She is followed by Dessas and the small group of young Noitibma Korak.

Bryzon takes in a deep breath of unconcealed relief, he is elated to see Namow has managed to escape the horror of not only Pishdrah, but also the fierce battle that was fought to save her kind. She turns her head from side to side, he knows she is seeking out only his face among the many. Those nearby are fascinated by the Korak woman and the strange transporter that brought her to Ambition.

When she spots Bryzon her thin lips curl into a smile, she makes her way towards him as quickly as her legs allow her. The scene playing out in front of him once again confirms that he did the right thing by insisting on saving these passive beings. He feels whole for the first time since the Eslaf invasion so many years ago.

Tears fall freely from Namow's large eyes as she hugs Bryzon, wrapping her arms around him, and holding him tight for a long time before she releases him.

"Tank you Brizo, you good fren, you brave and honor man," she praises, bowing her large oval head in respect. She reaches for Raine's hands folding her large calloused alien hand over them before bowing to her.

"Namow know you mans die to save Korak, Namow sad, Namow cry faw you," the alien tells her. Woman to woman Raine can feel the alien's apology is without any doubt sincere.

They find a place to sit in a room just off the main flight deck. Namow tells Bryzon that they wish to depart as soon as Sonder's crews have transported the goods needed by the Korak. She seems anxious to leave Kearthat, and Bryzon understands her urgency.

When Bryzon asks after the Korak fatalities, she lowers her eyes and tells him there were many.

"You try Brizo, we win becuz no maw die now," she tells him and Bryzon knows that only leaders think that way.

They are interrupted by a knock at the door, it is Remek.

"It is the Korak who grew up in Noi, as requested, Bryzon," he says.

"Oh, my apologies, greetings Namow, it is good to see you," Remek expresses, smiling.

"Remy, you good boy," she tells him and smiles. She demonstrates her gratitude with an enormous hug. Remek is quite startled at her reaction, pleased when she releases him, he smiles and slips out of the room.

Only thirteen of the fourteen Korak who grew up in Noitibma Colony enter the room. One look at Dessas tells the story of the missing Korak male, Hadvah.

The Korak, despite their losses are wide-eyed with anticipation after being called back so soon after returning from battle to attend a gathering with a Korak woman they had never met until this day.

Raine goes over to Dessas, "I am so sorry," she says. "We all loved Hadvah with all of our hearts," she tells him. Tears sting her eyes, she knows that Dessas and the male Korak Hadvah were great friends. Dessas finds it hard to control his emotions, he cries softly and openly in front of everyone.

Namow comes forward and with one of her long fingers she touches his face and the tears before she bows her head to Dessas. "My haat feel yaw haat," she tells him, then steps away, tilting her head as she looks at the broken-hearted olive being who is so much like her, yet so different.

She walks down the line stopping to look at each one of them for a few seconds, taking their hands in hers, greeting each one in a language they had never been given the opportunity to learn.

When she gets to the last male in the line she stops and asks, "What yaw name?"

"My name is Orsoh," he tells her, bowing his head in respect.

"Ohso," she repeats and the young Korak male smiles briefly at her pronunciation of his name.

Namow lingers for a moment, tilting her head from side to side, looking intently into the eyes of the Korak male.

When Namow turns away, she walks to where Bryzon is sitting but still does not sit down. Instead she says, "We go now Brizo, my house long time far, Korak say tank you for free fuud, and for free my Korak. Namow say tank you Brizo for look good my brudda Mehtevas son of my fadda," bowing her head she smiles, she knows that Bryzon knows she had lied about who she was. But, he knows they are one for one now that Namow knows that he had been Xennes for the seventeen years they slaved side by side.

The last thing Namow says to Bryzon before she leaves to board her ship comes as a huge surprise to him.

"You look good Namow son Ohso, he need strong mans, Brizo teach him good," before she strides away towards her transporter. The walkway retracts and the

Korak leaders, Namow and Mehtevas leave for their home on Dirha, leaving Bryzon stunned by Namow's decision to not try and convince her son to leave with her. As the hatch closes, familiar faces wave at Bryzon, it is Nam and Dulf. Bryzon waves back at the Korak men who had likewise been a good friend.

The enormous bay doors on Ambition begin to close and Bryzon's thoughts about his alien friends are interrupted by the com.

"Bay doors open, bay doors open," Ameka's usual calm voice is raised and hurried as she speaks into the device in front of her. "Fighter craft prepare, Eslaf incoming, incoming!" she announces frantically.

The doors that were halfway closed now reverse. The squeal of sirens going off, red warning lights on the homeship add to the chaotic urgency as fighters run for their craft. The sound of the ships as they ignite into action fills the air. At the same time, Ambition rocks violently from side to side. Kearthat is dying and fast.

Then the desperate command follows, "Fighters go, go, go!" and the fighters file out into the ominous orange sky. It is time to leave Kearthat.

"Bay doors close, close!" Ameka repeats. Raine is sure the same frenzied orders are being issued on Sonder as she and Bryzon take the elevator to the Command Deck. Ambition moves ever so slightly under their feet as the big ship begins to ascend, slowly at first then speeding up. Bryzon and Raine rush to join Marcus as they leave the elevator. What greets them takes Raine's breath away for a second as she looks on the screen in front of her. There are Eslaf craft heading straight for them, at least thirty, perhaps more, and Kearthat is on fire.

Raine holds her head, and Rence screams at her.

"What is it Raine, what is wrong?" as he shakes her by the shoulders. She does not answer straight away but when she does look up she has a curious look on her face.

In the silence her voice is calm as she tells them, "The It-Ha have assured me that the aliens cannot see our fighter craft. It is The Veil, they are hiding the fighters but we are exposed. Faster, Ameka, we must retreat," Raine says. "We must keep moving, we are in much danger from the Eslaf, and Kearthat."

The alien fighter craft gain, and soon they are closer and closer but it is not long before they are attacked from behind as the Xennes craft fire mercilessly on them. The Eslaf are shocked, they turn around in wide arcs but they cannot see their enemy. They are at a loss.

On the Command Deck they watch as the Eslaf are shot down one by one, but the aliens are single-minded. The last two Eslaf fighters try to make a run for the homeship to the detriment of their lives, they are hoping to slam into Ambition. Relentless, Leyashe and Xandr pursue the aliens as they get closer and closer to

Ambition and Sonder. Before long, two explosions fill the sky and it is over, they have been eliminated, the alien craft have been stopped.

"Talk to me, brother," Raine shouts in her mind, and Leyashe's voice comes to her immediately. "They are no more, sister. Open the bays, Raine," adding, "We are coming home."

Chapter 50 - The Message

As if in a dream everyone near a window is looking out into the distance where the power of Ante Mountain is destroying everything on Kearthat. Feeling relieved and heartbroken, a strange mix of sadness and elation at the same time makes it final. They beat the Eslaf but their planet is destroying itself.

Explosions, plumes of lava, and fiery ash spew high into the dark purple sky. From their vantage it is a spectacular and frightening sight as they race to put some distance between Kearthat and the two homeships.

Suddenly the brilliance of one mighty explosion blinds them, and they know it is the end of all life on the sphere. Seconds later the homeships rock from side to side as the waves caused by the giant explosion reach them, but they are too far away for it to cause damage. Transfixed by what has happened, there is silence on the Command Deck for a few moments.

Raine Seeks It-Ha Layrrah's mind as she wipes the tears from her cheeks. "Stop The Veil, we are safe," she tells her.

A moment later Raine hears the High Yraif Laathria in her head.

"Do not cry for Lan~Igiro child, you were destined to journey since the day of your first breath," Laathria tells her.

Raine makes her way to her quarters. She sits on the bed and looks at the drawing of her parents, reaches for the Trungo fur and pulls it closer to feel its familiar softness. It smells like her little bedroom in the cabin in Noitibma Colony. The odour calms her and she lays back on her pillow.

"If only you were here," she says, talking to the picture of her parents. She cries silently for a short while before drying her tears and placing the drawing next to her on the bedside table. A feeling of exhaustion envelopes her, and she closes her eyes. 'Ten minutes,' she tells herself, "Then I will go to see what I can contribute."

When the knock and the 'bing bong bong' of the door sounds, Raine finds she is disoriented for a few seconds. She presses the button that opens the entrance to her quarters and struggles to focus on her brother's face.

"Rai, how are you feeling? Everyone wondered where you disappeared to, but when Rence found you sleeping we decided to let you rest," he tells her.

"Where are we?" she asks.

"On Ambition," he answers and flops down onto her bed.

"No silliness, please, Ash," she says, sounding slightly irritated while yawing several times.

"Sorry, but you have been asleep for six hours, and we have not moved an inch. We are waiting for Number One to tell us which direction she would like to take," he chuckles.

"The Eslaf?" she says, looking at him.

"Nothing, we have not seen a thing," he tells his sister.

"And the Korak ship?" she asks.

"No one can be sure, but Bryzon spoke to High Yraif Laathria, and she assured him she could feel they had escaped to safety."

Raine walks over to the window and looks to find Kearthat. She sees a reddish-brown planet in the distance. All life on their world destroyed in a matter of hours.

"Brother, our home is gone," she says, turning to face Leyashe. "All the animals, the birds and our Trigga tree, all gone," suddenly profoundly sad. Leyashe walks over to his sister and puts his arms around her, she rests her head on his chest. Although he is younger than her he has been towering over her since his fourteenth year.

"Sssh sister, we are safe, there is sadness in my heart too for everything that we have lost, but we must be brave. We have our people to lead, they look to us to for strength."

Then she hears something familiar, and at first, she can't believe her ears.

"What is it Rai, what are you looking for?" Leyashe asks as he watches his sister searching her room, a big smile on his face that she does not seem to notice. Finally she peeks into the washroom.

She cannot imagine how it is possible. Sitting in the middle of the small room, Regor stares up at her.

"Leyashe!" Raine shouts, come and look who I found, but as she turns around she knows it is his doing.

"How?" she asks with a smile.

"A gift from Remek and myself to you, Rai. We know how you love the silly Eninac."

"The Veil," she says, "Who?" she questions and is shocked when her brother answers.

"High Yraif Laathria."

Raine rubs Regor under the chin. Without invitation, the Eninac finds a comfortable spot on her bed and curls up.

Raine and Leyashe call for a meeting in the Arc Room.

An hour later they arrive to find, Bryzon, her cousins Krom, Remek and Nedai waiting. After a short while It-Ha Sayhran and It-Ha Layrrah join them but the High Yraif does not accompany them. They are soon followed by Marcus, Ohre, Dourok, Kadez and Rence, then Nor~han comes through the door.

"Where is everyone? I sent word for many more to attend, this gathering is very important" Raine says sounding confused, but before anyone can answer Leyashe cuts in.

"Be calm, sister; they will be here soon. It takes time, this is a big ship and those from Sonder must be brought to Ambition by transporter."

Nor~han raises his hand to speak.

"If I may," he asks.

"Of course, Nor~han, go ahead," Raine tells him, stifling a yawn.

"The Xennes and Yraif of Sonder have spoken and I bring you their message," he begins. "They asked that I express their wish that The Liberators who are all present at this table, represent the people. This opinion includes those of the Korak, who have chosen to take quarters on Sonder" he adds.

"But that…" Raine begins to say but is interrupted again, this time by Marcus.

"I bring a message from The Xennes and Yraif of Ambition," he says, "They too, chose The Liberators to be the members of their new council."

"It is the decision of all that you and Leyashe lead us, Raine. We all support you; we will be at your side."

Leyashe and Raine look at each other, they are stunned at the decision of the people, this was not the way she had planned it.

"You two should be proud," Bryzon tells his niece and nephew.

"But why would they do that? Ash and I want the people to be free, we want to give them the right to choose ...," Raine begins to say and then stops, clearly confused at what has happened as she shakes her head.

"Raine, the people have chosen; they choose you and Leyashe, and us to stand with you," Nor~han repeats to the shocked siblings.

Remek breaks the awkward silence that seems to have taken hold of the room.

"Well then Ash, I suggest you willingly give the number one spot to Raine," Remek chuckles, looking at his cousin. "That way, when things go wrong, number two can blame number one for all the mistakes."

Laughter erupts, and Raine notices that even the normally subdued Nor~han joins in with a dignified smile as he sits down between Dourok and Kadez, completing the members of The Liberators.

After they settle down, the group discusses immediate actions that need to be taken. A noise causes some of them to look under the table.

"Regor!" Sayhran shouts out with a confused look on her face and smiles.

"A gift from Remek and Ash, the High Yraif Laathria helped them," Raine admits openly, smiling.

"You have the deference of the High Yraif, Raine. You are the first to receive that tribute," Nor~han announces and It-Ha Layrrah can feel that Nor~han finds it difficult to believe the High Yraif would agree to participate in such a mortal act as gifting an Eninac, things had indeed changed.

Bryzon addresses the ceremonies for the fallen after he shares the names of those lost.

The decision to go about burial the way the earthlings did on their long journey to Kearthat is immediately adopted. It seems to be the most practical and deserving of the warriors. They move on to the next matter after a period of silence is observed to honour those who gave their lives in the battle.

Raine and Leyashe soon encounter the reality of delegating the responsibilities of running two homeships. Refreshments are brought to them while they work. Plans are set in motion, and the siblings try to remain impartial in each decision. Some decisions take longer than they should because Raine is adamant that ruling by fair choice is the only way. It is a busy day.

Marcus remains in the position of overall Commander of Ambition, and Ohre is appointed Commander of Sonder.

Raine and Leyashe suggest that the homeships keep putting distance between them and Kearthat to avoid any Eslaf that may have made it off Kearthat. There is no particular direction at this point, and when asked, Raine simply says, "Just keep going forward." This remark earns her some laughter and teasing from Remek.

Things move along smoothly considering Raine and Leyashe's inexperience. After many hours Raine calls the gathering to an end, but not before it is decided that the words, elder and council are never to be used again, declaring the new council will be known as the Om~ada. The word's meaning; 'Leading Together' is in the Yraif language. The suggestion by Nor~han is eagerly adopted, to his surprise and noticeable delight at his contribution.

Raine and Leyashe insist that Dessas join the Om~ada to represent the Korak presence, they vote, and Dessas is included in the newly formed leadership.

Then Raine speaks from her heart.

"Bryzon, you are very important to us, to me and Leyashe, to everyone. I have pondered many hours to know what most suits your many talents, and where your heart rests. Ash and I would be very honoured if you would be the advisor to The Selected and remain as Commander of The Xennes Starfleet."

Bryzon, not expecting any particular designation, is overjoyed by Raine and Leyashe's decision. "If that is what you want, I would be happy to accept," he says, bowing his head first to Raine, then Leyashe. Ohre starts a round of knuckle rapping to show their support for a deserving man.

There is a knock at the door and Keeland peeks in. "I wish to speak to the It-Ha Layrrah. I will be brief," he requests. Layrrah looks surprised but follows Keeland out of the door. When she returns, she puts her hands on the back of the chair. Bryzon looks at Raine. Something has happened.

"Keeland has just informed me that Moss has passed to the next world. He was found in his bed. His old age claimed his life. He knew he was going to die. He left a short note," she says as she unfolds the piece of paper brought to her by Keeland.

"To all of the people of Kearthat. I wish you well on your quest for a new sphere. Know that I am truly regretful of my deceit. Forgive me.

"The note is signed," Layrrah tells them. "It reads, 'Farewell, Moss, son of Dreyba.'

The news is neither sad nor otherwise. Raine decides Moss will have a respectful committal, but it will be quick and quiet. Later, Raine is surprised to learn that only ashes remain where Moss lay in his bed. Only then did it dawn on her that she too would die exactly as Moss had when her years were spent, it was part of being Xennes.

It reminds her that she has a story to tell Leyashe. Recently, Raine had discovered the secret of how It-Ha Layrrah and High Yraif Laathria had been able to conjure the 'undoing spell' that took away Moss's power over It-Ha Layrrah.

The two brave women, High It-Ha Solaarr and It-Ha Sihuun, who had saved her grandfather's spaceships, had left a powerful gift behind. Armed with the knowledge that their physical forms would simply become dust the moment their hearts became untrue to the Great Elder, they had found a way to hide something of great value. They put snippets of their hair in a bottle made of strong glass, glass created by the mighty power of Ante Mountain's explosion thousands of years ago. The waters of the Cigam, and root from the Enoce tree preserved their hair and the magic contained within it.

Raine had more questions about the timing of using the bottled magic, but It-Ha Layrrah refused to divulge more, only promising that one day she would explain it all.

Back to reality, happy members of the Om~ada file out of the room, each with lists that will set many things into motion. Each decision has been reached to maintain an orderly society with equal say and freedoms. Rence does not leave Raine's side and remains in the Arc Room with her once everyone has left, but he is denied a chance to speak.

"I have much to do for the next two days," she tells him, and Rence senses immediately that she wishes to be alone. "I have not forgotten my promise to you. I have spoken to Xandr, and he will be guiding you when the time comes to be a fighter craft pilot. I need you on the Command Deck for now," she says, holding his hands in hers and looking into his eyes.

"I ask your patience for a while longer," she tells Rence, leaning forward. Their lips meet, and for a short while, everything is lost around them. It is Regor who eventually decides to break up their embrace as he jumps up on Raine as if to say, enough, thank you, and they both laugh at the antics of the jealous Eninac.

"Of course, I will wait until everything has settled," Rence agrees, kissing her on the cheek before he leaves. He gets a smile and a gentle squeeze on his arm, and he knows that their love prevails.

The Arc Room seems larger now that Raine is on her own. Regor, for some reason, chose to follow Rence. She walks over closes the door, and finds herself being drawn to the soft chairs in the back corner of the room. The long, comfortable bench that looks out through the enormous round window has become her favourite spot-on Ambition.

She and Leyashe have been left with a huge decision. Where to next? Raine sits down and stares at the darkness in front of her. She can see thousands of stars in the distance, but where between those millions of glints of light is a planet that could be called home.

Kearthat, now the size of Raine's thumbnail is in the distance, and getting further and further away. She finds it strange that when she requested Nor~han tell her more of Lanrete, he had waved the matter away for now. She found it strange that he would not give his people a chance of a normal life among their own people. Something did not feel quite right.

Suddenly, It-Ha Layrrah finds her way into Raine's head. "I will not linger, Raine," her voice says. "Look under your seat," is all the It-Ha says before she disappears from Raine's mind.

Raine huffs, making sure to shut her mind before she stands. She looks at the bench with the nice-smelling pillows. "There is no "under" it, Layrrah," she says aloud. Raine bends down and lifts the long cushion. She spots a latch similar to the one at the Trigga tree cavern, but it needs a triangle key.

"Rence has the key or had the key last," she says to herself. She knows he had been the last to pass through the cavern entrance, but did he keep the key? If not Nor~han has one, she knows. When Raine finds Rence, he is working on a schedule Kadez asked for and looks surprised to see her. Regor wags its big Eninac tail excitedly.

"Have you the key we used to get into The Below?" she asks him.

"Yes, I kept it as a remembrance, but you may have it if you like," he offers.

"I would like that. Is it possible for me to have it now?" she asks gently, putting her palms together in a begging motion.

"Now?" he replies, wrinkling his forehead, as she nods in the affirmative.

"Yes, of course, I will retrieve it for you immediately." Rence is a little confused but still manages a smile for the woman he loves.

"Can you bring it to the Arc Room for me, please?" She shouts as he rounds the corner, and a hand with a thumbs-up appears and then disappears.

Raine feels guilty that she is taking the one thing Rence decided to bring with him from Kearthat. She immediately makes up her mind to find someone else to take over his duties. She would talk to Xandr and have Rence begin his training on the fighter craft as soon as possible.

She opens the door when Rence knocks, takes the key from him and smiles. The silence that follows indicates that she wants to be alone. Rence nods, then closes the door softly behind him. He is two steps away from the door when he hears the lock engage.

 Raine inserts the triangle key into the recess on the bench, and it lights up briefly. Then, the top of the seat slides away, revealing dozens and dozens of neatly stacked books. She takes out a few and soon sees they are numbered. They are her Grandmother Farron King's Journals.

She looks for Journal number one and closes the hiding place. Arranging the cushions, she sits down, glances at the blackness of space, then crosses her legs and begins reading.

Earth Year 2071

Dear Journal,

Day One. I feel the need to document our journey into space, and to share for the first time a secret I have kept all my life.

So here goes.

I have had vivid dreams for as long as I can remember. In my dreams, a 'shadow' makes his appearance; often, he goes by the name of Jaenus. He has been part of my dreams since I was a child.

Leaving me cryptic messages,...

The first Journal leads to the next, and eventually, Raine has them all lined up in the correct number order as she completes one after the other. Time disappears as she ploughs through the journals. She naps here and there but keeps at it. Knocks come and trays are left with meals, but she barely looks up.

She reads about the three homeships and the many lives that simply vanished. The recounting of the events in her grandmother's Journals makes Raine wonder if there were bigger forces at play that directed these events. She has seen powerful magic in the past few weeks. Is it possible that the missing earthlings simply slipped into space and time? Are they still alive somewhere? Her thoughts do not linger long as she moves on to the next Journal.

At the end of day two, Leyashe appears. When she answers the door, she has a letter in her hand, written by her grandmother. Draped between her fingers are two neck chains. So engrossed, Raine does not realise that she knew it was Leyashe at the door.

Leyashe puts his hands on his hips, his face frowning at his sister. Stepping over several food trays, many still laden with food, he enters, pushing the door closed behind him.

"You have been locked in here for two days, Raine. What ails you, sister?" Leyashe asks. "I, we," he corrects, "Have been patient, but I come here with everyone's concern for you and to plead that you leave this room immediately," he demands.

"Come in, Ash," she invites calmly, reaching past him to lock the door.

"What is ailing you, sister? We are all concerned that you are losing your mind," Leyashe conveys with a soft, compassionate tone. "Why are you ignoring us?" he keeps questioning, looking at his sister for an explanation. He looks down at the variety of dishes at his feet and shakes his head.

"Have you eaten in the last two days? Did you even notice that we stopped moving hours ago? We are waiting for you to make decisions, Raine, daughter of Dayson," Leyashe pleads, using his father's name to try and bring his sister to her senses.

"I have made a discovery," Raine tells him, smiling; it is clear she had not heard a word he had said to her.

"Will this discovery get you out of this room? Will it help you direct our people? Will it make you eat something? Will it make you brush your hair and your teeth, bathe your body?" he pleads, wrinkling his nose.

"I have only a few minutes ago found this," Raine says, holding up the two gold chains, each with what looks like half of a moth wing hanging from them.

"Where did you find it?" he asks, taking the two necklaces from her.

He holds the adornments up, swapping them around to complete what clearly is a golden Firemoth. The delicately moulded wings, exact copies of each other glint in the bright light of the room as they swing from his hand.

Raine comes over and hugs her confused brother.

"They were in the back of the last Journal started by Greatmother Farron, the last few journals were written by Greatfather Jon," Raine explains and proceeds to show Leyashe the many Journals that were hidden under the long seat. The journals lie scattered on the floor in piles that obviously only make sense to Raine.

"I have been reading, brother," she tells him as she bends down and hands Leyashe the final Journal.

"Greatmother Farron had a special power or was guided by this shadow person in her dreams. It is how the earthling spaceships came to Kearthat. She saw Kearthat in a dream, believing she had a destiny. But hold onto your boots, brother. The voice she heard in her dreams had the same name as the young man who fell in love with the Yraif girl in Bryzon's story."

Raine stops talking and looks at Leyashe, "Grandmother referred to him as Jaenus. It is what we thought when we were in the blue box; this confirms it," she tells her brother.

It takes Leyashe a few seconds to remember Sayhran saying that their mother Caite called her necklace 'her Jaenus.'

"Is this going to help us understand what grandmother meant?" Raine asks Leyashe as she passes him a note she found in the last Journal their grandmother wrote in. It simply reads, 'Believe what you see Rain and Ash.'

Before Leyashe has time to discuss it with her, Raine slips one of the necklaces over her brother's head and then does the same.

"Hold my hand brother," Raine tells him.

"Why, Rai?" he asks rolling his eyes.

"Patience, Leyashe," she says in a gentle voice. "With your other hand put your half of the golden moth to my half. Zoh~ren and Layrrah's runes were trying to tell us something, now we have the key I think," she says, hoping for a result of some kind.

Leyashe takes Raine's hand and with the other hand, they put the two halves of the Firemoth side by side until they touch evenly. Immediately the pieces come together as if by some magnetic force and a light green aura appears around them.

"Leyashe tries to pry the pieces apart but they are stuck together. Then they both see it. In the middle of the green aura generated by the pendant, numbers and letters appear. Leyashe's quick mind captures the script to memory as he reads the message aloud, 'DWR20FL01PG17.'

Now he knows why he has always been fascinated with numbers, it was all for this very moment. As quickly as the aura appeared it dissipates and the wings of the golden moth fall away into two pieces.

"I think I know where to find the message," Leyashe tells his sister smiling.

"Well, are you going to tell me, or am I to grow old while you stay silent?" Raine asks impatiently.

"We are meant to find something that Greatmother Farron left for us. Perhaps it will tell us where our journey is meant to begin sister," he says, taking her hand they head for the door.

Chapter 51 - The Ya~zeld

Leyashe finds the drawer in the room where all the schematics are.

"Drawer number twenty, containing File number one, look on page seventeen," Layashe says out loud as he reaches for the contents.

The drawer has a recess, it is a triangle, Leyashe looks at his sister and she reaches into her pocket and produces the key that seems to unlock many things.

The box is bigger than the one in which they discovered the Code to Freedom. It contains a single celestial chart and a yellow file folder. While Leyashe opts to look at the chart Raine reaches for the file. She opens it at a random spot, immediately recognising her grandmother's handwriting. At the same time, a small piece of irregularly shaped paper falls to the floor.

Raine picks up the piece of folded paper and studies it, it is a spaceship she realises. On closer inspection, she can make out that there are tiny little windows drawn in at the very point of the folded craft. Further scrutiny reveals that someone took the time to write the word 'Courage' on the one wing it reads, 'I love you' and a number, '2043'. She shakes her head as her eyes well up. It is Farron Brands's paper rocket she folded when was only five years old, she had read it somewhere in her Grandmother's Journals.

There are several tall stools in the room arranged in front of the many computer screens. Raine hops onto the nearest one, her feet barely reaching the footrest as her brother opens the chart and sits down next to his sister.

After looking at the chart for a bit, not having any idea what they are meant to find Leyashe notices his sister looking around as if disinterested.

"Why do you not help me, sister? Perhaps you will see something I do not," he asks, sounding a little bothered.

"What is wrong, Rai? You look unhappy, sister. I thought you would be pleased to find purpose by studying the star chart that Greatmother Farron drew out and the contents of the yellow folder."

"It is all too easy brother, it is too easy," Raine repeats.

"From the day you took me to see your secret door until now. It was all too simple," Raine repeats. "The It-Ha and the Yraif answering to The Order of Lanrete, I feel that we have yet to gain our freedom. There is something strange happening." But, before Leyashe can reply, things change abruptly. They do not have time to discuss anything further or discover the secrets of page number seventeen. There is mayhem.

The com has clicked, and Ameka's frantic voice is calling out, "All fighters to the bays, ready for take off. Eslaf fighters incoming, incoming."

"Bay doors open, bay doors open," Dourok's voice continues. In the background, Raine can hear Bryzon giving Learridy instructions on Sonder.

Raine jumps off the stool, shoves everything into the drawer and closes it, by the time Raine turns around Leyashe has hurried away without a word. When Raine gets to the Command Deck, Bryzon's face reveals the seriousness of their predicament.

"Tell me Bryzon, how bad is our situation?" Raine asks.

"It is definitely the Eslaf, they have found us, one of their large spaceships and many fighters. Our reconnaissance ship discovered them not far from our ships. Ohre and Pateeo came back as fast as they could on a slow transporter to warn us, the Eslaf have followed," Bryzon tells her.

Raine looks at the screen that projects their surroundings. Her eyes quickly make out the shape of the Eslaf homeship closing in on them, around it are dozens of small craft. They have come prepared.

Just then, the fighter craft from Ambition fly over the homeship. Filing into formation, they head towards the danger; not long after, the fighters from Sonder follow. They are less than sixty craft against almost twice that of the Eslaf force.

Raine's knees feel weak. She thought they were safe. She closes her eyes and calls out to It-Ha Layrrah. "The Veil is protecting them, Raine, is the only response she gets, and then the It-Ha closes her mind to Raine.

They wait and watch on the screens in front of them. Seven long minutes pass before the fight against the Eslaf begins and Sahdmar's voice reports back. "The Eslaf seem to be retreating, it is not normal. We await your orders, Bryzon. They cannot see us but they fire randomly while they retreat."

It-Ha Layrrah cuts into Raine's thoughts.

"I fear the Eslaf may know that distance is to their advantage, they have guessed that the powers that keep the fighter craft in The Veil will wane if we follow them. Tell our men to return Raine, do not let the Eslaf draw them in. There could be many more fighters on their mothership waiting for us. Do not make this error," she warns.

Immediately, Raine tells Marcus and Ohre to recall their fighters."

"We must plan, Raine. We cannot let them follow us any longer. We must devise a strategy to evade them or fight," Bryzon suggests.

"Bryzon, we must be careful, the It-Ha feel that the Eslaf may be hiding fighters to trick us. We cannot follow if The Veil wanes, if we do so, our fleet is too small," Raine cites relaying Layrrah's premonition to Bryzon.

As they debate their dilemma there is a development. Leyashe reports back that the Eslaf are being attacked from behind by an unknown force. "Whoever it is they are helping us, the Eslaf are making a run for it. The aliens are outnumbered," Leyashe reports back to control.

It does not take long before the Eslaf spaceship and all its fighters disappear from the screens, the mysterious fighting force has saved Ambition and Sonder.

In all the confusion, Sayhran interrupts with a message that the High Yraif has requested to see Raine and Leyashe in the Arc Room, insisting it is a matter of great urgency. She also requests the rest of the Om~ada.

"It is an inopportune time, Rai," Leyashe protests, rolling his eyes when Raine tells him of the High Yraif's request.

"An impending attack on our homeships is more urgent? Do you not think, sister? We have much to deal with, these other craft whoever they are could be more dangerous than the Eslaf? That is what is important," Leyashe repeats while Raine waits for her brother to end his tirade.

"Brother, have you considered that perhaps Laathria can give us the answers we seek? She asks Leyashe, but his response is silence as he shrugs his shoulders.

"I will be there, sister. I must remove my battle suit," he says and stomps off.

It is the first time Raine and Leyashe have disagreed and the first ever encounter with the High Yraif sitting down as they enter the meeting room. Raine is immediately concerned as Laathria's staff casually rests against a chair nearby, it is most odd.

"High Yraif Laathria, what can be more important than what is happening with the Eslaf and the strange craft we are now encountering? Why is it that you do not see this? Leyashe asks.

"Sit child, the time has come for me to speak with honesty. We will wait until all have arrived for this gathering, the Eslaf will not be back, and the other craft that came to our assistance will stand aside for now, I tell you this because I know this to be true," Laathria informs the now horribly confused siblings.

When Nor~han and the other members of The Om~ada arrive Laathria moves to the end of the table so that everyone can focus on her. With her staff in hand, she starts talking.

"I know you think me foolish to call you here," Laathria says, her tone measured.

"You must explain your intrusion, High Yraif Laathria. Not only are you taking us from important talks but you are also directing us as if you command Ambition and Sonder. It is highly unsettling," Bryzon interrupts bravely."

The High Yraif goes silent until all of the Om~ada are seated waiting for her to speak her mind.

"I have come to share a story that affects all who live on Ambition and Sonder," the Yraif says, "A story that some of you know part of, but will soon fully understand," she sighs, something else Raine finds strange. Laathria sounded tired to her.

The High Yraif begins to tell the story of two young people who fell in love high up on the mountains of Kearthat. Those who have heard these tales respectfully stay silent. It does not take long before she divulges how she had conjured the last living breath of Su~nev to travel to another being, on a faraway planet to save her for the future. This statement has everyone leaning in to hear the rest of Laathria's story.

"I sent Jaenus to Lanrete, I gave him *The Endless Life*, and he became immortal." A low murmur can be heard in the room but the mystic is unperturbed and continues talking.

When she tells Raine that she holds Su~nev's breath within her, Raine chokes on a sip of water she has just taken from a glass she is holding. Visibly upset she immediately looks at Bryzon.

"I, hold the last living breath of this Su~nev? Raine repeats.

"Yes, Raine," Laathria confesses. "Your grandmother carried this breath and so did your mother Caite. When you were born it was passed onto you. You are a long line of the descendants of 'Ama-e,' the first earthling who guarded Su~nev's breath," Laathria clarifies. "None knew that they held within them such an important purpose," the Yraif mystic divulges and silence persists as all eyes rest on her face.

"Two thousand and twenty-four years ago, I used my one special gift to save Jaenus and Su~nev. Now it is time for Su~nev to return to Jaenus and to Lanrete.

"Jaenus is the Leader of The Order of Lanrete. Earlier it was the Starfleet of Lanrete who aided in removing the danger that the Eslaf brought to us," Laathria tells them, and whispers can be heard in the room as those of the Om-ada talk amongst each other.

"The Ya~zeld has finally opened," the High Yraif tells them.

"Jaenus has overcome many difficulties to bring Su~nev's breath to him. He discovered its existence on Earth when The Order of Lanrete were deliberating if the species known as humans, were worth saving. A species, who were destroying their sphere with their hate, wars and greed.

Jaenus used his powers to help Frederick King discover a way to leave Earth, to save many earthlings and bring Farron King to Kearthat, and with her, Su~nev's breath."

Raine has kept silent as she absorbs what the High Yraif is telling them, but now she wants answers. As she is about to ask a question a knock comes to the door. It is Ethlah who, until recently, had been a leader in Accedes Colony and, more recently, nowhere to be seen.

Laathria looks up and smiles at Ethlah.

"I have chosen Ethlah to be the third It-Ha to The Xennes people. It will complete the full force of powers that you will need on your journey to find a new world Raine. Once it is done, Jaenus will come to you; he awaits my signal," she informs Raine, and the room erupts with conversation.

Ohre bangs his fist on the table and there is immediate silence.

"Where is he, this Jaenus, and where is this Lanrete, is it close ...? Raine asks suddenly confused, sounding somewhat silly.

"Child, you must listen, not speak, I have little time," the High Yraif reprimands and immediately Leyashe fights back.

"If you wish us to understand, then you must not command us, It-Ha of the Yraif. I will not hand my sister's life to you," he says adamantly, a scowl on his face showing his anger, his hand resting on his sidearm.

"I beg your forgiveness Leyashe, but you must understand that I speak as someone who has little time to complete my charge," the Yraif answers calmly.

"When Jaenus comes, I will take Su-nev's breath from you Raine. You will not be harmed. It will not change you, you will not be harmed, it will simply feel as if nothing happened," Laathria promises as she looks at Leyashe.

"You have nothing to fear. My life has reached its time of forfeit," she confesses to the confused faces glued to her every word. It is the first time anyone has seen the High Yraif Laathria smile that broadly in two thousand years.

"Su~nev and Jaenus will be together in Lanrete, the Ya-zeld will close, and my conjuring of many years will be completed. I will pass to the next world, my time has come. I have lived a long life, I am ready." There is silence. Laathria has managed to dumbfound the members of the Om~ada. She appears genuinely happy.

"When will this Jaenus arrive?" Bryzon asks as he rubs his face as if washing it. "So much to fathom, one minute reality, the next ... I cannot keep my mind straight" he admits aloud in an almost whispered voice.

"So let me ask this," Remek says.

"Jaenus has been waiting all these years for the many who came after this Ama-e. When he found it to be inside my grandmother he helped Greatfather Jon and Frederick King to accomplish an escape from Earth. Did he not know that the Eslaf would come and invade Kearthat and kill my forefathers?" Remek looks at Laathria and the expression on everyone's face is of anticipation as to her answer.

"It is so Remek, Jaenus, our leader, could not foresee the attack on Kearthat. When it did happen, as you know, the Ya~zeld was closed. There was nothing he could do. He had tried to warn your Greatmother Farron but she mistakenly did not see her dreams as a vision; after that, we hid her when we could from the Eslaf, and The Veil prevailed as it protected Su~nev's breath."

"The gateway only opens when the chaos of the forces in the realms allow time and space to create an orientation. Only then can the void linking the realms make itself known; it happens every one hundred and seven years. Jaenus was saddened by the destruction brought by the Eslaf," she explains. "But there was little he could do, "Laathria says, recalling how Solaarr and Sihuun had unselfishly given their lives.

"If there is blame, then we can look to the Supreme Elder Council who did not take Bryzon's warnings seriously, but this too may not have been enough to prevent the invasion," she says, making sure not to lay blame.

"Laathria, you do not seem saddened that you will be giving your life," Raine asks bluntly.

"I am relieved to unburden myself of the secret I have kept for so many years. I am old and tired child," the High Yraif confesses. Suddenly Raine feels very sorry for her, Laathria had gone through her life with no partner, it had to have been very lonely.

"We are stopped," Ameka tells them, sounding breathless as she reaches the Arc Room. Everyone's attention is diverted to her, and she speaks without asking for permission.

"There is a big spaceship right in front of us and it is not the Eslaf. A man calling himself Jaenus has asked for permission to come aboard. What do you want me to do?" Ameka repeats, sounding highly flustered and winded.

"Permission granted," Raine says loudly and next to where Laathria sits, a figure begins to materialize before Ameka even leaves the room. The silence in the room is so loud it is breathtaking. It takes a few seconds before the ear-ringing quiet is broken by Nor~han.

"This is our leader Jaenus, he comes to us from Lanrete, beyond this realm," Nor~han introduces then bows deeply to the man in front of him.

Raine looks at the man. If he is over two thousand years old he certainly does not look it. He has long white hair tied in a knot such as Leyashe wears, the rest of his hair hangs at least twelve inches below his shoulders. He is dressed as a leader of the Yraif would. He does not look  Drennan at all. His forehead holds different symbols to those of Nor~han. The clasp that holds his cape depicts a gold moth. His boots are soft-soled and reach to his knees, and his tunic is a light greyish colour with a blue hue. He is nothing like Raine expected.

"Raine, Leyashe and the members of the Om~ada, we finally meet. I knew your grandmother and mother well, Raine," the young man says, smiling. The way he speaks makes him sound much older somehow.

"Laathria has told you what I wish from you Raine," Jaenus says. "In return, you will have my gratitude for my lifetime, I will be at your service always. Whenever you call my name, I will answer. I shall always remain indebted to you, you have my word," the man pledges.

Raine suddenly feels she needs to confer with Nor~han.

She excuses herself, taking Nor~han by the arm. She leads him out of the Arc Room, closing the door behind them. Leaving a room full of people to stare at Jaenus while Raine consults with Nor~han behind a closed door.

"Tell me the truth, Nor~han," Raine demands, looking into the pale face of the Yraif from Telmah.

"He speaks of fact, Raine, he was born Drennan, but Jaenus is our leader. The leader of the Yraif and the Leader of The Order of Lanrete."

"Is he the one you do not speak of?" Raine asks bluntly.

"That is so, Raine, but now we shall always be able to say his name."

"Why is it that you and your people did not return to Lanrete to be with your Yraif?" Raine asks, not holding back.

"My father followed Oreh~itna when he chose to leave Lanrete many thousands of years ago, my brother and I had no choice. There was a disagreement and he and many followed to make Lan~Igiro their home. Those who left Lanrete were banished and could never return, one of them was my father."

"When the Drennan came to Kearthat my father had passed to the next world. Ore~itna, Su~nev's father was our leader. After the agreement with the Drennan Elder, Luvian, Oreh~itna lured Jaenus to the mountains pretending that he was regretful of his decision concerning his daughter," Nor~han sighs as if it just happened the day before.

"He took Su~nev and Jaenus to the cave where the Cigam spring flows and the Enoce grow, high in the mountains above the Freelands. Oreh~itna cast a spell on Jaenus that would make him sleep into his old age, it was a cruel punishment," Nor~han tells Raine as she stands listening, mesmerized by all the mystery.

"When Su~nev found out what her father had done she spent many days sitting by Jaenus's side in the deep cave. Her father thought his daughter would return and forget the young man but she did not. She drowned herself in the waters of the Cigam stream." Raine flinches when Nor~han tells her how Su~nev died, it must have been horrible.

"Su~nev had by then given Jaenus the water of the Cigam and he had tasted the root of the Enoce tree roots but nothing would wake him. Oreh~itna was unaware that Jaenus would wake up from the action that Su~nev took by drowning herself."

"So the spell was broken because Su~nev drowned?" Raine asks.

"When Jaenus saw Su~nev's lifeless body his heart held such pain in that moment that Laathria could feel his suffering. She was too late to bring Su~nev back to our world but in that moment decided that she would use her one special gift."

"Is this the one gift that the It-Ha of Kearthat do not get?" Raine asks.

"It is so, Raine," Nor~han confirms, before he takes a deep breath and continues.

Laathria cast a spell that would save Su~nev's last breath for a time in the future. She gave Jaenus *The Endless-Life*. She turned Jaenus's appearance to that of a Yraif. She knew that immortality guaranteed him a seat at The Order of Lanrete, once there he would find a way to bring Su~nev's breath back when it was safe.

"His appearance puzzled me, I was going to ask you for an explanation," Raine confesses. "So what happened next, Nor~han," Raine asks, eager for the Yraif to continue the story.

"There was a difficulty, Jaenus would have to wait until the High It-Ha's gifted life was close to its end. Today is that day, Raine. Laathria has lived her *given-life*, if she does not take Su~nev's breath it will leave you of its own. But it will have nowhere to go. The breath needs Laathria." Raine is shocked when she understands that no matter what, Laathria is going to die.

"After the madness took hold of Su~nev's father, when he understood what he had done, the Yraif Assembly took his power and imprisoned him on the mountain. When Jaenus left to be with The Order, we banished Oreh~itna. He was returned to Lanrete for his punishment."

"How did Jaenus get to Lanrete? Raine wants to know.

"The Yraif hid Jaenus until the next Ya~zeld opened, Laathria dealt with the matter," Nor~han explains.

"Hundreds of years passed before Jaenus became our leader. He asked that we stay and wait for Su~nev's last breath. He promised we would be welcomed back on Lanrete. We knew that Ante Mountain would erupt again, but we stayed." Raine is stunned at the wave upon wave of secrets.

"I have been waiting for today, Raine, so that I can be free, free of my oath," Nor~han admits. For the first time in his long life, Nor~han can be unburdened. All has been revealed.

"What of Laathria, why must she die to take this thing out of me?" Raine asks.

"It was her gift to give, and her time of ending has come," Nor~han's pale face wrinkles into a pained expression as he shows a rare expression of emotion.

"You cannot stop it, Raine. Now that Su~nev's breath is near, the breath will find its way out. You must let Laathria take it. It will not harm you; I give you my word. If you give it willingly, you will be safe," Nor~han promises.

When Raine returns to the room, the lights dim. The High Yraif already knows the outcome of Raine's conversation with Nor~han. She is ready for the ceremony.

Laathria calls on Sayhran and Layrrah as they begin the chant that will change Ethlah to become Layrrah's newest Tiro. She reaches for Raine's hand, and with the other hand, she holds her staff. In a corner, away from the proceedings, Jaenus stands quietly, almost hidden in the shadows of the semi-darkened room.

Many things happen at once when Laathria stops chanting. Raine feels suddenly relieved, and a feeling of lightness comes over her. Seconds later, Laathria begins to change, her features slowly merge into that of Su~nev. As the High Yraif's image begins to diminish, she manages a smile and mouths the words 'farewell, my old friend,' as she looks at Nor~han. Within seconds, the High Yraif is no more, but her staff finds life as it makes its way moving by itself into Nor~han's left hand. Then, right in front of everyone, green wisps emanate from the staff in his hand and encircle him. When all is done, Nor~han is undoubtedly the new High Yraif. His eyes are a light green, gone are the sparkles his eyes used to have.

When Su~nev sees Jaenus, she runs over to him. They embrace and Raine knows she will never forget what just happened.

"It has been too many years? Su~nev says, looking at Jaenus. Everyone notices the tears as the once Drennan man and Yraif girl are together again.

Raine excuses herself, saying she will be back in an hour. She whispers to Krom to tell Jaenus that she wishes a meeting with him. Her cousin nods as Raine heads for her quarters. On the way out she whispers to Nor~han, smiling, "I suppose this makes you the High Yraif now," and squeezes his hand.

"Sister, you must not let this be a weight on your mind," Leyashe begs, running after his sister. "It was Laathria's choice, as Nor~han explained. You should be happy that you no longer carry this silly breath around with you," Leyashe says with a tiny smile to cheer Raine.

"Be on time when I meet with this Jaenus, brother, please," Raine says before she disappears into her quarters with a smile to reassure her brother that she feeling fine after what just took place.

When she is finally alone, Raine sheds tears for her friend Laathria, the woman who took her under her wing and taught her so much in such a short time.

Chapter 52 - The Vote

"There are many questions, I know," the man from Lanrete says as he meets with Raine and Leyashe.

"I will tell you what I came to say, then you may ask anything you wish of me, daughter and son of Dayson and Caite. The Om~ada has my word that I will tell only the truth."

Raine is caught unaware by Jaenus's use of her father's name and she has to remind herself that he was born a Drennan of Kearthat, and of course, he knew everything about them.

Jaenus tells them that the realms are joined by interlinking voids. Somehow, as these universes are drawn together at different times by the great forces of chaos and correction, wormholes open. The voids have for many thousands of years been used by the Yraif to navigate between these enormous creations of time and space.

"That is why they called them the Ya~zeld, meaning tunnels in Yraif," Jaenus informs the siblings.

"Our ability to navigate the voids and contact those in different worlds was a gift shared with me by the First Ones of the Yraif people. It enabled me to find Su~nev, it allowed me to talk to the It-Ha and High Yraif of Kearthat, and speak to your mother throughout her life until the invasion of Kearthat," he confesses.

"I would wish for you to bring your people and live among us on Lanrete. You will be safe from the challenges of this universe. This realm has many like the Eslaf of Ludinia. It is not a safe place," he cautions.

I gave "The Code to Freedom" to your Greatmother. I hoped it would give her and Jon the courage to wait for the Ya-zeld to open. It saddened me when I was told of the Eslaf's cruelty, and the losses that were suffered. It was hard for me to endure, I suffered greatly under the burden of knowing the Lanrete were unable to stop the cruelty that the Eslaf brought to Kearthat."

Raine and Leyashe can see from the look in the man's eyes that he is trying to make them understand how desperate he felt not being able to help their forefathers.

"When Caite became ill I was alarmed that Su~nev would be lost to me forever. I reached out to It-Ha Layrrah to watch over your mother, making sure that you were close, so that the breath would pass to you," he admits as the secrets continue to emerge.

"I have spoken with Nor~han. He tells me you will let your people decide their own fate; this is virtuous. I congratulate The Selected on their choice of leadership," his compliments and his admiration ringing of sincerity.

"I have as little as four days before the Ya~zeld will close to my world. If your people are in favour of it, you may return to Lanrete with me immediately. You will find that we are peaceful. We are kept safe by our great celestial fleet. I offer this safety to you and your people."

Raine has waited patiently while Jaenus has talked but now she has questions.

"Do you know what ALUSIL56MM is? She asks as her first question. Immediately Raine can see Jaenus has no clue, what she is talking about.

"I do not," Jaenus admits, shaking his head as if confused by the question.

"It is of no matter, I will continue," Raine quickly responds and moves on. Leyashe smiles, he knows what Raine is talking about. She is going to be very disappointed when she discovers what it represents. He does find it odd that Raine felt it was perhaps a message from their Grandparents in some way.

"Where is this universe where Earth can be found?" Raine asks next.

"No Raine, you cannot possibly be thinking of returning to the sphere from which Jon and Farron fled?" Jaenus adds, clearly confused at Raine's intentions.

When Jaenus seems to recover from the question he tells Raine and Leyashe they will have to pass through the void. The gateway to reach Earth he explains opens every seven years, and it will be opening soon.

"If you have solved the riddle of the necklaces Farron hid for you, you have found the star charts that will lead you there," Jaenus confirms.

"Does Earth still exist, do you know?" Leyashe fires off as he looks at his sister, his eyes begging her to let him get an answer from Jaenus.

"The Order declared Earth of no consequence. The earthlings were a mostly flawed species. They continuously fought over what belonged to all, they did not advance enough to save themselves. Frederick King was different. I see it was an excellent choice to bring so many earthlings to Kearthat. You and Leyashe are indeed remarkable, as mixed-bloods your species will be stronger now," Jaenus forthrightly tells the siblings.

Raine does not know if she should be angry or happy at Jaenus's summation of her forefathers. It is all so confusing, and she decides to let it go. She does, however, get the feeling Jaenus is sincerely concerned about those on Ambition and Sonder.

"But do you think Earth still exists, or is it gone?" Leyashe asks again.

"Every time the Ya~zeld has opened the realm that leads to Earth I have tried to Seek those Yraif who many hundreds of years ago were sent to Earth to observe. I was not successful," Jaenus tells them, as Raine just about falls off her chair.

"There were Yraif on Earth? Do you think they could have survived? Did my grandmother know about them?" Raine exclaims with a string of questions.

"No Raine, daughter of Caite, Farron was not aware. The Yraif were granted permission by The Order to return through the Ya~zeld and bring their mixed-blood families, but they rejected our offer. We do not know their reasoning. When I Seek their minds now, they do not answer."

Raine can see that Jaenus feels greatly troubled by the actions of the Yraif on Earth.

"Do the Eslaf know of the Ya~zelds?" "Would they be able to navigate them?" Raine asks next.

Jaenus chuckles, "The Eslaf are beasts; they have progressed but have become like stinging insects. They multiply and bring misery; they move from planet to planet because they destroy everything. They are dangerous, Raine. If you decide to remain in this realm, get as far away as possible from where you are now," Jaenus warns, and it is clear to Raine that Jaenus does not know for certain how the Eslaf move about the galaxy.

"Are there spheres other than yours that we can explore from your universe? Raine asks next.

"There are. We could help you find a new home, Raine. You and Leyashe will have all my aid at your disposal," Jaenus offers.

"Leyashe and I have discussed the safety of our people. We will put forward the proposal that they can return with you to Lanrete if they so choose. Those who volunteer will journey with Ambition and Sonder to find the path of our forefathers. We will journey back to Earth." Raine watches Jaenus for a reaction but his demeanor remains unchanged.

Two days later, the Om~ada accepts the newest It-Ha, and Ethlah takes her seat at the table in the Arc Room, no one speaks of Laathria.

The Xennes have voted. High Yraif Layrrah asks a surprised Remek to read the results of the vote that has been counted and verified by Nor~han, Dessas and the High It-Ha.

Remek opens the neatly folded piece of paper that contains the result. At first, he sees nothing, the page is blank. He smiles and looks over at Layrrah. When he looks back, the message has made itself known. The jesting between Remek and Layrrah goes unnoticed but the young man is thrilled to know that the It-Ha has become his friend.

"The Xennes, and Korak of Ambition and Sonder who hail from Kearthat, have chosen not to enter the Ya~zeld to Lanrete. They would journey through the void that will take them to the planet called Earth," he reads. Remek's face lights up.

Raine looks at Nor~han. "Are you and your people going with Jaenus to Lanrete?" she asks the High Yraif bluntly.

The vote of the Yraif is on the note that Remek read out. "We will follow The Selected," he tells her. Raine is overjoyed. She jumps up and hugs Nor~han; the confused Yraif pats her back as he tries to absorb the strange ways of the younger generation.

Raine and Leyashe look at each other. They are explorers now. If they do not find Earth habitable they will return and enter the Ya~zeld to Lanrete, then explore the other universes until they find a suitable home.

That night, Raine's dreams are confusing, but somewhere in the tangle of it all, she hears a now familiar voice. 'I am always with you,' the leader of The Order of Lanrete promises. 'I thank you for returning Su~nev safely to me, and wish you well on your quest,' Jaenus's voice trails into the distance before it fades. The muddle gives way to a vision of Raine and Leyashe walking in a green meadow, strange-looking birds twitter, and one sun warms their arms as they walk beside each other. The clouds are white and the sky is light blue, and when night comes there is only one moon.

The next morning, Raine wakes up feeling as light as a feather. Regor sits up and licks her chin. She tries to swing her feet off the bed but the Eninac pounces, its large yellow tails wagging furiously as it manages to lick her on the arm before lying on its back next to her.

A new morning ritual, Raine first rubs Regor's tummy as she ponders her day. But today she notices that Regor is looking rather round. She feels the Eninac's belly, something is moving.

Regor is going to have a pup. She knows instinctively that the pup was a parting gift from the High Yraif Laathria.

Today is the day that the Om~ada will plan their entry to the Ya~zeld that will take them to Earth. Nor~han would have no difficulty finding the void when the time came. The clue that had appeared so many times in runes and symbols, and was now confirmed by her grandmother's charts.

Jaenus has left Nor~han with the knowledge of how to use the Ya~zeld, and promised that in time Nor~han will pass on the ability to her and Leyashe to use effectively.

It is a perfect day at last.

The door chimes and Raine opens it to find a tray with a glass of fruit juice and a note, she looks up and down the hall but there is no one around. She picks up the tray and puts it on her bedside table and opens the note. It is from Leyashe.

Number One

ALUSIL56MM is a rune the earthlings put on the homeship's windows to show its strength. It is unimportant, sister.

 Signed, Your clever Number Two.

Raine laughs, bounces out of bed, and begins to get ready for the day.

Then something catches her eye in the mirror, on her left upper arm she sees a mark. On closer inspection, she sees it is a rune.

She sits down, straining her neck, squinting to get a better look at the mark. Her pulse begins to race as her mind tries to fathom a reason for what she is seeing. Slowly it comes back to her. She had a dream, in her dream a strange shadow told her that he would always be there for her.

"The rune is to reassure me that his word is true," Raine whispers and smiles. It is a triangle with the outline of a moth inside of it. She finds it quite pleasing. It will go well with the half-moth necklace that she and Leyashe wear around their necks.

Raine has a dream shadow now, and his name is Jaenus.

UNTIL WE MEET AGAIN

Glossary

Abeona -Pronounced Ay-be-oh-nah. Comes from the Latin verb *'abeo'* in Roman mythology. As a goddess Abeona was believed to especially guard children, as they took their first steps away from their home to explore the world, whether literal or metaphoric.

Adarra - Pronounced as Ah-dah-rah. Freelander and Leader of Ytineres Colony, Ex Kearthat Starfleet, Engineer, Spaceship pilot and Drennan Xennes, wife of Auwzen the Lesser Leader of Ytineres.

Ade~mordna - Pronounced Ah-day-mord-nah – The fictitious galaxy in which the Planet of Kearthat resides.

Ae~ranh - Pronounced as Ay-ran. A Yraif girl of The Below.' She is also a member of the Yraif Assembly headed by the Yraif Leader Nor~han.

Agnak - Pronounced as Ag-knack. A large docile six-legged creature that lives deep in the forest and feeds on moss. It could have some resemblance to Earth's Kangaroo.

Ama-e - Pronounced as Amah-eh. The first woman on Earth that carried the breath of Su~nev. Conjured by the High Yraif Laathria the breath moved to each new generation until it made its way to Kearthat carried by first Farron, then Caite and finally Raine.

Ameka - Pronounced as Ah-meh-kah. Freelander and Lesser Leader of Laeredis Colony, Ex Kearthat Starfleet, Engineer, Drennan Xennes woman.

Anish - Pronounced as Ah-nish. Freelander and Leader of Noyclah Colony, Ex Kearthat Starfleet, Spaceship pilot and Drennan Xennes man.

Annrev - Pronounced as Un-rev. Freelander and Lesser Leader of Arorua Colony, Ex Kearthat Starfleet, Spaceship pilot and Drennan Xennes man.

Ante Mountain - Pronounced as Ant-tee. Gigantic Mountain on the Planet of Kearthat, a 'supposed' dormant volcano.
Ardyh - Pronounced as Ahr-dee. A Small yellow and green slithering, a three-headed creature of Planet Kearthat.

Arorua - Pronounced as Ah-roar-rua. Eastern Colony of the Freelands.

Ashok - Pronounced as Ash-shock. Freelander and Lesser Leader of Ytineres Colony, Ex Kearthat Starfleet, Spaceship pilot, Drennan Xennes man.

Assembly, The - Pronounced as written. Council of the Yraif of The Below.

Atolf flowers - Pronounced Ay-tulf. Purple flowers resembling the water lilies of Earth.

Auwzen - Pronounced as Ou (as in ouch)-zen. Freelander and Lesser Leader of Ytineres Colony, Ex Kearthat Starfleet, Spaceship pilot, Drennan Xennes man.

Below, The - pronounced as written. – The lava tubes in Ante Mountain where the Yraif live, The Below.

Bailea - Pronounced as Bay-lee-ah. A Korak female brought to Noitibma Colony as a baby to be raised by the colonists.

Bennat - Pronounced as Ben-nat. Freelander and Lesser Leader of Noyclah Colony, Ex Kearthat Starfleet, Spaceship pilot, Drennan Xennes man.

Bouchard, Jean- Earthling Commander of the second homeship that landed on Kearthat.

Brann - Pronounced as written. Freelander and Lesser Leader of Elbaffeni Colony, Ex Kearthat Starfleet Spaceship pilot, Drennan Xennes man.

Bryzon - Pronounced as Brigh-zin. Ex-Commander of the Kearthat Starfleet, leader of the rebel uprising. Brother-in-law to Sayhran and Caite, he was a lesser leader of the Rednos Colony before he relocated to Noitibma Colony, the uncle to Krom, Remek, Raine, and Leyashe.

Caite - Pronounced as Kate. Earthling woman, daughter of Jon and Farron King, wife of Dayson, mother of Raine and Leyashe, sister-in-joining to Bryzon. Sister to Sayhran and Nick King

Cigam Spring - Pronounced as Sea-gam. An underground stream of water with magical powers.

Cirabrab - Pronounced as Sir-ah-braab. Alien Eslaf Leader that invaded the Planet of Kearthat.

City of Etah - Pronounced as Et-ha. The name was given to The City of Seccus after the Eslaf invaded the planet Kearthat.

Dayson - Pronounced as Day-sun. Twin brother to Bryzon, husband of earthling Caite, father to Raine and Leyashe, brother-in-law to Sayhran and Nick King. Ex Kearthat Starfleet spaceship pilot, a Drennan Xennes man.

Dehrazz - Pronounced as Day-raz. Freelander and lesser leader of Elbaffeni Colony, Ex Kearthat Starfleet Spaceship pilot, Drennan Xennes man.

Dessas - Pronounced as Day-sass. A Korak male brought to Noitibma Colony as a baby, to be raised by the colonists.

Dexim Refinery - Pronounced as written. The Zraphite Mineral Refinery is not far from the Zraphite mines on Kearthat.

Digger - Pronounced as written. An underground machine operated by the alien Eslaf digs tunnels to extract the mineral Zraphite.

DIPPAR, Speed - Pronounced Dip-paar - Enhanced speed developed by Frederick King to propel the earthling spaceships through space at mindboggling speed. (*Also see* DIPPS)

DIPPS - Pronounced as written - Acronym for 'DIPPAR, Speed.'

Dirha - Pronounced as Dur-ha. The planet from which the Korak aliens derive.

Divaad - Pronounced as Dee-vaad. Freelander and lesser leader of Sedecca Colony. Ex Kearthat Starfleet freight Spaceship pilot, Drennan Xennes man.

Dreyba - Pronounced as Dray-baa - Elder Moss's father.

Dourok - Pronounced Doo-rock. Freelander and lesser leader of Sonder Colony, father to Rence. Ex Kearthat Starfleet freight Spaceship pilot, Drennan Xennes man.

Drazil - Pronounced as written. Type of lizard of creature that lives on Planet Kearthat.

Drennan - Pronounced as Dren-nan. The Drennan are the people of Planet Kearthat.

Droid - Pronounced as written – Droid derived from Android.

Endless Life, The - Pronounced as written. Immortality.

Ekans - Pronounced as Ee-cans. A harmless eel-like water creature found in the Elin River that flows from The High Mountains to Planet Kearthat's ocean.

Elbaffeni - Pronounced as Elba-fen-knee. A Western Colony of the Freelands.

Elfradah – Pronounced El-fray-dah. A Xennes woman of Elbaffeni Colony. Ex pilot of the Kearthat Star Fleet.

Elin River, The Great - Pronounced as Ee-lin. A big river that starts in The High Mountains making its way through the Freelands then flowing to the ocean on Planet Kearthat.

Ellpa Fruit - Pronounced as El-pah. A bright red round fruit. Much like apples on Earth.

Eninac- Pronounced as Any-nack. Similar to a dog on Earth.

Enoce tree - Pronounced as En-know-chee. The Enoce roots, combined with the water of the Cigam Spring form a potion, combined with the magic of an It-Ha it grants 'long-life'.

Enscriptor - pronounced En-script-tor. Alien technology of a material that resembles glass. Similar to a 'tablet computer' found on Earth. Used by the Drennan of Plant Kearthat.

Eslaf - Pronounced as Ez-laugh. Alien creatures hailing from the Planet of Ludinia, in the Yawa Galaxy. The Eslaf invaded the planet of Kearthat for their mineral, Zraphite.

Eslaf Spotter Craft - Small two and four-man spaceships used by the alien Eslaf to patrol Kearthat.

Es~Roh - Pronounced Ez-row. An Inop of "The Below." A creature on Planet Kearthat that somewhat resembles horses of Earth, but for their multi-horned foreheads and their incredibly long manes.

Ethlah, It-Ha - Pronounced It-Hah, Eth-Lah. Ethlah was a Drennan, and ex Kearthat Starfleet spaceship pilot. Later, Ethlah was chosen by the High Yraif Laathria to become an It-Ha.

Evalc - Pronounced as Ee-valk. A gathering or meeting held by the Drennan Xennes.

Evas - *see* **Mehtevas.**

Farron (Brand) King - Pronounced as written. Daughter of Richard Phillip Brand benefactor of Project P25K. The earthling wife of Jon King, mother to Caite, Nick and Sayhran, and grandmother to Krom, Remek, Raine and Leyashe. Great-grandmother to Marcus King, and great-great-grandmother to Nedai King.

Firemoths - Pronounced as written. Harmless large orange-red and black moths that glow in the dark, they live underground and only come out at night to feed on the Lattgrass of the Freelands.

First Ones, The - Pronounced as written – Another name for the Yraif who were the first to inhabit Planet Kearthat.

Flutterbugs - Pronounced as written. Kind of large butterfly that frequents the flowers and shrubs of Planet Kearthat.

Freelanders, The - Pronounced as written. The farmlands, and prairies of Kearthat.

Gip - Pronounced as Jip. A fragrant meat from a large grey and black snorting creature found on Kearthat.

GoTrike - Three-wheeled cart that transports up to two persons around the large bays of the earthling spaceships.

Great Elder - Pronounced as written. A Great Elder is the *oldest* elder of the Supreme Elder Council of Kearthat. When a Great Elder passes, the next oldest takes on the burden of 'secrets' kept for thousands of years on the Planet of Kearthat.

Hadvah - Pronounced as Haad-vah. The only Korak raised in Noitibma who refused the potion of long-life and perished in the battle that took place in Seccus.

Hy-Ox - Pronounced as High-ox. A name for the means by which the earthlings are able to produce water and breathable air on the homeships.

High It-Ha - Pronounced as written. A mystic woman who possesses the power to create magical feats. High meaning the mystic in charge. It-Ha are chosen by the High Yraif of The Below.

High Mountains - Pronounced as written. The giant mountain range on Kearthat of which Ante Mountain is the tallest.

High -Yraif - Pronounced as High Ee-rayf. The High Yraif is the mystic woman of the Yraif people who live in the Village of Telmah in The Below.

Ibromne - Pronounced as Ee-brom-nee. Planet in the same visible Universe as Kearthat, a trading Post that traded metal for Zraphite with the Drennan of Kearthat.

ICSS - Abbreviation for the Inter-Colony Shuttle Service.
Idler - Pronounced as written. A name that the survivors of Kearthat gave to the drones brought to Kearthat to watch over them by the alien Eslaf after the invasion.

Idna - Pronounced Id-nah. Freelander and Leader of Arorua Colony, Ex Kearthat Starfleet, Engineer, Spaceship pilot, Drennan and Xennes.

Idah - Pronounced Eye-dah. The only Xennes woman who died in the final battle on Kearthat.

Ikud - Pronounced Eye-could. A water bird, much like the ducks of Earth.

Innocent, an- On Planet Kearthat being 'an innocent' means that you have a kind and good heart.

Inop - Pronounced as Inn-op. A large sleek muscled animal of Kearthat used as a means of transport when tamed. Similar to Earth's horses but for their multi-horned foreheads and incredibly long manes. They are black on The Above, but white in The Below.

Inmo, The - Pronounced as In-mow. An ability given to the mystics (It-Ha) of planet Kearthat, also known as 'The Eye that sees all.'

Jaenus - Pronounced Jay-nis - The name of Farron King's 'dream-shadow/friend' that appeared in her dreams. Jaenus is the Leader of the Order of Lanrete, the home planet of the Yraif.

Joined as one - Pronounced as written – The Kearthatian way of describing, being/getting married.

Jon King - Pronounced as written - Earthling leader, husband of Farron, father of Caite, Nick and Sayhran, and the son of the Earthling Frederick King who built the spaceships. Grandfather of Krom, Remek, Raine and Leyashe. Great grandfather of Marcus King and Great-great grandfather to Nedai King.

Ju~neh - Pronounced as Joo-nay - Brother of Nor~han, the leader of the Yraif of The Below.

Kadez - Pronounced Kah-dez. Freelander and Lesser Leader of Rednos Colony. Ex Kearthat Starfleet fighter craft pilot, also a Drennan and Xennes man.

Kahldeh - Pronounced as Kull-day - Freelander and lesser leader of Niamod Colony, Ex Kearthat Starfleet, Spaceship pilot, Drennan and Xennes man.

Kaldu - Pronounced as Kull-doo. Planet in the same visible Universe as Kearthat, a trading Post that traded metals for Zraphite with the Drennan of Kearthat.

Kao Tree - Pronounced as Kay-oh. Large tree with leaves of varying colours.
Kearthat - Pronounced as Kurr-that – The planet on which most of this story takes place.

Korak, The - Pronounced Core-rack. Docile aliens whose planet Dirha was invaded by the Eslaf. They were brought to Kearthat to work in the Zraphite Mines.

Keazan - Pronounced as Key-zan. Husband to Sayhran, Father to Krom and Remek, Ex Kearthat Starfleet Member, Drennan and Xennes man.

Keeland - Pronounced as Key-land. Freelander and Lesser Leader of Noitibma Colony, Ex Kearthat Starfleet, Spaceship pilot, Drennan and Xennes man.

Kergann - Pronounced as Kur-gan. A young boy of Noitibma Colony who stutters badly, a Historian's son, and *runner* for the Noitibma Council members.

Kristoh - Pronounced as Chris-toe. Young man and Gatekeeper of Rednos Colony.
Krom - Pronounced as written. Son of Keazan and Sayhran, brother to Remek and cousin to Raine and Leyashe, and Nephew to Bryzon.

KSF – Abbreviation for 'Kearthat Starfleet.'

Kuldab, City of - Pronounced as Kull-daab. The 2nd largest city on the planet Kearthat, was destroyed during the alien invasion.

Laathria, The High Yraif - Pronounced as Lah-three-ah. The mystic woman is known as the High Yraif Laathria of the Yraif people of The Below.

Laeredis - Pronounced as Lah-ray-dis. A Western Colony of the Freelands.

Lan~Igiro - Pronounced as Lahni-ghee-roo. What the Yraif call the planet of Kearthat.

Lattgrass - Pronounced as Lat-grass. Type of tall wispy grass that grows on Kearthat's Freelands.

Layrrah, The High It-Ha - Pronounced as It- Haa - Lay-Rah. Mystic Woman of the Planet Kearthat.

Learridy - Pronounced as Lear-riddy. Freelander and Lesser Leader of Ygyzys Colony, Ex Kearthat Starfleet, Spaceship pilot Drennan Xennes woman. Bryzon's girlfriend.

Layhne, Tutor - Pronounced as Tutor Lane. Tutor (teacher) in Noitibma Colony.

Leyashe - Pronounced as Lee-ash. Son of Dayson and Caite (King), brother to Raine and cousin to Krom and Remek, nephew to Bryzon and Sayhran.

Lido - pronounced Lie-doe. Huge, yellow cup-shaped flowers that produce sweet nectar. They resemble the tiny Daffodils of Earth.

Luvian, Great Elder - pronounced Loo-vee-en. The first recorded Great Elder of the Drennan who came to Kearthat.
MagnoA Energy - Pronounced as Mag-no-ay. Never-ending power source discovered by the earthling scientist Frederick King.

Marcus King - pronounced as written. Leader of Rednos Colony. The son of Nick King, and grandson of Jon King. Father of Nedai, husband of Zaviah.
May the Day Welcome you - pronounced as written. A greeting on the planet Kearthat.

Mehtevas - *nicknamed Evas.* Pronounced as May-tah-vas (Ay-vas) – A Korak spaceship Pilot and brother to the Korak female Namow, a prisoner working in the colonies.

Meirah - Pronounced as May-ee-rah. Bryzon's bride-to-be, ex-Kearthat Starfleet, was killed during the alien invasion by the Eslaf.

Mezka - Pronounced as Mez-kah. Freelander and leader of Laeredis Colony, Ex Kearthat Starfleet, Spaceship pilot, Drennan Xennes man.

Mixed-Bloods - Pronounced as written. The offspring of the union between Drennan and earthlings.

Moss, Great Elder - Pronounced as written. Oldest, and only surviving member of the original Supreme Elder Council of Kearthat.

Mura Flowers - Pronounced as Mew-rah. Large red fragrant flowers.

Naylon - Pronounced as Nay-lon. Leader of Ygyzys Colony, Ex Kearthat Starfleet, Spaceship pilot, Drennan and Xennes man.

Namow - Pronounced as Nam-oh. Female Korak prisoner at Pishdrah Zraphite Mine, originally a leader of her species from the planet Dirha.

Narom - Pronounced as Nah-rom. Freelander and Lesser Leader of Sigae Colony, Ex Kearthat Starfleet, Spaceship pilot, Drennan Xennes woman.

Nedai King - Pronounced as Ned-day. Son of Marcus King, grandson to Nick King and great-grandson of Jon King.

Nedwon - Pronounced as Ned-one. Freelander and leader of Sedecca Colony, Ex Kearthat Starfleet, Spaceship pilot, Drennan and Xennes man.

Nedyar - Pronounced as Ned-yaar. Freelander and Lesser Leader of Temsik Colony, Ex Kearthat Starfleet, Spaceship pilot, Drennan and Xennes man.

Nemzah - Pronounced as Nem-zah. Freelander and lesser leader of Arorua Colony, Ex Kearthat Starfleet, Spaceship pilot, Drennan and Xennes man.
Neraz mazeiz livoz, Neraz mazeiz livoz. Pronounced as Ney-raz, May-zays, Lee-woz – The chant used by the It-Ha during the ceremonies to bestow the 'gift of long life' to become Xennes.

Nerrab - Pronounced as Nay-raab - Barren Desert of Kearthat beyond The High Mountains.

Nexo - Pronounced as Nex-oh. Domesticated animals that somewhat resemble cattle on Earth but for their extremely arched backs, and large eyes.

Nezray - Pronounced as Nez-ray. Freelander and Lesser Leader of Temsik Colony, Ex Kearthat Starfleet, Spaceship pilot, Drennan and Xennes man.

Niamod - Pronounced as Nia-mod. An Eastern Colony of the Freelands.

Nick King - Pronounced as written. Son of Jon and Farron King, brother of Caite and Sayhran, father of Marcus King, and grandfather to Nedai King.

Night Creature - Pronounced as written – Part Animal, part machine this creature resembles a black panther, but is much larger, with huge fangs, and a short tail. Brought to Planet Kearthat by the alien Eslaf, they patrol the Freelands from dusk to dawn.

No-Go-Zones - Pronounced as written. Areas where the Freelanders are not allowed to enter and are patrolled by drones 'Idlers.'(*see* NGZ)

NGZ - Abbreviation for No-Go Zone.

Nobrac - Pronounced as No-brack - Weapon carried by the alien Eslaf.

Noitibma - Pronounced as Noy-tib-mah. Eastern Colony of the Freelands.

Nor~han - Pronounced as Nor-haan - Leader of the Yraif of The Below.

Nowber - Pronounced as No-burr - Freelander and Lesser Leader of Noitibma Colony, Ex Kearthat Starfleet, Spaceship pilot, Drennan and Xennes man.

Noyclah - Pronounced as Noy-klah. Western Colony of the Freelands.

Nulling - Pronounced as written. Removing powers and status from those who possess 'abilities' or power on Planet Kearthat.
Nusflower –pronounced Nus, (as in 'nut'). Crop of blue flowers containing large seeds that are grown for the Korak prisoners on Kearthat.

Nut~Ca - Pronounced Nut-kuh. The river that flows Below to Telmah.

Observer - Pronounced as written. A Freelander (Raine) appointed by the Xennes Leaders to observe and record everything about the alien Eslaf who invaded Kearthat.

Ohre - Pronounced as Oh-ray – Xennes man of Temsik Colony, a friend of Bryzon. Ex Kearthat Starfleet, Spaceship pilot, Drennan and Xennes man. Confidante of the It-Ha, Layrrah.

Orsoh - Pronounced as Or-so - A young Korak male brought to Noitibma Colony as a baby for the colonists to raise, the son of Namow.

Om~ada, The - Pronounced as Om-ah-dah. A word meaning 'Leading Together' in both the Yraif and Drennan languages. The Xennes 'council' of Ambition and Sonder.

Oreh~Itna - Pronounced as Or-ray-it-nah. The 'Ancient One' or first of the Yraif who came to Lan-Igiro, also known as Kearthat.

Otatop - Pronounced as Oh-tay-top. A root vegetable crop grown on Kearthat, that resembles the potato of Earth.

Oznay - Pronounced as Oz-Nay. Freelander and Lesser Leader of Ytineres Colony, Ex Kearthat Starfleet, Spaceship pilot, Drennan and Xennes.

Pa~esh - Pronounced Pay-esh. A type of long-haired cross between perhaps a goat and a sheep of Earth, Pa~esh have long curly wool that grows down to their hooves.

Pateeo - Pronounced as Pah-tee-oh. Ex Kearthat Starfleet member, Spaceship pilot, Drennan Xennes man.
Pishdrah - Pronounced as Pish-drah. One of three Zraphite Mineral Mines on the planet Kearthat.

Radec - Pronounced as Raa-deck. A type of tree that grows on Kearthat that has a wonderful scent when cut.

Raine - Pronounced as Rain. Granddaughter of Jon & Farron King. Daughter of Dayson and Caite (King), sister of Leyashe and cousin to Krom and Remek. Niece to Bryzon. (*see* Rai.)
Rai - Pronounced Ray. Short for Raine.

Recon Ships - Pronounced as written. Reconnaissance spacecraft.

Rek~cus - Pronounce Reck-kus. A white slithering creature with a feathery body found in the river of The Below.

Rednos - Pronounced as Red-nos. Eastern Colony of the Freelands.

Reeb - Pronounced as written. A type of beer brewed by the Freelanders of the colonies.

Reggit - Pronounced as Ray-ghitt. A fierce animal on the planet Kearthat that resembles a Sabre-toothed cat.

Remek - Pronounced as Rem-eck. Son of Keazan and Sayhran, brother to Krom and cousin to Raine and Leyashe, and nephew to Bryzon.

Rence - Pronounced as written. Son of Dourok and Lesser Leader of Rednos Colony.

Rick Brand - Pronounced as written. Richard Phillip Brand, earthling and father to Farron King. The benefactor of Project25K.

Sahdmar - Pronounced as Sahd-maar. Ex Kearthat and Starfleet pilot, Drennan Xennes man.

Sanction Stone - Pronounced as written. The black shiny stone used by the It-Ha during the ritual granting long-life.

Sanew - Pronounced as San-new. Freelander and lesser leader of Sedecca Colony, Ex Kearthat Starfleet, Spaceship pilot, Drennan and Xennes man.

Sayhran - Pronounced as Say-ran. Wife of Keazan, daughter of Jon and Farron King, sister to Caite and Nick King, mother of Krom and Remek, Aunt to Raine and Leyashe and sister-in-law to Bryzon.

Seccus - Pronounced as Sec-kuss. The name of the main city on the Planet of Kearthat. After the invasion, the aliens renamed the city to, Etah.

Sedecca - Pronounced as Say-deck-kah. Western Colony of the Freelands.
Senrah - Pronounced as Sen-rah. Freelander and leader of Temsik Colony, Ex Kearthat Starfleet, Engineer, Spaceship pilot, Drennan and Xennes man.

Shiftaf - Pronounced as Shif-taf. A type of broad fish that is found in the rivers of Kearthat. The oil of this fish is harvested for cooking and the oil lamps on Kearthat.

Spaceba - Pronounced as Space-bah. A round Android Vacuum Cleaner that moves about the floor picking up dust and small particles on Ambition and Sonder.

Sigae - Pronounced as See-gay, and Eastern Colony of the Freelands.

Sister-in-joining - Pronounced as written. The Drennan way of saying sister-in-law.

Solaarr, It-Ha - Pronounced as Sow-laar – The first mystic woman of the planet of Kearthat. Chosen by the High Yraif Laathria.

Sontarr - Pronounced as Son-tar. Freelander and lesser leader of Niamod Colony, Ex Kearthat Starfleet, Spaceship pilot, Drennan and Xennes.

Stal Settlement - Pronounced as Staahl. A remote, secret town built in the far North boreal forests of North America, where the earthling spaceships were built.

Sihuun, It-Ha - Pronounced See-hoon. One of the original three mystic women known as the It-Ha of Planet Kearthat

Sixa - Pronounced Zigh-Za - A creature on Kearthat, the size of a Whitetail deer on Earth it has narrow stripes when young and broader stripes as it ages.

Su~nev - Pronounced Sue-nev. The daughter of the Yraif leader Oreh~itna of the Yraif.

Telmah - Pronounced as Tel-mah. Yraif village, home of the Yraif people of The Below.

Temsik - Pronounced as Tem-sick. An Eastern Colony of the Freelands.
Tenlegs - Pronounced as written. An enormous, poisonous spider-like creature of Kearthat with ten legs, and many huge eyes, it has green blood.

The Endless Life - Pronounced as written. - Immortality.

Tibbar - Pronounced as Tee-bar. A smallish friendly animal with four floppy ears, a curly tail and huge feet that resemble a rabbit on Earth.

The Cooling & The Darkening - Pronounced as written. The eclipses that occur on Kearthat.

The First Ones - Pronounced as written. A term for the Yraif who were first to live on Lan~Igiro.

The Order of Lanrete - Pronounced as Laan-reet. A Yraif planet in another *Realm*/Universe.

Time-of-learning - Pronounced as written. The period dedicated to youth education on Kearthat.

Time-off - A break from chores on Planet Kearthat

Tiro - Pronounced as Tea-row. An apprentice mystic.

Tiro~pedah, The - Pronounced Tea-row-pay-dah. The time it takes for an It-Ha or mystic to learn how the use 'The Inmo,' or 'The Eye that sees all.'

Toakez - Pronounced as Toe-kez. Freelander and Lesser Leader of Sigae Colony, Ex Kearthat Starfleet, Spaceship pilot, Drennan and Xennes man.

Torrak - Pronounced as Tore-rack. A root brown vegetable that resembles carrots on earth.

Torrap Bird - Pronounced as Tore-wrap. A bird with very long tail feathers that squawks very loudly. They have bright yellow, green, and red feathers.

Tremblay, Lieutenant Colonel - Pronounced Trem-blay. The Government representative that oversaw the contract signed by Frederick King.

The Nothing - Pronounced as written. - A mysterious place, emptiness.

Traxid - Pronounced as Trax-sid. A multi-wheeled transporter, with rugged multi-axle units and Omni-directional capabilities. The vehicle has similarly capable trailer attachments sometimes referred to as a 'worm' by the colonists.

Treival - Pronounced Tray-vell. The wife of Lesser Leader Dourok of Rednos Colony and the mother to Rence.

Trigga tree - Pronounced as Trig-gah. Tall trees that grow on the planet Kearthat, with large purple and green leaves that only once in their lifetime.

Trungo - Pronounced as Trung-go. Very large hairy, six-legged animals of planet Kearthat that were hunted to extinction by the alien Eslaf that invaded Kearthat. They have a very slight resemblance to the elephants but are much larger.

Udo - Pronounced as Ooh-dough. Freelander and Lesser Leader of Elbaffeni Colony, Ex Kearthat Starfleet spaceship pilot, Drennan and Xennes man.

Untru - Pronounced as Untrue. A Doll made of Ylock leaves owned by a child on the Freelands. (*see* Ylock)

Va~had - Pronounced as Vaa-had. Yraif Male, Member of the Yraif Assembly led by Nor~han.

Xandr - pronounced as Zan-durr. Freelander and lesser leader of Laeredis Colony, Ex Kearthat Starfleet, Spaceship pilot, Drennan and Xennes.

Xennes - Pronounced as Zen-nes. Some of the Drennan people of the planet Kearthat who are gifted with 'long life,' and can regenerate when injured, they can live for a thousand years or more.

Xiso - Zigh-sow. A kind of bovine found on the Planet of Kearthat.

Ya~zeld, The - Pronounced Yaa- zeld. The Void, tunnel or wormholes that join the Realms or Universes that the Yraif travel.

Ygyzys - Pronounced as Ee-ghee-sis. An Eastern Colony of the Freelands.

Ylock - Pronounced as Ee-lock. A husk vegetable with red kernels cultivated to produce flour for bread much like Earth's corn cob.

Yraif, The - Pronounced Ee-rayfe. A species living on Kearthat in the lava tubes under Ante Mountain. The Yraif were also known as the First Ones of Kearthat. Their Leader is known as Nor~han.
Ytineres - Pronounced as Eye-tinner-ris. An Eastern Colony of the Freelands.

Zari - Pronounced Za-ree. The wife of Lesser Leader Udo of Elbaffeni Colony.
Zaviah - Pronounced as Zah-vee-ah. Wife to Marcus King, mother to Nedai, healer of Rednos Colony.

Zoh~ren - Pronounced as Zor-ren. Advisor on the Assembly of Nor~han leader of the Yraif of The Below, and Sentinel to the High Yraif Laathria.

Zraphite - Pronounced as Zra-fight. A natural mineral found only on the planet of Kearthat.